A DEATH IN THE FAMILY

ALSO BY MICHAEL STANLEY

A Carrion Death

The Second Death of Goodluck Tinubu

Death of the Mantis

Deadly Harvest

A DEATH
IN THE
FAMILY

A DETECTIVE KUBU MYSTERY

MICHAEL STANLEY

MINOTAUR BOOKS
A THOMAS DUNNE BOOK ✖ NEW YORK

A THOMAS DUNNE BOOK FOR MINOTAUR BOOKS.
An imprint of St. Martin's Publishing Group.

www.thomasdunnebooks.com
www.minotaurbooks.com

The Library of Congress Cataloging-in-Publication Data is available upon request.

ISBN 978-1-250-07089-0 (hardcover)
ISBN 978-1-4668-8155-6 (e-book)

First Edition: October 2015

10 9 8 7 6 5 4 3 2 1

To Andy Taylor, principal of the extraordinary
Maru-a-Pula school in Gaborone

NOTE

The peoples of Southern Africa have integrated many words of their own languages into colloquial English. Most of the time, the meanings are clear from the context, but for interest, we have included a Glossary at the end of the book.

For information about Botswana, the book, and its protagonist, please visit http://www.detectivekubu.com. You can sign up there for an occasional newsletter. We are also active on Facebook at www.facebook.com/MichaelStanleyBooks and on Twitter as @detectivekubu.

CAST OF CHARACTERS

Words in square brackets are approximate phonetic pronunciations. Foreign and unfamiliar words are in a Glossary at the back of the book.

Banda, Edison	Detective in the Botswana Criminal Investigation Department [Edison BUN-duh]
Bengu, Amantle	Kubu's mother [Uh-MUN-tleh BEN-goo]
Bengu, David "Kubu"	Assistant Superintendent in the Botswana Criminal Investigation Department [David "KOO-boo" BEN-goo]
Bengu, Joy	Kubu's wife [Joy BEN-goo]
Bengu, Mzilikaze (Mzi)	Kubu's step uncle [M-zilly-CAH-zi BEN-goo]

Bengu, Nono   David and Joy Bengu's adopted daughter [NO-no BEN-goo (no as in nor, but without the "r")]

Bengu, Tumi   Joy and Kubu's daughter [TOO-me BEN-goo]

Bengu, Wilmon   Kubu's father [WILL-mon BEN-goo]

Dlamini, Zanele   Forensic expert [Zuh-NEH-leh Dluh-MEE-nee]

Hong Zhi Peng   Manager of the Konshua Mine

Khama, Samantha   First female detective in the Botswana Criminal Investigation Department [Samantha KAH-muh]

Khumanego   Bushman childhood friend of Kubu [Ggoo-muhn-AY-go (gg=guttural sound like clearing one's throat)]

Koma, Julius   Son of the tribal chief in Shoshong [Julius KO-muh (O as the o in or)]

Koma, Rankoromane   Tribal chief in Shoshong [Run-koro-MAA-neh KO-muh (O as the o in or)]

Kunene, Goodman   Assistant Director, Department of Mines [Goodman Koo-NEH-neh]

Mabaku, Jacob   Director of the Botswana Criminal Investigation Department [Jacob Mah-BAH-koo]

MacGregor, Ian   Pathologist for the Botswana police

Mopati, Albert   Director, Department of Mines [Albert Mo-PAH-ti (O as the o in or)]

Newsom, Peter   American mining representative

Ngombe, Mma and Rra   Wilmon and Amantle's neighbors and friends [En-GOM-bee]

Serome, Pleasant   Joy Bengu's sister [Pleasant Seh-ROE-meh]

Shonhu Wei Long   Executive at Konshua Mine

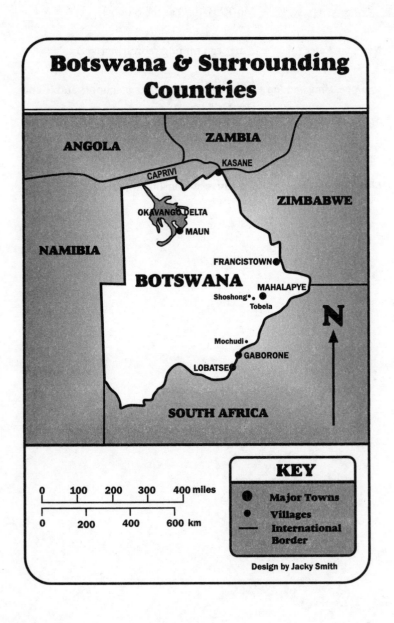

Botswana & Surrounding Countries

ANGOLA

ZAMBIA

KASANE

CAPRIVI

OKAVANGO DELTA

MAUN

ZIMBABWE

NAMIBIA

FRANCISTOWN

BOTSWANA

MAHALAPYE

Shoshong•

Tobela

Mochudi•

GABORONE

LOBATSE

SOUTH AFRICA

N

| 0 | 100 | 200 | 300 | 400 miles |

| 0 | 200 | 400 | 600 km |

KEY

● Major Towns

● Villages

— International Border

Design by Jacky Smith

PART 1

CHAPTER 1

Assistant Superintendent David "Kubu" Bengu was enjoying his dream. He was at an all-you-can-eat buffet at The Palms hotel. His table was on the patio away from the noisy bar, and Joy, his wife, was visiting her sister, so she couldn't limit how much he had to eat.

A smile flitted over his sleeping face as the bowl of shrimp on the buffet table slowly morphed into a platter of lobster in front of his eyes, and a man with a chef's hat put two enormous tails onto his plate. Then his plate grew to the size of a tray, and there was room for cold, poached salmon and a delicious white sauce he didn't recognize, as well as a large piece of smoked trout. That's enough for a starter, he thought as he gazed at the lamb on the spit and the mountain of rare beef surrounded by crisp roast potatoes and horseradish sauce. He picked his way back to his table past the other diners and their dainty helpings, where his half-empty glass of Sauvignon Blanc miraculously changed into a silver ice bucket with a bottle of Moët champagne, already open.

A white-gloved waiter with a red sash pulled back his chair, then slid it forward as he sat down. Kubu nodded, and the waiter poured the bubbling nectar into a flute that stood a foot tall.

Even though he was fast asleep, Kubu let out a quiet sigh of pleasure.

Joy rolled onto her side, trying to move away from the twitches of Kubu's arm as he drained the flute in a series of toasts to the other diners on the patio.

Now Kubu watched a man nearly as huge as himself trundle a large trolley of desserts toward him. Sherry trifle, apple pie, malva pudding, chocolate cake, carrot cake, jugs of custard and bowls of whipped cream delicately laced with cognac. Kubu groaned with pleasure as it approached. Thank God, there was no fruit salad or fresh fruit.

He opened his mouth, and the man wheeled the trolley right into it. Why choose, Kubu thought, when you can have it all?

Just as he was about to wash it all down with a bottle of port that had appeared in his hand, an alarm went off, and a doctor ran onto the patio holding a clipboard. He pointed at Kubu, and the alarm rang again. Kubu looked around, and the piles of food shrank in front of his eyes, and the diners evaporated into thin air. Kubu became frantic. Where was the food going? What was he going to eat?

"Wake up, Kubu!" Joy shook him. "Wake up. It's the phone. It'll be for you."

Kubu shook his head trying to orient himself back to reality.

"Okay. Okay," he grumbled, and stretched over to pick up the phone next to his bed.

"Bengu." His voice came out like a hoarse whisper. He cleared his throat.

"Bengu." This time he recognized his own voice.

"Kubu, this is Jacob Mabaku. I have some bad news."

Kubu sat up, trying to think which of his cases could have blown up so badly that the director of the Criminal Investigation Department had to call in the middle of the night.

"What's going on, Director?"

"There's no easy way to say this, Kubu. Your father's dead. I'm afraid it wasn't natural causes. He's been murdered."

CHAPTER 2

"My father? Murdered?" A band of tightness squeezed Kubu's chest. "It must be a mistake. That's impossible. No one would do that." The band tightened, and Kubu found it difficult to breathe.

"Your mother phoned the police in Mochudi about three hours ago to say he was missing. She was worried he'd lost his way because he's been absentminded lately. Anyway, they started looking, and about an hour ago they found his body about five blocks from here, on Litabi Street. Some neighbors identified him. They phoned me. I'm at your mother's house now."

Kubu couldn't think—couldn't breathe. A huge sob shook his body. His beloved father murdered? It was not possible.

"What . . . what happened? How did he die? Do they know who did it?"

"He was stabbed. And there's no indication at the moment either who did it or what the motive was."

Kubu sucked in a deep breath. He wasn't prepared for his father to be dead.

"My deepest sympathies, Kubu. He was a wonderful person. One of a kind."

Kubu couldn't speak. Only a croak came out of his mouth.

"Kubu. Please put Joy on the line."

"What time is it?"

"It's just after midnight. Please give the phone to Joy."

Kubu turned to Joy, who was sitting up, tears streaming down her face. She put one arm around Kubu's shoulders and took the phone.

"Is it true?" she whispered.

"Unfortunately, it is, Joy. It's a terrible tragedy. But I need you to look after Kubu. He's not going to take this well."

"What can I do?"

"I've sent a car to bring him up here. His mother needs him, and you too if you can get someone to take care of the kids."

"It's late. I don't know . . ."

"The car will be there in twenty minutes."

"What happened?"

"We don't know anything at the moment, except that he appears to have been stabbed."

"Who would do that? He wouldn't harm anyone."

"I'm sorry, Joy. We've no information at all. Please tell Kubu to be ready for the car." There was a pause. Then Mabaku continued. "I'm so sorry, Joy. I don't know what to say. Call me at any time if you need to talk. Anytime—day or night. Kubu has my cell phone number."

"I'M NOT WAITING for any car!" Kubu shouted. "I'm going now!"

Joy grabbed Kubu's sleeve. "Please, Kubu. Please wait. You're not in any state to drive."

"I've got to get to my mother. She needs me."

"So do I, and so do the kids. We can't have you killing yourself driving up there."

"I'm fine!"

"Please, Kubu, I'm frightened something will happen to you."

Kubu stared at her. Then he put his arms around her. "I'm sorry for shouting at you, darling. But I can't just sit here and twiddle my thumbs. I'll be careful." He picked up the keys to his Land Rover and headed to the front door. "Please call Pleasant to see if she can look after the kids. Mother will need you too."

Then he turned and left.

MABAKU'S FEARS WERE well founded. Kubu's mind was not on the road as he raced north to his mother. He went through the stop sign at the end of Acacia Street and narrowly missed another car as he failed to yield at the circle on the A1.

This can't be true, Kubu thought. Why would anyone want to kill Father? He doesn't carry any money unless he's going shopping. And he doesn't wear a watch.

Kubu didn't even notice the pair of donkeys eating grass right at the edge of the road as he left Gaborone.

Maybe he lost his temper with someone—Alzheimer's can do that to a person. Kubu was trying desperately to make sense of the senseless. But why kill him? He's old and frail—a shove would've taken care of any aggression.

Kubu increased his speed now that he was out of town.

How was his mother going to survive? They'd been married for nearly forty years. Done everything together. Depended on each other.

Kubu's eyes filled with tears. He took a deep breath, trying to get hold of himself.

His mother would have to come and live with them. They'd have to add on another room—the kids were already sharing the second bedroom.

Where would they get the money for that?

The turnoff to Mochudi was just ahead, and Kubu barely had time to slow down to make the turn. He shook his head. I'd better be careful on this next stretch of road, he thought. There are usually cows wandering around.

Ten minutes later he pulled up in front of his parents' house. There was a police car there, as well as Mabaku's Toyota Camry.

As he climbed the stairs to the veranda, he heard voices inside. He opened the front door and went in. It was obvious the neighborhood had come together to support Amantle. Several men and women were in the living room, some in dressing gowns. Amantle was on the sofa, head in her hands, sobbing quietly.

Mabaku was standing to one side looking very uncomfortable. When he saw Kubu, he took him by the arm and pulled him back outside.

He put his hand on Kubu's shoulder. "I don't know what to say, my friend," he said. "This is a terrible night."

Kubu just nodded, unable to respond.

"Before you go and speak to your mother, I need to say a couple of things. One, you are to take the next week off. Your mother will need help with the funeral arrangements. We'll take care of your cases. And two, you are to keep completely away from the investigation into your father's murder. And when I say completely, I mean completely." He paused and looked Kubu right in the eye. "Understood?"

"But, I can . . ."

"No 'buts'! You're to stay out of it. No investigating on the side. No talking to people about it. Nothing! Am I making myself clear?"

Kubu nodded. "Who will you put on the case?"

"I will lead the investigation myself," Mabaku replied. "And Samantha will do most of the legwork. I'm giving it top priority on the grounds that it may be an attempt to intimidate a police officer."

"Thank you, Jacob." Kubu's voice came out as a whisper.

"I'll call you to arrange a meeting tomorrow afternoon. We need to see if you've given anyone a reason for doing this."

"Yes, Director. Thank you."

With that Kubu turned and went in to console his mother.

CHAPTER 3

For Detective Samantha Khama, it was only her second call out to the scene of a murder. The first time had been dreadful, the still body proclaiming that a life was over, violently ended with no time to put affairs in order, no chance for good-byes. But this time was much worse. The body lying in the alley under the police flood-lights was a defenseless old man and, worse still, the father of a colleague.

Samantha wiped her eyes and tried to focus on the job at hand. She and Kubu had had their disagreements, but she counted him as a friend and looked up to him. Their work together on the witch-doctor case had been close and intense, and although she wouldn't use that word, Kubu had become her mentor. She could imagine the turmoil he was going through now. She'd never met his father, but she'd heard Kubu talk of him and had deduced how close they were. And she could imagine how she would feel if something like this happened to her father.

Everyone at the scene was upset. There was little conversation except what was necessary to carry out the job efficiently. They were taking every care with the scene itself. Forensics had photographed the area around the body and checked for footprints. They had a couple of clear prints in the dusty section opposite the body, but they seemed to match those of Constable Tohe, who had discovered the body.

Ian MacGregor, the pathologist, was kneeling next to the body. He was usually unflappable, but she could see that he, too, was badly shaken.

Ian hauled himself to his feet, shaking his head. "Looks like three or four stab wounds to the chest and one into the neck. One probably went into the heart. Of course I won't be able to tell until we do an autopsy. My guess is that the assailant was right-handed and struck downward."

Samantha nodded, but didn't respond.

"Well, you can search the body now."

"I think I should wait for the director. He said he would head over here as soon as Kubu was with his mother." She hesitated, then rushed on, "Dr. MacGregor, this is so awful! Who would attack an old man and knife him to death? He was just a frail old man and deserved respect."

"Well, that's your job to find out. But in my experience, people who commit murders aren't usually very concerned about age and frailty. The less likely the victim is to fight back, the better."

They heard a car drive up, and soon Mabaku joined them.

"How is Kubu taking it, Director?" Ian asked.

"How do you think? He's seems okay on the surface, but he's in shock. And his mother's distraught, of course. It's a hell of a mess." He turned to Samantha. "Drop everything else. This is now top priority. I don't care if he was mugged or if this is somehow connected to one of Kubu's cases. Whoever did it is going to hang. We're going to make it absolutely clear that we won't tolerate anyone hurting one of us through our families."

Samantha wondered how much that was going to help Kubu and his mother, but she just nodded.

"So what have we got?"

Ian shrugged. "He's been dead for around three hours, I'd say. Died somewhere between eight and ten o'clock. There are several stab wounds, one of which went into the heart as far as I can tell. I'll do a preliminary autopsy first thing in the morning. Not much more I can do here." But he made no move to leave.

"Forensics?"

"Zanele's people haven't come up with anything yet. No murder weapon, no clues. But they're working on it."

Mabaku could see that for himself. Zanele was talking to her fingerprint specialist and sounded frustrated.

Mabaku cursed. "We should have something by now!" He took a deep breath and watched the activity. Then he said more quietly, as though to himself, "We have to be careful to keep perspective on this. Routine procedure and hard work. That's what we need. That's what solves cases." He didn't add that they'd miss Kubu's flashes of inspiration, but they were going to have to do without them. "Let's take a look." He put on his overalls, booties, and gloves and went over to the body.

Kubu's father was wearing a white shirt with long sleeves, and a gray jacket open in front, as if to frame the browning crimson of the wound. The pockets of his trousers were turned inside out. Mabaku bent over and started searching. He rolled the body on its side to see if there was a wallet in the back pocket. There wasn't, but lying on the ground was a cell phone.

"That's funny," Samantha said. The two men looked at her, surprised. "I mean it's odd. Kubu told me that Wilmon never takes his cell phone anywhere. He just uses it to get calls from the family. Kubu told me it once fell in the toilet, and his father pretended it was lost . . ." Her voice trailed off, and she felt her throat close. She swallowed.

Mabaku thought for a moment. "We must check that with Kubu and Amantle. Maybe he was expecting a call. He doesn't seem to have anything else with him." He turned to Samantha. "Please check the phone for calls made and received for the past month and check with the telecom company as well, in case any of the records on the phone have been deleted."

Samantha nodded, then asked, "No wallet?"

Mabaku shook his head. "Hardly surprising. If he was mugged, the wallet would be gone. Or the assailant could have taken it to make it look like a mugging. Wilmon must have dropped the cell phone when he was stabbed and fallen on top of it."

Zanele joined them looking tired and depressed.

"Nothing yet. A dirt street is about the worst murder scene you can imagine. It's been windy, so stuff blows away. People walk through here all the time, so anything we find might have nothing to do with the murder at all. I've already got a whole bag of junk. And I don't think we'll get any fingerprints." She glanced at the rough brick walls.

"Keep at it, Zanele," Mabaku said. "Collect everything. Some of your junk could turn out to be important later on. In the morning we'll search the whole area. Maybe the killer threw the knife away. And we'll start checking right away if anyone in the area saw or heard anything."

Suddenly, Samantha had an awful thought. Suppose they never got to the bottom of this? Suppose Kubu had to live without knowing what had happened here and why? Then she pulled herself together. That wasn't going to happen. Mabaku wasn't going to let it happen and neither was she.

The director turned back to her. "If this is just an opportunistic mugging, we'll get him through the local police. Check with them in the morning and get them to see if their contacts have any information that could be useful. But if this is something to do with Kubu, then we're going to have to get at the motive through him.

That's going to be painful for him because he'll blame himself for his father's death."

Samantha thought about it. "What if it's neither a mugging nor connected to Kubu?" she asked tentatively.

Mabaku shook his head. "Wilmon was as straight as an arrow. He would never have been involved in anything that would get him killed."

Samantha said nothing, but she wondered about that cell phone.

CHAPTER 4

Kubu walked into the tiny living room, where his mother was sitting. Two elderly neighbors were next to her, and the rest were standing, talking quietly.

"Thank you all so much for being here," he said. Despite his grief, he couldn't help wondering how they came to be there. Had Amantle gone next door to get support, or had Mabaku called them?

"Oh, Kubu," one of the ladies said. "I am so pleased you are here. It is such a tragedy. What is the world coming to?"

Kubu, he thought. Even among my parents' friends, I'm Kubu. Somehow tonight he wanted to be David, the name his father and mother had given him, rather than his childhood nickname of Hippo that had stuck. But he said nothing like that to the kindly neighbor.

"Thank you so much for being here, Mma Ngombe," he said instead as he sat down next to his mother, who was struggling to stand to greet her son.

"Don't get up, Mother. I'm here." Kubu didn't know what else to say.

He put his arms around her and held her close. They both started crying.

"It is so terrible," Amantle whispered. "Your father never hurt anyone. Everyone loved him. Why would someone want to kill him?"

The two of them rocked gently back and forth.

"I cannot believe he is gone. What am I going to do?"

"Mother, you'll come and stay with us. You can't stay here alone."

"You do not have the room, and all my friends are here."

"Let's not talk about it now, Mother. We can discuss it in the morning."

Kubu looked up at the two neighbors. "Who told you?"

Mma Ngombe shook her head. "We woke up because of the lights on the police car. I think it was your boss. Edwin went out to see what was happening. When he heard, he thought Amantle would need me. He went and woke up Lizzie and her husband, and the two of us came over."

"Aaii! I thought Amantle would die also," Lizzie said. "It is a tragedy."

Kubu pulled his mother closer. "Mother, did Director Mabaku ask you any questions?"

"Yes. He was very kind. He just asked if Wilmon said why he was going out tonight or where he was going. Or if he seemed nervous or different."

"What did you say? *Was* Father behaving strangely?"

"Well, you know he has been struggling recently. But tonight he seemed excited. He did not even finish his supper. And he kept looking at his watch. He said he was going to meet a friend. I told him he should not go out alone at night. That he would get lost. But he just said he would not be long. And about eight he left."

She started to cry.

"I told him he was being an old fool. I should never have said that."

Her body shook in Kubu's arms.

"I never saw him again!"

"It's not your fault, Mother. He knew you always loved him. And he loved you too. More than he could show, I think."

Kubu patted his mother on her back.

"I think you should try to get some sleep now. I'm sure the police will want to talk to you again tomorrow. I'll pull the other bed out of your bedroom and sleep here."

He turned to everyone in the room. "Thank you all for being here. I really appreciate it."

Kubu let go of Amantle and stood up. He took her by the hand. "Come on, Mother. Try to get some sleep."

EVEN THOUGH IT was two in the morning, Kubu knew he wouldn't be able to sleep, so he went out to the veranda and sat in the cool air.

I owe everything I have to my parents, he thought.

It was his father who had insisted that Kubu have the best education available; it had been his father who had approached their priest to arrange a scholarship for Kubu to Maru-a-Pula school—a school no poor family like Kubu's would ever be able to afford.

He took a deep breath.

And it was his father who had served the community for years as a wise man and excellent traditional healer. Everyone trusted him.

He brought his fist down on the arm of the chair.

"Damn you! Damn you, you bastard."

He stood up and gazed across the sleeping houses. Somewhere out there is a murderer, my father's murderer, he thought.

He kicked at the veranda wall.

"Damn you, whoever you are. Damn you!"

"There's nowhere for you to hide!" Kubu said, anger boiling inside him. "You're not going to get away with this!"

Suddenly, he wanted to see his father's body. To see what the murderer had done. And to say good-bye.

He hurried down the steps and walked briskly toward where the body had been found. He hoped it was still there and hadn't been taken to the mortuary at Princess Marina Hospital.

As he rounded the corner on Litabi Street, he stopped. Halfway down the block was the familiar sight of police cars with flashing lights, people milling about, constables keeping a few gawking spectators in pajamas and dressing gowns from encroaching on the crime scene, and a solitary ambulance, rear doors open.

He took a deep breath and walked toward where his father must be lying.

As he approached the yellow police tape, a constable he didn't recognize stopped him. "Sorry, rra. You can't go any further. This is a crime scene."

"I know it's a crime scene," Kubu snapped. "I'm with the CID."

"I'm sorry, rra. I've orders not to let anyone in."

"It's my father who's been murdered!" Kubu shouted. He pushed the constable aside, ducked under the tape, and strode toward the center of the action.

"Stop him!" the constable shouted. "Stop him."

Everyone turned to see what the shouting was about.

A second constable joined the first, and they grabbed Kubu's arms and pushed him back.

Kubu tried in vain to break free, but the men were young and strong.

"Go back, rra," the one said. "You're not allowed in here."

Suddenly, Kubu saw Mabaku striding toward him.

"Let him go," Mabaku told the constables.

They dropped Kubu's arms but stayed close.

"Kubu, you can't come in here. I know you want to see your father, but you'll have to wait for a few days. This is off-limits to you."

"But . . ."

Mabaku put his hand on Kubu's shoulder. "Go home, Kubu. Get some sleep. There's nothing you can do here except cause problems later on. Go home, my friend." He turned to one of the constables. "Get a car and take him home."

Mabaku turned Kubu and led him away.

Kubu's head dropped, and his anger was replaced with resignation.

"I'm sorry, Jacob. I can't believe he's gone."

"None of us can. But we'll catch the bastard who did it."

CHAPTER 5

The next morning, Kubu and Amantle were up early. Kubu had managed a couple of hours sleep, but Amantle had tossed and turned in grief. Amantle made a pot of tea and a stack of toast with jam, but neither felt like eating. To be polite, Kubu nibbled at a single slice, washing it down with tea, but couldn't face any more.

While they had a second cup of tea, Kubu said gently, "Mother, you shouldn't be here on your own. I know the neighbors are kind, but you should be with your family. Come and spend some time with us in Gaborone."

Amantle said nothing for a few moments, and Kubu was afraid she'd reject the idea out of hand. Then she said, "There is no room in your house. Where will I sleep?"

"You can use the kids' bedroom. They'll sleep on mattresses in the lounge. They won't mind; it'll be like a camping adventure for them."

Amantle finished drinking her tea. "All right," she said at last. "I will go and pack some things."

Kubu breathed a sigh of relief, surprised she'd agreed so easily.

"But I will come for only a few days," she continued. "I must be here to receive all the condolences and to prepare for the funeral next Saturday. It will be a large gathering because your father was known and respected by many people."

Kubu had expected that Amantle would insist on a traditional funeral—a weeklong event that involved the whole community. Although surprised she was willing to curtail the preparations, he was happy she was going to spend time at his home—it would be good for her.

His thoughts were interrupted by a loud knock on the door. He sighed and went to answer it. It was sure to be the first of the neighbors looking in.

"Ah, Kubu. This is a sad day indeed. The first day without our beloved Wilmon. How are you? How is Amantle?"

"Mma Ngombe. How kind of you to come. We're as well as can be expected. My mother will be staying with us tonight. She's busy getting ready at the moment."

The woman nodded doubtfully. "But what of the funeral arrangements?"

Kubu parried her questions as best as he could, but it was nearly five minutes before the well-meaning woman finally left. As soon as Amantle came out with a cloth bag of clothes and toiletries, Kubu helped her into the Land Rover and left quickly before any other sympathizers could arrive to pay their respects.

Amantle was uncharacteristically quiet in the car. She answered if asked a question; otherwise, she had little to say. She didn't cry, but Kubu knew tears were very close. And when they arrived at his house, and Joy rushed to open the gate for them and helped Amantle from the car, both women dissolved into uncontrollable sobs as they hugged each other.

Kubu left them to their grief and took Amantle's bag inside. Ilia, their fox terrier, sensed something was wrong and, instead of her usual enthusiastic welcome, sat quietly on the veranda, whining softly.

When Joy and Amantle eventually came inside, Kubu left them in the lounge and went out into the small garden of succulents and acacias. Ilia trotted up and put her front paws on Kubu's thigh, hoping to have her ears scratched. But Kubu didn't notice. He, too, was lost in grief.

AT THE CID headquarters at the base of Kgale Hill, most of the people around the table were bleary-eyed. The only exceptions were the detectives who hadn't been involved in the late-night investigations of Wilmon Bengu's murder. Ian MacGregor sat with his eyes closed, his head rocking slowly left and right as though in time to a Scottish dirge. The women in the room, forensic specialist Zanele Dlamini and Detective Samantha Khama, both normally wide-awake and chatting to each other, sat quietly with their eyes open but minds far away. Edison Banda, who had helped Samantha go door-to-door in the early hours of the morning, was slouched forward, arms on the table, head on his arms. No one was talking.

The door opened, and Director Mabaku walked in and sat down at the head of the table. The chair next to him, normally occupied by Kubu, was vacant.

"Good morning." Even Mabaku's voice was tired. A murmur of responses came from around the table.

"I'm going to keep this as short as I can. We've got a lot of work to do today." He turned to MacGregor. "Ian, do you have any updates for us on Kubu's father?"

Ian shook his head. "Unfortunately not, Director. I did a preliminary autopsy before I came in this morning. As I thought, he died from a single stab wound to the heart. The other blows all missed and did mainly surface damage. The stab to the neck narrowly missed the left carotid artery and would not have been fatal. The knife was about three-quarters of an inch wide at most and at least seven or eight inches long. It penetrated the heart and went right through it." He took a sip of his coffee. "The perpetrator doesn't appear to be professional—the overhand stabs and the multiple wounds probably indicate he didn't really know what he was doing."

"Or she . . ." Samantha interjected.

Ian glanced at Samantha with a slightly irritated look. "Or she."

"Did you notice anything else about the body?" Mabaku asked.

"I didn't have time to do a thorough examination. I'll do that after the meeting. I've juggled my caseload to move this to the top. I thought you'd want that."

"Thank you. Let me know immediately if anything new turns up." He turned to Zanele. "Has Forensics come up with anything?"

She shook her head. "It wasn't a good crime scene. There were lots of footprints in the sand, and it's very hard to make sense of them. Anyway, I sent one of my men up there at first light this morning to take a closer look in daylight. We also have Rra Bengu's clothes and are looking at them closely to see if there's anything there—hairs, threads, etc. We won't be able to get any prints off them, but sometimes things cling . . ."

"So you don't have anything at the moment," Mabaku growled. The meeting was not going the way he'd hoped. He needed progress. He needed his best detective back.

"And you, Samantha and Edison. I hope you have something positive."

Samantha and Edison looked at each other. Samantha pointed at Edison.

Edison cleared his throat. "We've got people searching a wide area around where Rra Bengu was killed looking for the murder weapon or any other clues. But nothing has turned up as yet." He glanced at Mabaku and then quickly went on: "Of the people I spoke to last night, only one had any information. A Rra Mulale saw Rra Bengu leave his house at about eight fifteen and walk down the street. He's known Rra Bengu for many years, so he's sure it was him. He said Rra Bengu was walking faster than usual and that he was alone."

"Where does this Mulale live?"

"He lives on the road where the body was found, halfway between it and the Bengus' home."

"Did he notice if anyone was following?"

"I asked him that. He said he didn't notice anyone. Not much help, I'm afraid."

"And you, Samantha?" Mabaku's patience was wearing thin. "I hope you've something useful."

"I have two things, but I'm not sure they're useful." She opened her notebook. "A Mma Pooe was walking her dog just before nine. A man ran past her, away from where the body was found. She noticed mainly because the dog tried to chase him and nearly pulled her off her feet. She said the man had a hood over his head."

"Where exactly—"

"What sort of hood?" Mabaku interrupted Zanele's question.

"She said the hood was like the one you get on some tracksuit tops."

"Not a mask or balaclava, then?"

"No. Just a hooded top."

"I wish you'd mentioned this last night, Samantha." Zanele's voice was uncharacteristically tinged with irritation. "We might have been able to get some footprints. Where exactly did she see him? It may not be too late."

"I'm sorry, Zanele. It was long after you'd left, and it didn't occur to me to get you out of bed at that hour. I kept going to homes until about two thirty in the morning. Pooe's was my last house. She saw the man opposite Plot 327 on Limpopo Street, just down the road from where Rra Bengu was killed."

Zanele stood up. "Excuse me, Director, I'll get someone there immediately. Footprints from a runner are much easier to find." She turned to leave the room.

"Get reception to phone the constable who's guarding the crime scene and have him cordon off the block where the man was seen. We may still be able to find something."

"I'm so sorry, Director," Samantha said. "I should have phoned Zanele. It's my fault."

Mabaku stared at her, not quite sure what to say. Samantha had certainly made a big mistake, but it was unusual for a low-level detective to admit it. And she had stayed out longer than anyone.

"Be more careful next time. If we're lucky, there may still be something there." He looked around the table. "Anything else?"

"Yes." Samantha consulted her notes again. "Rra Bengu was carrying a cell phone. Apparently, that was very unusual for him. I checked the logs on the phone. Over the two weeks prior to his death, he'd made no calls, but he'd received six: three were from Kubu and the others from landlines. I'm having those numbers traced. I've also asked Mascom for a printout of all his calls for the past three months."

"Let me know as soon as you've any information."

Samantha nodded.

Mabaku looked around the table. "Anything else?"

Everyone shook their heads.

"I have something else to say," Mabaku continued. "First, this case has top priority. Until I have reason to believe otherwise, I regard Rra Bengu's murder as a strike against the CID because he's Kubu's father. We have to find out whether the murder is connected with any of Kubu's current cases. I'll do that after this meeting. I'm meeting with Kubu at his home. Second, Kubu is to have nothing to do with this case. NOTHING!" He banged the table with his fist, startling everyone. "If he tries to get involved in the investigation in any way, you let me know immediately! If you hear that he's doing stuff on his own, you let me know immediately! Understood?"

Everyone nodded.

"He's going to want to be involved, to help. That's understandable. But any involvement is through me only. No one else! Understood?"

Again, everyone nodded.

"God help you if I find anyone disobeying me on this. Even if I don't fire you, you'll be investigating petty crimes in the most remote village I can find. If Kubu gets involved, it'll prejudice any case we've got."

Mabaku took a long drink of water from the glass in front of him.

"The press is going to be all over this story. I'll hold a conference this afternoon after I've seen Kubu. No one else should talk to them. Refer all questions to me. Understood?" He looked around the room of nodding heads. "Okay. Enough of that. What else is going on?"

Each person at the table updated the group on the cases they were working. For the most part, they were relatively minor incidents: bar brawls, a few tourists pickpocketed, three stolen vehicles, some shoplifting, and two burglaries with minor losses. When it was Edison's turn, he said that he'd heard from a friend at the Shoshong police station that there was the potential for trouble there as the nearby mine was planning to expand into an area of small holdings where a lot of people lived.

Samantha reported five incidents of domestic violence. "We need to start locking up men who beat up their wives or girlfriends," she said angrily. "You should see the state some women are in when they arrive at the women's shelter. It's disgusting that it happens in this day and age, and even worse that nothing happens to the men. If women retaliated and hit the men with a heavy stick, the police would arrest them and charge them with assault."

She glared at one of the detectives across the table. There were rumors that his wife had been trying to hide bruises on her face. He looked away.

The exchange wasn't lost on Mabaku, but he let it go.

"All right," he said. "We've got work to do. Let's catch that murderer."

CHAPTER 6

Samantha and Zanele drove to Mochudi in separate cars, which was a good thing as Zanele was still fuming over Samantha's oversight the previous night. They met at the home of Mma Pooe, Samantha to question her further, and Zanele to ask the woman to point out exactly where she'd seen the shadowy figure the night before.

"I was just minding my own business, walking Phiri before going to bed, when this man came running down the road. I think Phiri thought I was being attacked. He jumped at the man and nearly pulled me off my feet. I thought my arm was going to come off. Lucky for the man, I was able to hold on; otherwise, he would have been mincemeat. Phiri has jaws like a hyena."

"It's too bad you didn't let go," Samantha said. "We may have solved the case already."

They walked the short distance to Litabi Street, which Zanele was pleased to see had been cordoned off. A constable checked their credentials before letting them through.

"I was over there," Mma Pooe said, pointing to a spot about fifty yards away. "I saw him at the end of the block. It was dark, you know. Most of the lights aren't working around here. He was running straight at me. Then he saw me and swerved to get past. That's when Phiri went after him. By the time I'd controlled Phiri, he'd gone. He must've run around the corner down there, but which way I don't know."

"Mma Letita, if he had a hood, how do you know it was a man?"

"By the way he ran. Women don't run like that."

"Mma Letita, please show me exactly where he ran." Zanele was eager to search for footprints.

The three walked up the road.

"He ran close to that hedge." Mma Letita pointed to the other side of the road. "I'm sure you'll see Phiri's prints as well. He was very quiet next to me until he went after the man."

Zanele opened her forensics bag and took out a camera. She walked over to the other side of the sandy street, carefully picking her way. Just after the middle, she pointed to the ground.

"I see dog prints here, going toward the hedge."

She continued slowly, scanning the ground carefully. Suddenly, she stopped and pointed to the ground. For the next few minutes, she photographed a number of footprints. Then she walked back to where Mma Letita had first seen the man. A paved road crossed Litabi Street there. She walked to the other side and looked carefully, but saw no more prints.

Then she went to the other end of the block, where the man had run around the corner. She took more photographs. Eventually, she came back.

"I'm sure they're the prints," she said. "Definitely someone running. The heel is much deeper than if he was walking. The problem is that the road has sand that's very granular. The boots don't leave a decent print. But there is one print just before the corner that's left a decent imprint of the sole. The sand is much finer there.

It's partially obscured by another print, but I think there's enough to ID the shoe or boot."

"You can find out who the man was from his footprints?" Mma Letita asked.

Zanele smiled. "No, mma. But we can find out what type of boot or shoe. If we're lucky, we may be able to find out who sells them in Botswana. And if we're luckier still, we may get a list of customers. It's unlikely, but it may be all we have to go on."

"I'll go back with Mma Letita and go over everything again," Samantha said. "Then I'll follow up with other people in the neighborhood. I'll see you at the meeting in the morning."

Zanele nodded. "Okay. I want to make a cast of the footprint, and then I'm going to see if I can follow the tracks anywhere else."

She turned to leave, then stopped and turned. "Samantha, I'm sorry I snapped at you this morning. I know you want to find the murderer as much as I do."

"That's okay, Zanele," Samantha replied. "I should've called you when Mma Letita told me about the prints." She frowned. "Let's do Kubu proud."

CHAPTER 7

By the time Mabaku arrived at Kubu's home, things had settled down, and Amantle was able to thank him for his kindness the night before. Then Kubu took the CID director into the garden so they would have some privacy. Once they were seated, each with a glass of ice water, Mabaku got straight to the point.

"Kubu, we need to explore every possible motive for your father's murder. Most likely it was an opportunistic attack. Maybe some thug thought he was carrying money."

"An elderly man in old clothes? It seems unlikely. Father never walked around with much cash. What would he use it for?"

"But a mugger wouldn't know that, would he?" Mabaku paused. "But we need to look at other options too. Think back over your cases, your arrests. Has anyone threatened you? Said they would get even or something like that?"

Kubu thought for several moments. "There was that gang of bank robbers. One of them shouted, 'I'll get you for this,' but he shouted all sorts of stuff as the guys handcuffed him. I didn't take any notice at the time."

"Was there any evidence that they were connected to a wider group? A sort of mafia-type thing?"

Kubu shook his head. "Anyway, why my father? If they wanted to hit me, why not do just that? It doesn't make sense, Jacob."

Mabaku had to agree. Nevertheless, he made Kubu go back over all his recent cases, and some not so recent, noting every possibility for later checking. At last he said, "That seems to be it, Kubu. But I need to talk to your mother again. Maybe she remembers something more. At least she can give me a bit of background. Is she up to it?"

Kubu nodded. "I think she'll be okay. She'll want to help in any way she can." He hesitated, then asked, "What have you got so far? Anything?"

Mabaku sighed. "Not as much as I'd hoped. I wanted an early breakthrough and a quick arrest for both our sakes. I've got that Interpol conference coming up in New York in a couple of weeks, and I want the satisfaction of seeing the culprit locked up before I go. Last thing I need at the moment is a trip halfway across the world." He shrugged. "Anyway, Zanele is working through all the forensics stuff. We went house to house last night. A few leads but nothing really helpful." Kubu had a suspicion that Mabaku might have more information, but clearly he wasn't going to share it.

Mabaku put his hand on Kubu's shoulder. "I know how you're feeling, and I know what you want to do. But remember what I said last night. Keep out of this. Don't even talk to anyone about it."

Kubu sighed. "Yes, Director. I understand. I'll take you in to Mother now."

AMANTLE HAD SETTLED on the couch in the lounge and was drinking tea. Joy offered Mabaku a cup, which he accepted. Kubu joined them and went to find the biscuits, which he passed around, keeping a few for himself. But in the end he didn't eat them and left them on his saucer.

"Mma Bengu," Mabaku began, "do you know why your husband

went out last night and where he meant to go? He was found at Litabi Street. That's quite a way off."

Amantle shook her head. "He said he was going to meet a friend. I said it was late and he might get lost. His mind . . . it is not so clear anymore. Sometimes he is fine, but other times he gets very confused, even angry. It is because of the illness, because of . . ."

Kubu rescued her. "My father was in the early stages of Alzheimer's. On bad days he didn't know who he was or where he was."

Amantle nodded. "I was afraid he would get lost. It was already quite late."

"He didn't say who he was going to meet?"

"I asked him, but he said it was someone I didn't know. That was strange because I know all his friends. But that's all he would say."

"And he didn't say where he was going to meet this friend?"

Amantle shook her head.

"Was there anything about your husband's behavior over the last few days that surprised or puzzled you? Or something strange that he said?"

Amantle shrugged. "Since he started to get sick, he was always saying strange things. Sometimes he went out and said he needed to meet people about his herbal medicine. I thought that was odd because he used to bring people to our home, and he would talk to them, and I would make tea. Now it was different. I was afraid he would get confused or lost when he went out. But he always came back when he said he would. Until last night." She paused and thought for a moment. "But he *was* behaving strangely at dinner. He seemed in a hurry and even left some of his food. He kept looking at his watch."

"What time was it when he left?"

"About eight o'clock."

"And when did he say he would be back?"

"He just said he would not be late. But when he had not come back after two hours, I was sure he was lost. So I went next door to Rra Ngombe and woke them up so I could use their phone. I do not have one myself."

Kubu cursed himself for not thinking of that. They should each have had phones, and he should have persuaded Wilmon to have his with him at all times. How had he missed that? But it was too late now.

"I phoned Constable Tohe at the police station," Amantle continued. "He knows Wilmon and knows about the trouble with his mind. He grew up with Kubu and is a good friend to us. Anyway, he promised to look for Wilmon. And he found him." Tears started to run down her face. Joy gave her a tissue, and she dabbed at them ineffectually. "I am all right," she said, and sipped her tea. "I am all right."

Mabaku waited for her to finish the cup. "Did you try to call him on his cell phone?"

Amantle shook her head. "He never takes his phone with him, and anyway I do not know the number."

"Did he have any money with him?" Mabaku asked.

"Why would he take money? What for? It was too late to shop."

"Didn't he have a wallet? Wouldn't he have taken that with him?"

Amantle shook her head again. "If he took money, he put it in his trouser pocket."

Mabaku made a note of that, then changed the subject. "Mma Bengu, please think carefully. Did anyone ever threaten your husband? Or did he have any bad enemies? Someone who hated him enough to do this?"

Amantle shook her head in annoyance. "No one. Everyone liked him! He helped so many people with his medicines. You can ask anyone. He would spend hours talking to people and giving them advice. I think you should go and find this wicked man who killed my poor husband. I have nothing more I can tell you." The tears started to flow again, and Joy put her arm around her.

Mabaku realized that there was no point in continuing to question the poor woman. He stood up and asked her to call him if she thought of anything else, anything at all. Then he thanked them all and headed back to the CID.

As he drove, he breathed deeply. He had to prepare himself for the press conference at five.

CHAPTER 8

It was nearly suppertime when Ilia raced out of the house, barking excitedly. *Must be Pleasant and the kids*, Kubu thought.

He heaved himself out of his deep armchair and went to greet them. By the time he was out of the house, Tumi had already opened one side of the gate and was pushing away a jumping Ilia, who was trying to lick her face. Nono, the Bengus' adopted daughter, was standing quietly next to the other half of the gate, which she'd opened unmolested by the enthusiastic fox terrier.

Pleasant drove in, climbed out of the car while the children were closing the gate, and hugged Kubu.

"Oh, Kubu. I'm so sorry. I can't believe it. Your father was a father for Joy and me too. We're going to miss him terribly."

Kubu patted her on the back. "It hasn't really sunk in yet. It's so unbelievable that someone would kill him!" He shook his head. "Thank you so much for looking after the kids. We've decided to tell them right away. But I'm not sure they'll really understand."

He let Pleasant go and called out. "Come on, Tumi; come on, Nono. Let's go and say hello to your grandmother."

The kids ran over and each held one of Kubu's outstretched hands.

When they reached the living room, Joy said, "Girls, go and give your grandmother a hug and a kiss."

Tumi and Nono walked over to the old woman and both hugged her at the same time. She kissed them on the tops of their heads.

Tumi looked around. "Where's Grandfather?"

Kubu looked at Joy.

"Come over here, please," Joy said. "Come and sit with me."

She put her arms around both of them.

"I have something very sad to tell you." She hugged them closer, fighting back her tears. "You know your grandfather was old and having difficulty remembering who you were?" They nodded. "It is so sad. He died last night. I'm afraid you won't see him again."

Tumi and Nono stared at her, then at Amantle.

"Will Grandmother find someone else?" Nono asked. "Like I did when my sister died?"

Joy shook her head. "No, my darling. I think Grandmother will live alone. But she's going to stay here with us tonight."

"Did Grandfather leave us a present before he died?" Tumi asked.

"No," Joy said with a smile. "But he sent you both his love and a big hug." She pulled the two girls close to her. "Grandfather is now with Jesus and is very happy. You must remember him in your prayers. Now he can watch over you all the time."

Tumi and Nono looked at each other. "Will he see us when we're being naughty?" Nono asked with wide eyes.

For a moment there was silence. Then Kubu smiled for the first time since the evening before. "Yes," he said. "I think he will."

DINNER THAT EVENING was a somber affair. Although Amantle had been stoical during the day, when the family sat down to eat, she broke down. Tumi and Nono were unsure what was happening and started crying also, so Pleasant suggested they go outside and turn dinner into a picnic. That immediately cheered them up, and they dashed into the garden.

Joy sat down next to Amantle and put her arm around her, patting her gently. She let Amantle weep without saying a word. Kubu wasn't quite sure what he could do, so he picked at his plate of food. He had long ago learned that keeping quiet was a better strategy than attempting to help.

After about ten minutes, Amantle sat upright. "I am sorry for behaving like a schoolgirl," she said. "But I miss him so much."

Kubu leaned over and took her hand but said nothing.

"Thank you." Amantle squeezed his hand. "Thank you both."

Joy stood up, took Amantle's plate, and replaced the now cool food. When she put the plate down, Amantle said, "I must go back to Mochudi tomorrow. I can't wait any longer. I have to prepare for the funeral. That is what Wilmon would want."

Kubu frowned. "Mother, as I said this morning, I think you should stay a few more days. The funeral arrangements can wait."

"No. I have made up my mind. I am all right now, and my friends will expect a proper funeral. They will be with me all week to help me." She dried her eyes and smiled. "It will be a big day with many people coming. Sometimes I thought Wilmon knew everyone in Mochudi. I would not be surprised if there are five hundred people."

"Where will you hold it, Mother?" Joy asked. "Your house is too small for that many people."

"I will speak to our priest," Amantle replied. "I am sure he will let us use the church hall. And it has a kitchen big enough to cook for everyone."

"Are you sure you're ready to go back?" Kubu asked.

"I have made up my mind." Amantle's voice was now strong. "We will return to Mochudi in the morning, if that is convenient for you."

Kubu glanced at Joy, who nodded.

"Then we'll leave after breakfast tomorrow, Mother. And I'll stay with you until the funeral. I want to help with the preparations, and I'll pay for all the food."

"That will not be necessary," Amantle said sharply. "We have a funeral policy to pay for it."

Kubu decided not to pursue the matter, even though he knew that the payout of such policies seldom kept pace with inflation.

"As you wish, Mother. You and Father planned so well for this sad occasion." He stood up. "We should all get an early night, so I'll go and pack. You and Joy can have some tea on the veranda; then I'll join you."

"You are a good son, David. Thank you."

As he was packing, Kubu realized that an early return to Mochudi was actually a win for him. Whether Mabaku liked it or not, he was going to poke around, even if it was behind the scenes and unofficially.

PART 2

CHAPTER 9

After breakfast, Kubu took his suitcase and Amantle's cloth bag to the Land Rover and put a couple of bottles of chilled water in a cooler.

"When will you come up?" Kubu asked as he kissed Joy good-bye.

"On Thursday evening with Pleasant and the kids. I'll borrow some foam mattresses, unless you can get some from the neighbors. We can all sleep on the floor."

"Can't you come up sooner?"

"I'll try, but I've so much on the go at work at the moment." She saw the disappointment in Kubu's eyes. "I'll do my best, darling. But I'm sure your mother will keep you busy."

Kubu shrugged. He could really do with Joy's support during the week. It was going to be a long few days looking after Amantle and putting up with her friends.

They kissed once more. Then Kubu lifted Tumi and Nono, hugged them close, and gave them a big kiss each. "Be good, girls. I'll see you in a couple of days."

With that he and Amantle climbed into the Land Rover and, with a tap on the horn, they set off for Mochudi.

FOR THE MOST part, the trip to Mochudi was quiet. Amantle didn't speak much, and Kubu did little to encourage her. They both used the time to reflect on the man they had loved—loved in different ways, of course, but loved with similar intensity.

As they turned into Kgafela Drive, Amantle said, "Thank you for coming to Mochudi, David. It will be a big help to me."

He nodded. "It's what I want, Mother. So it's not a problem for me."

Kubu stopped the Land Rover in front of his parents' house. He climbed out and went to open his mother's door. He could see that she was struggling to keep from crying. He took her by the arm and walked up the stairs to the veranda.

"Give me your key, Mother."

She rummaged in her handbag and handed it to Kubu. He inserted the key and tried to open the lock. The key wouldn't turn. He put a little more force on it, but it still wouldn't move. He turned the door handle, and the door opened immediately.

"Are you sure you locked the door when you left, Mother?"

"I think so."

"Well, it was open. Your mind was elsewhere, I'm sure."

He pushed the door open and gasped. "You've been robbed, Mother. Someone has ransacked the house."

Amantle pushed past Kubu and walked in. She looked around at the chaos and burst into tears. Drawers had been pulled out of cabinets and dumped on the floor. Sofa cushions had been ripped open and their stuffing strewn everywhere. And through the open bedroom door, Kubu could see that the two mattresses had suffered the same fate.

"Don't touch anything, Mother," Kubu said. "Please go and sit outside for a few moments. I need to call the police here in Mochudi and some people at work."

This is no ordinary robbery, he thought. It has to be something to do with Father's murder. He wondered what on earth Wilmon could have been up to. What did he have that somebody wanted so much?

He called the Mochudi police station and reported the break-in. Then he called Director Mabaku.

"Director, my parents' house has been torn apart. Obviously, someone is looking for something they think my father had." Kubu's voice started getting louder. "And what's next? My mother killed? My wife and children attacked? I need to be on the case. I know everyone around here. You've never lived here, and Samantha hasn't lived here for years."

"Kubu, calm down! We're doing everything we can. I've put everyone possible on the case. It's top priority. You know full well we can't have you involved. If you're part of the team, and we prosecute someone, the defense will shred your objectivity to pieces. They'll say you're biased and prejudiced. And they'll be right."

"But you've accomplished nothing so far. You've—"

"Shut up, Kubu. We've been on the case just over a day. And you expect—"

"Director, you know as well as I do, that the chances of catching a perpetrator go way down after the first forty-eight hours. It's nearly two days now, and you've got nothing. You've got to put me on the team."

"I'll call you right back."

Kubu couldn't believe that Mabaku had cut him off. Didn't he understand that everything was urgent?

His phone rang again. It was Mabaku.

"I've arranged for Zanele and Samantha to go to Mochudi immediately to see if they can find any sign of the intruder. And I've arranged twenty-four-hour protection at your home and your mother's. Just in case. You'd better let Joy know." Mabaku paused, then continued, "Listen to me carefully, Kubu. You are not to go back into the house until I say so. You are not to go snooping around talking to neighbors. You are not to contact any member of the team investigating your father's murder. Do you understand? Take your mother back to your home in Gabs—she's had a bigger loss than you, and she's behaving a lot better. Pull yourself together, man. We'll do our job as well as we can, and having you interfering is only going to slow things down."

Before Kubu could respond, Mabaku hung up.

Kubu stood for a few moments, cell phone in hand, seething with anger. His father had been murdered, his mother's house broken into, and he was meant to do nothing about it.

"We'll see!" he snorted. "We'll see."

CHAPTER 10

Kubu called Joy and told her about the break-in. He did his best to persuade her not to worry, but she was understandably concerned. When he'd finished talking to her, he turned to his mother, who had buried her face in a handkerchief.

"Come on, Mother. Let's go next door and get a cup of tea." He took her by the arm, but she shrugged free.

"I am not leaving. This is my house, and I have things to do."

"But, Mother—"

"It is my husband who has died. I have a responsibility to—"

"Mother, you can come back later. You can't go in now. It's a crime scene. Let's go next door for the moment."

"I do not know what this country is coming to. Everything is getting worse. Nobody is safe."

"Come along, Mother." Again he took her by the arm. This time she let him help her to the neighbor's house.

"Hello again, Mma Ngombe," he said when the front door opened. "Would it be possible for my mother to stay here for a couple of hours? Somebody's broken into her house, and we're waiting for the police."

Mma Ngombe frowned. "But aren't you with the police?"

"Of course, mma, but we can't go in until the forensic people have taken fingerprints and so on. And I can't do that. Besides, they won't let me do anything because I'm personally involved."

"Oh dear. That must be hard for you." She turned to Amantle. "Amantle, my dear. What is the world coming to?" She patted her friend on the back. "Come on in."

"She was at my home in Gaborone last night, thank God. Did you hear or see anything unusual?"

She shook her head. "No. As you know, there are people in the street until nine thirty or ten every night. I'm sure someone would have seen whoever broke in if it was before ten."

"And after ten?"

"Well, you would have to speak to everyone in the neighborhood. We were on the veranda until just before ten, and we saw Rra Seema and his wife, and old Rra Nini. And Mma and Rra Macha. And a few people I didn't recognize. But they looked as though they were just out for a stroll. Nobody paid any attention to Amantle's house as far as I can remember."

"And did you hear anything after you went to bed?"

"No, I slept very well, but you should speak to my husband. He's a light sleeper. And I'm told that Rra Roze doesn't sleep well either—probably too much beer, I think. He lives on the other side of Amantle's house."

"Thank you, mma. You're very kind. I'm sure Mother would like a cup of tea. It's been a very difficult time." He hesitated. "And I'd like one also, if it isn't too much trouble."

"And now they do not want me to go into my own house," Amantle said. "My own house! And I have to prepare for Wilmon's funeral."

"Don't worry, my dear," Mma Ngombe said. "All your friends will be here to help. Go and sit down."

. . .

"MOTHER, WHERE DID Father keep his front door key?" Kubu asked as they waited for Mma Ngombe to brew the tea. "Would he have taken it with him the night he was killed?"

Amantle shook her head. "I do not know if he took it. Usually, if one of us is in the house or if we go for a walk, we do not lock the door. But that night . . ." She broke off as she tried to regain her composure. "But that night, he was acting so strangely, I do not know what he did."

"Where do you normally keep the keys?"

"There is an old clay pot on the table in the living room—"

"The one with the piece missing? I know it," Kubu interrupted.

Amantle nodded. "It was a gift from my parents when we got married."

"I'll be back in a minute."

Kubu heaved himself out of his chair and walked next door to his parents' house. Before he went inside, he walked slowly around the building to see if there were any signs of a break-in. It would be ironic, he mused, if the intruder had broken in instead of just walking through the unlocked front door. However, there were no signs of anything having been forced.

When he reached the front again, he climbed up on the veranda and pushed the front door open, making sure not to touch anything. He picked his way through the debris on the floor, and then, using his handkerchief, he lifted the pot and turned it upside down. It was empty.

Kubu put the pot back in its place, carefully left the room, and returned next door to his cup of tea.

"I'll arrange to have the locks changed today," Kubu told his mother. "The key is missing, and I don't want you worrying when we go back home. I'll get both outside doors changed."

Amantle nodded. "Why are they doing this to us?" she asked. "We have nothing valuable."

"Are you sure Father didn't say anything about a person he was meant to meet or an arrangement he was making?"

Amantle shook her head. "He never said anything to me."

WHEN HE'D FINISHED his second cup of tea, Kubu took his leave and went to speak to the people Mma Ngombe had suggested. He learned absolutely nothing, drew a complete blank. Nobody had heard or seen anything. Mostly, they wanted to talk about the funeral arrangements and were concerned that Amantle would have to get a move on to complete the rituals in time.

As he was walking back to Mma Ngombe's house, he noticed that Director Mabaku's car was parked in front of his parents' house, but Zanele's wasn't.

He'll have to wait for her before he can take a good look around, he thought. But when he walked into Mma Ngombe's house, he was surprised to find Mabaku there, also having tea.

"Sit down, Kubu." This was a command rather than an invitation. Kubu settled himself on the sofa, mentally bracing himself for a typical Mabaku tirade.

"Where have you been?" Mabaku snapped.

"I just went to see if Father's front door key was in its usual place."

"You did what?" Mabaku jumped to his feet.

"I went to see—"

"I told you to stay out of the house!" Drops of saliva flew out of Mabaku's angry mouth. "What don't you understand about what I told you?" Mabaku was close to shouting. "You could contaminate the crime scene and wreck the whole investigation! What makes you so important that you don't have to listen to me?"

"The door was unlocked . . ."

"So what? I told you not to get involved." Mabaku took a deep breath. "And what were you talking to the neighbors about? I saw you. From my car and from this window."

Kubu squirmed uncomfortably in his chair. "I just wanted to know if they had seen anything last night. I was just trying to save you some time."

"What did I tell you?"

"You said I should keep well away from the investigation into my father's murder."

"And don't you think this break-in is linked to your father's murder? And don't dare say no!"

"But, Director—"

"This is my final warning, Kubu. One more time, and you'll be stationed in Tshane or Kang. For five years! With no chance of an appeal. Do you understand?"

Kubu decided discretion was the better part of valor and nodded. "Yes, Director. I understand."

Mabaku turned and thanked a shocked Mma Ngombe and stalked out.

As Kubu watched through the sitting room window, Mabaku strode toward Amantle's house and Zanele Dlamini, who had just arrived.

I hope she finds something, Kubu thought. If she doesn't, Mabaku's going to rip her to shreds.

KUBU STOOD UP and thanked Mma Ngombe. Then he turned to Amantle.

"Come on, Mother," he said. "We'd better go home. I'll phone Joy and tell her we're going to be there for dinner."

"I am not going back to Gaborone." Amantle's voice was firm. "I need to prepare for your father's funeral on Saturday. And now I have only four days left to do it. You go home, and I will stay here and arrange everything."

"But, Mother—"

"I have made up my mind, David. I am staying. If I cannot use my own home, Mma Ngombe will let me stay here, I am sure."

Mma Ngombe nodded.

"Then it is settled. When will you return to Mochudi, David?" his mother asked.

Kubu sighed. He couldn't argue with his mother over something as important as her husband's funeral.

"All right, Mother. You win. We'll both stay as planned. And we'll stay in your house. We'll just have to wait until they've finished with all their work. I'll see you in an hour."

With a nod to Mma Ngombe, Kubu turned and walked out, hoping he could persuade someone at the hardware store to come and install the new locks.

CHAPTER 11

When Mabaku and Zanele left Amantle's house, Kubu took his mother back. They found the house in far better shape than it had been earlier in the day. His colleagues had tidied things up.

"Director Mabaku is such a nice man," Amantle said as she saw what had been done. "And Detective Khama is very nice too."

"How do you know Detective Khama, Mother?"

"While you were sorting out the locks, she came and said she would pray for your father's soul. And for me as well."

Kubu frowned. That didn't sound like the Samantha he knew. "Is that all she said?" he asked.

"Oh no. She also asked about your father's friends. She wanted to talk to them. She was very kind."

Kubu felt a flash of resentment that a junior detective was trying to find his father's murderer rather than himself. What experience does she have? he thought bitterly. It should be me on the case.

He took a deep breath and set to work putting everything back in order, while Amantle stitched the mattresses and pillows so the stuffing wouldn't come spewing out when they lay down. The sofa would have to wait until the next day.

Among the papers that had been stacked on the dining room table, Kubu came across the funeral policy that his mother had mentioned. He opened it and found what he had expected. The policy was twenty years old and paid a mere five thousand pula—barely enough for a coffin at today's prices and certainly not enough to cover the costs of the food. *At least it is something,* he thought.

Another thought struck him as he sifted through the papers. "Mother, did Father have a will?"

Amantle stopped sewing. "Yes, he did. I remember he got one of the elders to help him with it when you turned twenty-one. He said it needed to be changed. That seems a long time ago now."

Kubu knew it was a long time, over fifteen years. "Do you know where he kept it?"

Without a word, Amantle put aside the cushion and walked to the bedroom. He heard her open the cupboard and pull something out. "They are gone!" she exclaimed. "All his papers!"

She returned to the lounge carrying a metal lockbox with rust around the hinges. "He kept his private papers in here, like his will and his identity document and his savings book from the bank. It is all gone! These *skelms* have stolen it. They kill him and then they come and steal his things . . ." She collapsed into a chair and started to weep.

Kubu went to comfort her. "Mother, that may not be it. I found his identity card on the table with the other papers. Maybe the detectives just picked the things off the floor and put them here for us to sort out. Don't worry. I'll go through everything." But Amantle shook her head and continued to cry.

Kubu returned to the table and sorted the papers. "Ah!" he said, pleased. "Here's the savings book! I'm sure the will is here too."

But it wasn't. And although they searched the whole house, they could find no trace of it.

I should really let Mabaku know, Kubu thought. But let's see how long it takes them to *ask* us if anything's been taken.

CHAPTER 12

The meeting at the CID the next morning was not pretty. Mabaku was in a foul mood because there had been little progress, and Zanele had found nothing at Amantle's house that she could use.

"There were no signs of a forced entry," she said. "I think the murderer must've taken the front-door key from Kubu's father." She glanced nervously at Mabaku. "We have nothing to go on," she continued, exasperated. "We've picked up a lot of hairs and will start going through them today. But I doubt they'll be any help. There've been dozens of people there over the past few days. And the same goes for fingerprints—lots of them, but we'll have to eliminate them one by one by checking on everyone who's been at the house. Even then, it's unlikely we'll get a match. Whoever broke in was pretty careful."

She looked at her notebook. "We've also been trying to identify the maker of the boot that left the partial print near the crime scene. The tread is very unusual and doesn't match any of our records. We sent a print to Interpol so see if they could help. They responded very quickly for a change. It's a common boot made in China. I have one of my people going to all the Chinese general stores in Gabs to see if they carry them."

Then it was Samantha's turn. She reported that she had just received information from Mascom about the calls on Wilmon's phone.

"The three calls not from Kubu came from pay phones in Mahalapye. Two from the same phone and the third from a different one."

"Mahalapye?" Mabaku interjected. "Kubu's father's half brother lives there. They didn't get on apparently. Go on."

"I also made a list of Rra Bengu's closest friends," Samantha continued. "I'm going back to Mochudi later today to talk to them."

She closed her notebook and leaned forward.

"There is one other thing, though," she said. All heads turned toward her. "It's just an idea that I had. When the director, Zanele, and I were going through the house, everything had been searched—cupboards, drawers, pillows and mattresses, you name it. Including books. That got me thinking. If the intruder was looking inside books, he had to be looking for something flat, like a photograph or piece of paper. It couldn't be something with bulk."

There was silence in the room.

"That's a very good idea," Zanele said.

"I agree," Mabaku chimed in. "I'm not sure how it helps at the moment, but let's keep it in mind and see if it leads anywhere. Check with Kubu's mother if anything like that is missing."

He stood up to leave, but Edison put up his hand.

"Director, I have an update on what I reported yesterday."

"Yes, Edison. What is it?"

"I told you about the unrest in Shoshong. My friend now thinks that there could be real trouble at a *kgotla* they're going to have at the end of the week. Apparently, the chief is going to make some people move to another part of town, and they don't want to."

Mabaku grunted. "Well, what the chief decides has nothing to do with us. But give the station in Shoshong a call, Edison, and make sure they're on top of it. They may want to have some constables at the *kgotla*. Now, let's go and find who killed Kubu's father."

CHAPTER 13

At the same time that the meeting at the CID was in progress, Kubu was finishing a small breakfast of bread and jam accompanied by a cup of strong tea. Not enough, he thought. I'll have to go into town for a little more.

His mother was making a list of things to do to ensure her husband's funeral was a success.

"I am going to the church, David," she said. "I have to make sure that the priest is available for the funeral, as well as the church hall for the meal afterward. And I want to use their kitchen on Friday—it will be a big funeral, so we will have a great deal to prepare."

"Let me take you, Mother. I'll drop you off while you talk to the priest; then I'll come and pick you up afterward. I'm sure you'll want to visit the butcher too—you'll have to order a huge amount of meat. I'll tell him that I will be paying. And the supermarket, of course. And we should have lots of drinks. It will be hot, and people will be thirsty. Will cold drinks, beer, and a little wine be okay?"

No wonder it takes a week to prepare for a funeral, he thought. So much food to prepare, so many people to socialize with.

"Thank you, David. That is very kind of you," Amantle responded. "I will be ready in fifteen minutes."

KUBU WAS FEELING pleased with himself that he'd finessed a chance for a real breakfast without upsetting his mother. He knew that her visit to the priest would be prolonged, so he'd have time for a substantial portion of eggs, bacon, sausage, and fried tomatoes, followed by toast and marmalade. But when he arrived at the restaurant and considered the menu, he realized that he wasn't really hungry. The thought of the food had occupied his mind but not whetted his appetite. "I'll just have a large cappuccino," he told the waitress.

To pass the time he read the latest copy of *Mmegi* but found little of interest. Just as he was about to leave, his phone rang. It was Samantha. A wave of irritation hit him.

"How are you doing," she asked softly.

"I'd be a lot better if I was helping."

There was a silence. Then Samantha continued. "Did your mother notice anything missing from her house after the break-in?"

Kubu hesitated. Part of him wanted to protect his small piece of information—the only thing he knew that Samantha and the others didn't. Eventually, he realized he had to tell her.

"As far as she knows, the only thing missing is my father's will."

"His will?" Kubu could hear Samantha's surprise. "Is she sure that he had one—that's a very strange thing to steal. There's usually a copy somewhere, at the lawyer, whatever."

"She's sure. She didn't know what was in it. Apparently, my father had it drawn up when I turned twenty-one—that's a long time ago. My mother says he consulted an elder, not a lawyer. Would you like me to try and find out who it was?"

"I'll have to speak to the director about that. I'm sorry, Kubu, but you know how it is."

There was another silence. At last Kubu asked, "Have you made any progress?"

It took a few seconds for Samantha to answer. "I know how hard it is for you, Kubu. But I have to do my job. I can't say anything. Good-bye." The line went dead.

Kubu wanted to crush his phone, he was so angry.

For the next ten minutes or so, he just sat at the table and tried to calm himself down.

Eventually, he paid his bill and drove back to the church, where he found his mother and the priest wrapping up the arrangements. Kubu greeted the priest and took him aside.

"I know you are in charge of the burial, Father. I expect there will be quite a number of people who want to say a few words at the graveside. I want to be last."

Before the priest could say anything, Kubu followed up. "I know it's traditional for me to be the first to speak after your service, but given the circumstances of my father's death, it's important for me to have the last word."

The priest looked at Kubu, puzzled, but agreed.

Kubu turned to his mother and said, "Come on, Mother. We have shopping to do."

THE SHOPPING TOOK much longer than expected, partly because that's the nature of things and partly because Amantle kept remembering things she'd forgotten to put on her list. So it was early afternoon by the time they had finished. As they pushed the carts to his Land Rover, he was shocked both by the sheer quantity of what they'd bought and, of course, by the cost. He'd probably have to take out a bank loan.

On the way home, they stopped at the church hall and filled the refrigerator with as much of the meat and marrow bones as would fit. The rest would have to be split between Amantle's fridge and Mma Ngombe's. Kubu hoped that his mother knew what she was doing. He'd been told that cooking for three hundred to four hundred people was much more than multiplying the recipe for four by a hundred.

It didn't take long for Kubu to decide that he could be most helpful by keeping out of everyone's way. So he retired to the veranda, where he collapsed on a chair, exhausted by the comings and goings. A quick power nap will do me good, he thought, and closed his eyes. It only took a few moments before he drifted off.

"KUBU, WAKE UP! Wake up!"

It took a few moments for him to return from his dream, where the boy Kubu and his father were climbing the rough trail on Kgale Hill. "You can see all of Botswana from the top," his father had said.

When he opened his eyes, Rra Ngombe was standing over him.

"Ah, Kubu, my friend," Ngombe said. "You have a fine set of lungs! I could hear you from my house."

Kubu shook his head and rubbed his eyes.

"Once again, please accept my sympathies for the loss of your father—a great man, so well liked and so humble. I still can't believe that he died in such a terrible way."

Kubu didn't have the energy to stand, so he gestured to Ngombe to sit down.

"Do the police have any idea who did it?" Ngombe asked after he'd made himself comfortable.

Kubu shook his head. "I don't know," he muttered. "My boss is keeping me out of the loop. Forbidden me to get involved in any way."

"Why's that?"

"He thinks if I'm involved, it will give the defense a chance to claim prejudice or whatever, if it ever gets to trial."

"Is there anything *I* can do?" Ngombe asked.

Kubu perked up. He realized that Ngombe had provided a perfect way to subvert Mabaku's ban on getting him involved.

"Actually, there is. I want to invite Father's friends to the shebeen tomorrow night to have a drink or two—to remember Father and celebrate his life. His murder will certainly come up. I'm not allowed to ask questions, but you can. I'd appreciate it if you could ask if anyone has seen anything unusual over the past few months. You never know in these cases. Sometimes even the smallest thing can be the key."

"That should be easy enough. I'll go and see who I can find. I'm sure they'll all want to come." He stood up.

"What time should we say?"

"Six would be good."

"Excellent. See who you can find, then come back for a beer before supper."

Ngombe shook his head. "Aaii! I would like to do that, but I have to see a detective, a woman. I don't know why she wants to see me. I already told her I don't know anything when she phoned me."

"They'll talk to everyone," Kubu said sourly. "Well, go ahead then. Don't be late."

Ngombe nodded. "Okay. I'll see you tomorrow."

Kubu nodded, disappointed. He needed some male company, and the reminder that Samantha was doing the job he should be doing had soured his already bad mood.

CHAPTER 14

Samantha had asked Ngombe to meet her at the church, where she'd already arranged to see Wilmon's priest. She was having a cup of tea with him when Ngombe arrived. The priest hurried off to fetch another cup and give them privacy.

"Rra Ngombe," Samantha began, "we're trying to find out if Rra Bengu said or did anything out of the ordinary over the past month or two. His wife says his behavior recently was a little strange, so I wonder if you noticed anything."

"He seemed a little more impatient lately. He couldn't sit still, even when we were at the shebeen. He would stand up and walk around a bit, then sit down again. But he never said anything. We all thought it was his Alzheimer's getting worse."

"Have any of your friends mentioned anything? Maybe about something Rra Bengu said to them or something that he did that was unusual?"

Ngombe thought for a few moments. "Alfred—that's Alfred Vilikazi—Alfred told me a couple of weeks ago that Wilmon said he was meeting some long-lost relative from Tobela at the shebeen one afternoon. When Alfred asked about it later, Wilmon said it'd been a mistake, and the man wasn't a relative at all. He never said anything to me though."

"Tobela? Where's that? I've never heard of it."

"Apparently, it is west of Mahalapye, close to Shoshong."

Samantha didn't show her surprise at hearing of Shoshong again. "I'm seeing Rra Vilikazi in half an hour," she said, "so I can ask him directly about that. Anything else you can think of?"

Ngombe shook his head. "No. I'm sorry I can't be of more help."

"Which shebeen was Rra Bengu going to, to meet his relative?"

"It's called the Welcome Bar No. 3, and it's about eight blocks from Wilmon's house on Giraffe Street."

Samantha made a note of that. "There's one other thing, Rra Ngombe. It's very important that Kubu keeps completely out of this investigation. Any involvement could jeopardize the case against the man who killed his father. You are not to discuss any of this with him."

Ngombe shifted uncomfortably in his chair, thinking of the arrangement he'd just made with Kubu.

Samantha noticed his hesitation. "This isn't my idea, rra. This is an order from my boss. And he's Kubu's boss too."

Ngombe nodded. "All right," he said.

Samantha stood up. "If there's nothing else, Rra Ngombe, I have to go. I've got a number of meetings this afternoon. Thank you for your time, and please remember, you are not to say anything to Kubu."

Ngombe nodded. "I hope you find the bastard that did it."

SAMANTHA LEARNED NOTHING more from Wilmon's other four friends. Even Alfred Vilikazi couldn't add to what Ngombe had told her about Wilmon's supposed relative. "It's very strange," she said to him. "It's as though he had something else in his life that no one

knew about—not even his wife. Kubu not knowing, I can understand, but his wife?" She shook her head. "Well, my last stop is the
shebeen. Maybe someone there heard something or saw something,
but I'm not optimistic."

After thanking Vilikazi, she set off for the Welcome Bar No. 3.

CHAPTER 15

Wednesday was a frustrating day for Kubu. He had to be polite to all the visitors his mother received, accepting their well-meaning sympathies; he had to contain his anger that he hadn't heard anything from Mabaku and was nervous about calling Samantha for information; and he had to be patient as the clock crawled toward six o'clock and his meeting at the shebeen.

To pass the time, he walked around the neighborhood but didn't bump into anyone he knew. Eventually, he decided to visit the museum situated at the top of the hills behind Mochudi.

It was a steep climb up rough-cut steps from the parking lot, and more than once, he paused to rest under the guise of admiring the view. Once at the top, he clambered over the granite rocks to the edge of the plateau, where all of Mochudi spread out below him. He paused under a rock fig tree, which grasped a boulder with roots like prehensile fingers. On a clear day, I'd be able to see Gaborone's tall buildings twenty miles south, he thought. This spot has the best view in the country. I just wish I could relax and enjoy it.

But he couldn't.

Why was his father murdered? What had he been up to? Who was he meeting? What could he have done to incite such violence?

Kubu shook his head. Nothing made sense.

Can I see his house from here? he wondered. He squeezed between the boulders to look in the right direction, but he couldn't pick out the house. It was too far away.

He thought about going into the museum, but he'd been there before, explaining the ancient artifacts and displays to the wide-eyed Nono and Tumi. He wasn't in the mood; his mind was elsewhere. So after fifteen minutes, he headed back to his mother's house to sit on the veranda and enjoy a large steelworks.

KUBU HAD HIS eyes closed and was remembering some of the good times he'd enjoyed with his father when his phone rang. He had to heave himself to his feet so he could pull his cell phone from his trouser pocket. It was damned Samantha again.

"Yes?"

"Kubu. It's Samantha."

"I know."

"How are you doing?" she asked.

"How do you think?"

"I'm sorry to disturb you again, but I need some information. Apparently, a few weeks before he died, your father met someone from a village called Tobela. They apparently didn't agree on whatever they were talking about, and your father lost his temper. He was overheard saying to the man, 'It's for my son. It will stay in the family.' Do you have any idea what he was referring to?"

"I have no idea what he meant. Where did they meet?"

"In Mochudi."

"Yes, of course, but where in Mochudi?"

"Kubu, you know I can't give you any details."

Kubu gritted his teeth.

"Did your father know anyone from Tobela?"

"Not that I know of," he replied. "Where is it? Or can't you tell me that either?"

"It's a small place between Mahalapye and Shoshong."

There was a silence. "Kubu, I have to go," Samantha said. "I hope you realize that I dislike this situation just as much as you. Look after yourself. Good-bye."

Kubu breathed deeply for a few moments, then went to find his mother. When he asked her about what Samantha had just told him, she replied, "I told her that I did not know what he was talking about. I told her she should talk to you."

"When did she speak to you?" he asked, puzzled.

"Oh, this morning, when you were out. I told her to call you because you always have your phone with you."

"Why didn't you tell me, Mother?"

"She said I should not say anything to you."

"Goddammit!"

"There is no need to swear, David."

Kubu took a deep breath, then continued, "Mother, did Father know someone from Tobela?"

Amantle frowned. "The lady detective asked me the same thing this morning. I do not think so. Not that I can remember. You know your father was born in Mahalapye, but his ancestors came from Tobela. But they moved away many years ago. More than a hundred, I think. Your father said that one of his ancestors was an elder at the *kgotla* of Kgosi Khama the Third."

Kubu decided not to pursue the matter but started wondering whether he needed a short vacation—in Tobela, for example.

"Thank you, Mother," he said, and walked back to the veranda.

AT HALF PAST five, Ngombe arrived, and the two of them walked to the shebeen. Along the way Kubu turned to him and asked what had happened at the meeting with Samantha.

"Nothing," Ngombe said. "As I told you, I don't know anything." But he didn't meet Kubu's eye.

"What did she ask you about?"

"Just who Wilmon's friends were. She wanted to talk to them too."

"That's all?" Kubu knew there had to be more. Samantha would do better than that.

Ngombe hesitated. "Look, Kubu, I don't know anything important. And she said not to talk about it anyway."

Kubu frowned, feeling frustration build. But he let the matter drop. He was sure Ngombe didn't know anything useful, or he would have said something long before Samantha shut him up. Let's see what they let out after a few beers, he thought.

When they arrived, two of Wilmon's friends were already there, beer in hand.

"*Dumela*, Rra Vilakazi. *Dumela*, Rra Kgole," Kubu said. "I'm pleased you could join me this evening. You know Rra Ngombe, of course."

They nodded and greeted their old friend.

"I'm so pleased to have a reason to come here," Kubu said. "I feel totally helpless at my mother's. She won't let me do anything."

"Aaii! It's not your place to help at the moment. You must get yourself ready for Friday night. You won't get any sleep." Rra Kgole laughed. "But we'll come and keep you company. And Saturday's going to be even worse. It's hard work to fill a grave in Mochudi because there are so many stones. And, of course, you will say goodbye to your father for the last time."

"I'm surprised that Amantle wants him buried here in Mochudi," Rra Kgole interjected. "People his age usually want to be buried at their ancestral home."

"I think my mother wants to be able to visit his grave, and Mahalapye is too far for her. She doesn't drive, of course, and taking a bus would be very difficult."

"Mahalapye?" Rra Vilikazi frowned. "He was born in Mahalapye, but the ancestral village is Tobela, near Shoshong. I think his grandfather was an elder at Khama the Third's *kgotla*."

"That's what my mother said too," Kubu said. "I don't remember my father telling me that."

"Fathers are like that," Ngombe said. "Their friends know more about them than their sons." He laughed and lifted his glass. "Here's to Wilmon—what a good friend he was to us."

Just as they were drinking to their old friend, three other elderly men arrived.

"Look who has arrived," Rra Kgole said. "What is this shebeen coming to?"

Kubu heaved himself out of his chair. "Thank you all for coming. I know my father didn't drink much, but I'm sure he's watching us now and happy we're remembering him."

BY THE TIME the men were on their third beer, they'd had one beer too many. The stories flowed about Wilmon's many successes, and a few failures, with his herbal remedies.

"Do you remember the time Mma Ramote went to see him for her runny tummy? He was confused and thought she was constipated. He gave her a special *muti* he made from an aloe he'd imported from South Africa. It was a laxative! She couldn't leave the toilet for a day and a half."

"She didn't speak to him for months!"

Kubu smiled. It was so nice to hear stories about his father, some he'd never heard before.

"And what about the time the mayor came to him for *muti* to help him get reelected?"

"Wilmon couldn't stand the man!"

"He gave him something that made him fart a lot. Every time he spoke to a group of people, they had to run for cover." He guffawed.

"The mayor still won though!" one of the others said.

The six men, who had known Wilmon for years, laughed until they had tears running down their wrinkled faces. Then there was a silence as they reflected on their old friend. Kubu felt the moment had come to see what the beers and good fellowship might produce in the way of information. Maybe Samantha hadn't spoken to all of them.

"I don't think he had any enemies," he began. "He was such a popular man. Why do you think he was murdered?"

The others all shook their heads but said nothing.

"Did any of you notice anything different about him recently?" Kubu continued. "Did he say anything to you?"

"Only that he couldn't remember who I was," said one.

"He got very angry with me last month when I told him we'd been friends for years," said another. "He told me that we'd never met."

"What about someone visiting him recently? Maybe a man from the village of Tobela?"

There was a silence. Kubu glanced at Ngombe, who looked away. Kubu turned to the others, and they also couldn't hold his gaze.

"Rra Ngombe, what's going on? You don't look happy. Nor do the rest of you."

Ngombe looked down but said nothing.

Kubu banged his fist on the table. "What's going on? Tell me, please."

"We can't tell you, Kubu. I'm sorry," Ngombe muttered. "The detective said—"

Kubu jumped to his feet. "Detective Khama? She's the most junior detective in the CID! What right does she have to tell you what to say to *me*? Damn it! I'm Wilmon's son!"

Ngombe put a hand on Kubu's arm. "She said it was important. That the murderer might get off. That it was an order from your boss!"

"We can't say anything, Kubu," Vilikazi said. He hesitated. "But you may want to speak to the bartender," he added quietly.

Kubu frowned. "Order another round. I'll be right back."

Kubu walked over to the counter and accosted the bartender.

"You knew my father, Wilmon Bengu?"

"Of course, rra. A wonderful man."

"My friends tell me that you may be able to tell me something that could be related to his death."

The man stared at Kubu. "You mean about the man from Tobela? I can't do that, rra. I was told not to tell you anything."

"Goddammit!" Kubu shouted, and leaned forward to grab the man's shirt. The bartender jumped back.

"I'm his son!" Kubu slammed the counter with his fist, causing glasses to rattle along its length. Patrons stared at the large man, and those close by moved away.

Ngombe jumped up and came over. "Come on, Kubu," he said, grabbing his arm. "I'm sure the police told him the same thing. You have to keep out of it."

At first, Kubu didn't move, then he acquiesced and walked back, head hanging.

"I'm sorry," he said as he sat down. "It's just so hard to be kept away from what is going on."

The others nodded. "We understand," Vilikazi said.

"Let's finish the drinks, my friends," Kubu said. "Then I must get back to my mother."

The group finished their beers and moved unsteadily toward the exit. Kubu paid the bill, glaring at the manager as he did, and left, wondering how he was going to extract information from Samantha without jeopardizing his future at the CID.

AS KUBU AND Ngombe approached Amantle's house, they heard singing.

"The prayers have started," Kubu said. "We'd better go inside."

But when they reached the house, they realized that going inside was pointless, probably impossible. At least fifty people were on the sidewalk and even on the street below the veranda. Amantle, Mma Ngombe, and several others were on the veranda overlooking the crowd. A man Kubu didn't recognize was leading the singing.

"*Lumelang! Kea tsamaea,*
Ke ea lefatšeng lela.
Jesu oa mpitsa,
O ntokisetsa,
Sebaka sa ho lula."

Kubu joined in with gusto. Every Motswana knew the song.

When the song ended, the man on the veranda said a short prayer praising the Lord and offering salvation to all believers.

"Amen," he shouted.

"Amen," came the response from the crowd.

The man started singing again.

"*Greetings! I am leaving,*
I am going to that world.
Jesus is calling me,
He is preparing me,
A place to stay."

Again the crowd joined in.

IT WAS WELL past midnight when the singing stopped and the crowd dispersed. It's amazing, Kubu thought, how music is at the core of everything we do. We sing when a baby is born, we sing at birthdays and weddings, we sing at work, and we sing when people die. Everyone just loves to sing. It's amazing.

And what happened today will happen again tomorrow. And on Friday, the activities will last all night. What a send-off for Father.

Then he went inside and found Amantle making a cup of tea.

"I need something to make me sleep," she said. "It has been a long day, but I keep thinking of your father. Forty years together. It does not seem that long."

"You two were very lucky," he said.

Amantle shook her head. "There was no luck. If you believe in God and never give up in hard times, a marriage will last. Just remember that when you and Joy have problems."

"Yes, Mother," he said quietly. "I would never want to lose her. She's the only person I could ever love."

"I will take my tea to the bedroom. Tomorrow will be tiring again. Please take this cup to the constable outside."

Kubu had forgotten about the guard Mabaku had ordered. He delivered the tea, then came back and sat down.

It was the first time in hours that he'd had time to reflect. He wondered who the man from Tobela was and if Samantha had learned anything that would really help to find his father's killer.

What if I never find out? he wondered. What if I have to spend the rest of my life not knowing?

He shook his head, trying to banish these insidious thoughts.

What if the killer comes after Joy or the kids?

What if he comes after me? What will my family do if I'm dead?

He stood up and started undressing.

Dear God, please let me sleep.

CHAPTER 16

Director Mabaku was so frustrated at the lack of progress that he called Thursday's meeting for seven in the morning. He hoped that would send a strong message of urgency.

He looked very tired as he brought the meeting to order. "Well?" he asked. "I hope someone has made some progress. Zanele, what about you?"

"As I expected, the boot print we found is from boots that are sold in every Chinese store in town. They sell hundreds a year. But the interesting thing is that they are not sold in any of the ordinary shoe or clothing stores. The manager of one told me that they would like to carry them because they are so popular, but the distributor always tells them that it is out of stock. He's convinced that it only sells them to Chinese stores."

"That doesn't help us at all," Mabaku said. "I assume that they do not have a list of all their customers?"

"I asked about that. I was told most sales are for cash."

"And probably not reported on their tax forms either," Mabaku growled.

"We're not making much progress with all the hairs we found at Mma Bengu's house. So many people were there after her husband was killed. We'll just keep at it."

Mabaku turned to Samantha.

"I have a lot of information, but I'm not sure I've made any progress." She opened her notebook. "I went to Mahalapye yesterday and spoke to Mzi Bengu—Kubu's half uncle. He's a surly, unhelpful man. He lives near one of the pay phones but denies knowing anything about calls to his half brother. He claims he hasn't spoken to Kubu's father for years."

Mabaku grunted. "Do you believe him?"

Samantha shrugged. "I met him at his favorite bar. He was there last Saturday too. He left when they threw him out. He definitely wasn't in Mochudi."

"What about the pay phone itself? Maybe someone saw him use it."

Samantha sighed. "There are no CCTVs in the area. I asked some people who live around there, but nobody can remember anything out of the ordinary." She shrugged.

"On Tuesday, I spoke to all of Rra Bengu's friends. He told them he was going to meet a relative from Tobela—that's a small village close to Shoshong. They had some sort of disagreement, and Bengu stormed out of the shebeen, calling the man a fraud. Anyway, they came back, talked for a while, and when Bengu left, he said something about *it* being for Kubu. Nobody knows what that means."

"Does Kubu's mother know anybody in Tobela?" This time it was Zanele who asked.

"She told me that she doesn't but that it's Rra Bengu's ancestral home, so maybe it could have been some distant relative. She also had no idea what it could be that Rra Bengu was referring to when he said *it* was for Kubu."

She paused. "I spoke to Kubu and asked if he knew. He also said he had no idea what his father was talking about. There is one small piece of information I'll follow up on—the bartender saw the man drive away in a silver Toyota. I'm sure there are plenty around, but I'll see what I can do."

Mabaku grunted. "It's probably nothing, but ask the newspapers to say that the police want to interview a man who visited Rra Bengu last week, who came from the Tobela area and drove a silver Toyota. Maybe the man will come forward, and then we can close the issue. Or maybe someone recognized him."

Samantha glanced nervously at Mabaku. "I'm sorry I haven't made any useful progress."

"This is how most investigations go," Mabaku said. "It's slow work gathering information. We hope suddenly a pattern will emerge that will lead us to the killer. It's always hard work. Keep on it."

CHAPTER 17

On Thursday morning, the need to know what was going on proved too strong for Kubu, and he decided to call Mabaku and ask for permission to speak to Samantha.

After the pleasantries were over, Kubu took a deep breath.

"Jacob, I was at the shebeen last night with some of my father's friends. We were having a drink to his memory. The bartender mentioned that Father had recently met with a man from Tobela. He wouldn't say anything more but said that he had told Samantha everything. I wonder—"

"No, you can't! And I don't believe for one moment that the bartender told you that without some encouragement from you."

"But, Director—"

Kubu heard Mabaku take a deep breath and let it out with a sudden whoosh. "I told you to keep out of this case, Bengu, and the first thing you do is start questioning the neighbors, and then you start interrogating people in bars! I TOLD YOU NOT TO GET INVOLVED!" The last sentence was so loud that Kubu had to move the phone away from his ear.

Kubu decided that attack was the best form of defense. "Well, Director," he said angrily, "how can you expect a young detective with little experience to make progress? You need me on this case. Otherwise, it's not going to be solved!"

For a moment Kubu thought he'd gone too far. The silence on the other end of the line made him think the director had hung up on him. But when the director eventually spoke, it was in an icy voice.

"This is your last warning, Assistant Superintendent Bengu. If I hear of one more breach of my instructions, you will not like the consequences. Good-bye."

Kubu was left holding his cell phone, which was deathly silent. He wanted to scream.

THE REST OF Thursday was very frustrating. There was little Kubu could do to help his mother and her army of friends prepare for the funeral, although he did go and buy two pounds of salt to put in the beef *seswaa*. Even his hopes of seeing his family later in the day were dashed when Joy phoned to say they would only arrive on Friday afternoon.

So Kubu had to while away the rest of the day. He sat on the veranda; he walked around the block; he had a couple of beers at the shebeen and wasn't sure if he was happy or disappointed that the manager wasn't there; and he chatted to some of the numerous visitors to Amantle's home.

The only positive time came after dinner, when people drew together to pray and sing. The throng gathered around Amantle's house was so large that Kubu could sing at the top of his voice without embarrassment. Normally, he only sang in his Land Rover when no one could hear him. But tonight, he let loose.

CHAPTER 18

It felt as though he had barely gone to sleep when he was abruptly awakened.

"Wake up, David. Wake up, please." Kubu opened his eyes to see his mother shaking him by the shoulder.

"I have made a big mistake," she continued. "A big mistake."

"What is it, Mother?" Kubu muttered.

"When we went shopping, we bought food for four hundred people. I thought it was enough. But everyone is telling me that it is likely to be closer to one thousand."

"One thousand?" Kubu sat up. This was going to cost a fortune. "That's not possible, is it?"

"Today is Friday, and the funeral is tomorrow. We will have to go shopping right away, David. And we will have to buy two large pots as well. The church only has two. We can donate them to the church afterward."

Kubu tried to get his mind around this news.

"But we will not have to buy as much meat as we did before,"

Amantle continued. "Wilmon's friends have brought a cow, and they will kill it this evening. Then we can carve it up and use it. It is so very kind of them."

THAT AFTERNOON, THE funeral festivities—there really was no other name for them—moved to the church kitchen and hall. Dozens of women helped Amantle prepare prodigious amounts of *pap*, beef *seswaa*, and *samp* and beans—a process that would last all night with waves of helpers coming and going.

The men, on the other hand, had it easy. Mochudi was a big enough town that there was a small backhoe at the cemetery to dig the graves. So they had the time to sit around, talk, and enjoy a lot of beer, both St. Louis and Shake Shake. Kubu would have preferred a glass of red wine but decided against opening a bottle because he would have had to share it with people he didn't know, whose taste buds were better attuned to the revolting Shake Shake beer.

When Joy, Tumi, and Nono arrived in the late afternoon, he only had time to give them each a hug and a kiss before they all headed to the church kitchen to be with Amantle. He felt a bit put out. His mother had lots of company, and he felt quite lonely in the crowd.

Early in the evening, a hearse arrived with an elaborate coffin. Here was an opportunity for the men to help. They put down their beers and carried the coffin into the church, where the funeral-home attendant unscrewed the top and slid it open so that Wilmon's face could be seen. Almost immediately, women began to ululate and shout prayers. A line formed, and people shuffled up to pay their last respects. Kubu stood at the back of the church, overcome with emotion. This was the last time he would see his father.

It's amazing, Kubu thought. His mother had arranged everything, and he, Kubu, had done virtually nothing. But that was the way of things in traditional funerals.

· · ·

THROUGHOUT THE NIGHT, preparations progressed, punctuated with prayers and singing, not organized, but rather different groups spontaneously standing and lifting their voices. Kubu found it very moving even as he felt exhaustion slowly taking hold. He didn't dare to lie on one of the couches in the hall lest he fall fast asleep. His mother would never forgive him.

As dawn broke, a *bakkie* arrived with several men on the back, holding large urns. "I hope it's coffee," Kubu said to the man standing next to him—a man Kubu had never seen before. Fortunately, it was, and lines soon formed. People needed something to keep them going until ten a.m., when the service was due to start. When Kubu reached the urn, he filled three Styrofoam cups with coffee, milk, and sugar—two for him and one for his mother.

Around eight, people started to drift home to change into their finest clothes for the service. Amantle only had one black dress, so she stayed, but Kubu went and donned his only suit.

THE CHURCH WAS full for the service. Fortunately for the hundreds of people outside there were a few clouds to break the oppressive heat. When the service was over, the crowd moved toward the grave in a long procession, led by Amantle, Kubu, Joy, Tumi, and Nono. The air was filled with songs and ululations.

At the grave, the casket was poised above the hole, ropes in place. Close by was a small awning, erected to protect the dignitaries from the sun. When all in the procession had arrived, the priest said a few final words and asked if anyone would like to speak. It was an hour before he turned to Kubu. "It is your turn," he said.

Kubu pushed himself to his feet, mopped his brow, and took the microphone.

"*Dumela*. Amantle, Wilmon's wife, and I want to thank you for your support. It is overwhelming." He used both his arms to illustrate the extent of the crowd.

"Our family will miss Wilmon a great deal, as I know you will."

A murmur ran through the crowd.

"Those who spoke before me praised my father as he deserved, and I'm not going to repeat what they have already said. But I have to say, as his son, that I couldn't have had a better father. He brought me up to respect the traditions of our people, but he also saw the future and made sure that I had an education that would enable me to raise a family in a changing world. He was wise and tolerant and fair. But he also demanded obedience." He paused. "I remember the first time I came home late for dinner—I had been playing with one of my friends in the hills—and the time slipped away from us. He took me behind the house, made me bend over, and gave me six lashes with a reed. I don't think it was actually sore, but I thought it was and cried for about an hour. And I didn't have any dinner." Kubu smiled. "I never missed dinner again!"

As the crowd laughed at the thought of him missing a meal, Kubu looked around, trying to locate Mabaku, whom he knew would be there. Fortunately, Ian MacGregor's white face stuck out from the throng, and Kubu saw Mabaku standing next to him.

"But I do have something to say which I ask you all to listen to very carefully." He paused and surveyed the faces in front of him.

"My father was murdered, as most of you know." There was a buzz from the crowd and several shouts and ululations.

"As of today, we don't know who did it. We don't know why he was killed. We don't know why such a man, whom we all loved, was taken from us."

Kubu had to pause as the noise swelled.

"He was a good man!"

The noise level increased.

"He was a man of and for the community!"

He had to wait again.

"He was a man who respected every one of you. And helped you with his medicines when he was able. Helped you with his wisdom when he could."

Kubu looked at Mabaku, but he was too far away to tell the director's mood.

"And someone killed this man whom you all loved. Murdered my father. Took him away before his time."

Now the crowd was getting agitated and angry.

That's enough, Kubu thought. Now I must bring them down. He used his arms to indicate he wanted quiet.

"My father would ask you to do what he would do if a friend of his was killed. If you have any information that may help the police find the man who murdered my father, please tell Director Mabaku, who is standing over there." Kubu pointed in the direction of his boss. "Or any policeman anywhere. But don't tell me because it will make me more angry than I am already. And I don't want that."

He looked over the crowd.

"We will now lay my father to rest. *Ke a leboga*. Thank you. *Tsamaya sentle*. Go well."

Kubu and a group of Wilmon's friends took hold of the ropes and slowly lowered the casket into the grave. Amantle stood up, walked to the grave, tears flowing freely, and threw the first bunch of flowers onto the casket. And for the next hour and a half, people filed by the grave throwing in a handful of dirt or some flowers. They then offered Amantle and Kubu their condolences and worked their way to the church hall, where mountains of refreshments awaited.

Eventually, the line disappeared, and Kubu and a few of Wilmon's friends took turns using the solitary shovel to fill in the rest of the grave. When it was finished and the canvas cover moved into place, Kubu stood alone at the grave.

"Good-bye, Father," he whispered. "Everything I have, I owe to you."

He turned and headed to the much needed refreshment table.

PART 3

At the same time Wilmon's funeral was taking place in Mochudi, another gathering was convening a three-hour drive north in the village of Shoshong. Constable Polanka hadn't seen anything like it before. Dust rose into the air from the hundreds of feet moving along the sandy roads, and the air was full of babble as arguments flared up between different groups. It seemed as though every person in Shoshong was headed for the *kgotla*. He wondered what the chief would decide.

Polanka didn't know what to think. He'd heard all the arguments, and whatever position someone took, he found himself agreeing with it. When he'd asked the station commander his opinion, the man growled, "It's trouble either way. Don't get involved. Don't give people your opinion."

If what they said was true, he thought, Shoshong would benefit from many more jobs. That would be good for a village where many men spent their days sitting in shebeens drinking Shake Shake beer. But what if it wasn't true? What if the promises were empty? Then so many people would have to move for nothing. The only people to benefit would be the people who owned the mine.

He shook his head. He was pleased he wasn't the chief, who had to make the decision.

He was about to head for the *kgotla* himself when a well-dressed white man wearing dark glasses walked up.

"*Dumela*, rra," the man said with a broad smile.

"*Dumela*," Polanka replied, wondering who the stranger was. He didn't recognize the accent.

"Are these people all going to the cottler?"

"Cottler? You mean the *kgotla*?"

"Yes, the meeting."

Polanka frowned, wondering why white people had such difficulty pronouncing simple words like *kgotla*. "Just follow the people," he said.

"Thank you." The man turned and joined the crowd.

Must be from the newspapers, Polanka thought. Or maybe from television, since he was good-looking. Then he, too, headed for the meeting.

THE GRAYING CHIEF, leaning on his carved staff, walked slowly through the throng to the low platform that had been set up at the front of the *kgotla*. He was followed by his son and the four elders who comprised his advisory council. They climbed the two steps and sat down, thankful for the canvas tarpaulin that provided shade from the broiling sun.

A young man lifted a microphone onto the platform and set it up in front of the chief. He tapped it and, hearing nothing, spoke into it. "One, two three, four." Still nothing.

"We do not need that thing," the chief said. "I can just speak."

"*Kgosi*, only the people in the front will hear you. That's fine for most meetings, but this is different. The whole village is here, and everyone wants to hear what you have to say."

"We have never needed it before."

"*Kgosi*, let me make sure it's working. Then I'll turn it off. You can start speaking without it." He jumped off the side of the platform and fiddled with some knobs. He stepped back up and tapped the microphone again. Dull thumps reverberated from the speakers he'd tied to the trees.

"It's ready, *Kgosi*. If you need it, I'll turn it on."

THE CHIEF WAITED for another ten minutes before he decided to start. He lifted his staff and brought it down sharply onto the platform. He repeated this three times. Slowly, the hubbub subsided as the people in the front turned and shushed those behind.

"*Dumela*," the chief said. The first couple of rows responded.

The chief looked at the crowd. "Thank you for attending this important *kgotla*. I have an important and difficult decision to make. I need to listen to what you think."

"We can't hear you!"

"Talk louder!"

"Use the microphone!"

The shouts came from the younger members of the crowd, who were standing at the back.

The young man next to the stage looked at the chief expectantly. Eventually, the chief frowned and nodded at the man, who turned on the microphone. Then he jumped up and set the microphone just in front of the chief's face.

"Please. You must talk into the microphone, *Kgosi*. Otherwise, people won't hear."

The chief didn't look pleased with this intrusion of modern technology into the traditional *kgotla*. He cleared his throat.

"Thank you for attending this important *kgotla*. I have an important and difficult decision to make. I need to listen to what you think." He looked around and saw people throughout the crowd nodding in agreement.

"As you know, the mine to the east of Shoshong wants to expand. The director of mines for Botswana, Rra Mopati, has told me that the mine expects to hire another two hundred men and twenty-five women if the expansion takes place. That would be very good for Shoshong, because there are many people here without work, and families are suffering."

A number of young men at the back of the crowd cheered.

The chief, not used to being interrupted, lost his train of thought and glared at them. He banged his staff into the platform.

"For the mine to expand," he continued, "it will need to take land between the existing mine and the village. There are about eighty homes where the mine wants to go. The mine has told the director that it will provide better land for the people who live there and build better homes for every family that is displaced."

There were more cheers from the back.

"And it will also give each family ten thousand pula to help make the move."

"Let's do it!"

"Why are we waiting?"

The chief looked angrily at the back of the crowd. "Please, please. Let me finish." He leaned forward toward the microphone again. "The offer appears to be a fair one, and the director says that the government is supporting the application by the mine because it will help the people of Shoshong, and it will bring many millions of pula into the country, which can be used to benefit everyone."

He pulled out a dirty handkerchief and coughed into it—a deep, rattling cough that lingered for some time.

"On the other hand, some of the elders on my council are not in favor of the proposal . . ."

That brought a chorus of jeers from the back.

"This is the last time I will say this," the chief said angrily. "If you cannot behave in a manner befitting a *kgotla*, I will have to ask Constable Polanka to remove you." He pointed at the policeman, who was standing at the side of the stage. Polanka stuck out his chest and tried to look official. The chief tried to locate where the sniggers were coming from, but his eyesight wasn't good enough to make out individual faces at the back of the crowd.

"I will ask Rra Maedze to speak to you."

The young man jumped onto the stage again and moved the microphone in front of one of the elderly men, who remained seated.

"Speak into the microphone please, rra."

The old man cleared his throat.

"*Dumela.*" He looked around and was gratified that he heard a few *dumela*s in return.

"Last summer, my granddaughter was to be married. Several weeks before the ceremony, the father of her betrothed brought the agreed-upon *lobola*." He smiled. "It was a good amount of cattle. Some he had to buy because his family did not have enough.

"I was with my son when the cattle arrived, so we inspected them together. Of course, we could have just sat down and enjoyed many beers, but it was our responsibility to make sure that the *lobola* contract had been satisfied." He looked around but didn't notice that the men at the back were getting fidgety at the story that appeared to have nothing to do with the purpose of the meeting.

"When we looked carefully, three of the cattle were not well. It was quite embarrassing for everyone. When we pointed this out, the father said they were among the ones he bought, but he had been in a rush to get them to us and had not looked at them carefully enough. He was an honorable man and took the cattle away. When he returned the next day with healthy cattle, he told us that he was able to make the man he bought them from give him healthy ones. So all ended well."

Once again, he looked around.

"I know some of you wonder why I tell this story. Mainly you young men at the back." He waved his hand dismissively. "As we consider the proposal from the mine, we must think of it like a marriage. What the mine is offering us is *lobola* for the village of Shoshong and for those who will have to move. We must make sure that the number of cattle offered is enough, and we must check that all the cattle are healthy."

He shuffled in his chair trying to get comfortable.

"Let me tell you a story," the old man continued, to a chorus of groans from the back. "Before some of you were born, there was no mine here. And officials from the government and from a mining company approached us because they needed land for the mine. Land where many people lived. Just like today. They made a promise to the chief that the people who moved would have better land and better houses. And they would receive some pula for their trouble. It was just like today. The chief—*Kgosi*'s father—agreed. So did the elders. And the village was excited.

"The mine took the land, knocked down the houses before new ones were ready, and then took a year to build the new houses. And they were poor in quality—no better than shacks—on land that could not be used for cattle, only for a few goats. And this happened even after the government spoke to the owners of the mine." He cleared his throat.

"My family was one of those moved. Where we lived before was a fine house with good grazing around it. The new house was bad. So bad, we left the house and had to stay with relatives. And we had no money.

"So what I say is this: we must make sure that all the *lobola* cattle are healthy. If we agree to this move, it is *we* who must select the land that will be used for the new houses, and it is *we* who must approve the quality of the houses before the old houses are knocked down. And it is *we* who must be given the money right away. If we wait until the mine expands, I fear what happened before will happen again. Thank you."

Constable Polanka noticed that many of the people who applauded were elderly and seated at the front.

A young man at the back put up his hand. "*Kgosi*, I would like to speak."

The chief nodded, and the man came onto the platform. For several minutes he urged the chief to accept the offer. "I want to work," he said, "but there is nothing here in Shoshong for me. And many of my friends feel the same. We need jobs and money."

Shouts of approval and clapping erupted from the back of the crowd.

Another young man ran down from the back.

He grabbed the microphone. "We're wasting our time," he shouted. "There are more young people than old in Shoshong. We need the mine. We shouldn't listen to these old men who have nothing better to do than to dream of the past. We need jobs. I say we tell the mine to go ahead." The young people roared their approval.

"Yes! Yes! Yes!" they shouted.

The chief struggled to his feet and went to the microphone.

"I am the chief of Shoshong," he spluttered. "It is I who makes the decisions with my council. The government will not listen to you. You—"

"Jobs! Jobs! Jobs!" The chief's voice was drowned out.

Constable Polanka realized that things were getting out of control. He walked in front of the stage and held up his hands. Nobody paid attention. He waved his arms, but the crowd ignored him.

"Please," he shouted. "Let *Kgosi* speak." He waved his arms more vigorously. Eventually, the hubbub diminished until the chief could be heard.

"We have had *kgotla*s for many hundreds of years. They have served us well."

A chorus of boos came from the back.

The chief banged his staff on the platform.

"Does anyone else want to speak?"

A hand shot up, and a woman with a baby strapped to her back with a blanket walked forward. Everyone was suddenly quiet. It was unusual for a woman to speak at a *kgotla* that was discussing land and jobs. Those were matters for men.

She clambered onto the platform, grabbed the microphone, and glared at the elders. "You speak of *lobola* and history and tradition. Your children are grown up. What about my children? This is only one of them!"

The crowd laughed, enjoying the feisty woman and the discomfort of the council.

"Look there!" She pointed at a man nearby in the crowd. "That's my husband. He's not a bad man, but he can't find a proper job, a job to support our family. He spends his days with his friends. He does odd jobs, and the money he gets he drinks!"

The crowd laughed again, and the men muttered jokes to each other about this man needing some lessons about showing his wife who was boss. But many of the women clapped. When the crowd was quiet again, she said, "*Kgosi*, you must get us these jobs. Otherwise, stand aside and let someone else find them for us." Then she climbed down from the platform and returned to her husband's side.

The chief was speechless with anger at her insolence, but there was little he could do as another man had already taken the microphone and had started talking. And so it went on for another hour, some people for the proposal and some against. In general, younger people supported the offer enthusiastically, but older people, while not rejecting it out of hand, were much more cautious.

Eventually, the chief put up his hands.

"That is enough! We have heard fine arguments for and against the offer. My council and I will take everything into consideration. We will meet here next week at the same time for my decision. Thank you for attending the *kgotla*." He looked toward the back of the crowd. "We would like the young men—and women—of the village to attend all our meetings, not just the ones that may affect them."

He, his son, and the other elders stood up, descended the stairs, and shuffled through the crowd.

PART 4

CHAPTER 20

Petrus Towane was elderly, but he believed in exercise to keep healthy. So every morning he would start the day with a long walk with his dog. Lenny was a mongrel, his silky brown coat suggested spaniel, but the shape of his head and often erect ears suggested something more like a border collie.

This morning Petrus chose the road along the Gaborone dam that led past the yacht club. It was quiet with little traffic, and Lenny could run free. The walk started as usual with Lenny noting and replying to messages left by other dogs. However, when they came to the dirt-road turnoff to the dam, Lenny started to behave strangely. He sat on his haunches at the intersection and stared down the track with his ears pricked up. Petrus followed his stare and could see the rear of a car tucked into the bush a short way down the track. It seemed an odd place to park.

"Let's take a look, Lenny."

Petrus started down the track. Lenny walked along behind, still alert and with his tail steady.

From some distance away, Petrus thought that the vehicle was empty, but Lenny sat again and stared at the vehicle. Intrigued by the dog's odd behavior, Petrus walked up to the passenger side of the car and looked through the window. The glass was tinted, which made it hard to see clearly, but he realized there was a man sprawled across the front seats. It was too uncomfortable a position for the person to be asleep.

"He's drunk, Lenny," Petrus told the dog. "He pulled off here and passed out."

He shook his head and was about to turn away when he spotted a garden hose sticking through the top of the driver's window. He swore and tried the door, but it was locked. Rushing to the other side, he yanked the hose out of the window and tried the driver's door, but it was also locked. Lenny came to life and ran around the car barking.

"Quiet, Lenny. We have to get him out! He may still be alive."

He could get his fingers through the gap at the top of the window by pushing through the duct tape sealing it, but he couldn't force the glass down. "Damn it, Lenny!"

Petrus looked around for something to use to break the glass and settled on a rock tapering at one end. Closing his eyes, he slammed it into the middle of the window, but it just bounced. Cursing, he tried again, as hard as he could but without success. Then, aiming at the exposed edge of the window, he managed to get the window top to shatter. He reached in and unlocked the door, cutting his arm in the process. Flinging open the door, he reached in, grabbed the man's shoulders, and dragged him out of the car. He put his hand on the man's forehead. It was warm. Then he felt for a pulse but couldn't detect any signs of life. Leaving the body where it lay, he phoned for the police.

CHAPTER 21

Kubu had known that his first day back at the CID was going to be painful. He made his way to his office through a gauntlet of sober-faced detectives. He knew his colleagues meant well, but all the condolences, all the vows to get the murderer, just made Kubu feel worse. He didn't want to keep being reminded. Now that the funeral was over, he wanted a semblance of normalcy. He wanted to sit in his office and think about something else.

He started catching up with e-mail and paperwork, a job he usually hated, but one he found almost relaxing now. He was glad to be left alone, and it was nearly lunchtime before he was disturbed. There was a knock on the door, and he looked up warily. It was a relief to see Ian MacGregor.

"How are you doing, Kubu?"

Kubu shrugged.

"Yes, well, it's going to take time, my friend, a lot of time. There isn't anything else that helps."

The words were clichéd enough, but the way he said them

sounded as though he'd been there himself. Kubu realized that he'd never asked Ian about his family. The Scotsman seemed happy enough living alone in Botswana, being the state pathologist and indulging his passion for painting watercolor scenes of the Kalahari. But what history lay behind that?

"I've got a story for you, Kubu. I've just been to see Mabaku, and he sent me to you. He's busy himself with . . ." Ian's voice trailed off. Kubu just nodded. He knew what Mabaku was busy with.

"Anyway," Ian continued after a moment, "it's that suicide. Kunene. A high-up in the Department of Mines."

Kubu looked puzzled. He had no idea what Ian was talking about.

"It's been all over the news," Ian added.

"I haven't been following the news much lately."

"I suppose not. Well, I'm talking about Goodman Kunene. He is, or rather was, the assistant director of the Department of Mines. On Friday, he was found dead, gassed in his car. It was down a quiet road near the yacht club. It seems he connected a hose to his exhaust, fed it into the driver's window, sealed it with duct tape, and ran the engine. When he was found, the car had run out of fuel, but Kunene had run out of breath long before that. I did the autopsy this morning."

Kubu wondered why Mabaku had sent Ian to him. He wasn't really interested in suicides.

"Was there a note?"

Ian shook his head.

"Problems at home? At work?"

Ian shrugged. "I don't know any of that stuff. You'll have to ask the investigating officer. The point is that I have doubts about it."

"That he was killed by the car fumes?" Kubu wished Ian would be less obscure.

"No. No question about that. The fingernails and lips had the

characteristic reddish hue of death from carbon monoxide poison-
ing, and I confirmed it with blood tests from a sample we took
when the body was brought in. The blood alcohol level was also
quite high. He'd had a wee bit too much to drink—about seven or
eight drinks, I would estimate. I was surprised that he was sober
enough to set up the whole suicide scenario after that."

Kubu thought about it. "Maybe something depressed him, and
he went on a binge. That would just make him feel worse. Maybe
he couldn't see any way out." But it seemed wrong. This had been
planned down to the hose and the duct tape.

Ian seemed to share the thought. "That's not really consistent
with a suicide like this."

"Could someone have got him drunk and then put him in
the car?"

"I doubt he was drunk enough to pass out, and it would've been
very risky. Suppose he came around and escaped? But I've sent off
some samples to the lab. Maybe the drinks were mixed with something else."

Kubu digested that and then asked, "Any signs of a struggle?
Bruises or blood on him?"

Ian shook his head. "There was blood on his jacket, but that
came from the man who found him. He cut his hand breaking the
window."

Kubu felt a stirring of interest. "I'd better go and chat to the
director about this."

MABAKU SAW HIM at once. He waved Kubu to a chair and looked
him over critically.

"You look tired."

Kubu forced a smile. "I'm not sleeping too well. Don't worry. I'm
fine."

"Kubu, you can take some more time off if you like. We can
cope for another week."

Kubu shook his head. "Better to get back to work. I'm interested in this Kunene story."

"Ian spoke to you?"

Kubu nodded.

"It's a bit of a mess, Kubu. Goodman Kunene was a senior civil servant. It's a big deal. A man who lives in the area found him. He thought Kunene might still be alive, so he broke into the car to get him out. And the policemen who came to the scene didn't do a great job. To be fair, they naturally thought it was a straightforward suicide. So they got an ambulance to take him to the morgue and had the car towed to the police vehicle lot. Not exactly a perfect crime scene, if that's what it is."

"Who is working on the case?"

"Edison."

Kubu sighed. Edison would follow procedure. He was a good enough detective, but he lacked flair.

"I'll talk to him. And I'll ask Zanele to have her people check out the car and the place it was parked."

"Look, Kubu, this could blow up in our faces. It's very high profile, and we can't afford to go crashing around. That's why I want you to take over from Edison. Suicide is one thing, but murder . . ."

"I'll be careful, Director."

Mabaku nodded and waited for him to leave, but Kubu wasn't going anywhere just yet.

"Jacob, what have you got on my father's case? It's been over a week. And what about the break-in at the house? We should have something by now."

It was Mabaku's turn to sigh. "Nothing much yet. You know it takes time. I realize this is hard for you, Kubu, but we'll get to the bottom of it. The whole department is working on it."

"The whole department, except me." Kubu hesitated. "Did you get any leads on the man who upset my father so badly at the shebeen?"

"Samantha got a decent description, but the man was apparently from out of town. She hasn't been able to find anyone who recognized him, but she's circulated the description to other police stations. If the man's a criminal, they may recognize him. Also she's trying to trace the silver Toyota, but there're plenty of those. No luck so far, but she's working on it."

Kubu thought that was a long shot, but he didn't have any better ideas. Still, he might get some if he had all the information.

"Look, Jacob, I want to be in the loop on the case. Sit in on the meetings, offer suggestions." He held up both hands as Mabaku frowned and started to interrupt. "I won't do anything. I'll leave everything to you and Samantha. But at least that way, I can follow what's happening and feel that I'm helping."

Mabaku thought about it. Kubu was back in the office, and everyone talked about the case; CID meetings focused on it. And, in fact, he could do with Kubu's insights.

"All right, Kubu. If I have your word that you'll do *nothing*. No more talks to neighbors. No more chats to bartenders. Nothing!"

Kubu promised and rose to leave. He was relieved and pleased. Mabaku had been fair, and now he could get a detailed report from Samantha about what was going on. He was sure he'd be able to persuade her to follow up on any ideas he had. It was almost as good as being on the case himself.

KUBU WASTED NO time contacting Samantha, who immediately called Mabaku to check that she could answer Kubu's questions.

"You don't trust what I say?" Kubu asked after she hung up.

Samantha didn't answer, but she pulled out her notebook. "From what the director tells me, I don't have much to report that you don't already know," she said. "We are still looking at silver Toyotas, but that's going to take us a while yet. There are lots of them, especially because it probably came from somewhere other than Mochudi."

"How are you going about it?" Kubu growled.

"We're trying to speak to the owners of all silver Toyotas in the Mochudi, Mahalapye, and Gaborone areas to see where they were on Monday, the twenty-seventh of January. We also cross-checked this with our Known Criminals database. It's very tedious, and several people are working on it."

Samantha hesitated. "I went up to Mahalapye to check out the public phones where the calls to your father were made, and I spoke to your uncle, Mzi. I must say he wasn't very helpful, but he was at his favorite shebeen—Kalahari Oasis—the whole night when your father was attacked. I also stopped at Tobela, but I didn't discover anything." She looked at Kubu. "That's all I have. I'm sorry."

Kubu stood up. "Thank you, Samantha. Please let me know when you learn something."

He returned to his office frustrated by the lack of progress, but he acknowledged a little sheepishly, at least to himself, that Samantha was doing a good job.

CHAPTER 22

Kubu realized he had to talk to Kunene's wife. For the first time in his life, he felt that he really understood what she was going through, and he was reluctant to trespass on that grief. But there was no option, so he found her address and headed to the house.

Tasela Kunene was drinking tea with a neighbor. She was a stout woman, dressed formally in black. Her eyes were red, but what struck Kubu at once was that one eye looked swollen, and she had a crepe bandage on her left forearm.

Kubu introduced himself, and the neighbor retired to fuss in the kitchen and allow them some privacy. Feeling strangely embarrassed, Kubu offered his condolences. She nodded and offered him a chair opposite her. He wasn't sure where to begin.

"Mma Kunene, I'm sorry to disturb you at a time like this, but the police need to investigate any death not due to natural causes. It's standard procedure."

Tasela surprised him with her response. "I hope you don't believe that Goodman committed suicide like that other detective did."

Kubu hesitated. "The circumstances seemed to suggest suicide, mma."

She shook her head. "You don't know him. Goodman got a promotion about six months ago, so he was making good money. We have two fine sons and a fine house. Why would he kill himself?"

"There was no indication of depression? The two of you were happy?"

She nodded.

"Was your husband on any regular medication? Was he under the regular care of a doctor?"

She shook her head firmly.

"So what do *you* think happened, mma?" Kubu asked gently.

She shifted about in her chair, obviously uncomfortable. "Could it have been an accident?"

Kubu shook his head. Although he didn't explain, she accepted that.

"Then someone killed him!"

"Why would anyone do that? Did he have any enemies? Has anyone made threats?"

"He was a senior man in the government. Such people always have enemies. People after their jobs."

Kubu nodded, but in his experience, politicians and senior administrators tried for each other's jobs by stabs in the back rather than by asphyxiation.

"Had anyone threatened him?"

Mma Kunene looked around the room as if she expected to find the answer written somewhere there. At last she said, "I don't know. But there was the insurance policy."

Kubu leaned forward. This was an interesting development. He waited for her to continue.

"He took out a new life policy about six months ago. He said it was just in case something unexpected happened, but I'm sure he was worried about something. I'm sure there was more behind it, but he refused to tell me." She looked down and fiddled with her jacket.

"How much was this policy for?"

"One million pula."

Kubu was careful to show no reaction. A million pula was a lot of money! He spotted a possible reason for Mma Kunene's concern about the cause of death.

"And the company won't pay for suicide?"

She shook her head. "No, because the policy is so new. But that's not the point, Assistant Superintendent. I don't care about the money. Something happened to my husband, and I want to know what."

Kubu watched her face for several seconds, but she didn't look away. Maybe it was true. Maybe the money wasn't the issue.

Kubu leaned forward. "How did you hurt your arm?"

"I fell." Now she avoided his eyes.

"And your face?"

"The same fall."

Kubu frowned. Obviously, she was lying. It was almost certain that it was her husband she was protecting, and it was too late for that now anyway. "Mma, you believe we're dealing with murder here, and you may well be right. Lying to the police is a very serious matter. It could even make you a suspect. Don't make me ask your boys what really happened. You all have enough to deal with at the moment."

Tasela turned away from him, and tears ran down her face.

Feeling awful, Kubu went and asked the neighbor for more tea and a few tissues. She gave him a dirty look and bustled in, but Tasela seemed to have pulled herself together. Nevertheless, she added three spoons of sugar to the tea, stirred, and sipped it in silence until the neighbor left again. Only then did she answer Kubu's question.

"We had a fight. It was my fault, really. Goodman sometimes

has to work very late, meeting people for drinks and so on. Last week, he missed dinner and came in a bit drunk. I accused him of having another woman. He denied it and said he had a special contact he had to see after work, but he wouldn't tell me who it was or anything about this person. I got angry and screamed that I didn't believe him, that he was sleeping with another woman. I . . . I called him bad names. It got out of hand. He was very sorry afterward. Said it would never happen again."

"Has it happened before?"

"Only once before. Look, Assistant Superintendent, we were happy. Really. He wouldn't kill himself over a fight, would he? Everyone has them . . ."

"Certainly not a week later, mma. There's nothing to blame yourself for."

"He hit me in the face, just once. I fell and cut my arm. That was all there was to it. He just lost his temper. It's not as if he beat me or something." She looked away again.

Kubu sighed. The case was getting more complicated rather than clearer.

"When was the last time you saw him?"

"At breakfast. He was in a hurry. He had a busy day. He usually did."

"Did you expect him home for supper that night?"

She shook her head. "He phoned me around lunchtime and said he had a late meeting, and I should just leave something in the oven for him."

"Did he say who he was going to meet?"

She shook her head again. "He just said it was the special contact."

"And what did you do that night?"

She gave him a surprised look. "I was here with the boys. They had to have their dinner."

"When did you get concerned?"

"When I woke up the next morning and he wasn't here. I gave

the boys their breakfast and sent them off to school. Then I phoned his office, but they hadn't seen him either. I was thinking what to do next when there was a knock on the door, and your men were there. Then I knew. I knew something was terribly wrong." The tears started to run again, but she brushed them away angrily. "Is there anything else, Assistant Superintendent?"

"Not now. Thank you, you've been very helpful. I'll have to send someone to take your fingerprints—the boys also—just so we can eliminate those when we check the car. Will that be all right?"

Mma Kunene nodded, and shortly afterward Kubu took his leave.

AS HE WAS driving back to the CID, his cell phone rang. He saw that it was Zanele, so he pulled over and answered.

"Hello, Zanele. What have you got?"

"The problem is that we've got too much," she replied. "Too many fingerprints, hair samples, cloth fibers. That car hadn't been cleaned for some time. We'll have to follow up with the family and eliminate all sorts of things before we can see if anything sticks out." She added with disapproval, "And the policemen on the case handled everything and trudged all over the scene!"

"What about the section of hose?" Kubu asked. "Where did it come from?"

"It's ordinary garden hose. It'll be hard to trace. I'll tell you one thing though. It's not the same as the one Kunene has at his house. Edison checked."

Kubu realized that Edison deserved more credit than he'd given him. "Any fingerprints on it?"

"There were some prints and some smudges, but we haven't identified them."

"What about Kunene's prints?"

Zanele paused while she checked her notes. "Not unless it was a smudge."

"If it was suicide, you'd expect Kunene's prints on it."

Zanele hesitated. "I suppose so."

"Keep working on it, Zanele. Thanks. And see if you can find out where the hose was bought."

He pulled back into the traffic, thinking about Goodman Kunene. The insurance policy seemed to be key. Why suddenly take out a large policy? Mma Kunene had said he seemed worried about something. He must have perceived a threat if he thought he needed extra life cover. That didn't fit with suicide. And where did he get the hose? His prints should have been clear on it. There was no reason for him to clean it off.

The phone rang again; this time it was Ian. Once more Kubu pulled over and took the call.

"Kubu? It's Ian. I'm afraid I was right. The lab found benzodiazepine in the samples from Kunene."

"Benzodia-what?"

"Benzodiazepine. It's a class of sedative drugs. Like Valium. Like Rohypnol, which has made a bit of a name for itself as a date-rape drug. It's likely it was used to knock Kunene out before he was dumped in that car. Nasty business."

Kubu was convinced. Goodman Kunene had been murdered. And he'd bet that the mysterious special contact Kunene had met on the evening of his death was an important link. Possibly even the murderer.

CHAPTER 23

The next morning found Kubu fretting in the reception area of the director of mines. He'd been waiting for over half an hour and had only been offered *rooibos* tea. Not even a biscuit. The director's secretary ignored his glances at his watch and occasional sighs. He passed the time reexamining Kunene's phone records, which Edison had obtained for him. He sighed again. Samantha would have identified the people by how they fitted into Kunene's life. However, Edison just gave the names and left it at that. Mma Kunene had assisted by identifying some as friends and family, but quite a few were left. It would have helped if they could actually find Kunene's cell phone with its contact list, but the phone was missing. Another puzzle.

Kubu concentrated on the day Kunene died. At around nine in the morning there was a call to a number that Edison had identified as "US Embassy." After that there were several office contacts, an incoming call from an unidentified number, and then, at lunchtime, a call to Kunene's wife—presumably the call where he told her he'd be home late. The unidentified one was interesting because it lasted nearly ten minutes. Edison noted that he'd requested more information from the phone company.

At last the secretary's phone buzzed, and she waved him through to Director Mopati's office.

"Assistant Superintendent, my apologies for keeping you waiting. Things are upside down here since Goodman passed away. My people are doing their best, but . . ." He shrugged and motioned toward a seat facing his desk.

"I understand, Director. And I won't keep you long. I'm investigating Rra Kunene's death." Kubu hesitated. "Certain aspects have come to light that aren't consistent with suicide."

Mopati sank into his executive chair opposite Kubu. "I thought suicide was obvious from the circumstances," he said.

"Perhaps, but we want to check all the possibilities. Did Rra Kunene ever give you any indication that he might want to take his own life?"

Mopati shook his head. "Absolutely not. It was a great shock to us all." He hesitated, rubbing his chin. "To be honest, he sometimes did seem disturbed in recent months. I once asked him about it, but he said he was just going through a bad time at home. That everything would be fine. He apologized, but his work was always excellent. Nothing was too much trouble. His work always came first. He was a very impressive man."

"Did he tell you about his domestic problems?"

Mopati shook his head. "He was having some issues in his marriage, I believe. I'm sure his wife didn't tell you that."

Kubu nodded. Kunene *was* having issues at home, and maybe more than his wife had suggested. But nothing that sounded like a reason for suicide. He waited for the director to continue.

"Women can be difficult, Assistant Superintendent."

"Did he sometimes seem nervous or depressed?"

Mopati took his time. "Now that you mention it, perhaps. He always kept his own council, so maybe I didn't realize it at the time."

Kubu made a few notes while he collected his thoughts. "What was he working on in the days before he died? Could it be related to that?"

Mopati shook his head firmly. "Absolutely not. Routine stuff about applications for mining permits and the like. Nothing dramatic."

"I have his phone records for the week before he died. Some are friends and relatives. I checked with Mma Kunene this morning. Some are other members of staff here, but there are a few less obvious ones. For example, would he have had any reason to call the US embassy?"

The director shrugged. "Of course we have contacts with other governments. Goodman was in touch with someone in the economic section there—I can't remember the person's name. But there was no reason I can think of for him to brief them right now."

Kubu made a note of that. "I also want to check his appointments. Can you please arrange that for me?"

"Why do you want to do that?"

"I only want to know who he saw in the last couple of days. Just routine."

The director looked unhappy, but all he said was "My secretary will help you with that."

"I'd like to look at his office too. His cell phone is missing, which seems very odd for a suicide." Mopati nodded but didn't comment.

Kubu tried another approach. "Did he have any serious enemies here? I'm talking about someone who really hated him, someone who would be glad he's dead. Not someone who just didn't like his opinions or personality."

Mopati shook his head. "No one. He was well liked, although he tended to keep to himself."

"Do you know who he was meeting on the night he died?"

The director shook his head again. "I didn't know he was meeting anyone. He didn't say anything about it. Was he meeting someone?"

Kubu ignored the question and flipped back through his notes.

There were a few things that puzzled him. Kunene had called the US embassy, yet his boss didn't know of any reason why he should have. Kunene was sometimes depressed and kept to himself, yet he explained to his boss that he was having personal problems at home. Which he was, but why had Mopati been in such a hurry to say Kunene's wife wouldn't have admitted it?

"Mma Kunene said that her husband had recently received a promotion. Is that correct?"

"No, he's been my deputy for some time. I wonder why he would tell her that."

"And the insurance policy?"

"What insurance policy?"

Kubu rose to his feet. "It doesn't matter. I've taken enough of your time, rra. I know how busy you are. I hope this will all be cleared up soon." He offered his hand, and the director shook it, but Kubu could tell that the man was dissatisfied by the sudden way the interview had ended.

THE SECRETARY TURNED out to be quite helpful. She even pulled up Kunene's appointments on her computer while Kubu was looking through the office.

"We share our calendars on Outlook," she said. "Much more efficient."

And much less private, Kubu thought. The secretary could and did tell him who was involved in all of Kunene's meetings. He'd had a long meeting with the director and representatives of a mining company on the afternoon that he died, but there was nothing scheduled for the evening.

"He wouldn't note his private appointments here," Kubu mused. "He'd put them on his phone or something." He'd looked through Kunene's office, but there was no cell phone or anything else helpful for that matter.

Disappointed, he took his leave and headed back to the CID.

• • •

WHEN HE GOT back to his office, Kubu called the US embassy number. It turned out to be their general-inquiries number, and he had to wait as the recorded voice offered various options before eventually defaulting to a human. Explaining he was from the CID, he asked to be put through to the head of the economics department.

"That would be the Political and Economic Section," the receptionist informed him, and put him on hold. After a moment, another woman answered, this time with a strong American accent.

"Assistant Superintendent? I understand you wanted to talk to me. My name is Connie Olsen. How can I help you?"

"Good morning, Ms. Olsen. I'm investigating the death of Goodman Kunene. Did you know him?"

"Yes, I did. He was at the Department of Mines. He was our contact there for mining and exploration matters. His death is a great tragedy."

"It is. Did you speak to him last Thursday? The day of his death?"

"As a matter of fact, I did. He phoned me in the morning. I was so sad the next day when I realized that we'd never speak again."

"Did you know him quite well then?"

"No. We met a few times. Business and a couple of embassy functions. That's all."

"When you spoke to him on Thursday was there any indication that he was upset?"

"Not at all. We just discussed a routine matter. He seemed fine."

"And what was that routine matter?"

Olsen hesitated. "It was in connection with a mining lease that had been applied for by an American company. He told me the matter was still being considered. They needed more information."

Kubu thought about that for a few moments. "Why didn't he just go to the company concerned?"

"It's complicated, Assistant Superintendent. The lease is important for strategic reasons. The United States is offering certain guarantees to support the applicant company. That's what he wanted to check with me."

"What's the name of the company?"

"Uranium and Nickel Exploration. It's applied for quite a large lease in the region of Shoshong."

Kubu had never heard of the company, and this conversation didn't seem to be going anywhere. The call to the embassy was a dead end; Kunene was just doing his job. He thanked the woman, who told him he was welcome, and he hung up.

But he would have been very interested indeed if he'd heard the next call Connie Olsen made on the embassy's secure line.

CHAPTER 24

The six men were sitting under an acacia tree at the far end of the Shoshong cemetery. "Father, you have no choice," the youngest said. "Your people need jobs! Half the village is out of work." He pumped his fist to emphasize the point. "There will be two hundred new jobs at the mine. Well-paying jobs. Shoshong will start growing again and be a place where children want to stay, not get out of as soon as possible."

"That is true, Julius, my son."

"*Kgosi*, you must remember what happened last time." It was the man who had spoken at the *kgotla*. "I and many others lost our homes. The ones we were promised were nearly a year late, so we had to live with my daughter-in-law." From the look on his face, it was clear what he thought of her. "And then they were so badly built that we couldn't stay in them, and even the cows wouldn't go in. It was a disaster for the village."

The chief nodded, eyes closed.

"That is true, my friend."

Julius jumped in. "We can insist on the conditions the people talked about—money for moving paid at once, and we can start building the new houses right away. There's no risk. The real risk is that the mine may change its mind!"

The chief looked at his son and decided not to respond. He closed his eyes once again.

"If you accept this offer, *Kgosi*," another elder said, "the whole of Shoshong will change. We will lose our traditions. We will see drugs and drunkenness more than we have now." He spat in the dirt.

"It may happen."

"This is ridiculous, Father. There's chaos now because there are no jobs. We already see more crime because people need to eat. More money and more jobs help the village."

For a long time the chief said nothing. Then he lifted his cane and brought it down hard onto the ground. "Enough!" he said. "Enough!"

He stood up and looked at the group. "Thank you for your opinions. I will give my decision at a *kgotla* on Saturday afternoon."

Julius jumped to his feet. "Father, I've spoken to the management at the mine. They say there'll be trouble if you don't accept the offer. The young people need jobs. They'll be very angry if you don't agree."

The old man turned toward his son. "And why are you talking to the mine management? That is not your role. It is mine. And why did you not tell me? That weakens my position, and I do not like that." He cleared his throat. "And what will they do for you if we accept? A new car? A big house? Do not speak to them again." He turned and walked away.

Julius stared after him, his face hot. He saw the looks on the faces of the elders; they were pleased to see him put down by his father. He felt that they despised him. He turned and walked away without a word of farewell. Then he pulled out his cell phone and punched in a number that he'd recently memorized.

CHAPTER 25

The day was getting old when Kubu had his second afternoon cup of tea and only a single biscuit. He didn't feel like two. The afternoon had been frustrating. He'd waited impatiently for input from Zanele, but when she'd called he was disappointed.

"The crime scene is a write-off, Kubu," she'd told him. "The policemen who responded to the callout assumed it was a straightforward suicide, of course, and trampled everywhere. They didn't even mark the area as a crime scene, so there've been newspaper photographers all over it and people gawping. Sometimes I think people don't have enough to do with their time!"

"What about the car?" That was where Kubu hoped to find some clues.

"Well, we've got lots of fingerprints, but most are from Kunene and his family. There are some others, but Edison discovered from Kunene's wife that the car was at the garage for service a few weeks ago. We'll have to check them against the mechanics'. Then there are soil and dust samples, but nothing special there. They could come from anywhere around here. And lots of hair, most from the family pet." She'd sounded irritated about that. "But obviously some human hair also. We'll have to check those too."

They discussed the situation a bit more, and then Kubu switched to a topic that was more important to him.

"Zanele, have you made any progress with my father's case?"

There was a pause before Zanele answered. "Not really, Kubu. The print we found in the sand was made by a boot manufactured in China—and they're sold in a number of shops in Botswana. So that's not much help. Samantha is following up on the other stuff. You'll have to speak to her."

Kubu felt anger welling up, not at Zanele, who he knew was doing her best, but at the total lack of progress. "Thanks, Zanele. You'll let me know as soon as you find something useful?"

"Of course."

Reluctantly, Kubu hung up and let her get back to work on all her data.

Then there was the cell phone company. All they could say about the untraced call was that it was from a cell phone with no ID. They said that was impossible, so there must be a mistake. They were looking into the matter. Kubu sighed. He didn't expect further information anytime soon.

I might as well head home, he thought, cheering up at the thought of supper. I can help Joy with the kids and the food, and I need to talk to my mother. He sighed again. Under protest, Amantle had agreed to spend a few days with them in Gaborone, but Kubu wanted her to stay permanently. He was worried about her in Mochudi alone, even with the constable guarding the house, and he knew the police wouldn't keep that up for long. Yet they needed a proper room for the girls. They couldn't sleep in the lounge on a long-term basis.

Just as he was packing up, the phone rang. It was the desk sergeant who told him that there was a man at Reception who wanted to talk about the Kunene case. Kubu told him to bring the man up. A minute later, there was a knock on the door, and the desk sergeant ushered in a white man, who was tall and well built, with a touch of gray in his hair. He looked fit and carried no excess weight.

"How are you, Assistant Superintendent?" he asked with a strong American accent. "My name is Peter Newsom." He walked up to the desk and shook hands firmly. He took the seat facing the desk without waiting for an invitation.

"I'm sure you're a busy man, Assistant Superintendent, so I'll come straight to the point."

Kubu nodded. He was in favor of that; he wanted to get home.

"I'm a friend of Goodman Kunene, or rather I should say I *was* a friend of his. We'd known each other for about a year. I believe I may have been the last person to see him alive. I thought I should report that to the police. The desk sergeant told me you were the person to speak to."

All thoughts of family vanished from Kubu's head. "When was that exactly?"

"It was on the same evening that he died. Last Thursday."

"Exactly when did you see him?"

"We met for a couple of drinks at my apartment after work at about seven. We chatted, and then Goodman left to go home. That's about it. As I said, I don't want to waste your time."

"I appreciate your coming forward. Please start at the beginning. How did you know Mr. Kunene in the first place?"

"We met at an embassy function. I'm a mining engineer and consult for a number of US companies interested in working here. I have friends at the embassy, and sometimes I make useful contacts through them." He presented Kubu with a business card.

Kubu glanced at it and said, "And Mr. Kunene, being a senior person in the Department of Mines, would be a useful contact."

Newsom nodded. "Yes, it started like that. We were both golf nuts, and the Phakalane course is fantastic. So we arranged to play and had a great afternoon. After that we'd meet occasionally for a coffee or a drink. Just to chat. And we played golf a couple more times."

"And what did you chat about?"

"Maybe this will sound strange, Assistant Superintendent, but I admired Goodman. He had strong family values and great commitment to his country. But things don't always go quite the way they should here. Or in the US for that matter." He gave a rueful chuckle. "I felt it important that he focus his energy and not become cynical. I guess you could say I mentored him. But very informally. When he needed to talk, I made myself available. I know you're thinking it's odd for a guy from Botswana to choose a white American as a mentor, but I think that was the whole point. Our different perspectives enabled us to ask each other questions that we might not have thought of otherwise. And it was a two-way street. I learned a lot about the culture here from him. I'm going to miss him a great deal."

"And what were the issues that bothered him so much?"

Newsom shrugged. "The usual things. Friction with his boss. A feeling that matters could be better managed and that he should have more responsibility. Dissatisfaction that some of his colleagues did their jobs badly and got away with it because they had the right connections."

"Did he ever discuss personal problems with you?"

Newsom hesitated. "Just once. Everything wasn't smooth sailing at home. But it wasn't a crisis."

"You said you had a couple of drinks. How many is a couple?"

"We had two beers each over about an hour and a half. That was it. Then Goodman went home. Or I thought he did."

"The problems don't sound that severe. Did you have any idea that he might commit suicide?"

"Absolutely not," Newsom said at once. "No, I had no inkling he might do such a thing. In fact, I can't believe it. When he was feeling down, he talked about getting another position—leaving his work for the government—not killing himself. In fact, that evening he was quite positive. Can there be any doubt about the suicide story? It makes no sense to me."

Kubu decided to tell Newsom that Kunene had been murdered. They couldn't keep it a secret much longer. Pretty soon everyone would know. But first he was curious about something else.

"When did you arrange this meeting with Rra Kunene?"

"In the morning. I called him and suggested a drink."

"From your cell phone?"

"No, I used Skype. I'm on my computer a lot. It's convenient."

Kubu wondered if that was the unidentified call. It might add up. "Mr. Newsom, what did you do after Mr. Kunene left?"

"I made some supper and went back to work. I'm a bit of a workaholic." He gave an easy laugh.

"No one was with you? Did you speak to anyone on the phone?"

Newsom shook his head. "This sounds like a murder inquiry, Assistant Superintendent. You don't normally need an alibi for a suicide."

"We're also finding it hard to believe that he committed suicide. So let's say it wasn't that, and it certainly wasn't an accident. Mr. Kunene spoke to you about his enemies. Were any of them really dangerous?"

Newsom shrugged. "Some of his work colleagues were jealous of him. If they had a chance to show him in a bad light or block a promotion, they'd jump at it. That's a very long way from wanting him dead, let alone doing something about it."

Kubu leaned back in his chair. Newsom had the right answer for everything, said with confidence and little hesitation. Was he too confident, too prepared? Normally, someone asked about an alibi would show some reaction however innocent he might be. But it hadn't phased Newsom one bit.

Kubu had another thought and tried a little fishing. "Did you speak to Ms. Olsen this afternoon?" For a moment Kubu saw a reaction. This was a question Newsom hadn't expected, but he recovered quickly. "Connie Olsen? At the embassy? This afternoon? No. Why?"

Kubu folded his arms and stared at Newsom. "Mr. Newsom,

Mr. Kunene did not commit suicide. He was murdered. I don't know who did it or why. But as far as I know, you were the last person who saw him alive. Other than the murderer, of course." He paused and waited for that to sink in. "Now, would you like to add anything to what you've told me already? Anything that might throw some light on those questions I have?"

Newsom frowned. "Am I a suspect?"

Kubu didn't reply.

"I was his friend. I thought very highly of him. If I could help catch his murderer, I'd jump at the chance. But there's nothing more I can tell you."

Kubu pushed some more, but Newsom didn't change any aspect of his story. They met at seven; they each had two beers; they talked about matters related to Kunene's job and Newsom's interest in Botswana. Kunene left to go home at around half past eight.

Eventually, Kubu gave up. "Mr. Newsom, I'm grateful that you volunteered to help the police, but I'm not convinced you're telling me everything you know. It would be very helpful if you did. Do you have plans to leave the country?"

Newsom hesitated. "Not at the moment. I have enough work here for quite some time."

"Please let me know if you plan to do so."

"I'll do that." Newsom rose to his feet. "Have a good evening, Assistant Superintendent."

After Newsom had gone, Kubu thought over the interview. Probably Newsom was exactly what he said he was. There were no slips, no hesitations, no concerns. Except for the moment when he'd reacted to Connie Olsen's name. Kubu gingerly lifted Newsom's business card by the edge and set it aside. More fingerprints for Zanele to check.

Logic dictated that he owed Newsom an apology or even a beer. But his instincts were telling him something quite different.

CHAPTER 26

The next morning Kubu felt, if anything, more inclined to trust his instincts. He sat at his desk with his chair pushed back and his feet stretched out. He was once more studying Kunene's telephone records, but this time he was comparing them to the man's bank records.

There were no calls from the cell phone number that appeared on Newsom's business card, but over the last three months, there were five calls from unidentified numbers. Was it really likely that Newsom contacted Kunene every few weeks when sitting at his computer rather than using his phone? And then there were the deposits. There were quite large cash deposits within a few days of three of the calls. It could be coincidence; the pattern wasn't perfect. But it was an odd coincidence, and Kubu didn't believe in coincidences, although he was willing to admit that sometimes they did happen. However, he wasn't willing to admit that until he'd checked every other possibility.

Was it possible that Kunene was blackmailing Newsom? That

was a good motive for murder. But what could Kunene have on him? Or maybe Newsom had got the information he wanted from Kunene and thought it was time to cover his tracks so he got rid of Kunene. Either way, if Newsom was the murderer, why would he insist that the death wasn't suicide when he'd carefully set it up to look like that?

With a grunt, he dumped the paperwork on his desk and picked up the phone. It was time to nag Zanele.

"Good morning, Zanele. Any joy on those prints?"

"Well, Kubu, it would've helped if you'd given the man a glass of water rather than collecting a business card. At least you didn't smudge the prints when you picked it up."

Kubu was disappointed. He'd been rather pleased with himself for thinking of picking up Newsom's prints from the card. "It was no good?"

"I didn't say that. I'm pretty sure the thumb print matches one on Kunene's car."

"On the car? Where on the car?"

"On the roof."

Outside the car. That could be explained by Newsom saying good-bye to Kunene.

"Can you tell how old it is?"

Zanele hesitated. "That's not so easy. The whorls start to thicken after a while, but—"

Kubu interrupted. "What about the service station? Didn't you say they'd cleaned the car?"

"Yes, three weeks ago."

"So the prints must be more recent than that." Kubu quickly checked the records. There had been only two Skype calls in the last three weeks. "Other prints?"

"There are still a few we can't confirm as belonging to the family or the service station people. But they aren't very clear. We're working on it."

Kubu sighed. "Anything else?"

"The hair. None of the mechanics had straight hair. So there's no obvious explanation for it."

Kubu leaned forward. "European? What color?" Newsom had chestnut hair, quite an unusual color.

Zanele hesitated. "It's black, and we think it's probably Asian. But we can't be sure at this point."

Kubu had already been thinking about how to get a sample of Newsom's hair. But now this seemed another dead end.

Zanele had nothing else for him at the moment, so he thanked her and went back to the records. Going back six months, the first cash payment coincided with the first debit order for the large life insurance policy. That was around the time Kunene had told his wife that he'd received a promotion. It all seemed to fit. But did it have anything to do with Newsom? That was less clear.

Frustrated, his mind returned to his father's murder. He wondered if he should phone Samantha and see if any progress had been made in finding the silver Toyota. There can't be that many, he thought. But his heart sank when he realized that rental agencies used them.

There was a knock on the door, and Mabaku came in. As usual he wasted no time on preliminaries.

"Have you seen this?" He tossed a copy of the *Daily News* onto Kubu's desk. Kubu glanced at it. The headline read: KUNENE DEATH—POLICE SUSPICIOUS. Kubu sighed. The CID kept few secrets from the press.

"Kubu, I told you this was sensitive stuff! I've had the commissioner on the phone, and he wants to know whether we're a hundred percent sure about this. He had some questions I need to check with you." Kubu knew he'd better have the answers.

"You told me that Kunene had been drinking and that he'd taken Rohypnol. Right?"

"Yes, his blood alcohol level indicated that he was intoxicated at the time of his death. And we also found the residue of a strong sedative in his blood. Not necessarily Rohypnol."

"So maybe it was just Valium? Is Ian certain that it knocked him out? What if he took it after he attached the hose and so on to make his suicide easier?"

Kubu shook his head. "Ian felt that Kunene probably had too much to drink to carry out the careful placement of the duct tape and so on. And there was no bottle in the car—with or without alcohol—and no sedatives. And apart from the forensic evidence, there are other issues. For example, there were no fingerprints on the hose, yet he wasn't wearing gloves. How could that be explained?"

"Perhaps by the driving gloves we found in the glove compartment," growled Mabaku. Kubu cursed under his breath. Why hadn't he checked the list of contents found in the car? Mabaku had.

"But why wear gloves in the first place? Just to confuse us?"

"The exhaust would've been hot. He'd driven to the dam. He was being careful."

"I can't see someone intent on committing suicide fiddling with gloves. All he had to do was shove the hose into the exhaust. He didn't need to touch it." Kubu shook his head. "And what about his cell phone? It's missing."

"Maybe he got rid of it. All part of the same behavior. He didn't want to have a way out at the last minute." Mabaku shook his head, looking unhappy. "The commissioner isn't buying it, Kubu. He wants this to go away. And now it's all over the press!" Mabaku sighed. "Get Edison onto the hardware stores. The hose wasn't from the house. If Kunene *did* commit suicide, then he bought that hose and probably the duct tape at the same time. Or maybe someone else did that. How many hardware stores can there be in Gaborone?"

"Unfortunately, there are quite a lot," Kubu said. "Edison has already visited about half but has come up with nothing so far." He was pleased someone else was doing the legwork around the city.

"Anyway, there's a development you don't know about." He filled Mabaku in on the Newsom interview.

"You realize that Newsom could have slipped him the drug, forced him to drink some alcohol, and driven him to the dam?" Mabaku said.

Kubu thought about it. "He would've needed an accomplice to get him back to his apartment from the dam. It's quite a way. I must admit that I didn't like Newsom, but I don't think he's the murderer. He was adamant Kunene wouldn't commit suicide."

Mabaku brooded about that. "We should check the bars along the route from Newsom's apartment to the dam. Maybe he did have a few drinks along the way. And maybe he met up with someone else there."

That was another good point, and one that Kubu had already thought about. Another job for Edison.

"I'm going to tell the commissioner and the reporters we're covering every possibility," Mabaku continued, "although we still regard the death as suicide at this point. Still, we may as well make a virtue of this necessity. I'll also ask them to call on people to come forward if they saw Kunene that evening or anything unusual around the dam."

With that he headed for the door.

Kubu's mind returned to the phone records and bank statements, thinking about the Skype calls and the often coincident payments. If he couldn't discover what was behind that, he had a suspicion about how this case would end. The commissioner would be happy to declare it a suicide. No scandal, no embarrassing revelations. A man unhappy at home, who decided to end it all in a painless way. Case closed. However, Kubu was sure that Goodman Kunene had been murdered, and he wasn't going to allow that to go unpunished. And right now there was only one person who could help him with that. He needed another meeting with Peter Newsom.

CHAPTER 27

Newsom had no problem with another meeting. "Of course, Assistant Superintendent. Look, I'm heading out to Mahalapye for an important meeting with one of my clients this afternoon, and it's already nearly lunchtime. There's a nice Chinese place in Africa Mall. Let's meet there. I'll buy you lunch."

Kubu wasn't really keen to have lunch with Newsom; he wanted a more formal context. On the other hand, it was going on for midday, and he had to eat.

"Okay, Mr. Newsom. I'll meet you there, but I'll buy my own lunch."

"As you like, Assistant Superintendent. See you in half an hour?"

KUBU EASILY FOUND the Hong Long restaurant. Dusty red banners with Chinese characters hung outside, and a red dragon with gilded teeth straddled the door. Many of the customers were Chinese, shoveling their food with chopsticks at impressive speed, but there were also Batswana clients and even a few white people. Newsom was already there, nursing a Tsingtao beer. Kubu joined him and waved for a waiter. Asking for a steelworks would be hopeless, so he ordered green tea.

"Amazing how the Chinese population has grown in Gaborone," Newsom said. "Look at all these people. And this restaurant is quite good. They have more and more genuine ingredients these days."

Kubu had noticed the Chinese presence increasing. The debacle, where a Chinese company had half built the new Gaborone airport and then infuriated President Khama by walking away, didn't seem to have slowed them down. They were doing all sorts of business. One of Joy's friends was going to Shanghai next month to select a container full of doors, windows, tiles, carpets, and plumbing fixtures—in fact a whole new prefabricated house—apparently at much less cost than building locally. Kubu was a bit uncomfortable about the growing Chinese influence, but they seemed to mind their own business and not cause trouble.

"I recommend the sweet-and-sour pork. That's what I'm going to have."

Kubu ordered the chicken with cashews and got down to business.

"I'm curious about your work, Mr. Newsom," Kubu began. "What is it that you actually do here?"

Newsom hesitated and took a sip of beer before answering. "My background is in mining engineering, Assistant Superintendent. But I've found that mining nowadays is as much about knowing the country where you operate and how to manage the political context as it is about the mine design. A good relationship with the government, the workers, the local people, the environment is what really counts. They're all critical. I advise clients on that sort of thing."

Kubu wasn't sure that he knew much more than before. "You said you were seeing a client in Mahalapye. The only mine up that way is the one near Shoshong, isn't it?"

Newsom nodded. "But there are a lot of new prospects in the area. I'm working with an American company that's trying to develop a new mine—and having some problems, but that's another story."

"Is this what you discussed with Mr. Kunene?"

"Only in very general terms. Our meetings were mainly social."

Kubu sipped his tea. "I have a few points I'd like to clarify about your social meetings with Mr. Kunene." He took out his notebook. "When Mr. Kunene came to see you last Thursday, was he driving his own car?"

Newsom looked surprised. "I suppose so. We met at my apartment. I already told you that."

Kubu nodded. "And the previous time you met? When was that and where did you meet?"

Newsom hesitated. "It was the Saturday two weeks before. We played golf."

"And did he use his own car that time also?"

"I presume so."

"You can't be sure?"

Newsom shook his head, looking confused.

"I'm wondering why we found your fingerprints on his car then."

Newsom thought about that, then nodded. "Oh, yes, we sat in his car after golf for a few minutes discussing an issue about his work. He didn't want to do that in public."

He recovers quickly, Kubu thought. He would check that they'd been at Phakalane that day, but he was sure it was true. He suspected Newsom was too smart to set himself up to be caught in a lie.

He changed tack.

"Did you always phone him from Skype on your computer?"

Newsom hesitated and then shrugged. "I can't really recall. It's possible. I don't get good reception at my apartment. But if I was driving or something, I'd use my cell phone."

"You always phoned him?"

"No, he'd contact me sometimes. By phone or send me an e-mail."

"Strange. There is no call from him to you listed on his phone records."

"Maybe he called from the office. Why is this important, Assistant Superintendent?"

"I'm just following up on everything." Kubu thought for a moment, wondering what Newsom would do if offered an easy way out. "Actually, it seems quite likely that he did kill himself after all. Some of the issues that worried us before can be explained in other ways. We'll keep digging, but I suspect his death will eventually be declared suicide at the inquest."

"And what would have been his motivation?"

"Things weren't always smooth at home. You told me that yourself."

"It wasn't that bad! And he doted on his boys. He'd never desert them that way. Never."

"Maybe money was an issue. That's another thing I want to ask you about. About six months ago, he started getting fairly regular cash payments. Sometimes around the times he spoke to you. Can you explain that?"

Newsom put his glass down firmly on the table. "Absolutely not. Are you suggesting I was bribing him? I'd no reason to do that and wouldn't in any case. And if you'd known Goodman at all, you wouldn't even suggest it."

"I didn't suggest anything. He told his wife he'd received a promotion, but that wasn't true. However, he did receive this extra money, which he paid into his account in cash. He also took out a large life insurance policy at about the same time. And you say you mentored him, helped him with his career decisions. I'm asking you what that money was about." Kubu waited, but Newsom refused to be drawn out.

"I told you. I know nothing about it," he said.

Kubu had had enough. "Mr. Newsom, I don't think you're tell-ing me all you know. You and I both think I'm dealing with a mur-der here. The victim was found drugged and drunk in his car. As far as we know, you were the last person he saw. You admit he was drinking with you. You had the opportunity to administer the drug. Your fingerprints are on his car. Money was changing hands. I advise you very strongly to tell me the whole story."

Newsom didn't flinch. "I've told you everything I can. I've got nothing more to say."

The food arrived, and they ate in silence. Newsom seemed com-fortable with chopsticks, but Kubu used a knife and fork. He was certain the man knew a lot more than he was letting on. Yet it would have been easy for him to say that Kunene had been depressed, up-set, and spoken of suicide. Instead he'd reacted strongly against the suggestion that the death was self-inflicted. What game was he playing?

Kubu found the chicken quite good and enjoyed the Chinese cabbage, which was new to him, but he ate slowly, playing with the food.

Newsom shook his head at the mention of dessert and asked the waiter for his bill. "I have to get on the road, Assistant Super-intendent. So, if there's nothing more?"

Kubu took his time replying, but he couldn't see how to press the man further. "Not for the moment. No."

Newsom headed for the cash register, where a harried Chinese lady was dealing with waiters and payments. Kubu watched New-som pay and leave without a backward glance. Either he was of-fended, or he was making a good show of it. A man, who had been sitting by himself drinking tea, also went to the desk, dropped his bill and a handful of pula notes, and left. Kubu took no notice. He was forcing himself to finish the chicken.

• • •

IT WAS AFTER ten when Newsom returned, weary from the long drive to Mahalapye and back. He was worried that his efforts to persuade the police that Kunene had been murdered had backfired; their focus was now on him as a suspect. The large, lumbering detective was much sharper than he appeared. And his meeting with Uranium and Nickel Exploration had not gone well. They saw their big discovery slipping away between obfuscation and bureaucratic delays. They wanted action. He'd explained that his key contact was gone, murdered, but they hadn't been satisfied.

When he pulled his car up in front of his apartment building, he was tired, and so he was careless. He used the remote car lock and walked toward the main door of the complex without checking the street. His only warning of the attack was the slightest sound behind him, only heard at all because of his combat training. He started to turn, and the kick to the back of his knee that would have dropped him hit it on the side instead. He staggered backward, but managed to maintain his balance and swing around to face the assailant. The man was already on top of him, and his right hand held a knife aimed to strike upward into the chest cavity. Newsom twisted away and felt a searing pain as the knife sliced into his stomach muscles. He screamed, lashing out with his right leg while going for the knife arm with his left hand. The attacker easily avoided the kick, dancing out of reach.

Newsom knew he was in trouble. He was losing blood from the stomach wound, and although his assailant was shorter than he was, the man was obviously trained in martial arts, and he had a knife. All Newsom could see of his face were dark eyes watching through the slits in the ski mask covering his head. Newsom absorbed all this in the instant before the man was at him again, slashing with the knife to keep Newsom occupied, while he aimed a vicious kick to the groin. Newsom, punching the knife arm away, twisted, and the kick took him on the thigh. He bellowed and staggered back, feeling the knife slash his right arm. His training took over, and his left hand shot out for the knife arm, and against the odds, he felt his fingers close on the wrist. He grabbed at the man's other hand, but it was too quick for him, snatching the knife from the imprisoned hand and digging the blade into Newsom's bicep. Newsom yelled again, and this time he heard an answering shout and the sound of someone running toward them. The attacker heard it too and was distracted for the split second it took for Newsom to slam his fist into the man's head. He staggered back and wrenched his hand free, avoiding Newsom's kick aimed between his legs. Then he started to run down the street away from the approaching shouts. Newsom took a few steps after him, but the pain was too much, and he sank to his knees. Blood soaked his trousers. He pressed his right hand against his stomach, trying to stanch the bleeding.

A moment later a young Motswana man ran up to him. "Rra! What's happened to you? I heard the shouts . . ." But Newsom was slumped on the ground and didn't reply.

PART 5

CHAPTER 28

"You tell me you make problem go way." The man behind the desk showed no emotion, but his eyes signaled his anger. "But problem still problem. What you do?"

"I'm sure the chief will approve the mine expansion," the young black man said. "I've been working very hard to make sure of that."

The man sitting at the side of the room translated. The man behind the desk didn't react, didn't say anything. It was impossible to read what he was thinking.

Julius wasn't used to silence and began to sweat. "And I have a plan if he doesn't. But I think he'll accept your offer, because it's very generous. There are many people who want it."

Again a translation. Again no reaction.

"Mr. Hong, the chief is going to tell us at a *kgotla* on Saturday—that's a meeting of the village. I think he'll do what the young people want. They want jobs. He'll accept your offer."

Julius swallowed, his throat dry. There was still no response after the translation.

"There'll be trouble if the chief says no," he continued. "The young people will be very angry and won't listen to the chief. Then he'll be gone, and I'll be the new chief, and I'll do what you want."

This time the translator spoke for some time—more than a translation would have required. Julius wondered what he was saying. Hong frowned. "The chief is your father. You must agree with his decision," he stated.

Julius shook his head. "He does not understand his people anymore. But I think I've persuaded him. It's only the elders who don't want change because of what happened last time."

"When will the village give an answer?" the translator asked.

Julius looked at him. "On Saturday, Mr. Shonhu, if the chief agrees. Another week if he says no," he said quietly.

"Sure?"

Julius nodded nervously. "Yes. I promise. By the end of next week you will have permission. Then you must move quickly to provide the money for moving and building the new houses. That's what we've promised."

There was no immediate response from Hong after the translation. Eventually, he spoke. "Go with Shonhu."

"Come," Shonhu said to Julius, pointing at the door.

Julius stood up and started to leave. Then he turned to the man behind the desk. "I promise."

A FEW MINUTES later, Shonhu returned to the office and stood in front of the manager's desk.

"The chief's son is scared," he said in Chinese. "I don't think he's tough enough to get us the right answer."

Hong nodded. "We'll see by the end of the week. Until then there is nothing we can do. We must be patient. In China it would be easy. But here? These black people . . ." His voice trailed off without finishing the sentence.

"But what if the chief says no?" Shonhu asked.

Hong shrugged.

"The chief's son says he can fix the problem," Shonhu said. "We will see, but I don't think he can. So we'll make our own plan."

He turned to the door. "I will take you back to the village."

HONG SAT IN the back of his Gilan car as Shonhu drove from the mine toward Mahalapye. After about ten minutes, they turned off the main road toward a high barbed-wire fence that encircled a large cluster of prefabricated homes, most of which had Chinese flags fluttering above them or red pictographs on their walls. Here the road was unpaved and corrugated. The manager wished he had a Toyota Land Cruiser rather than a Chinese vehicle totally un-suited to rough roads, but he couldn't be seen in a vehicle made outside his homeland.

They turned under an ornate arch that sported a pair of heavy gates. A guard walked over, peered into the car, nodded, and pressed a remote. The gates slid back, letting the manager's car enter. The manager was pleased. The guard's firearm was not visible. It wouldn't be good for the locals to see the man was armed.

JULIUS WAS NOT a happy man when he left the mine. Despite what he'd told the manager, he wasn't confident that his father was going to accept the offer. And if the mine didn't expand, he wouldn't be paid his consulting fee—a sum that was the equivalent of several years' salary in the area.

He decided it was time to buy some insurance, to make sure that the village accepted the mine's offer. He headed to the shebeen in the center of Shoshong, where he knew a large group of unemployed young men would be drinking.

"Dumela, dumela," he said as he walked in. Heads nodded in response. "The next round's on me," he shouted. "Get a drink; then come over here." He walked to the corner of the room and sat down at one of the tables. There was a rush for the bar as the men took advantage of the offer, switching from cheap Shake Shake beer to whisky or brandy. It was the chief's son, after all, who had made the offer.

When most of the men had gathered around, Julius raised his hand to quiet the group. "I'm worried about the *kgotla* on Saturday," he said. "I'm not sure that my father, the chief, will listen to us and accept the mine's offer." The men listened intently.

"As you know, I think that's the wrong decision," he continued. "It's the decision of old men with their eyes and ears closed to your needs." There was a murmur from the crowd. "It's the decision in favor of the past rather than your future." The crowd murmured again, showing signs of restlessness.

"We must show my father and the elders that the future is with us, not with tradition. We must show them that their way is wrong."

Heads nodded and several men shouted, "Show them. We must show them."

Julius looked around, pleased at the reaction. He needed to get the men worked up, willing to take the situation into their own hands.

"On Saturday at the *kgotla*, you must listen to the chief. If he agrees to what the mine offers, you must show him your support. But if he doesn't agree . . ." He paused and looked around. "If he doesn't agree, you must show your anger. You must show the old men that it's your lives they're taking away, your future they're stealing."

"They are thieves. Show them!" The crowd was getting agitated.

Julius raised his hand. "If the chief turns down the offer, you must take the elders and shake them and make them afraid, so they will change their minds, so you can have jobs."

"We want jobs. We want jobs." Now there was anger in the shouts.

It took Julius several minutes to stop the chant.

"You must show them, but you must not hurt them, because

they are our fathers and our elders. Make them understand. But don't hurt them."

This was met with silence.

He stood up. "Soon we have jobs!" He turned and walked out to the cheers of the young men.

As he opened the door of his Toyota, he heard another chant from the shebeen. "Julius. Julius."

This is what it felt like to be chief-in-waiting. He smiled, closed the door, and drove off.

CHAPTER 29

Kubu woke with a start to the shrill ringing of the phone. He grabbed it, his heart pounding. Joy sat up in the bed, also wide-awake.

"Yes?" He cleared his throat. "Assistant Superintendent Bengu here."

He listened for a moment and then interrupted. "Just wait a minute." Joy was listening to every word and holding his arm. "It's all right, darling. It's Edison. Nothing to worry about." He felt her relax and lie back, and he returned his attention to the call.

"Who? Are you sure? Is he alive?" He listened a bit longer, then said, "I'll head out there now. Keep the witnesses at the scene till I get there."

He hung up, switched on the bedside lamp, and turned to Joy. "A man's been stabbed. An American. I have to check it out." Seeing the look on her face, he added, "Don't worry. Try to go back to sleep."

But she was already getting up. "I want to check on the girls.

See that they're all right. And your mother may have woken." In the past, even if Joy had answered a late-night call, she would have handed the phone to him and been instantly asleep again. But that was the past.

KUBU'S MIND WAS still foggy with sleep, so he missed the turnoff to the apartment block where Peter Newsom lived. At last he found the street he was looking for and could see police activity a few blocks down. As he reached the taped-off area, he sat in the car for a few moments and took in the scene lit up by the police floodlights. Several uniformed policemen were keeping back a small crowd of onlookers. Edison was speaking to a group of young men, and Zanele and her team were inside the tapes scouring the area for clues. Kubu clambered out of his vehicle, walked over to Edison, and greeted him.

"This is Mandla Towene," Edison said, pointing to a young man in an orange Illinois T-shirt. "He's the man who reported the attack. He was leaving a shebeen on the next block with some friends and heard shouts. They ran over to see what was going on." He paused. "How's the victim?"

Kubu knew that Edison's interest was not concern; he wanted to know if they were on another murder case.

"I phoned the hospital, but they couldn't tell me anything. The doctors are putting him back together. It'll be quite a while before we know much more. How did you know it was Newsom?"

"A lady identified him. His neighbor apparently." He checked his notes, holding them to catch the light. "A Mma Kamanga. She saw the attack. She's waiting in her apartment; I spoke to her, but I told her you'd want to talk to her too."

Kubu nodded and looked around. The apartment building was on three levels and wasn't in an expensive neighborhood. Somehow he'd imagined Newsom in a more upmarket area. The residents' cars were parked on a paved area in front of the building.

Kubu felt a twinge of disappointment. There would be no footprints for Zanele to work with. On the other hand, it was nearly a full moon, so maybe they'd get something from the witnesses. He turned to Towene, who was now sitting on the curb surrounded by his mates.

"You found the victim here?"

"Yes, well, like I told the detective," Towene said, indicating Edison, "we heard this guy screaming. So I ran over, and when I got here, he was lying on the ground with blood all over him. He didn't look good, so I phoned 999. Josh, here, has done a first-aid course, so he checked if the guy was still alive and said we shouldn't move him."

"Did you see anyone?"

Towene nodded. "There was someone running up the road, but he had a start on us. And we were more worried about the guy who'd been attacked."

"Can you describe the man? The one who was running off?"

Towene shook his head. "He was running fast and was quite far away from us already." He shrugged.

Kubu tried a few more questions, but it was clear that the group had responded to the cries but observed little. The white man collapsed in the parking area had attracted all their attention.

Kubu told Edison to get their names and addresses. "Oh, and check the underside of their shoes to see if they stepped in the blood. It might be important for Zanele to know. Then they can go home." Perhaps they would recall something more in the morning, but Kubu doubted that, especially if they'd had a lot to drink.

"Where will I find the woman who identified him?" he asked Edison.

"She's in number three on the first floor."

MMA KAMANGA WAS an elderly lady with gray creeping into her hair. She opened the door at once when Kubu knocked, and she nodded when he introduced himself. "Come into the kitchen. We can sit at the table. I just made myself some tea to calm down. Would you like a cup? It's bush tea." Her voice wasn't steady, but Kubu couldn't tell whether that was due to age or the shock of the evening's events. He wasn't fond of *rooibos* tea, but he accepted a cup to make her feel more comfortable.

"Is Rra Newsom . . . ?"

Kubu nodded. "He's alive and at the hospital. We won't know anything for a while, but I think he'll be okay."

The woman relaxed a bit, and Kubu decided he could get to the point.

"Please tell me exactly what you saw."

She thought for a few moments. "I'd switched off the television and was going to bed. I remember hearing a car pull up. The window was open because it was quite warm. I suppose it was a few minutes later when I heard a scream, and I went to the window to see what was happening. A man was attacking Rra Newsom! I think he had a knife." Kubu nodded and waited for her to continue. "I had to find my cell phone in my bag so I could call 999. It only took a few seconds, but by the time I got back to the window, the attacker was running away, and then that group of young men arrived."

"How did you know it was Rra Newsom being attacked?"

"I know Rra Newsom. And they were just outside my window!"

"Can you describe the man, the attacker?"

She paused, thinking. "I think he was wearing dark clothing. I can't really describe him. It was hard to see even with the moonlight, and it was all over so quickly. The man was smaller than Rra Newsom, but he was rushing him and slashing at him. That's why I thought he might have a knife."

"What happened after that?"

"I went out to see if there was anything I could do. I stayed with Rra Newsom until the ambulance came. Later I spoke to your detective."

"Weren't you concerned about joining a group of strange men with the victim of a knife fight?"

She shook her head. "I'm old," she said.

Kubu then asked her about Newsom himself. She had chatted to Newsom a few times and even invited him to tea once but really didn't know much about her neighbor. He worked for some mining company. He was an American. He kept flexible hours and was sometimes away on a trip for several days. He was friendly and polite. He didn't have many visitors.

Kubu scrounged in his wallet and found a picture of Goodman Kunene and passed it to her. "Have you ever seen this man?" he asked.

She shook her head at once. "No, I've never seen him. Who is he?"

"Someone Rra Newsom knew," Kubu replied. He checked his watch. By the time he reached the hospital, there should be news of Newsom. He thanked Mma Kamanga for the tea and her help and asked her to call him in the morning if she remembered anything else.

AS KUBU DROVE to the Princess Marina, he considered what he'd learned from Newsom's neighbor. It wasn't much. He'd hoped for an insight into the American but had been disappointed. And, of course, the fact that she hadn't recognized Kunene proved nothing one way or the other.

When Kubu arrived at the hospital, the news was good. Newsom's wounds were not life-threatening, and he was recovering in a private ward. Kubu sat in the waiting room, nodding off from time to time, until the doctor agreed he could see Newsom, provided it was only for a few minutes.

The American was barely awake. The anesthetic was wearing off, and he'd been given painkillers and a tranquilizer.

Kubu pulled a chair up to the bed and sat down heavily. "How are you, Mr. Newsom? A lucky escape, I think."

Newsom nodded. "I'm okay." His speech was slow and slurred. "But I'm in pain. Up to my eyeballs in drugs. Come back later. I don't want to talk now."

Kubu made no move to leave. "I won't be long. We need to start looking for the person who attacked you right away. By tomorrow, the trail may be cold."

Newsom sighed and tried to concentrate. "All right. I got back around ten, parked, and started for my door. The man attacked me from behind. With a knife. He knew what he was doing. Meant to kill me." He stopped talking and closed his eyes. After a few moments, Kubu was worried that he'd fallen asleep. Eventually, he opened his eyes and continued. Kubu had to lean forward to hear him. "Some young guys came, I think. I remember lying on the ground, and they were looking down at me. Then the ambulance came. I don't remember much after that."

"Can you describe the man?"

"He was wearing a ski mask."

"You said he knew what he was doing with the knife. How do you know that?"

"I was trained in hand-to-hand combat. In the marines."

Kubu eyed Newsom's bandages and his arm in a sling. "But you couldn't handle him?"

"Marines was long ago. I'm rusty. And an attacker with a knife is a big problem."

Kubu changed tack. "I'm worried that this attack is linked to the Kunene issue. We don't know what was behind that. Now someone comes after you."

Newsom just shook his head.

"I don't believe in coincidences, Mr. Newsom. A close contact of yours is murdered, and a couple of weeks later someone tries to kill you. You said yourself your attacker was a professional."

It was a few moments before Newsom responded. "Maybe I was wrong. Maybe I was taken by a thug after a few bucks."

"And he never demanded money or your cell phone? Look, Mr. Newsom, don't waste my time. I was pulled out of bed in the middle of the night for this."

"You think I got cut up to ruin your night?"

Kubu sighed and stood up. Kubu was sure Newsom knew a lot more than he was letting on, and he was determined to get that information first thing in the morning. "Okay. Let's pick this up later. You need some sleep. And so do I."

KUBU PHONED EDISON and told him what he'd learned. Then he drove home, bone-weary. It was around two a.m., and he hoped he could still get a few hours' sleep. Despite his exhaustion, his mind was active, turning over different ideas, mixing them up, and then rearranging them. Intuitively, he was sure there was a link between the murder of Kunene and the attack on Newsom. But what was that link? They knew each other, and both were involved with mining, but that was as far as it went. And the attacks were very different—Kunene abducted and gassed in a quiet road, Newsom assaulted outside his apartment by a trained knife fighter. Who would gain by eliminating a civil servant in the Department of Mines and a consultant, he wondered? Perhaps they'd stumbled on something that was supposed to remain hidden?

Then he tried to put it all out of his mind as he concentrated on driving, easing through the red traffic lights in the sleeping city.

CHAPTER 30

Kubu woke with a start to the Grand March from *Aïda*. As he grabbed for his cell phone, he checked his watch. It was after eight! He had a vague recollection of deciding on a few more minutes in bed when Joy rose to manage the kids. That had been over an hour ago.

"Hello?" he croaked. Then he cleared his throat and tried again. "Assistant Superintendent Bengu here."

The voice on the other end was respectful almost to the point of obsequiousness. "Assistant Superintendent, this is Constable Kanye here. I was sent to the Princess Marina Hospital to provide security, sir. Thank you for trusting me with that assignment, sir."

Needless to say, Kubu had had nothing to do with the assignment other than phoning the previous night to request a constable to keep an eye on Newsom. "Yes, Constable. Get to the point. I'm very busy this morning." Kubu had meant to report on the Newsom matter to Mabaku first thing.

"Yes, sir. Of course. Sir, I was sent to provide security for a Rra

Newsom. But he's not here, sir. I thought I should let you know at once."

Kubu sat up. "What do you mean he's not there?"

"Well, the nurse said he left early this morning. He's not here."

Kubu was now fully awake. "Let me talk to her."

Kanye put the nurse on the line. "Yes, Assistant Superintendent, Mr. Newsom checked out early this morning. It was just after my shift started."

"Nurse, please give me the details. When exactly did he leave?"

There was a pause as she consulted her records. "Quarter past six this morning. He signed all the documents and paid his account with a credit card."

"Did he leave alone?"

"No, two people came to fetch him. Not Batswana. Americans, I think."

"And where did they go?"

"I've no idea. Maybe to his home. I have the address he gave us."

Kubu knew where Newsom lived, so he brushed that aside. "He looked pretty bad when I saw him last night. Was he well enough to leave the hospital?"

The nurse sniffed. "I can't tell you anything about his injuries. It's patient privilege."

"He was cut up with a knife. Anyway, that isn't what I asked you."

"He left in a wheelchair. They brought their own."

"Please put Constable Kanye on the line again. And tell him to hold on. I'll be right back."

Kubu put down the cell phone and scrabbled in his wallet for Newsom's card. He dialed his number on the landline and waited, but it went to voice mail immediately: "Hello, this is Peter Newsom. I'm returning to the United States. I will check my e-mail, but for urgent issues you can contact me at my office number 00-1-212-555-0188. Thanks." The phone cut off without the option of leaving a message. Kubu jotted down the number, obviously a US one.

Kubu switched phones. "Constable Kanye? Are you there?"

"Yes, sir."

"Why did it take you till now to get to the hospital?"

"I only came in to the station an hour ago, sir."

Kubu cursed under his breath. It was his own fault. He should have emphasized that he wanted the protection immediately, but he hadn't imagined someone would try anything with Newsom in the few remaining hours of the night.

"All right, you can leave now. There's nothing more to do there."

Kubu hung up and tried to clear his mind. Why had Newsom left? Concern about Batswana doctors? He didn't think so. His injuries apparently weren't that bad. He recalled Newsom's reluctance to talk the night before. Either Newsom was spooked by the knife attack, or maybe he had done something illegal and felt that Kubu was getting too close. It was all very unsatisfactory. Kubu cursed again, aloud this time.

He picked up the cell phone and dialed the US number. After two rings, he heard a recording.

"This is Newsom Consulting. Please call during business hours, eight a.m. until six p.m., Monday through Friday, or leave a message at the tone. Thank you."

The phone beeped, and Kubu left a message asking Newsom to contact him, giving his cell phone number.

After a moment's thought, Kubu guessed who Newsom would ask for help. He phoned the US embassy and asked to be put through to Ms. Connie Olsen. He reached her immediately, and she responded without hesitation to his questions.

"Yes, Assistant Superintendent, that's correct. Mr. Newsom has returned to the US. His wife was understandably upset about the attack on him, and he preferred to be at home to recuperate."

"You make it sound as though he's there already! He was here in Gaborone two hours ago."

"He's in South Africa and will be leaving for the United States from Johannesburg later today." Olsen's voice betrayed no emotion.

"Damn it, Ms. Olsen, are you aware that he's an important witness in a murder case here? I believe that may have been connected to the assault last night."

"Exactly, Assistant Superintendent. He felt he wasn't safe in Botswana. That's why we assisted him with arranging the trip home."

"I need to speak to him immediately!"

"Assistant Superintendent, Mr. Newsom is a US citizen. There is no question that someone attacked him last night and injured him seriously. It's our responsibility to assist our citizens in danger in foreign countries. Have you found his attacker?"

"It's only been a few hours."

"Mr. Newsom hasn't been arrested or accused of anything, has he?"

"I asked him not to leave the country without informing me."

"I wasn't aware of that, but he's the victim here, Assistant Superintendent. Keep that in mind."

Kubu wasn't sure what to say. How had this matter got out of hand so suddenly? "How can I contact him? I need to speak to him urgently."

"Hold on a minute. I have phone numbers for him. A local cell number and a number in the US. I'll give you those." She read off Newsom's Botswana cell phone number and the same US number Kubu had picked up from Newsom's phone.

"I've tried both those numbers but just get recorded messages."

"Well, he's in transit. You'll have to wait until tomorrow."

"Do you have an address for him in the US?"

She hesitated for a moment, then said, "I'm sorry, Assistant Superintendent, I'm not allowed to give you that information."

"I can get the information from Interpol."

"Well, of course, Assistant Superintendent. Please go ahead with that."

Kubu thanked her as politely as he could manage and hung up. He would alert the border posts and the airport, but he didn't think Olsen was lying to him. They must have driven Newsom through the Tlokweng border or flown him out of the country in a private plane. And he had no hope of getting the South African authorities to hold Newsom on a few hours' notice; he wasn't accused of any crime and had presumably left Botswana legally. He cursed again. He should have insisted on holding Newsom's passport, but there'd been no justification for that at the time.

He dressed quickly. He was going to have to explain the whole mess to Mabaku, but he doubted that the director would be too upset. As far as Mabaku was concerned, the Kunene issue was already history, and with Newsom gone, the knife attack would decline in importance.

Kubu had an uncomfortable feeling in his stomach that he'd just lost his main connection to the Kunene murder and any hope of understanding how it linked with the attack on Newsom the night before.

CHAPTER 31

Constable Polanka was worried. There were just as many people headed toward the *kgotla* as the previous time, but now many of the young men had cartons of Shake Shake beer and were brandishing heavy sticks. The talk was aggressive.

"The chief had better say yes to the mine!"

"We need the jobs."

"We'll throw him out if he says no!"

"And the other old men also."

"I'll beat some sense into them!"

Constable Polanka was scared. He could never stop this crowd if it got out of control, so he pulled out his cell phone and called the station chief.

"Rra. I think there's going to be trouble at the *kgotla*. The young people are angry and are carrying big sticks. If the chief says no to the mine, I don't know what they will do. Please send some more men up here. Quickly."

• • •

THE STAGE WAS set as before. The chief's son and the elders were sitting under a canopy, and the people from the village thronged around it. However, this time much of the space close to the stage was occupied by young men, restless as they waited for the chief. The older men had been pushed to the back and were muttering at the disrespect. There were women scattered here and there, but the mood was quite different to the previous meeting; children and babies had been left at home. And Constable Polanka had been reinforced with the arrival of five other constables.

Eventually, there was a buzz as the crowd parted, and the chief walked slowly toward the stage and climbed the steps. He went straight to the microphone and waited for the crowd to quiet down.

"Thank you for your patience. I have consulted with the elders and have now made my decision." The chief looked around at the audience. If he saw the sticks, he didn't show it.

"As we heard last time, there is great opportunity in the offer the mine has made . . ." A growl of approval came from the young men. "But we also have had a bad experience in dealing with the mine—promises were broken and a number of families were thrown out of their homes with nowhere to go."

The elders onstage nodded.

"I have listened to many opinions from young and old and have considered the issue from all sides. This has been a very difficult situation because whatever decision I make will pit young versus old, the past against the future. So it will be impossible for all to be satisfied. So I ask everyone to accept what I have decided and to move forward without looking back." The young men leaned forward expectantly.

The chief cleared his throat. "This is what I have decided."

Constable Polanka was startled by the silence. How can so many people be so quiet? he wondered.

"Shoshong is a town with a great history," the chief continued. "It was the center of all of this part of what is now Botswana. It was the home of the great Khama the Third before the droughts forced him to leave. There is no doubt that expanding the mine will bring jobs." He paused to clear his throat. "But it will also destroy our heritage." He looked at the crowd. "I believe that a heritage is more important than jobs. So I will tell the mine we do not want it to expand. I have—"

The young men jumped up, bellowing in anger, and started to move forward.

Constable Polanka jumped in front of the stage, waving his arms, and shouted for the mob to stop. It did not. He pulled out his handgun and fired it into the air. "Stop," he cried. "Go back!" It had no effect. One of the other constables also fired into the air and, when the crowd continued to move, pointed at it and fired. A man fell, howling in pain. The constable fired another shot. Another man fell. There was pandemonium. People ran in all directions, and the screams of women could be heard over the din.

Some of the young men turned and charged toward the shooter. He panicked, fired again into the crowd, then turned tail and ran as fast as his legs could carry him. The rest of the mob rushed the stage and knocked Constable Polanka to the ground.

"Help!" he screamed, as he was trampled and kicked. Then he gave a second but weaker shout for help. But it was to no avail. No one heard him over the angry roar.

The men poured onto the stage. One of the elders was smashed to the ground and kicked and beaten with sticks. He writhed, knees to his chest, arms covering his head. But soon his arms were broken. And then his head. Blood oozed over the stage.

A second elder was dead before the crowd reached him—his heart stopping in terror at the wave of anger headed his way.

The third elder stood up and started to run, but his spindly legs were no match for angry young ones. He died from a single blow to the head from a hardwood *knobkierie*.

The incensed men then turned to the chief, who had jumped

off the back of the stage and was running away as fast as his ancient legs would carry him. Julius turned and followed his father. Several of the screaming men sprinted after them. A shot rang out. The mob closed on the chief. There was another shot, barely heard above the din, just before the first man reached the old man. The chief stumbled and fell. Nothing could stop the rampage. In seconds, he was nothing more than a bloodied, broken body facedown in the sand.

Like a flock of queleas, the crowd changed direction and surged toward the remaining constables, who were trying to get away. One turned and stood his ground, taking careful aim. The crowd didn't break its stride and ran screaming at the man. His courage evaporated, and he fled, firing over his shoulder until the magazine ran out. He knew he was running for his life, but it was not fast enough.

CHAPTER 32

"Let us pray."

Kubu, Joy, Amantle, Tumi, and Nono joined hands around the dinner table.

"Nono, will you please say grace."

"Thank you for this food, Jesus," Nono said. She hesitated a moment and then continued in a rush. "And-please-fill-the-tummies-of-everybody-who-is-hungry-because-it-is-not-nice-to-be-hungry.-Thank-you-Jesus.-Amen."

"That was very thoughtful of you, Nono," Joy said with a smile. She recalled how hungry Nono had been when they took her into their home, as thin as a rake, after her sister had succumbed to AIDS. "I'm sure Jesus will listen to you."

Amantle, who was sitting next to Nono, took her hand and gave it a squeeze. "That was very nice, my child."

"Daddy, Daddy, serve me first," Tumi shouted.

"Please don't shout at the table, Tumi," Kubu said. "I can hear you very well."

Tumi bounced up and down in her chair. "Please serve me first," she said in an exaggerated whisper. She picked up her knife and fork expectantly.

Kubu put a large spoonful of mashed potato on the top plate and covered it with steaming meat stew. Then he added a helping of boiled cabbage and passed the plate to Amantle, who put it down in front of Tumi.

"You can start," Kubu said.

He then served Nono, followed by the three adults.

Joy frowned as she saw how little Kubu put on his own plate. "Are you sure that's enough, dear?" she asked.

He nodded. "I'm not that hungry," he replied.

"If you carry on like this, you'll need to take in all your trousers," she said, attempting to make light of her concern. "At least can I get you a glass of wine?"

Kubu shook his head and started playing with the food on his plate. He built a wall of mashed potato and dammed the stew behind it. Then he stuck his fork into the dam wall, opening a hole through which the stew trickled onto the rest of his plate.

Joy shook her head but said nothing, and for the next few minutes, the only sounds were the clinking of knives and forks on the dinner plates.

Kubu had just finished his serving when the phone rang.

"I'll get it. I'll get it," Tumi shouted, and ran to the phone. "Hello. This is the Bengus' home," she said in a serious voice. She listened for a moment. "I'm fine, thank you. I'll call him." She laid the receiver on the table. "It's Rra Mabaku, Daddy. He wants to speak to you."

Kubu heaved himself out of his chair and picked up the phone. "Good evening, Director. I hope you've got good news."

For the next few minutes, he listened, saying almost nothing. Joy watched his frown grow. It's not about Wilmon's attacker, she thought. God, I wish they'd find him, so Kubu can get back to being himself.

Kubu continued to listen. It must be another damned murder, Joy said to herself. What's this country coming to?

Eventually, Kubu spoke. "Yes, Director. Right away. I'll meet you at the police station as soon as I can get there." He put down the phone and slumped back into his chair.

"Go on, children. Go to your room and play."

"But what about dessert? Mommy bought some ice cream."

"You can have it in a few minutes. I have some grown-up talk to say to your mother and grandmother. Go on."

When the kids had disappeared and shut the door of their bedroom, Kubu looked up at the two women. "There's been a riot in Shoshong. Several policemen have been killed, and so have the chief and some elders." He paused. "We knew there were tensions, so we had some constables at the *kgotla*, and they were armed. But we never thought things were as bad as they turned out to be." He looked at Joy. "Darling, I have to go to Shoshong this evening. We have to try to calm things down."

"But it will be very dangerous . . ."

"No, my dear. I'll be fine. The army has been sent to impose a curfew. I have to meet the director there at ten." Kubu stood up. "I'd better be going. I think it's about a three-hour drive. I'll stay up there tonight and phone you first thing in the morning to let you know what's happening."

"No you won't!" Joy snapped. "You'll phone me as soon as you get there. You know how dangerous the roads can be at night, especially when your mind is on other things. I'll be worried sick until I hear from you."

"Yes, dear. Please don't worry. I'll be fine." He walked over to Joy and gave her a kiss. She clasped his body to hers. "Please be careful, dear," she whispered. "I love you so much."

He went into their bedroom, dumped a few clothes in a carryall, took his service pistol from the safe, and stopped at the front door.

"I'll call you when I get there. I promise. And don't forget to give the kids their ice cream."

KUBU WAS FRAZZLED by the time he pulled up outside the police station in Shoshong. He had narrowly missed two drunks—black men dressed in dark clothes—who'd been staggering along the edge of an unlit road. No wonder the number of pedestrian deaths was so high, he thought. And there were more cows than usual, grazing on the grass at the edge of the pavement. The cows were the worst—totally unpredictable, they could wander onto the road no matter how heavy the traffic. And hitting a cow often did more damage to the car than to the cow.

Kubu pulled out his phone and called home.

"I'm safely at the police station in Shoshong, dear," he said to a relieved Joy. "The usual stuff on the way up but largely a clear run. I'll call you around lunch tomorrow and give you an update."

"Please be careful, dear. I'm so scared something will happen to you. I love you so much."

"I'll be careful, and I love you too."

WHEN KUBU WALKED into the small conference room that Mabaku had commandeered as his operations room, Kubu thought that war must have broken out. There was a senior officer from the army—what his rank was, Kubu didn't know—and his aide. They were talking to the head of the police helicopter squadron, whom Kubu knew quite well. The commissioner of police was there in full uniform, listening to an earnest-looking civilian. Kubu's colleagues Zanele Dlamini and Samantha Khama were standing near the window talking quietly. And Director Mabaku was in the far corner, glowering at everyone. He motioned for Kubu to join him.

"What an unmitigated mess," Mabaku growled. "That person talking to the commissioner—he's the local National Assembly member. Between the two of them, they can only make things worse with their politicking. What do they know about riot control? Neither of them would have thought to bring in a couple of helicopters."

He looked around the room. "At least Major Pule has his head screwed on straight. He knows how to handle men. He's fair but won't put up with any nonsense. We're just waiting for the station commander, who's gone to find the constables who survived the riot. Apparently, three constables were beaten to death, as were the chief and three of his elders, and four of the rioters suffered gunshot wounds. Fortunately, the chief's son was able to calm the mob, who then left the *kgotla* and went drinking. From what I hear, that's what they're still doing." He nodded toward Major Pule. "The army got here very quickly and secured the scene. They're in the process of imposing a curfew. The injured men were all taken to the local clinic and treated. Then they were taken to the hospital in Mahalapye. Your friend MacGregor is going to have to arrange to get the bodies to Gabs for his autopsies."

"I'm amazed at the reaction to the chief's turning down the mine's offer," Kubu said. "There must have been some ringleaders urging the crowd on. We'll need to find out who they were."

Mabaku nodded. "That may be difficult. Mobs have a mentality of their own. I think we'll find a great deal of denial when we talk to men who were at the *kgotla*."

He indicated toward the door. "Here's the station commander. I've got to go." He walked over to the commissioner, spoke to him, then clapped his hands. "Attention, please."

Immediately, the hubbub subsided.

The commissioner quickly introduced everyone, giving their credentials. Then he continued, "The president has ordered me to get to the bottom of this disaster as quickly as possible. Director Mabaku of the CID will be in charge of the investigation. He will work hand in hand with Major Pule to ensure there isn't a repetition. I will ensure that they have the resources they need. The President expects—"

Before he could finish the sentence, there was a knock on the door, and a constable stuck his head in. "The new chief wants to speak to you, sir," he said to the commissioner. "Shall I let him in?" The commissioner nodded.

A young man walked into the room, wearing an old brown jacket with a black armband. "Good evening, *borra*. My name is Julius Koma. My father was the chief here in Shoshong. He was killed at the *kgotla* today. I will be the new chief."

THE COMMISSIONER, MABAKU, and Kubu spent the next two hours interrogating the old chief's son. He told them of the schism that had developed in the community over the mine's offer. "Young men are desperate for work," he said. "But I understand why the older people are cautious. They were lied to once before by the same mine."

"But why did the *kgotla* get out of hand?" the commissioner asked. "What brought on the violence? What did it achieve?"

"I think it was years of frustration," Julius replied. "The government isn't listening to the people. These men want to work, but nothing is being done to provide jobs."

"There must've been a ringleader or several ringleaders," Mabaku said. "Who were they? We need to know. We have to find those responsible."

Julius shook his head. "It was like a landslide. Once it started, it just grew and grew. No one was leading it."

"Didn't you try to stop the mob?" Mabaku continued.

"What could I do? Nothing could stop them! I could see the anger in their eyes. I grabbed my father and jumped off the back of the stage and tried to run." He paused and took a deep breath. "He was an old man. He couldn't run very fast. They caught up to us very quickly."

"Why didn't they kill you?" Kubu asked. "You were part of the village council."

"I'm on their side. I wanted my father to accept the mine's offer. Everyone knows that!"

"When will the elders meet to appoint a new chief?"

"The elders will have to meet in the next few days," Julius responded. "Shoshong is a strange place. There are actually three groups in the area, and the elders of all three groups decide on the new chief. The position of chief normally moves from one group to the next. But the other groups don't understand what the men need. If the new chief is appointed in the old way, we'll just have more trouble. So I'll persuade them to appoint me. Otherwise, there could be another riot."

"What will the other groups say when they hear you've already taken your father's place?" This time it was the commissioner who asked the question.

"It's only until they elect someone. Somebody needs to be in charge until then, somebody who understands the situation, who knows the young men. Otherwise, more bad things will happen. When I go to them tomorrow to arrange the *kgotla*, I will sit with their elders and explain why I had to do what I did. They'll understand."

The commissioner frowned. "I hope so. Tradition runs deep in places like Shoshong that have a long and prominent history. The elders may want to preserve that tradition and use the riot as the reason why."

"I think the elders will support me," Julius said. He stood up. "I have to go now. It's been a terrible day, and I need to go and comfort my mother."

The commissioner looked at the other two, who both nodded, relieved that they might soon be in bed.

When Julius had left the room, the commissioner turned to his colleagues. "What do you think? Is he telling the truth?"

"About what?" Mabaku asked.

"That he needs to be chief if the unrest is to stop."

Both Mabaku and Kubu shook their heads. "I don't know anything about this area," Kubu said. "But what he claimed is easy to check out. Perhaps you can speak to the elders from the other villages tomorrow, Commissioner. They would respect a man of your position."

"It seems very strange to me that people would riot like that without someone urging them on," Mabaku said. "Were there any reports of strangers being at the *kgotla*? Could someone from the mine have stirred up trouble?" He looked at the other two. "And what's mined here anyway? I've never heard of a mine in this area."

"I seem to remember that my history teacher said there had been mines here for hundreds of years, but what was being mined, I've no idea," Kubu responded.

"I think I read that a uranium mine upgraded the *kgotla* last year, as a gesture of goodwill to the community." The commissioner sounded skeptical. "Probably smoothing the way for the offer they made."

"I need to get to bed," Kubu said, "and it's quite a drive back to Mahalapye. I'll check all that out in the morning."

The three men left the police station and headed for what they knew was going to be a short night's sleep. The press would have no mercy if they weren't on the job at dawn.

CHAPTER 33

As Kubu drove back to Shoshong early on Sunday morning, he tried to come to grips with what had happened the day before. The Batswana were known as peaceful people who respected traditions and believed in the wisdom of elders. They didn't settle their problems with violence and riots. Or so it was in the past. Now the youth were impatient for money and the things they expected for a good life—cars, smartphones, nice clothes, houses. They had lost patience. And why shouldn't they? Kubu thought. The diamond boom was over. The new generation had missed out. But to riot and kill weak old men and batter policemen to death? To him it was inconceivable, and he was going to find out who was responsible.

He was so focused on his thoughts that he almost missed the village of Tobela. The sign caught his eye as he was already driving past the entrance track. He braked and pulled over to the side of the road. He'd known that Tobela was somewhere along this road, but he'd missed it the night before in his rush to meet Mabaku, and by the time he drove back to Mahalapye, he was too tired to do more than watch for stray animals. But now that he was at the entrance, he wasn't sure if a detour into the village was a good idea. He wanted to get to work on the reasons why Shoshong had turned into a battlefield, and he knew that anything he did in Tobela would be frowned upon by Mabaku, but the lure of finding out who had visited his father proved too great. He should have carried on to Shoshong at once, but instead, he turned onto the dirt road that took him through a rusty gate into the village.

He bumped down what was really a donkey track until he reached what he guessed was the center of the village. People were already up and about, chatting in small groups. Some were dressed up for church—presumably in Shoshong—but others were in casual clothes. The mood was somber; only the children seemed happy, enjoying the weekend break from school.

"*Dumela*." Kubu approached a group talking in the road. They returned his greeting, but instead of introductions and polite questions about himself and his relatives, they at once wanted to know who he was and whether he knew the details of what was happening in Shoshong.

"Yes, I am Assistant Superintendent Bengu of the Botswana CID in Gaborone. I'm here to help the local police find out what caused this disaster and who was responsible." This wasn't the way Kubu had meant to introduce himself, but there was no option. Only one thing was of interest in Tobela on this Sunday.

"Aaii! So it is true then? Their chief is dead? Murdered? And all their elders?" It was an old woman who said this, shaking her head.

Kubu nodded. "There was some sort of riot at the *kgotla* yesterday. Some men attacked the chief when he told the gathering that he wasn't going to allow the mine to expand. Several people were killed, including the chief."

A man with a sour face looked at Kubu. "Their chief cared nothing for what the people need. He was stuck in the past. I'm not surprised his people got tired of him."

The woman sucked in her breath. "How can you say such a thing, Dithebe? And on the Sabbath. They did not depose him. They murdered him! Hacked him to pieces. It is shocking, and I cannot understand it."

The rest of the group joined in, and Kubu was flooded with questions. They expected him to know all the answers, but at last they ran out of steam. The elderly lady said firmly, "Well, I am not going to the church today. I do not know if it is safe, and I do not know what to ask God. I do not know." There was silence, and several people nodded agreement. Then she continued, "And you, Rra Detective, what are you doing here? As you see, no one here knows what happened yesterday in Shoshong."

"But I didn't know that before I came here." Kubu hesitated. His mission was hard to explain to these shocked people. "But I'm here for another reason too. My father's ancestors came from here, and I wonder if there's still family here. The name was Bengu."

Everyone looked at the old lady, but she shook her head. "No, I don't remember that name. How long ago did they leave?"

"It was a very long time ago."

"There is no one here with that name now."

"I ask because a man came to visit my father in Mochudi. He said he was a relative and that he came from Tobela."

"And what else did he say?"

"I don't know. But my father was murdered shortly afterward, and I'm trying to trace this man."

"Aaii! Even the family of the police are not safe now! What is the world coming to?" Tears started to run down the woman's lined face, and Kubu was touched by them, whether they were for his father or in reaction to the dreadful events of the previous day.

A man turned to Kubu and said, "I'm sorry for your loss, rra, but we know nothing of this here."

There was a murmur of agreement, and Dithebe spat on the ground, not at Kubu's feet, but the message was clear enough. Kubu realized that his timing couldn't have been worse. On any ordinary day, a visitor from Gaborone would have been a welcome event in Tobela, and people would have been interested in the historical family connections. But this was no ordinary day.

He thanked the group for their time and turned to walk back to his car. But Dithebe wanted the last word. "When you get to Shoshong, tell their new chief not to drive around in fancy cars while his people are hungry. Then maybe they will respect him."

"Shut up!" the old lady told him. "You know nothing. He didn't have a fancy car. It was just an ordinary Toyota. You have a foul mouth. You should wash it out with soap!"

"Well, it was a fancy silver color. And with fancy wheels! That costs plenty of money."

Kubu turned back. "The chief had a silver Toyota? He was here in Tobela?"

The old lady nodded. "Last month he came with his son and two of his elders to consult with our elders. And he even spoke at the *kgotla* here. He came in a silver car, but it was not a Merc or a BMW like all the big politicians." She turned on the hapless Dithebe. "It was not fancy. But you speak ill of everyone. Even the dead, who cannot talk back." The man turned away from her with a shrug and walked off.

Kubu climbed into his Land Rover and drove off, bumping over the pot-holed track through Tobela. A group of goats looked at him casually, but they moved aside to let him pass. And so he left his father's ancestral home none the wiser about his heritage, but with a piece of information he hadn't expected to find.

IN THE EARLY light, the protecting horseshoe of hills around Shoshong made a beautiful sight, the dolerite boulders piled one on top of another a rich gold. In the distance, Kubu could see the gorge where the river had brought water to Old Shoshong, before it dried up over a hundred years ago, forcing Khama III to move his people away.

When Kubu reached the police station, Mabaku was already in his operations room. He glanced up as Kubu entered. "How come you're so late?"

Kubu thought the question a bit unfair given how little sleep they'd all had. He started to reply, but Mabaku brushed it aside. "Never mind. Another man died last night from a gunshot wound. We're going to get to the bottom of this, Kubu. Who was behind it, who led that riot, who joined in. I'll get every policeman I can lay my hands on going door to door, finding out who was at the *kgotla*, and finding out what they saw. We'll get the bastards who killed our policemen and those elders."

Kubu started to comment, but again Mabaku interrupted. "What I want you to do is find out who or what was behind all this. It wasn't spontaneous. Some group must have set it up. Those are the people I want to get my hands on."

Kubu was relieved that he wasn't to join the door-to-door brigade. "Any idea where I should start?"

Mabaku nodded. "I've been talking to the station commander. *He* was here early. Good man. He knows what's happening in his town. It turns out one of the elders on the chief's council didn't go to the *kgotla* yesterday. Apparently, he's not well. Anyway, he should have some insight into what was going on between the chief and the different interests involved, if anyone does." As an afterthought, he added, "You'd better talk to the mine manager too."

Kubu nodded. It seemed like a sensible place to begin. "What's the elder's name and where can I find him?"

"It's Rra Nwako. I'll get a constable to show you where he lives. It's in the old part of town, and it's hard to find anything there." Mabaku sighed. "Kubu, this is a very big deal. It could affect tourism and the stock market—good thing it's closed today. And the commissioner just phoned me to say that the president wants to come and address the people at the very same place where every-thing blew up yesterday! That will be a security nightmare. He's agreed to wait a few days, but the commissioner knows him. He says the president won't back down once he's made up his mind."

A constable bustled in with some papers for Mabaku. He glanced at them and said, "Please take Assistant Superintendent Bengu to Rra Nwako's house right away." Then he turned his attention back to Kubu and added with a touch of sarcasm, "You'd better hurry, Kubu, or you'll miss your lunch."

It didn't seem to be the moment to mention the Tobela visit, so Kubu just nodded and followed the constable out to the car park.

RRA NWAKO'S HOUSE looked as though it had been built in the glory days of Khama III at the end of the nineteenth century, when Sho-shong was a trading post for travelers from all points of the compass. It was large with a view of the hills, but it had fallen on hard times and needed plastering and a good coat of paint.

An old man was sitting on the veranda eating porridge and drinking black tea. He greeted Kubu but didn't interrupt his breakfast.

"Would you like tea, rra? My daughter will make you some." Without waiting for a reply, he called out, "Funeka, will you come out here, please." Raising his voice was too much for him, and he started coughing. A woman appeared and watched the old man with concern.

Once he caught his breath, Nwako introduced Kubu to his daughter, adding, "The assistant superintendent would like a cup of tea. And I would like another myself." The woman nodded and left, and Nwako started coughing again.

"Funeka says it is the smoking. Maybe she is right. She will not let me smoke in the house. Do you have any cigarettes with you?"

"I'm sorry, rra. I don't smoke."

"It's a terrible thing that has happened here, rra." Nwako shook his head and swallowed another spoonful of porridge. "All these people dead. Young people with lives before them. Old people with much wisdom. This town will never be the same again. The trust is gone." He shook his head again and finished his breakfast in silence.

After a short while, Funeka brought the tea. She looked at her father with concern. "Emphysema. That's what the doctor called it," she said. "I know it's because of the smoking, but he won't stop."

"Just as well, is it not?" Nwako said. "If I did not have the excuse of being ill, I would have been at the *kgotla* yesterday, and you would be arranging my funeral this morning like the families of the others." His voice caught as he said it.

"He's completely impossible," she told Kubu, but it was said with affection. Then she left them to talk.

"Rra," Kubu began, "we're trying to understand what happened yesterday. We're hoping you can help us with that."

The elder met Kubu's eyes and said nothing for a few seconds. "It is impossible to understand what happened yesterday. But I can tell you what happened before." He paused. "You know about the mine and the jobs?" Kubu nodded. "Traditions are important, Assistant Superintendent. Our culture is based on our traditions. History is important too. Shoshong has a very long history. Many years before the days of Khama the Third, there were Tswana people here. Thousands of years before that, there was an Iron Age settlement in these hills. There are important relics from those people in the museum in Gaborone, pottery, iron tools. Perhaps you have seen them?" Kubu shook his head.

"You see," the old man commented, "people these days are not interested in such things; they live for the present." He paused. "But sometimes old people think that the past is all that is important. Our chief, rest his soul, was like that. He knew the town needed jobs, that the young men wanted to work—at least those who were not content to lounge around the shebeens all day—but his mind

was always on the past, preserving our traditions and our history. That was what was important. He said that the young men could go to Francistown for work." He shook his head. "If that happens, the town will die."

"So you supported letting the mine expand?"

Nwako nodded slowly. "It was the only way. But I was the only elder who thought so. Of course, the chief's son, Julius, supported it too. Very strongly."

"But that made no difference?"

Nwako shook his head. "Julius went to the mine management. He told us he was negotiating with them. That made his father very angry. It is the chief's role to do that; Julius went behind his back. I think it hardened the chief's resolve to turn down the mine's offer."

Kubu brooded about that. So there was tension between Julius and his father, and Julius had now all but declared himself chief. And presumably if Julius did become chief, the mine would get its way. So both Julius and the mine had much to gain from the chief's death. Another mining issue, Kubu thought. Newsom had come to Mahalapye to visit a mining company on the day he was attacked. Could there be a connection?

"I'm confused, rra. Why was this even an issue for the chief? It is the director of mines in Gaborone who decides on mining licenses and so on."

Nwako nodded. "Yes, but here people are living on the land the mine wants. The mine has to get our agreement. Julius told us the mine would get approval from the director if we gave our permission. I do not understand how he knew that."

"I suppose you will support him to be the new chief?"

Nwako raised his eyebrows. "In Shoshong, the chief rotates between groups, Assistant Superintendent. It doesn't automatically go from father to son." He shook his head. "As for Julius, I agreed with him on this issue, but I do not trust him." He coughed again,

hawked, and spat into his handkerchief. "Rra, you must excuse me
now," he said when he'd caught his breath. "I am old and much sad-
dened by all this. Now I must go and visit the families of my late
friends."

"Of course, rra. Thank you for your help. I may come back again
if I need to know more. But I have just one more question for now.
What sort of car did the chief drive?"

Nwako looked surprised. "The chief? He did not have a car. He
did not know how to drive. Why do you ask that?"

"I was just curious. Someone told me the chief drove to Tobela
to speak at the *kgotla* there."

Nwako nodded. "A group of us went to visit their elders. It was
about a month ago. Julius drove us in his car. It's a silver car. A
Toyota, I think."

Kubu took a deep breath. Now he recalled that the Mochudi
bartender had told Samantha about the age difference between
Wilmon and his visitor. Although he had no real evidence, Kubu's
gut told him that it was Julius Koma who visited his father in
Mochudi the week he was killed.

CHAPTER 34

Kubu sat in his car and wondered what to do next. He was itching to challenge Julius about whether he'd been to Mochudi, but should he rather show the bartender Julius's picture first? That would be the cautious strategy, probably the right strategy. But Kubu felt time was getting short, and everyone was tied up in Shoshong trying to discover what had happened at the riot and preparing for the president's visit. Also, if he told Mabaku about his hunch, he would be sidelined again—perhaps even on the Shoshong case. Kubu shook his head. He needed to do something. But what exactly? He couldn't very well question Julius about the car. Mabaku would have a fit.

While he was thinking about it, he scratched through his notes and found the details of the manager at Konshua Mine. At least he should fulfill Mabaku's instructions. He dialed the number, and just when he was about to give up, the phone was answered by someone speaking Chinese.

"Good morning. This is Assistant Superintendent Bengu of the Botswana CID. Can I speak to the mine manager, please?"

"I am Shonhu. Mr. Hong is not available. It is Sunday." The English was accented but easy enough to understand.

"There's been a lot of trouble in Shoshong. I need to speak to him urgently."

"He is available tomorrow, not today. I have an announcement from the mine. I will read it to you." There was a pause and the rustling of papers. After a few moments the man came back on the line and read, "The Konshua Mine management and staff express great regret at the sorrowful events in the historic town of Shoshong. The Konshua Mine had great respect and affection for Chief Koma. It is regrettable that a misunderstanding led him to believe that the mine was not concerned about the traditions and history of the great town of Shoshong. In fact, China has a great heritage and greatly respects the heritage of others. Once a period of mourning is past, we look forward to engaging with the new chief to resolve all misunderstandings to the benefit of the people of Shoshong and the Konshua Mine. The mine will be closed on Monday as a gesture of respect to those injured and killed. All workers will receive full pay."

There was a pause. I suppose I'm expected to clap, Kubu thought. They obviously have a good spin doctor there, but I could have read that in tomorrow's *Daily News*. "I need to speak to Mr. Hong at once," he reiterated.

"I regret. It is not possible." The connection was cut. Kubu immediately phoned back, but this time the phone just rang.

Kubu sat in his car and fumed. He started the engine and switched on the air conditioner. Who do these people think they are? They come to our country, exploit our resources, cause a riot, and then tell us they are not available to the police on Sunday. Perhaps Mr. Shonhu needs a call from the commissioner. Or, even better, Director Mabaku. In the meantime, I'm getting nowhere and still have no idea what to do about Julius Koma. Then, his problem was solved in an unexpected way. His phone rang and it was Samantha.

"Hello, Kubu. I'm so glad we're working together again. I mean . . . Anyway, I've been talking to bartenders in the shebeens around Shoshong, and I've picked up something you should know."

Bartenders seem to have become her specialty, Kubu thought grumpily. "What's that?"

"On Friday, Julius Koma—the chief's son—visited a number of bars and chatted to the locals. His message was that they must push the chief and elders hard at the *kgotla*. Threaten them, if necessary."

"You're saying Julius was behind the riot?" Kubu said, amazed.

Samantha hesitated. "No. He was very clear. No violence. No one gets hurt. But still! He was the chief's son, and he was stirring up the people against him. He must've known that if the chief ruled against the mine there could be trouble."

It seems that Julius isn't the good guy he's cut himself out to be, Kubu thought. And suddenly he knew what he needed to do.

"We need to talk to him, Samantha. Julius said nothing about this in the interview last night. We need to hear his side of the story. I have his cell number, so I'll call him and set up a meeting. I want you there; this is your lead. In fact, I want you to question him."

"You do?" Samantha was pleased.

"I'll call you right back."

IT WAS JULIUS's choice to meet at a coffee shop. He said his mother couldn't cope with anything more at the moment, and the house was full of relatives arranging the funeral. Kubu remembered how large Wilmon's funeral had been and imagined that the whole of Shoshong would turn out for the chief's. Old and young—even if they'd helped strike him down. In other circumstances, he would have felt a lot of sympathy for Julius.

When Kubu reached the coffee shop, Samantha was already outside, admiring a display of cakes in the window. "I can't eat these things," she said regretfully. "They're full of calories." Kubu thought he might manage a slice. Breakfast had been tea and a piece of toast.

"Samantha, you question Koma. But there's one extra question I want you to work in. Ask him about his car."

Samantha frowned. "His car? What's that got to do with anything?"

"You'll find out. Look, here he is now."

"Good morning, Assistant Superintendent. This better be quick. I'm glad to get out for a while, but I've got lots to do."

Kubu introduced Samantha, and they all ordered coffees with hot milk. Kubu selected a slice of the carrot cake. True to his word, he let Samantha ask the questions while he took the occasional mouthful. But Julius wasn't fazed. "Yes," he told them, "that's right. I went around the shebeens on Friday afternoon trying to calm the young guys down. My father was out of touch with the young people, Detective. I told them to make their points, demonstrate even, but that *no one should be hurt.* I was afraid things might get out of hand. You can see I was dead right." He nodded firmly.

He's lying, Kubu thought. Will Samantha see that?

Indeed, Samantha probed, asked for details, quoted what people had told her. Julius had an answer for all of it. At last Samantha snapped her notebook shut.

"Is that all?" Julius asked, and finished his coffee. "I should be getting back to my mother."

Samantha glanced at Kubu, then turned back to Julius. "Just one other thing. What sort of car do you have and where was it yesterday?"

"My car? What's that got to do with anything? Actually, it was at the *kgotla.* I drove my father there before the meeting. So what?"

"What sort of car is it and what color?" Kubu chipped in.

"It's a silver Toyota Avensis. This is stupid! Why do you care where the damn car was?"

Samatha had the scent. She knew that Kubu had set her up, and she wasn't pleased, but she also suspected that Julius wasn't the nice guy he pretended to be. And she assumed that Kubu had more information about the Toyota than its color.

"Where were you on Monday, January twenty-seventh?" she asked, opening her notebook again.

"That's three weeks ago! Look, what's this about? You're wasting my time here."

"I don't think we are, rra," Kubu said quietly. "I don't think we're wasting anyone's time here." His hands were tightly clenched.

Julius looked at him and said nothing for quite a while. At last he said, "Your name's Bengu. Are you related to Wilmon Bengu? That's where I was that day. I was in Mochudi visiting Rra Bengu."

There was silence again for several moments, and then Kubu said: "Yes, he was my father. And he was murdered the Saturday after you saw him."

"Terrible. I'm sorry. But what's it got to do with me?"

Kubu leaned back in his chair and looked at the half-eaten slice of cake. He's a liar, he thought. But he's a good liar. Maybe that's what he does best. But Samantha was angry and burst out, "Why didn't you come forward with this information? We've been looking for the person who visited Rra Bengu for weeks!"

Julius shrugged. "I didn't know that."

"It was in all the papers, and on the radio and TV!" Kubu exclaimed.

"Look, I've been busy here. You can see what we've been dealing with! You think I've got time for newspapers and TV?"

"So what did you talk to him about?" Kubu growled.

"It was about the mine, of course. Chief Koma thought he should be consulted. He told me to do it."

"Why? What had my father to do with the damn mine?"

"The chief thought your father was from Tobela. He thought he had land and family there. That he'd been an important person here in the past. He was wrong."

"What was the fight about?" Samantha asked.

"Fight? What fight?"

"The bartender said Rra Bengu shouted at you. He called you a fraud!"

"Oh, that. Yes, well, we thought he had relatives here, and that's how we set up the meeting. It was all a mistake. Once I explained to Rra Bengu, he calmed down and everything was fine."

"And what did he mean when he said, 'It's for my son. It will stay in the family'?" Kubu felt his blood pressure rising. "*I'm* his son!"

"I don't remember him saying that."

"Others heard him. It was as Rra Bengu was leaving," Samantha said.

"I didn't hear it. I was told later that Rra Bengu was not altogether with it anymore. He often made strange remarks or didn't recognize his friends." He shrugged and looked at Kubu. "Do *you* know what he was talking about?"

Before Kubu could respond, Samantha asked, "How did you set up the arrangement to see him?"

"I found his cell number and called him. My phone was causing trouble so I used a pay phone. There's one near the *kgotla*. Is there anything else? It's getting late."

Kubu started to ask another question, but Samantha interrupted. "No, rra, that's all. Thank you for your help this morning."

Julius nodded. "It's okay. Will you get the coffees? I'm late." With that, he walked out, waving to the cashier on his way out.

"Can't you see he's lying?" said Kubu, furious.

"Of course he's lying!" Samantha responded, equally angry. "But we're way out of line here. It was going to blow up in our faces! You set me up, Kubu."

Kubu calmed down. "Yes, you're right. I'm sorry. There wasn't any other way."

"Of course there was! You could've told me about the car and not let the whole thing be a big surprise."

"If I'd done that, you would've wanted to bring Mabaku into the story, and I would be sidelined again!"

"Yes, that's exactly right! Now we've alerted a possible suspect and important witness. How did you know it was his car in Mochudi anyway?"

"I didn't," Kubu admitted. "It was a hunch. It seemed to fit."

Samantha shook her head, speechless.

"Well," Kubu began, "now we know, the next thing we need to do is—"

But Samantha interrupted. "I don't care what you do next. The next thing I'm going to do is report this mess to the director. I want to keep my job, even if you don't care about yours!"

MABAKU HEARD THEM out without interruption. He asked a few questions calmly, then turned to Samantha, shaking his head. "I'm used to Kubu ignoring my orders, but I thought you at least might take some notice."

Before Samantha could respond, Kubu interjected. "It had nothing to do with her, Director. I didn't tell her about the car until we were into the interview."

Mabaku nodded, unsurprised. "All right, Samantha, you can go. I'll talk to you later." He waited until she left before he turned to Kubu, who was bracing himself for a Mabaku tirade. Instead Mabaku glared at him for several moments, and when he spoke, it was at normal volume.

"I can't tell you how disappointed I am in you, Kubu. I told you this morning how crucial it was to get to the bottom of the violence here. Did you listen? No. Instead you go off and compromise your father's case and this one also." Kubu waited for the outburst, but it still didn't come. "You gave me your word, Kubu. You promised that if you were in the loop, you'd keep out of the investigation. You've let me down, and I'm not going to forget that."

Kubu squirmed. He couldn't argue. It was true, and Mabaku's coldness hurt worse than being shouted at.

"I saw the commissioner this morning," Mabaku continued. "I can't go to the Interpol meeting this week. Not with the president breathing down my neck. The commissioner said the meeting was important and suggested you go, but I told him I needed you on the case here in Shoshong. But I was wrong. I need you *off* the case here." He shook his head. "Hand over everything you've got to Samantha. Call Miriam at the office and get her to arrange a flight for you to New York—I've already canceled mine. Then get back to Gaborone, pick up my speech from Miriam, and get packed."

"But Director, the Julius issue is a big breakthrough. We have to get to the bottom of—"

Mabaku chopped his hand through the air as if cutting the sound. "Get out of Shoshong *now,* Kubu! Or you're suspended. I mean it."

Kubu climbed to his feet. He knew that this time he'd gone too far. This time there was no arguing with Mabaku. "Yes, Director," he said, and went to find Samantha. He couldn't imagine anything that he'd rather do less than sit on planes for two days to deliver a paper he didn't care about in New York. Especially when he felt he finally had a real lead to whatever had culminated in his father's death.

CHAPTER 35

As Kubu drove back to Mahalapye from Shoshong, he brooded about the meeting with Mabaku. Had he been wrong all along? Instead of believing that he was the only one who could find the murderer, should he have trusted the team and left the investigation to them? He feared that his relationship with Mabaku was permanently damaged. And he didn't have much to show for his clandestine efforts. His gut told him that Julius was involved somehow, but he had no real evidence and no way of taking the investigation further. He was getting farther away from Julius with every moment.

When he reached the hotel, it was too late to cancel his room for that night, so Mabaku was committed to another day's cost. Too bad, Kubu thought. He intended to sleep in his own bed that night. But he didn't leave right away; there was someone he wanted to see before he left Mahalapye, and Kubu knew where he was to be found once evening came. He phoned Joy and told her what had happened, then called Miriam to make the travel arrangements to

New York. After that, he spent the afternoon relaxing in the air-conditioned lounge. Finally, he checked out, put his bag in the trunk, and went in search of the Kalahari Oasis Bar. A weird name for a shebeen miles from the Kalahari, he thought. Still, the oasis part of the name was probably more to the point. Apart from its name, the shebeen had another interesting feature: it was only a few blocks away from the pay phone that had been used twice to contact his father the week before he died.

When he eventually found it, he wasn't encouraged. It was in a rough part of town, and the bar was at least as shabby as the neighborhood. Kubu parked his car, wondering if it would still be there when he came back. For a few minutes he sat there and considered whether he should write off the meeting. The chances were that he'd learn nothing, and even if he did find something useful, he'd only have more angst with Mabaku. He decided that this time he'd follow the rules. He started the car, then realized he hadn't really come to get information. He actually wanted to see the man who might be the only remaining family member of his father's generation.

He turned off the engine, took his service pistol, and headed into the bar.

INSIDE IT WAS dingy and stiflingly hot. Plastic chairs, several broken, crowded around plastic tables decorated with empty cans. People were smoking—totally illegally—but no one seemed to notice or care. Kubu made his way to the bartender and asked for a St. Louis beer. The man shoved a lukewarm can toward him and demanded the money.

"I'm looking for Mzilikaze Bengu," Kubu said. The bartender pointed to one of the tables, where three elderly men were chatting with empty cartons of Shake Shake beer in front of them. They looked like street people, with ill-fitting clothes that could have done with a wash, but they seemed to have money for beer. Kubu doubted that the bartender gave drinks on credit.

Kubu was a boy when he'd last seen his half uncle, but he recognized him easily. A web of nasty scars twisted the left side of his face, the legacy of an attack with a broken bottle in a bar brawl.

"Hello, Uncle Mzi," he said.

The man looked Kubu up and down, but it was clear he recognized him. "You've grown, David. In all directions," he said with a smirk. For the benefit of the men with him, he added, "This is my half brother Wilmon's boy. A police detective." He didn't make it sound like a compliment, and neither of the other men offered a greeting. After a few moments, Mzi said, "You can join us if you're buying."

Kubu made no move to do so. "Can we talk in private?"

"Go ahead, Mzi," said one of the others. "I'm particular who I drink with anyway."

Mzi climbed to his feet and moved to a vacant table. "You can get me a brandy and coke. A double. Get yourself one too. Or are you going to drink that piss?" Kubu didn't answer but went to buy the brandy.

When Mzi had tested the drink, he turned his attention to Kubu. "Why?" he asked.

"Why what?"

"Why look me up after all these years? Why track me down."

"It wasn't hard to find you."

Mzi nodded. "Maybe not. So why?"

It was too complicated for Kubu to explain, so he said, "I thought you might know something. Something that would help us catch your brother's murderer."

Mzi smiled sourly at that. "Oh, *my brother*, is it? No one was keen to talk about *brothers* when your grandfather—my father—and your grandmother were doting on dear little Wilmon, and your grandfather had an affair and I came along."

"Look," Kubu said. "I don't know what happened in the past. I was young when my grandfather died, and my grandmother never spoke of that time. My father never did either."

Mzi shrugged. "They didn't care. Why should they? My mother found someone else, and they brought me up. After a fashion. They never got a thebe from my father."

Kubu felt the unfairness of that but put it aside and tried to change the subject. "Do I have any cousins?"

Mzi shrugged. "Probably." That seemed the end of that discussion.

Kubu sighed and got back to the point. "Can you think of anything that might have led someone to kill my father? Anything from the past, even long ago?"

Mzi seemed to consider it, then shrugged again. "I never knew him that well."

Kubu sighed again but felt obliged to push on, so he told Mzi about the visitor supposedly from Tobela. As Kubu told the story, the old man looked uncomfortable. He looked down at the table and focused on his empty glass. "I need another brandy," he said, shoving the glass toward Kubu. Without argument, Kubu bought him another.

Mzi grabbed it and took a gulp. "There was a man here looking for your father. Said it was a business proposition. I don't know how he found me, but people know me around here." He wouldn't meet Kubu's eyes.

"What did you do?"

"I told him Wilmon lived in Mochudi."

"You set up the meeting, didn't you? You called my father from the pay phone up the road."

Mzi nodded. "The man said there'd be something in it for me if the deal went through. That it would be a big windfall for Wilmon. Fuck it. I thought I was helping him!"

"How much did he pay you?"

Mzi shrugged. "A few pula. A couple of drinks."

"You made two calls to Wilmon to arrange the meeting?"

Mzi nodded.

"Why didn't you tell the police this? It's vitally important!"

"That snooty young girl? She only drank water and was rude because we didn't believe she was a real policeman at first. Why did you send her? Didn't you care enough about your father to come yourself?"

Kubu battled to keep his temper. After everything he'd gone through to try to help catch his father's murderer, this derelict was accusing him of not caring. And out of pique he'd kept information to himself, critical information. Mzi saw the anger on Kubu's face, pushed his chair back a bit, and swallowed the rest of his drink in one gulp. Without a word, Kubu grabbed the empty glass and headed to the bar. "Another brandy and coke," he told the bartender. "A single this time. And a brandy for me too."

"Single or double?"

"Single. Neat with ice."

By the time he got back, he'd calmed down. He took a sip of the brandy. "Who was this man?"

Mzi shook his head. "I hadn't met him before. Someone pointed me out to him."

"Did he have a name?"

"Called himself Rra Tau. Many people call themselves Tau. I don't think it was his real name."

"Would you recognize him again?"

"Sure. It was only two weeks ago." Kubu had a shrewd guess about who Mzi's visitor had been, but he knew it wouldn't get him any closer to the truth. Julius would just say he was following the chief's instructions and didn't want to give his real name in case Mzi tried to get more money. Kubu had to know what it was that Julius had wanted.

"What did he tell you about the deal?"

"Nothing. Just that it would be good for Wilmon. That's why I helped him."

"Think. There must have been something!"

Mzi frowned. "He said something about land for the mine."

That was consistent with what Julius had told them.

"Do you remember exactly what he said?"

Mzi shook his head.

"Well, they did meet. My father became very angry and shouted at the man. He said, 'It's for my son. It will stay in the family.' Does that mean anything to you?"

For many seconds, Mzi sipped at his drink. At last he asked, "Didn't you check his will?"

This time Kubu's frustration got the better of him, and he slammed his glass down on the table. "We can't find the damn will! My mother's home was broken into, and we think it was stolen from the house."

Again Mzi thought for what seemed a long time. "There was something. I remember my mother was very angry. Wilmon got something from our grandfather. Something to do with land. She felt it should've been shared, but of course it went to Wilmon. I didn't take much notice of what she said, though. When she was angry and she'd had a few drinks, it was best to keep out of her way."

Suddenly, Kubu felt sorry for this old man. Bitterness had spoiled his life. Bitterness and jealousy of a brother who'd started with little more than he had but who'd made something of his life.

Wilmon must have inherited something tangible, Kubu mused. It couldn't just have been a little money spent long ago on his house or Amantle's *lobola,* because in that case there would be nothing left now to "stay in the family." Mzi's mother had mentioned land. But not land that could be lived on, or at least his father never had. Could it be something to do with mineral rights? That would tie in with the mine, but all mineral rights belonged to the government of Botswana. And whatever it was, why had Wilmon never mentioned it to his wife or his son? His uncle's answers had just led to more questions.

"Mzi, thank you. You've helped me a lot. Tomorrow the police-woman will come to see you and take your statement."

"I've helped you. Why should I help her?"

"Just do it. Have a glass of water with her." Kubu offered his right hand, touching it with his left in a gesture of respect to an older person. After a moment Mzi shook Kubu's hand, and then, without a word, he turned and made his way unsteadily back to his friends.

Kubu was relieved to see that his car was still where he'd left it, and undamaged. He phoned Samantha, and although she was still cross with him, she promised to find the time the next day to take a statement from Mzi and see if he could identify a picture of Julius.

Then he sat in the car and puzzled about how mining in Sho-shong seemed to be at the center of, or at least connected to, all the cases. It had led to the riot; Newsom worked for a company with mineral interests nearby; Kunene had been a civil servant in the Department of Mines. And his father. His father would have had nothing to do with the mine; he'd used to say that what you take out of the ground ought to be something you can eat. But was it possible that somehow he'd had land rights important to the mine? Rights that would "stay in the family" and be "for his son"? Kubu shook his head. Wilmon had been a humble man—poor in money but rich in everything that mattered. Julius's story made more sense. It had all been confusion, a mistake. Except for one thing. A week after the meeting, his father was lying in a Mochudi street, murdered.

Then he phoned Joy to let her know that he was on his way and, with mixed emotions, turned onto the A1 and headed home to Ga-borone.

PART 6

CHAPTER 36

"It is going to be cold in America in February, David. You must take a jersey and your winter coat."

"Yes, Mother," Kubu replied. "I'm sure I'll be fine. Ten million people live in New York, and they survive."

"But I am sure they have good coats. And wear gloves too. Do you have any gloves?"

"The only gloves I have are gardening gloves, Mother. And I'm sure that they wouldn't be acceptable at an Interpol meeting. I'll buy some at the airport."

"And what about a hat? Everyone in the TV shows wears a hat in winter, or one of those ugly knitted things that they pull down over their ears."

"I think they call them stocking hats, Mother. Maybe they're made from old socks."

"And don't forget to take some boots, in case it snows. You could ruin your shoes if you have to walk in the snow. It can be very wet, I am told."

Kubu wondered who had told his mother about snow. And how did she know what people wore in winter in the United States? She didn't have a television. He shook his head. Mothers were amazing—they knew everything.

"Yes, Mother. I agree! I must be prepared for cold weather. I'll pack properly."

"What time do you leave this afternoon?"

"I catch the five o'clock Air Botswana flight to Johannesburg, then a nonstop flight to New York on South African Airways."

"Is South African Airways safe? I have heard that they have been having a lot of crashes since the government fired all the white pilots."

Kubu walked over to his mother and put his arm around her. The unexpected display of affection startled her.

"Mother, South African Airways is as safe as any airline in the world. And they haven't fired any white pilots. They're just training more black pilots, just like here in Botswana. Please don't worry. I'll be fine."

"Are you sure your coat is heavy enough?"

"Yes, Mother. I'm sure. Please would you go and make me a cup of tea."

"You must have a big meal, too. You have been eating too little recently, and my friends say that the food on airplanes is not good, and there is very little of it. I will make you something filling."

"Please, Mother. I'll be fine. Just a cup of tea, please."

AS AMANTLE SHUFFLED into the kitchen, Kubu walked onto the veranda and gazed at the garden of succulents. He didn't want to go to the Interpol meeting and was angry at Mabaku for sending him. He gritted his teeth. I'm no use ten thousand kilometers away, in freezing weather, talking about something I know nothing about.

He walked down the steps onto the gravel path that wound

through the garden. He kicked at the stones, disturbing a bird from a pawpaw skin that Joy must have put out. In Kubu's opinion, because of its strange assortment of colors, the bird could have been designed by a committee of detectives from the CID—each having a say but none having a plan. But what sort of bird it was, he had no idea, only that its prolonged trill had awakened him that morning far earlier than he'd planned.

As he wandered around the garden, he thought about all the cases. There appeared to be little or no progress with the investigation into his father's murder. And he could not come up with any reason at all why someone would steal his father's will. What was in it that had attracted such violence? Neither he nor his mother could imagine any scenario that made sense.

And he was no further along with the murder of Kunene—he was sure it was a murder. And what about Newsom? He was involved with Kunene in some way and perhaps attacked by the same person. And maybe his father was also killed by the same man. He could make no sense of it.

Kubu stopped. Perhaps there was a silver lining to the unwanted American trip. He could try to contact Newsom. Maybe the person who answered the phone would pass on a message if Kubu was actually in the country. A long shot, perhaps, but worth a try.

This new possibility lifted Kubu's spirits a little, and he headed inside for his cup of tea. He might even manage a biscuit, if his mother offered him one.

AFTER THE LAID-BACK security at the Sir Seretse Khama Airport in Gaborone, Kubu was not prepared for the rigorous screening in Johannesburg. He was taken aback when the alarm sounded as he walked through the metal detector.

"Please go back and take your belt off, sir. Then step through again."

"But it didn't go off in Gaborone!" Kubu exclaimed.

The security agent shrugged. "Please go back, sir, and take off your belt."

Kubu complied, holding his pants to prevent them slipping down, but the alarm went off again.

Kubu began to feel both embarrassed and irritated.

"Are you sure you don't have cash or a cell phone or something else made of metal in your pockets, sir?"

It took Kubu some time to check his pockets as he could only use one hand at a time.

"I'm sure there's nothing. I put my phone and my camera in the tray. And my cash."

"Walk through again."

Again Kubu went through the detector. Again, the alarm sounded. Kubu heard a groan from the line of people behind him.

The security guard pointed to a spot away from the X-ray machine. "Please stand over there. Face me and put both hands out to the side."

Now Kubu was acutely embarrassed. "Please can I put my belt back on?"

"When I've patted you down."

Kubu spread his legs as wide as possible to prevent his pants from slipping all the way to the floor. The security agent ran his hands over Kubu's arms and chest but couldn't reach his back, so he had to go behind Kubu to check. Kubu nearly jumped when two hands gripped the top of his thigh, slid down toward his knee, and finished at his ankle. He grimaced as the same procedure was repeated on the other leg.

"Must be your shoes," the agent snapped. "Take them off and put them on a tray."

"I'm sorry," Kubu said to the woman still waiting to go through the metal detector. "I haven't been through security here before. It's not like this in Botswana."

He put his shoes on a tray and pushed it through the X-ray machine. Then he stepped through the metal detector once again, holding his breath. This time the alarm did not go off.

"It's your shoes. Where are you going?"

"To New York."

"You'll have to take them off before you go through security there. They're much tougher than we are."

"Thank you, sir," Kubu said as he threaded his belt through the loops. He couldn't imagine anything more intrusive than what he'd just been through. "Thank you for the advice."

By the time Kubu had put himself together, gathered his belongings, and negotiated customs and immigration, he was completely frazzled. He ignored the glitzy duty-free shops and went in search of a bar. There was still over an hour before boarding, and after his ordeal at security, he needed a glass or two of wine.

CHAPTER 37

Ian McGregor adjusted his protective clothing and left his small office adjoining the morgue at the Princess Marina Hospital. He was deeply depressed, not because of the autopsies ahead—that was his job and he was used to it—but because his faith in the people of the adopted country he loved had been shaken to the core. The Batswana talked problems through, reached consensus, worked together. *Ubuntu*. How then the horrific blowup that led to the seven corpses chilling in the drawers next door? He wished he could chat to Kubu, who was a friend as well as a colleague. But he assumed Kubu was in Shoshong.

The bodies had been brought from Mahalapye by two ambulances overnight, so this was his first look. He knew Director Mabaku would want a preliminary report as soon as possible, so he decided to do a quick external examination of the bodies before he started on the autopsies. The two policemen and two old men—two of the elders at the meeting he supposed—had dreadful injuries. They had been battered with blunt objects, probably knobkieries. He would do complete autopsies over the next couple of days to see exactly what had led to their deaths, but he expected no surprises.

He took out the body of a young man who was not a policeman. One of the rioters, he supposed. There was no surprise here either. A bullet wound in the chest. Fortunately this was the only death from police fire, but he'd been told several people were in hospital also with bullet wounds. He sighed as he closed the drawer—the man had died so young.

There were two left: Chief Koma and another elder. He left the chief until last; he might as well start the autopsies with him. When he looked at the elder, he was intrigued. He had also been beaten, but not as badly as the others, and the lividity and lack of bleeding indicated that the wounds may have been postmortem. Ian's professional curiosity was peaked. Here was an issue worth investigating. Probably the old man had died of fright, as a layman might say. Ian would find the physiological cause of that.

Then he checked Chief Koma. He, too, had been battered, but there was a curious patch of blood on the back of his shirt. Suspecting a stab wound, Ian cut away the shirt to expose the flesh. Then he realized at once what the wound was.

MABAKU FELT THEY were making progress. Leads were coming together; people were starting to talk. He was hopeful that by the end of the week, they could tell the president that the investigation was essentially complete and the perpetrators of the violence brought to book. His positive mood was interrupted by his cell phone. It took him a moment to fish it out of his pocket, and he answered without checking the caller.

"Mabaku."

"Director, it's Ian McGregor here. I've taken a look at all the bodies. Very preliminary at this stage, but there's something you should know at once."

"Go on." Mabaku didn't like the sound of this.

"From a superficial examination, I would say that the two policemen and two of the elders died from repeated blows from a blunt weapon, possibly a knobkierie or the like. No surprises there. The other elder seems to have been battered *after* he died. I'm guessing he had a heart attack or a massive stroke. I'll be able to confirm that later. But Chief Koma . . ." He paused. "Chief Koma was shot. Shot in the back. The bullet lodged in the spine. That would have killed him. He was also battered, but maybe after he was shot. I can't be sure at this point, though."

For a moment Mabaku was speechless. Suddenly, the whole scenario had changed.

"Director? Are you there?"

"Yes, yes. Was it a stray bullet from a police weapon?" Mabaku realized this would be a public-relations nightmare, but at least that wouldn't be his problem.

"That's what I thought at first, but it's not right. I extracted the bullet. It's not police issue. The weight is more appropriate for something like a .22."

Mabaku sighed. Now it certainly was his problem. He asked Ian for more information, but the pathologist didn't have anything else to give him.

"I'll do a full autopsy on the chief now and try to determine whether the other wounds were postmortem. But I'll need some time, Director."

Mabaku sighed and signed off with, "Thank you, Ian. You've really made my day."

CHAPTER 38

The flight was every bit as uncomfortable as Kubu had expected, even though a flight attendant had offered the passenger next to him an alternative seat—an offer that was hastily accepted. After pecking at his tasteless dinner, Kubu had difficulty finding a comfortable position to sleep and anyway was concerned that if he did fall asleep, he would start snoring. So he read every word of the in-flight magazine, perused the emergency procedures, and read *The Star*, which he borrowed from a neighboring passenger.

Even walking up and down the aisle was problematic, though Kubu attempted it every thirty minutes or so to keep a promise he'd made to Joy, who was concerned about deep vein thrombosis. It was almost impossible to progress without brushing against the shoulders of passengers who were trying to sleep or stepping on feet that had strayed from under the seats. Kubu found himself apologizing at every step of the way.

The situation worsened when the plane landed at Dakar, which Kubu had not realized was a scheduled stop. Nobody left the plane, but quite a few boarded, filling the plane completely. The passenger originally seated next to Kubu was forced to return, and Kubu had to lower the armrest between them, which was no mean feat.

After takeoff, Kubu asked a flight attendant whether, in the interests of harmony in his row and the one in front of him, he could use one of the flight-attendant seats until they started the descent into New York. A quick glance at his bulk convinced her that a small violation of the rules was acceptable, and Kubu at last found a modicum of comfort.

WHEN THE CAPTAIN announced that they had commenced their descent into New York, and Kubu had returned to his seat, he started to feel excited. The Big Apple! JFK! Manhattan! The Metropolitan Opera! Central Park! The Empire State Building! Forty-Second Street! The Museum of Modern Art! Carnegie Hall! Broadway! All these places that he'd heard about for years were now going to become real.

He closed his eyes and imagined himself standing in the snow, eating roasted chestnuts and warm pretzels on the pavement—sorry, sidewalk. He smiled. He would go and watch people skating at Radio City Music Hall, wrapped in colorful scarves and holding hands, Strauss waltzes playing over the loudspeakers. For the first time in weeks, he felt a pang of hunger as he saw himself walking into a deli and ordering a Reuben sandwich and a blintz, whatever that was, to be washed down by a root beer float. And he would sit there and read the *New York Times* review of the current opera at the Met, surrounded by visitors from all over the world speaking languages he didn't understand. How sophisticated. And nobody would know he was just a boy from Mochudi.

HIS ENTRANCE INTO the land of the free was not quite what he'd anticipated. He noticed that passengers whose skin color was not white seemed to take much longer to clear immigration. And when he reached the front of the line, he was interrogated as though he were a terrorist—until he produced his police identification. "Why didn't you say so right away," the immigration officer muttered, banging his stamp onto Kubu's passport.

Then Kubu was pulled aside by a customs officer with an inquisitive dog and asked if he had any foodstuff. Kubu shook his head. "No, sir," he said politely.

"Open your suitcase, please."

Kubu complied, and the officer pulled clothes out and piled them onto the table. Eventually, his hand emerged grasping a small, gift-wrapped parcel.

"What's in here?"

"I don't know," Kubu said, beginning to feel a little guilty. "My wife must have put it in my bag."

"Open it."

Before doing so, Kubu read the little tag attached to the parcel. On it was written "I love you" in Joy's handwriting.

"See, Officer. It is from my wife."

"Please open it."

Kubu tore the paper to find a small packet of sliced biltong and another note: "You won't find any biltong in New York."

Now Kubu felt embarrassed.

The customs officer told Kubu that he couldn't bring meat into the country, even if it was cured. He took the packet and threw it into a large barrel. "Next time, remember you can't bring foodstuffs with you. Welcome to America." He walked off, following the sniffing dog, leaving Kubu wondering how he was going to get everything back into the suitcase. Next time, he'd watch Joy packing more carefully.

It was just getting light outside when Kubu emerged from the arrivals hall. He followed the signs for the taxi stand and walked through the sliding doors out into a cold New York winter's day. The few snowflakes didn't bother him, but he was totally unprepared for the cold. His coat was designed to ward off cold Botswana desert nights, where the temperature rarely fell below freezing. But it was nearly useless for the -3° F temperature that he had stepped into, made much worse by the howling wind that pushed cold air right through it. For the first time in his life, Kubu understood the meaning of the windchill factor. He gasped, thinking his lungs were going to freeze, and staggered back inside the terminal.

He stood recovering for a few moments, then decided he needed to find a place that sold hats and gloves. I couldn't care what I look like, he thought. I'm going to find a stocking hat—and a big one at that. And if all they have is garden gloves, that's what I'll wear.

"HOW CAN PEOPLE live like this?" Kubu asked the Somali cabdriver, as he unsuccessfully contorted his neck to see the top of the buildings. "Everyone living on top of each other."

"People don't see other people. Just concentrate on where they're going."

"And the traffic! We've moved two blocks in fifteen minutes. How long till we get to the hotel?"

"Nearly there. Only a few more blocks."

Kubu leaned back and closed his eyes. A power nap when I get to the hotel will be in order, he thought. But there was too much to see to keep his eyes shut, so he spent the rest of the time gazing in awe at the masses of people, the thousands of shops, the lights, and the slow-moving traffic, which was occasionally punctuated by cyclists weaving their way between the cars. And the noise! Everyone seemed to be hooting at everyone else. The cabbie behind nearly went apoplectic when Kubu's driver looked down for a few moments and failed to close the ten-foot gap ahead of him. As though it made any difference!

Eventually, they made it to the hotel on Thirty-Seventh Street. "Broadway is two blocks in that direction," the cabbie said, probably trying to be helpful to a fellow African. "If you go in the other direction, you end up at the Hudson."

"Thank you," Kubu said, paying him.

"You're welcome. Have a nice day."

The check-in was efficient, and Kubu soon found himself unlocking the door to his room on the twenty-seventh floor. He gazed around. I've paid over two thousand pula for this? he thought. The bed nearly takes up the whole room, and it's only a queen.

He put down his suitcase and squeezed past the bed to the bathroom. He stopped, trying to figure out how he could get in and shut the door. It seemed impossible. After a few seconds, he decided that since he was the only person in the room, it didn't matter if the bathroom door was closed. I understand now, he thought, how there can be so many people in New York. They're packed in like sardines.

Having a shower also posed logistical problems, and Kubu was worried by the amount of water that found its way outside the tiny stall. He hoped that it wasn't leaking into the room below. But what can I do? he wondered. The shower door opens inward, and once I'm in the shower, I can't close it.

After he had dried himself—in itself a difficult undertaking because there was no room to spread his arms—he decided to have a nap, even though it was only eleven in the morning. He reset his watch to local time, set the alarm for twelve thirty, slid between the sheets, and within minutes, the room was filled with the sound of his snores.

CHAPTER 39

It was nearly three o'clock when Kubu woke up. He'd slept far longer than he'd planned and was now feeling very groggy. What happened to the alarm? he wondered. He had to rub his eyes several times before he could focus on the numbers on his watch. The alarm *was* set for twelve thirty. Had he slept through it? He'd never done that before. He looked closer. It was set for twelve thirty a.m., not p.m. Damn it! In his fumbling, he must have switched the display from a twenty-four-hour clock to the more conventional twelve-hour one.

He squeezed into the bathroom and splashed water onto his face. Then he found the number Newsom had left on his Botswana phone and dialed it.

"Good afternoon. Newsom Consulting." This was a live version of the voice that invited people to leave a message, Kubu thought.

"Good afternoon. This is Assistant Superintendent David Bengu of the Botswana police. Please, may I speak to Mr. Newsom."

"I'm afraid he's not available. May I take a message?"

Kubu left the name and phone number of his hotel, as well as his Botswana cell number. "Please ask Mr. Newsom to contact me as soon as possible. It's quite urgent. It would be better in the evening, because I'm attending an Interpol conference from tomorrow."

"Certainly, sir. I'll leave him a message right away."

"Thank you."

"You're welcome. Have a nice day."

Kubu dressed and prepared to find a clothing store he could afford that had a coat for a real winter. The receptionist gave two recommendations, Marshall's on Sixth between Eighteenth and Nineteenth, and Big and Tall on Sixth between Fifty-Second and Fifty-Third. As he prepared to brave the cold in search of a cab, she shouted out, "I think Macy's also has a big and tall. West Thirty-Fourth between Sixth and Seventh." Kubu waved a thank-you, pulled on his newly acquired stocking hat and gloves, and pushed through the rotating door. Again, the cold nearly took his breath away.

He stood on the sidewalk and raised his hand when a cab approached. It went straight past. A few moments later, the same thing happened. And again. And again. There was a man nearby who had left the hotel a few minutes after Kubu and was also trying to hail a cab, so Kubu turned to him.

"Why don't those taxis stop?"

"They already have a passenger or are going to pick one up. Look at the cab number on the roof. If it's got a light, it's free. If not, you're out of luck."

Kubu thanked the man and continued waving his arm. Eventually, a cab veered from the other side of the road and stopped. Kubu moved forward, thankful that he would be protected from the cold for a few minutes. Just as he was about to open the door, the other man nipped in front of him, opened the door, and jumped in. "Have a nice day," he said as he closed the door. And the cab roared off.

For a moment Kubu stood in astonishment, then he retreated to the sidewalk. I'll try for another couple of minutes, Kubu thought, then I'll go inside and warm up. As luck would have it, two cabs stopped to disgorge a family—mother and three kids in one; father and two kids in the other. All the kids must have been under the age of ten, Kubu thought. How do the parents cope?

Kubu stepped forward and guarded the door of the first cab until all had alighted. Then he climbed in, enjoying a blast of hot air. "Big and Tall on Sixth Avenue between Fifty-Second and Fifty-Third," he said, feeling quite sophisticated. He leaned back and gazed in awe at the crush of people on the sidewalk and what appeared to be a perpetual road jam on the street. How do people do it? he wondered. No space to swing a cat.

AN HOUR AND a half later, Kubu returned to the hotel sporting an enormous winter coat that felt like something an explorer would wear to the North Pole and a scarf wound many times around his neck, mouth, and nose. He was exhausted. He was carrying two shopping bags from Big and Tall. One contained his thin coat; the other, two pairs of slacks that had fitted off the shelf, something that never happened in Gaborone, and two dressy casual shirts in strong colors. Everything was relatively cheap and well made, and they had given him a special 10 percent discount because it was his first time in New York City. Probably added 20 percent before giving me the discount, he decided. But nevertheless, the shopping was amazing—the service was good, and nobody questioned his credit card from Botswana.

"Are there any messages for me?" Kubu asked the receptionist as he headed for the elevator.

"You'll have to check your phone, sir. The voice mail is all automated."

Kubu nodded his thanks.

As he went up in the elevator, he wondered whether Mabaku would authorize the expenditure for a real winter coat. He'd tell the director that he would have frozen to death had he not bought one. Then he grimaced as he thought what Mabaku's response would be.

When he reached his room, he was excited to see the message light flashing. It took him a few moments to work out how to retrieve the message and, when he did, was disappointed to hear Mabaku's voice. "I thought you would want to know that the chief in Shoshong was killed by a shot in the back with a small-caliber bullet. Definitely not from the police. Make sure you don't screw up my speech."

Kubu was surprised at the message. It meant that someone at the riot wanted the chief dead, no matter what. It wasn't just a consequence of unruly behavior. He wondered what the implications were.

He tried to find a second message but was disappointed that there were no more. He wondered if Newsom had received his message. So he made himself a cup of tea and phoned the hotel reception for a recommendation for a good steakhouse, not too far away and not too expensive.

"Del Frisco's," came the immediate reply. "Sixth Avenue at Forty-Ninth. All cabbies know it."

"Thank you. Will I need to make a reservation?"

"I'll do that. How many people for what time?"

I'm sure people in a city like New York eat late, Kubu thought. "How about eight o'clock, just for myself."

"I'll take care of that, sir. I'll call back if there's any problem."

"Thank you."

"You're welcome."

To kill the time before dinner, Kubu turned on the TV. For the next hour he flicked through the channels, amazed at how difficult it was to find anything worth watching, despite there being a seemingly infinite number of stations. When he did find something that caught his interest, the program was interrupted every few minutes by advertisements. No wonder America is a consumer

nation, he thought. I'm sure people buy stuff in the hopes that the
ads will go away!

Eventually, he turned the TV off and lay down for another
brief power nap—being careful to make sure his alarm was properly set.

THIS TIME, KUBU had little difficulty hailing a cab, and he arrived
at the restaurant fifteen minutes early. Fortunately, they were able
to seat him immediately on the third floor. He gazed around at the
wooded opulence. Three tiers of dining, chandeliers, thousands of
bottles of wine, and immense windows with a view onto the city's
skyscrapers. Amazing, he thought. Probably more people lived
in one of those buildings than lived in the whole of Gaborone.

He perused the immense drinks list, wincing at the prices. He'd
planned to limit himself to two glasses of wine, but the sight of ex-
otic cocktails made him change his mind. One cocktail and one
glass of wine, he thought.

He ordered a pomegranate martini and a glass of a California
Cabernet Sauvignon that he'd never heard of to enjoy with his
steak. About 140 pula for the martini and 100 pula for a glass of
wine! He could get a bottle of a decent South African for that price.
Some of these bottles were over $1,000! He couldn't imagine that
they were really worth it. He did a quick calculation: $1,000 was
equal to about 10,000 pula. For that, he could buy between sixty
and eighty good South African reds. He shook his head. Why
would anyone spend that sort of money for only one bottle, when
they could have so many?

Then he turned to the menu. His mouth watered at the pictures and descriptions, even though he didn't understand some of
it. Tchoupitoulas sauce? Transmontanous caviar? Maque choux
corn? Chateau potatoes? Fortunately, the steak dishes needed no
elaboration, and he understood all of them except for the wagyu
longbone, which anyway was out of his price range at $95, even
though it was for thirty-two ounces. He scratched his head.

What was thirty-two ounces in real measurements? I think it's about a kilogram, he thought. That's a lot!

Eventually, he made up his mind. "I've never had oysters before," he told the waiter. "So I'd like to have them for a starter. On the half shell. Then I'll have the porterhouse—medium rare, please."

"Anything on the side, sir?"

"I'm not sure I know what that means?"

"You know, like vegetables."

"The steak doesn't come with vegetables?" Kubu asked.

"No, sir. They're extra."

Kubu glanced quickly at the menu again and ordered asparagus and sautéed mushrooms. As the waiter walked away, Kubu added up what this was going to cost. A martini and a glass of wine—$30. Oysters—$20. Porterhouse—$60. Veggies—$29. And probably $15 for dessert and coffee. Total about $155 before the tip. That was 20 percent, if the hotel receptionist was to be believed— another $30. He shook his head. This was going to cost him nearly 2,000 pula. For one meal!

The glimmer of a smile crossed his face. It wasn't going to cost *him* 2,000 pula. It was going to cost Director Mabaku 2,000 pula. "Serves him right for sending me away when I should be trying to find my father's murderer," he said out loud.

That thought immediately soured the evening. He'd put Wilmon's death out of his mind from the moment he'd boarded the South African Airways flight in Johannesburg. On arriving in New York, he'd been so overwhelmed by the whole environment—its size, its difference, its reputation—that he hadn't thought about it then either. But now, it insinuated itself once again into his head, and he knew it would be difficult to dislodge. Suddenly, the food didn't sound as appetizing as it had a few minutes earlier, and he didn't feel as hungry.

Well, it's too late to do anything about the order, he thought, so I'll have to do the best I can. That's too bad. I was looking forward to eating the director's budget.

• • •

WHEN KUBU LEFT the restaurant, it was snowing. He decided to walk at least part of the way back to his hotel so he could tell Tumi and Nono that he had walked in snow. Because he knew the kids wouldn't believe him, he needed a picture of the snowflakes coming down around him, so he gave a passerby his phone to take a photo. But he didn't last long in the cold and only managed one block before he started to shiver. He hailed a cab, which to his amazement stopped immediately, and ten minutes later, he pushed his way through the revolving doors of his hotel.

"Enjoy your meal?" the receptionist asked.

"Thank you. It was a very good recommendation. The food was delicious."

"Couldn't finish it, though?"

Kubu looked chagrined. "No. I ordered the porterhouse but only managed about half. It's a good thing they have doggie bags. Would you like to have it? I won't have a chance to eat it."

The receptionist thanked him but declined.

"Thank you. Good night," Kubu said as he stepped into the elevator. He pressed the button and watched the doors close.

A few minutes later, he opened the door to his minute bedroom and immediately checked the phone. The message light was not flashing.

Damn, Kubu thought. I wonder if I'll ever hear from Newsom.

He undressed, put on his pajamas, and climbed into bed. He set his alarm for seven and phoned reception for a backup wake-up call. He had to be at the Grand Hyatt at nine for the conference opening session and didn't want to be late.

I hope I can get to sleep, he thought. I've so many things on my mind.

But he needn't have worried. He was asleep in seconds, once again filling the room with his snores.

CHAPTER 40

Mabaku stared across the table at Julius Koma. Samantha was sitting to one side, taking notes.

Julius broke the silence. "I'm pleased to hear nine people have been arrested for the deaths of my father and the elders at the *kgotla*."

"And for the murder of the police constables," Mabaku added.

Julius shrugged that off. "Do you think that's everyone involved?"

"Everyone? Certainly not. There were more than nine rioters. But these have been identified by witnesses as being in the front wave."

Julius nodded. "Yes, well, as long as you have the leaders, we can move on. I want to get the chief issue sorted out quickly. The commissioner has been great. Having that constable with me at the meetings with the elders was very helpful. Of course, I said it was for our protection after the riots, but it got the message across. We need to get my appointment settled and do the deal with the mine so the men will have jobs. Then everything will get back to normal."

Mabaku digested that. "It's not quite that simple," he said at last. "Some issues have come up during our investigation that don't fit." He paused. "Two of the suspects have claimed that they received money to stir up trouble at the *kgotla* if the chief ruled against the mine. Do you know anything about that?"

"Did they say I gave them money? It's a fucking lie! I told people to make their voices heard, not to attack the elders!" Julius thumped his fist on Mabaku's table.

Mabaku shook his head. "They didn't say it was you. They said it was a man they didn't recognize, who said he worked for the Konshua Mine. Do you think the mine was behind it?"

"No, I don't. The mine has always been straight with us. The two men are murderers, Director. They're trying to shift the blame. What they say is worth nothing!"

Mabaku opened a folder and flipped through some pictures as he went on talking. "At least five people beat Mabula Tongwe, the first elder attacked. We've arrested three of the men, and we're still trying to identify the others. We know who used a knobkierie to kill Amos Moloi, the second elder, and we'll charge him with murder. Two of the others in custody will testify to that in exchange for reduced sentences. It seems the third elder there, Potter Masole, died of a heart attack, so probably we won't take that any further." He looked up at Julius and waited.

"What about my father?" Joshua asked when it was evident Mabaku wasn't going to continue.

In response, the director shoved a photo enlargement across the table. It was from a bystander's cell phone. Mabaku marveled that people would snap pictures in the middle of a riot with killings taking place, but that's what they'd done. And it had helped the police a great deal.

Julius picked up the enlargement and frowned. "I've looked at dozens of these pictures already, Director Mabaku. They're all taken from behind so they show the rioters' backs. What use is that?"

"We know what clothes they were wearing, and that's evidence supporting—or, in a few cases, contradicting—what witnesses have told us. And once we told the suspects we had pictures . . ." He shrugged.

"Yes, very clever. So why did you ask me to come here? I've told you everything I can already, and I'm very busy."

"You asked me about the murder of your father." Mabaku tapped a folder on his desk. "I have here a report from our pathologist on the cause of his death. He was beaten on the head, shoulders, and arms, resulting in trauma that would probably have been fatal." He paused for effect. "But he was also shot, and the bullet is probably what killed him."

Julius leaned forward. "Shot? That's impossible." After a moment he added, "It must've been a stray bullet from the police guns. Shooting into the crowd was what started the riot in the first place! There must be an investigation into that."

"The bullet wasn't from a police weapon," Mabaku said. "It was the wrong caliber."

Julius grabbed the picture again and studied it for a few seconds, looking upset. "How do you explain it then?"

"I was hoping you'd be able to help with that."

"Me? What would I know about it?"

Mabaku shuffled his documents. "This is your statement, Rra Koma. You say that you grabbed your father, jumped off the stage, and tried to escape. Is that right?" Julius nodded. "Were you holding on to your father, or were you behind him?"

Julius hesitated. "I was a bit behind him, I think. It all happened so fast."

"But you said you grabbed him."

"Perhaps it was more like a shove. I wanted him to run. I thought I might be able to reason with the mob."

"Did you try to do that?"

"I shouted, but no one listened. It was like a landslide. So I ran too."

"Please take another look at the picture." Mabaku leaned across the table and used his pen to point out the participants. "This is your father. He seems to have fallen. You are right behind him, here on the left in a sports jacket with your back to us. The mob is just about on you. This man is actually within striking distance of your father." He pointed to a man wearing jeans and a red T-shirt, who seemed to be reaching out for the chief.

Julius studied the picture and moistened his lips.

"We've questioned the five of our nine suspects who are in that picture. Two think they heard shots, but no one saw anything."

"Probably one of them did it."

Mabaku shook his head. "They led a bloodthirsty mob, but it wasn't premeditated, I think. Nevertheless, we're testing them for gunshot residue. Did you see anything, a flash, someone digging in his pocket, anything that struck you?"

Julius shook his head.

"Did you see your father fall?"

"Yes, I thought he'd tripped. I tried to get him up, but then they were on us. I couldn't save him." Julius buried his face in his hands. "Afterward, when I lifted him up, he was covered in blood."

Mabaku gave him a moment and then asked, "Did you hear a shot?"

Julius hesitated. "I think there was a shot. I thought it was the police."

"You thought the police were shooting at the mob?"

Julius threw up his hands. "Well, they did, didn't they? If it wasn't for that, the men would've had their demonstration on the stage, maybe pushed the elders around a bit to get the message across, and settled down. But your people overreacted and started shooting! Now we have dozens of people in hospital. And Petrus

Romade is dead. Who's going to pay compensation to his family? The whole thing was a disaster, Director Mabaku, and your men are to blame."

Mabaku swallowed an angry response. There was some justification for Julius's accusation, and the local police hadn't managed the situation well. So he contented himself with telling Julius, "We'll want you to take a gun residue test too."

Julius jumped up. "Are you suggesting—" he began, but Mabaku interrupted. "I'm not suggesting anything, Rra Koma. I'm doing my job. Sit down." He opened his notebook and started recording the relevant points of the interview. Samantha took her cue.

"Rra," she began once Julius had settled down, "I'd like to go back to the issue of Wilmon Bengu, the man you visited in Mochudi."

Julius brushed her aside. "We're finished with that issue." He turned back to Mabaku. "Director, it was wrong that Detective Bengu questioned me about what I was doing in Mochudi. It was *his* father who was murdered. He was very aggressive, and I'm going to talk to the commissioner about it." Mabaku didn't look up from his notes.

"Rra Koma," Samantha said icily. "*I* am conducting the interview now, so pay attention to what I say."

Julius continued to ignore Samantha. "Director Mabaku, I insist on talking to you, not to this junior."

Mabaku lifted his head. "Rra Koma, you may be an important man in Shoshong, but in here you're like everyone else. If you don't treat Detective Khama with respect and answer her questions fully, I will arrest you for obstructing a police inquiry. Understood?"

Samantha wanted to jump up and give Mabaku a high five but instead sat straight-faced until Julius reluctantly turned back to her.

"Rra Koma, how did you set up the meeting in Mochudi?" she asked.

"I told you. By phone."

"How did you get Rra Wilmon Bengu's number?"

"From his half brother in Mahalapye."

"Where did you call him from?"

"I didn't. This Mzi Bengu set up the meeting for me."

Samantha frowned. "Before, you told us you phoned from the *kgotla* here in Shoshong."

"I made a mistake."

"You lied about it?"

"I didn't want to bring Mzi Bengu into the story!" Julius said angrily. "Detective Bengu was upset already!"

Samantha frowned again. It was reasonable and exactly why Mabaku didn't want Kubu involved, but she wasn't convinced. "Did you speak to Rra Bengu on the phone yourself?"

"No!" He turned to Mabaku. "Look, Director, where's all this going? I thought we were talking about my father's murder!"

Mabaku looked up. "Exactly what did your father ask you to speak to Wilmon Bengu about?"

"I've explained that. Bengu is a name that's known here from the past. My father thought the man might have some status here. He thought he should be consulted. So that's what I did. The fact that he died shortly afterward has nothing to do with me."

"What do you think he meant about something staying in the family for his son?"

Julius shook his head. "I've no idea. The old man wasn't a full box of matches. The whole business was a big mistake, another example of my father worrying about the past instead of looking to the future. It was a complete waste of time!"

"And where were you on the Saturday night when Rra Bengu was murdered?"

Julius spluttered as though he were going to object but then calmed down and replied, "I was at home. It'd been a busy week. I watched some TV."

"Alone?"

Julius nodded.

"What was on the TV?" Samantha demanded.

"Do you know what *you* watched on TV two weeks ago?" Julius sneered.

Mabaku took over again. "Where were you on the next night? The Sunday night."

"I had a few drinks with some friends at a bar and then went home to bed."

"What time did you leave the bar?"

"I don't remember exactly. Maybe around ten. I had work the next day."

Mabaku asked him to give Samantha the names of the friends from the bar, and he waited while Julius did so. Then he closed the folder in front of him. "Rra Koma, someone stabbed Wilmon Bengu, someone shot your father, and someone was stirring up trouble before the *kgotla*. I'd like you to think hard about all these things. These cases aren't going to be closed until I have all the facts and all the people responsible. Is that clear?" He waited until Julius nodded, and then added, "A forensics officer is ready next door to do the residue test."

Julius was dismissed, but he had questions of his own. When could the funeral take place? It was urgent; it wouldn't be appropriate to appoint a new chief before that. When would the suspects be charged? What about an inquiry into the police use of excessive force? His parting shot was that he intended to speak to the commissioner about the rude treatment he'd received.

After Julius had left, Mabaku looked at Samantha for several seconds. "What do you think?"

Samantha didn't hesitate. "He seemed surprised about the chief being shot, but that could've been acting; he's had plenty of time to prepare his story. And I'm sure he knows more about the Rra Bengu issue than he's telling us."

The director nodded. "The chief was shot at close range with a

.22. Julius Koma was right next to the chief and was wearing a jacket that could've concealed the weapon. And he's the only person with an obvious motive. He stands to become the new chief and probably do pretty well out of the mine deal."

"He certainly doesn't seem really upset about his father's death," Samantha said, thinking of Kubu. She shook her head. "Much as I dislike him, I don't think he did it." She glanced at Mabaku to see his reaction to being contradicted, but he just nodded and waited for her to go on. "Why take the risk? Julius had just seen the mob kill two of the elders, and the chief was their main target. He was too old to get away. All Julius had to do was stand aside and let it happen. Which is pretty much what he did."

"Wouldn't the same argument apply to any one of the men in the mob?"

Samantha thought about it. "A .22 pistol is small. You could conceal one in a jacket pocket. Some of the men had knobkieries. Why not some guy who fancies himself with a handgun and uses it in the heat of the moment?"

Mabaku said nothing for a few seconds. "It's possible. We should question the suspects again, see if anyone would like to get out of the shit he's in by coming clean on a shooter. The man in the red T-shirt is in custody, and he would've had a pretty clear view, as well as opportunity himself. Unfortunately we'll get nothing from the residue test; it's way too late for it. But it stirred them all up. Julius too." He allowed himself a slight smile and then thought for a moment. "There's another possibility. Maybe someone came to the *kgotla* specifically to kill the chief, and if he was being paid to do that, perhaps he wasn't going to let a bunch of hotheads cut him out of his fee."

Samantha nodded. "In that case Julius could be behind it after all. He stirred people up, got someone to pay some money to a few *skelms* to cause trouble, and then took out insurance with a hit man."

"Yes," said Mabaku thoughtfully, "but there's another big winner with having the old chief out of the way and Julius in charge."

"The Konshua Mine."

Mabaku nodded slowly, frowning. He was thinking that this was the sort of mess Kubu was good at sorting out. And the thought irritated him.

CHAPTER 41

At the best of times, conferences were not on Kubu's list of favorite places to be, and in this case, he'd been forced to attend against his will. He nearly dozed off during a discussion of counter-counterfeiting techniques developed in Kazakhstan, and he *had* fallen asleep during an interminable talk on international art theft. It was only when his neck muscles lost their strength and his head fell forward that he woke up. He looked around guiltily, wondering whether he'd snored, and surreptitiously wiped saliva that must have drooled out of his mouth off the lapel of his jacket.

He shook his head, trying vainly to get rid of the heavy weights that appeared to be attached to his eyelids. What was the man saying? he wondered. Something about robberies in Monte Carlo? He adjusted his headphones and, to pass the time, tried to calculate how many translators were necessary for the thirty languages spoken at the conference.

There has to be a formula, he thought. So he tried first with three countries and then four, then five, hoping to find a pattern. But he couldn't. With three countries, you needed three translators; with four, you needed six, and with five, you needed nine. Or was it ten? Although he was intrigued by the puzzle, he didn't have the energy or the enthusiasm to do the calculations by hand all the way through thirty.

They must have a lot of translators, he concluded.

At that moment, a hand reached over his shoulder and deposited a note in front of him. "From a gentleman outside," a voice said. Kubu nodded and unfolded the paper.

"Starbucks. Entrance C. Ten minutes—Newsom"

"ASSISTANT SUPERINTENDENT BENGU. What a pleasure to see you again." Newsom stood up gingerly and flashed a smile. He offered his left hand; his right arm was in a sling. "What can I get you? A cappuccino? An espresso? A filter coffee?"

Kubu ignored the outstretched hand and sat down. "I told you not to leave Botswana."

"I know, but when I was stabbed, I needed to get stateside for immediate treatment."

"Bullshit! Your wounds were relatively minor. I checked. The hospital admits patients every weekend with injuries much more severe, and they don't have to go to the States to recover."

"My wife was worried, so—"

"It wouldn't have been too painful to lift a phone and—"

"Assistant Superintendent, that's water under the bridge. Let's talk about the future. I've something interesting to tell you. What'll you have to drink?"

"A cappuccino." Kubu paused as he tried to sort out his conflicting emotions—anger at Newsom's unannounced departure from Botswana, curiosity as to what Newsom was going to say. "Please," he added reluctantly.

A few minutes later, Newsom returned and put a cup down in front of Kubu.

"I apologize for not letting you know I was leaving," Newsom said as he sat down. "I was angry at being mugged. My gut was aching, and all I wanted was to get the hell out of Dodge."

Kubu wasn't sure what that meant but said nothing.

"As soon as you left the hospital, I called the embassy for assistance."

"At two in the morning?"

"Yes. The ambassador wasn't happy to be pulled out of bed, but one of his responsibilities is to help Americans in trouble, any time of the day or night. So he helped me. All I wanted was to get home, so he made that happen. That's all there is to it."

"Except for the fact that in the space of a few days, your friend in the Department of Mines is murdered, and right after you return from a visit to a mining company, you're attacked by someone who wants to kill you. I don't believe in coincidences, Mr. Newsom. And I'm sure you don't either. What's going on? What's this tidbit of interesting information you have to share with me?"

"First, let me tell you how I came about it. A friend of mine works in the foreign exchange department of a Botswana bank. He told me a couple of months ago that someone influential in mining in Botswana received a large wire transfer—over a hundred thousand pula—from the Standard Chartered Bank in Lagos, Nigeria. Of course, this piqued my interest, so I did some follow-up." He took a sip of his coffee. "I contacted a friend of mine here in New York, who did some digging around and found out that about nine months ago the same Nigerian account started receiving monthly deposits of five thousand US dollars from a bank in Shanghai." He paused and looked at Kubu expectantly.

Kubu decided not to get sucked into the game and said nothing.

"The person I'm talking about," Newsom continued, "is Director Mopati of the Department of Mines. And, in case you don't know, the headquarters of the Konshua Mine is in Shanghai."

Kubu wasn't surprised to hear a suggestion of corruption. Civil servants in Botswana, even directors, didn't make very much money and were often easy targets, particularly if the incentive was large.

"You seem to be very well connected, Mr. Newsom," Kubu said, holding Newsom's gaze. He thought he would bring into the open what was on his mind. "I assume that people working for the American government are better paid than their Batswana counterparts."

Newsom laughed. "You think I work for the US government? No, Assistant Superintendent. I'm not with the CIA or FBI or whatever you're thinking. I'm an independent contractor who needs the most accurate and current information in order to best help my clients."

Kubu reached for his cappuccino. How do they do that? he wondered as he admired the intricate fern-leaf pattern in the foam. It's a pity to destroy it.

He took a mouthful and set the cup down.

"Mr. Newsom, your so-called information solves nothing and only raises questions. One: Why didn't you tell me this when we met in Botswana? It could be very relevant to the Kunene case. Two: Even if Mopati received money from Shanghai, it could be a completely legitimate transaction. You haven't shown me there's a connection to the Konshua Mine. You only insinuated it. And three: Where's the evidence? All you've given me are words, and you know very well I can't use anything you've said without hard facts."

"I haven't finished, Assistant Superintendent. As I said, I first wanted to set the stage. I've something else for you—hard evidence that you can take with you."

Newsom pulled an iPod out of his pocket and handed Kubu a set of earbuds. "Put these on and listen to what I've got."

Kubu fiddled with the buds until they were in his ears. How can kids wear these all day long? he wondered. They're so uncomfortable.

When he was settled, Newsom touched the Play icon.

FIVE MINUTES LATER, Kubu realized he had just listened to a conversation that could potentially send two people to jail: Director Mopati of the Department of Mines and an unknown person at the other end of the call, whose voice seemed familiar. Although the details were vague, it was clear Mopati was being paid off to help some company obtain a mining lease.

"Where did you get this?" he demanded.

"It doesn't matter where or how I got it. You know it's Mopati, and I can tell you that the other person is a Mr. Shonhu, assistant to the Konshua Mine manager in Shoshong."

The man who read the statement about the riot, Kubu thought. That's who it is.

Newsom handed Kubu a flash drive. "It's all on here, Assistant Superintendent. Your hard evidence."

"Perhaps," Kubu countered. "But I won't be able to use it unless I can prove it was obtained legally."

"In a court of law, that's probably true," Newsom said. "But there are other ways of using evidence like that."

Is he just pointing the finger at Mopati again, hoping I'll pressure him to resign, or is he suggesting I use it to investigate and prosecute him? Kubu wondered. He leaned back in his chair as it occurred to him how Newsom could have got the recording.

"Since you know so much," Kubu continued, "perhaps you can tell me again what you know of big cash deposits into your friend Kunene's account every now and again."

Newsom took another sip of his coffee.

"I made those deposits."

"*You* did?" Kubu sat up. "You told me Kunene was totally honest. Now you tell me you were bribing him or maybe paying him to spy on his boss."

"Calm down, Assistant Superintendent. I never said anything of the sort. Kunene was worried that Mopati was taking money from the Chinese, so I helped him verify it. Naturally, that was useful information for me too. It was a sort of quid pro quo, so I gave him a little money for helping me. I didn't ask him to direct decisions my way or in the way of the companies I represent."

"You know, of course, Mr. Newsom, that recording another person's conversation without consent is a crime."

"Which is the bigger crime, Assistant Superintendent? Recording a private phone call or the corruption of a senior government official? Botswana has a fine reputation as a well-run country. Do you want that sullied?"

Kubu stared at Newsom. The old trap, he thought, that the end justifies the means.

"Mr. Newsom," Kubu said, changing direction, "all of this would have been very helpful to know when I asked you last time."

"But I obviously couldn't have told you while I was in Botswana. You would've detained me on some charge or other for trying to buy a government official or for illegal wiretapping."

"You're absolutely right," Kubu fumed. "And if I can find a way to detain you here, I'll do that immediately."

Newsom laughed. "Don't waste your time. It's not going to happen."

Kubu leaned back in his chair and stared at Newsom.

"What's in it for you, Mr. Newsom?" he asked after a few moments. "I don't see where you fit in."

"As you know, I consult for various American mining interests. One of them is interested in the area around Shoshong. All we want is fair consideration of our proposal to mine the area. If we get the rights, I get a nice bonus."

His nice bonus, Kubu thought, is probably more than I'll earn in my lifetime.

"Why is the area suddenly so appealing?" Kubu asked. "The Konshua Mine's apparently been there for quite a long time."

"As you no doubt know, Assistant Superintendent, nuclear power is not very popular after the Fukushima disaster. Konshua mines uranium, which, of course, has dropped dramatically in price. Germany has decided to decommission all of its plants, and many other countries will follow suit or are unlikely to build new plants because of public antipathy. To make money at these lower prices, Konshua has to increase its output. Hence its interest in the new land. It already has the processing capacity, so more raw material is very attractive. If it doesn't expand, it will probably have to close."

Newsom drained his coffee and used his teaspoon to scoop up the remaining foam.

"The company I work for," he continued, "wants to break into the mining world in Botswana because it likes the country's management, and it thinks uranium will rebound. It wants to start a mine now, while prices are down, so it can stockpile for when the time is right to sell. It'll be too late to start only when prices begin going up again. It's a big risk, but Texans are not averse to risk, and they've lots of money."

"Why don't they just buy the Konshua Mine?" Kubu asked.

"We approached them, but they don't want to sell."

"At any price?"

"Not at the price we were willing to offer."

"And that was?"

Newsom smiled but didn't respond.

"Okay, Mr. Newsom. Let's get back to you. Who do you think attacked you?"

"I don't know, but I suspect someone working for the Chinese. Mopati and the Konshua Mine must have discovered that Kunene and I were onto their cozy relationship. So they came after both of us. They got Goodman, and I escaped by the skin of my teeth. Are you still surprised that I was in such a hurry to leave Botswana?"

"What are your clients going to say?"

"Most of my work is done anyway for the formal presentations next week."

"Next week? Why next week?"

"Mopati has told the mine and us to make a final presentation next week—which will happen unless you use the information I gave you."

"But what can you do from here?"

"One of my colleagues can make the presentation, and I can join via telephone or Skype to help on the technical details."

"And you think that someone from the mine tried to kill you so there wouldn't be a presentation from the people you represent?"

"That's right. And because we were onto their corrupt relationship with the director of mines."

Kubu decided to change the subject.

"Did you have any contact with Chief Koma?"

Newsom shook his head.

"What about his son, Julius? He seemed to be very involved in the whole business."

"We were playing it by the book, Assistant Superintendent. We were going to talk to the chief only after the lease had been granted."

"I'm sure you're aware of what happened in Shoshong last Saturday?" Kubu said.

Newsom nodded.

"How does that affect your proposal? Surely, it's unclear what the new chief will decide—if there is a new chief by next week. I'm told it's a complicated situation, with three groups providing the chief in rotation."

Newsom shrugged. "Whoever becomes chief will support the mine's expansion. There's too much to lose if they don't."

"You seem very sure of yourself. I'm told that the riot has caused a lot of people to turn against the mine, because they blame it for the trouble."

Newsom shook his head. "I don't think the mine had anything

to do with the riot. That would be very stupid of them. They'd never get the mining lease if someone found out."

"So, who was responsible?"

"Wouldn't you be upset if someone took away your only chance to make a halfway decent living? I think the old chief was responsible by turning down the mine's offer."

"And the killings were a result of mob behavior?"

Newsom nodded. "I'm told things are getting desperate up there."

Kubu finished his cappuccino, wondering where the meeting was headed.

"Mr. Newsom," Kubu said, "you obviously want me to do something with the information you've given me, but I can't work out what that is. I have no proof, no evidence I can use, and all the accusations are coming from a direct competitor of the existing mine."

"It's simple, Assistant Superintendent. I want you to find out who killed my friend, Kunene, and who attacked me. And I want the company I represent to have a fair chance in getting the mining rights in Shoshong."

He stood up. "Enjoy the rest of your conference."

With that, he turned and walked toward the exit, leaving Kubu wondering what Newsom's real agenda was.

CHAPTER 42

Kubu returned to the conference but paid scant attention to the proceedings. His mind was working on what Newsom had told him. The only thing of which he was certain was that Newsom didn't just want a fair chance for his clients to get the mining concession. He would prefer that there was no competition at all.

So why did Newsom contact him? What did he want him to do?

Kubu closed his eyes as the current speaker droned on about something or other. He wasn't paying any attention to what was being said.

After a while, he opened his eyes and pulled a writing tablet from the bag Interpol had presented all delegates. He turned to the first page and wrote a large numeral *1* and circled it. Next to it, he wrote, *Mopati corrupt.*

Then he jotted down what Newsom had told him—the money transfers and the recording of Mopati's conversation with the mine manager's assistant. He stared at what he'd written for a few minutes. The allegations were useless in a legal sense but potentially useful in persuading the police to open an inquiry into Mopati and his dealings with the Konshua Mine. That would suit Newsom's purpose very well.

Then Kubu turned the page and wrote and circled a large *2*. Next to it, he wrote, *Kunene death—murder?* Again, he stared at the page for several minutes.

Then he jotted down the several points that indicated that the death was a murder and not a suicide. Next he wrote, *Suspects.* Below that he wrote, *Mopati, Newsom, and Konshua Mine.* If Kunene had discovered that Mopati was corrupt and Mopati had found out, that would be strong motivation for Mopati to get rid of Kunene. Or perhaps Kunene was blackmailing Mopati. Again a strong motive for Mopati to get rid of him. Similarly he could apply the same reasoning to the mine. Kunene would definitely be an obstacle to their plans.

For a few minutes, he couldn't come up with a plausible motive for Newsom wanting Kunene dead. Then he realized what a motive could be. Maybe Newsom was playing some double game, which seemed likely, because mining consultants don't usually tap cell phones and whistle up support from the US embassy at two in the morning. If Kunene had discovered it, that could be a threat to Newsom.

Kunene certainly threatened someone's plans, Kubu mused. But whose? At the same time, the payments into Kunene's account, apparently from Newsom, suggested that Kunene wasn't squeaky clean either.

He turned the page, wrote a large *3*, circled it, followed by *Chief murdered.* Does this have anything to do with Kunene and Newsom? he wondered. He shook his head. Something is wrong with all of this, he thought. Something doesn't fit. He closed his eyes once again and hoped his subconscious would bring something useful to the surface.

After a few minutes, Kubu was roused from his reverie by a loud round of applause. He glanced up as an elderly, uniformed officer left the stage and a young, blond woman entered. Kubu donned his headphones just in time to hear that the next speaker was the minister of justice in Denmark, the minister to whom the Danish police reported. She was going to speak on the topic of preparing for the inevitable protests about what Denmark was going to do with the radioactive waste and spent fuel rods from the various decommissioned nuclear facilities.

Kubu turned to the person next to him—a delegate from Bosnia. "I didn't know that Denmark had closed its nuclear plants," he whispered.

"Many years ago," came the heavily accented reply. "And Germany is doing same. It closed eight plants after Fukushima and will close rest over next ten years."

Kubu nodded his thanks.

This doesn't sound like an environment for starting or expanding a uranium mine, he thought. But maybe the Texans *were* willing to take a big risk if there was potentially a big payback. And maybe it *did* make sense for the Konshua Mine to make better use of its processing facilities. But he couldn't see why.

He shook his head. Who could I check with? he wondered.

A few minutes' thought yielded only one likely contact. And that was a long shot.

Several years before, Kubu had met a Professor Cretchley from the South Dakota School of Mines and Technology. He was a large Midwest farm boy, who was visiting the various Debswana diamond mines in Botswana. Kubu had met him in the unlikely place of Exclusive Books in Riverwalk Mall. Kubu was trying to find a copy of the *The No. 1 Ladies' Detective Agency*, and Cretchley was trying to find a travel book on Botswana to see how he could spend a week at the end of his visit. They had literally bumped into each other moving down one of the small aisles in the shop and ended up having coffee nearby.

• • •

BY MIDAFTERNOON, KUBU decided that he'd had enough of the conference and headed back to his hotel. As soon as he squeezed into
his room, he picked up the phone and dialed directory assistance.
After struggling to negotiate the automated menu, he eventually
was connected to the South Dakota School of Mines and Technology and asked for Professor Cretchley. Surprisingly, the professor
was in his office.

Kubu reminded Cretchley of their meeting, and they enjoyed
some small talk before Kubu asked him what he thought of the
future of nuclear power and the potential for starting a new uranium mine. Cretchley's answer was direct: "I'd put my money elsewhere," he said. "There's a chance that uranium will rebound, but
there's growing sentiment against the use of nuclear power due to
the tragedy in Fukushima."

"What about gold and diamonds?" Kubu asked.

"Gold is on a downward slope at the moment, but there is a good
chance it will recover over the next few years," Cretchley said. "As
for diamonds, starting a new mine now would be very risky. The
big mines in Botswana have already cut back on production, and
they could ramp up quickly if demand grew."

"Can you think of anything in Botswana that could get both an
American company and a Chinese company so excited that they
might be willing to go to extremes to get hold of it?"

There was a pause as Cretchley thought about the question.
"Well, a really large deposit of almost anything could be worth a
lot of money," he said, "but the only deposit I'd be excited about
would be rare earths. The issue would be grade. High-grade prospects, especially of the so-called heavy rare earths, would be significant. There are a couple of new mines being developed in South
Africa, which used to be one of the world's important producers.
Can you tell me where we're talking about?"

"An existing uranium mine near Shoshong in east central

Botswana wants to expand, and there's a group from Texas, I believe, who want to start a new mine in the same area. The Americans have told me that their interest is uranium. But there seems to be too much excitement for just uranium."

Cretchley was quiet for a few moments. "I seem to recall that a couple of rare-earth prospects are being investigated north of Francistown. That's pretty much right where you're talking about."

Kubu felt a twinge of excitement. "But what are these rare earths? I haven't heard about them."

"Well, you're obviously not in the minerals business! Actually, the name's a bit of a misnomer because most of these elements aren't rare at all. The problem with them is that they aren't often concentrated sufficiently to make mining them economical. And there's a big demand because they're used in all the important industries these days. Batteries for green energy. Phosphors for long-life lights. For computer screens and smartphone screens. You get the picture. This is a big deal."

"So they're really valuable?"

"It's more than that. They're hard to get. Ninety-five percent comes from China these days, and the Chinese watch them like a hawk."

Now Kubu was getting really interested. "The Chinese have most of these minerals?"

"Indeed. And they're not shy about throwing their weight around."

Kubu frowned. "But then they wouldn't be interested in a prospect in Botswana, would they?"

"On the contrary. They want to control the market. In 2011, they imposed export quotas on their rare earths, and the prices rocketed. And they're clamping down hard on illegal exports. It's the sort of thing you get executed for. A lot of businesses were forced to move to China to get access to them. And guess who's partnered in the new South African development."

"The Chinese?"

"Exactly right. So they'd be very interested in a new discovery in Botswana. Especially if it were a rich one."

"And," Kubu mused, "I guess you people would be very interested in a big new source not from China?"

"Certainly would." He paused, then continued, "Rare earths are often found in proximity to uranium, so it's a real possibility. If that's what they've found, I'm not surprised they're doing everything they can to get their hands on them."

"That might also explain why they're talking about uranium, wouldn't it? They wouldn't want anyone to know about it."

"That's right. If your Department of Mines knew, they'd work out a joint-venture type of arrangement like it has with De Beers—where the country really benefited from what was mined—in an open market."

They chatted for a few minutes, and after he'd thanked the professor for his time and insights, Kubu hung up. He was now convinced that the presence of rare earths would be a powerful reason for what had happened—the murder of Kunene and the attack on Newsom, the apparent corruption within the Department of Mines, and the riot at the *kgotla* in Shoshong.

Kubu thought about the ramifications of a rare-earth discovery for a few minutes and became more and more convinced that it could be the motive underlying the various events. He needed to speak to Mabaku as soon as possible.

However, there was one thing that the discovery of rare earths would not explain—the murder of his father.

CHAPTER 43

By the time Kubu had finished talking to Professor Cretchley, it was too late to call Mabaku. He would be asleep. Then Kubu smiled. He'd call really early Botswana time to get a little payback for being sent to New York. So he had a few hours to kill—an opportunity to explore the city, he thought.

So he bundled up and, for the next five hours, became a tourist—the Empire State Building, the observation area of which was probably higher than any point in Botswana; a carriage ride through Central Park, Kubu covered with extra blankets, listening to a sound he'd never heard before—the clip-clop of hooves—and wishing Joy was with him; a walk to Rockefeller Center with its Radio City Music Hall and outdoor skating rink, where hundreds of people floated in circles, scarves flying, and a group of Chinese tourists giggled as they kept falling down. He even bought a huge, salty pretzel from a vendor on the sidewalk and managed to eat the whole thing despite its lack of taste.

He ended up wandering around Times Square, where he could

see more lights than existed in his whole country and where he could feel the bustle and buzz of the theater district. Eventually, exhausted from his sightseeing, he found a small restaurant for a light dinner. But when he looked at the menu, he found that he wasn't tempted by the New York strip steaks or a rack of ribs and ended up ordering a carrot cake and a cup of coffee. As he waited for it to be served, he reflected that he had not thought of his father and the search for his murderer since he left the hotel. Will there come a time, he wondered, when I can go through a whole day or a whole week without thinking of him? It didn't seem possible.

The waitress arrived with a cup of coffee and a gigantic slice of cake. "Enjoy!" she said with a big smile as she put them down in front of him. Kubu lifted his fork and decided he would do as instructed.

WHILE HE WAITED back at the hotel for the time in Botswana to get late enough to phone Mabaku, Kubu played with Google to investigate rare earths. The more he read, the more intrigued he became. Apparently, only the financial collapse had rescued the rare-earth market from China's grip. The slowing world economy had allowed the prices to fall. But the Chinese had a long-term view and plenty of time. And prices were rising again. What China couldn't allow was a huge discovery outside its control.

Kubu checked his watch and phoned the director.

"Mabaku." He sounded half-asleep.

"It's Kubu, Director. I'm sorry to phone so early, but it's already half-past eleven here in New York, and I need a good night's sleep because I'm giving your presentation at nine in the morning."

"I assume you've called for reason. What is it?"

For the next few minutes, Kubu told Mabaku of his meeting with Newsom, telling him of Newsom's allegations of Mopati's corruption and giving a brief synopsis of the recording Newsom had given him. He also told the director how Newsom had paid Kunene for information—probably about Mopati's dealings with the Konshua Mine.

Mabaku listened without interrupting, but Kubu could almost feel the handset heating up the longer he spoke. Mabaku, Kubu knew, was very proud of how his country had pulled itself up from being one of the poorest countries in Africa to one of the most prosperous and well run. So even the hint of corruption in a government official put him in a foul mood.

"Where did Newsom get this fucking tape?" Mabaku asked at the end of the story.

"Good question. And how come he's so well connected at the United States embassy? And why can't we trace his calls to Kunene?" Kubu paused. "He's not just a mining engineer. I think he works for the CIA or some similar agency."

Mabaku grunted. "This gets better and better."

"But there's something else," Kubu continued. "One of the things I learned today at the conference was that countries like Germany and Denmark are closing all their nuclear power plants. I thought it strange that Newsom and the Konshua Mine would be going to such lengths to get access to more uranium in what appears to be a declining market. So I called an old geologist friend of mine here in the States and asked him. He also thought it was unlikely that they were after more uranium."

"So what are they after?" Mabaku growled.

"He suggested it could be rare earths. I spent a bit of time looking them up on the Internet. Every major industry uses them these days. You don't need a lot, but you have to have them. And, guess what? China controls almost all of the world's supply, and other countries are scrambling to find sources for themselves. That would explain why both the Americans and Chinese are so interested. I think they were planning to say they were mining uranium and then take the more important rare earths out of the country without telling us."

"So where do we go from here?" Mabaku asked.

"I had a free evening, Director, and gave it a lot of thought. This is what I suggest," Kubu said. "Although the voices on Newsom's recording sound like Mopati and the Chinese mine official I spoke to, we don't know for certain that it is them. I think our first step is to be certain of that. I think I know how to do that. Then, if it is them, we need to get a legal recording that we can use either in or out of court. I have a suggestion on how to do that too."

Then, for the next few minutes, Kubu outlined his plan, answering all of Mabaku's various questions and objections. When he finished, there was a long silence.

Eventually, Mabaku spoke. "It's risky, but I don't see a better alternative. E-mail me the recording, and I'll go and see the commissioner as soon as I can. There's a senior government official involved, so we can't do this without him knowing about it." He paused. "I think he'll go along with it—he hates corruption almost as much as I do."

There was a pause, and then Mabaku continued, "I have something for you. Two of the suspects we're holding for murder during the riot have told us that they were paid by some unknown man to cause trouble at the *kgotla*, to stir the men up. Of course, they deny any involvement in the killings, but we have strong evidence against them."

"Who do you think is behind it?" Kubu asked.

"We've no idea at the moment. Could be the mine. Could be the chief's son. After what you've told me, it could also be Newsom. Who knows, but we're working on it."

"I can't wait to get back and work on the case, Director," Kubu said quietly. "If you'll let me."

Mabaku grunted and hung up, leaving Kubu feeling far away from everything he loved.

KUBU'S PHONE CALL had put Director Mabaku into a foul temper, so he was keen to move on the plan immediately. *This is too im-*

portant, he thought, to talk to the commissioner by phone. I need to speak to him face-to-face. The problem was that Mabaku was in Shoshong and the commissioner in Gaborone. So Mabaku dressed, grabbed a cup of coffee, and set off for the capital.

At eight o'clock, he called the commissioner's office from the car to make an appointment.

"The earliest he can see you, Director, is tomorrow afternoon," the commissioner's assistant said.

Mabaku contained his irritation and replied that the issue was urgent and couldn't wait. "This is of national importance," he said. "It could have an impact on the president's visit to Shoshong next week."

"I'll speak to him and get back to you," came the reply.

Mabaku gritted his teeth and hung up. And for the next hour, he tried to keep his mind off what Kubu had said and on the road, where straying animals posed their usual risk.

NOTHING LIKE MENTIONING the president to get a high-up official's attention, Mabaku thought as he arrived at the commissioner's office a mere ninety minutes after his original phone call. And he only had to wait a few minutes before he was ushered into his boss's office.

Mabaku had known the commissioner for many years and thought he was an honest man, even though he was too political for Mabaku's taste.

"Sit down, Jacob," the commissioner said. "I hope you are not going to tell me that the president will be in some sort of danger when he goes to Shoshong."

"Not physical danger, Commissioner," Mabaku replied, "but potentially political danger."

The commissioner frowned. "It's not like you to pay attention to politics, Jacob. Are you beginning to learn something in your old age? What's up?"

For the next twenty minutes, Mabaku brought the commissioner up to speed on what Kubu had been told by Newsom, and he played the tape of the phone call supposedly between Mopati and the man at the Konshua Mine.

"The concern I have about the president's visit to Shoshong next week, Commissioner, is that he will make some commitment to the mine to appease the young men who are out of work. Given what we have just heard, I think that would be premature." He paused. "But I realize that I cannot suggest that the director of mines is corrupt unless I have incontrovertible evidence—which I don't."

"So what do you suggest?"

"I want your permission to try to corroborate what is on the recording. The first step is to make sure the voices are of Mopati and the Chinaman. What I want to do is leave a message for both of them to call me. We'll record their calls and do a voice match with what we have. If there is a match, then I want your permission to take the next step—that is, to see if I can get some evidence that they are working together in an unethical way . . ."

"And how will you do that?"

"I'll meet with Mopati, ostensibly to update him on our investigation of the mine riot. During the meeting, I'll tell him we have evidence that his deputy, Kunene, had been in the pay of the Americans and that he had been providing them with information about the tenders for the Shoshong mining concession. I'm hoping that he'll be so excited that we're investigating Kunene that he'll rush to tell his Chinese friends. I'll need you to get authorization for wiretaps on the business and private phones of both Mopati and the Chinaman, Shonhu."

"Based on the flimsy evidence you have or may get?"

Mabaku nodded. "Commissioner, we can't have this sort of thing undermine the progress Botswana has made. I'm sure you know someone you can persuade to give us this."

The commissioner sat silent for a few moments, then nodded. "I'll see what I can do."

AS HE DROVE back to CID headquarters, Mabaku pondered how to get Shonhu and Mopati on tape without raising suspicions. Mopati would be easy. He would contact him and arrange a meeting for the following day. He was sure there'd be enough conversation to compare it to the voice on Newsom's recording.

How to deal with Shonhu was more difficult. If he were to contact Shonhu directly, it might raise suspicions that the police were onto something. He didn't want that. He pondered various other alternatives and eventually decided that his assistant, Miriam, could speak to Shonhu under the pretext of inquiring whether he and the mine manager would be at the *kgotla* when the president spoke the following Sunday—the police wanted to be sure that they had all security issues covered. Again, Mabaku thought that they'd be able to get sufficient conversation to make a comparison possible.

He'd just settled down to handle the mountain of paperwork that had accumulated after the Shoshong riot when his phone buzzed. "It's the director of mines," Miriam said. There was a click, and Mabaku greeted Mopati and introduced himself. When the pleasantries were over, he said, "Director, I would like to brief you tomorrow about some of our findings concerning the *kgotla* fiasco. It's better done in person, and it's rather urgent. What time would suit you?" After a few moments of trying to coordinate schedules, they agreed on a time late the following afternoon and hung up.

That's plenty for the voice comparison, Mabaku thought with satisfaction, and returned to his pile of papers.

About half an hour later, Miriam walked into his office with a smile and said that she'd recorded several minutes of conversation with Shonhu, the Chinese mine executive.

"Excellent," Mabaku said. "Please send both recordings to

Zanele immediately. Please tell her I want her results back tomorrow morning."

He walked over to the window overlooking Kgale Hill and searched for the troop of baboons that often came into the CID parking lot looking for scraps of food, but they were nowhere to be seen. A pity, he thought. I like them more than some of the people I have to deal with. He turned and sat down at his desk. I wonder what tomorrow will bring, he thought as he picked up the next file needing attention.

CHAPTER 44

In the first session of the conference on Thursday morning, Kubu gave Mabaku's paper. He was very nervous, not only about speaking in front of a large and critical audience but also about being faced with questions he might not be able to answer. However, Mabaku's topic—the challenges of using high-tech detection and forensics in a developing country—appealed to many of the smaller and less affluent nations represented, whose problems were far away from art theft and nuclear power waste. The applause was warm, and the questions friendly and asked with genuine interest. Kubu enjoyed his moment in the limelight and returned to his seat with a warm feeling of a job well done. At least here, he'd not let Mabaku down.

His good mood was enhanced by the fact that he'd managed to change his flight to leave that evening. He'd persuaded himself that getting back to deal with the Mopati sting and what would develop from it was much more important than another day of boring talks. And returning to temperatures where you could walk outside without freezing was a bonus. However, he admitted to himself that the real reason for leaving a day early was that he wanted to get home. New York was great, and he was glad he'd had the opportunity to see a tiny part of it, but he wanted to be with his family. The next time I come to America, he thought, we'll come together and take the girls to Disney World! He knew it wouldn't happen— the cost would be far too high—but it was fun to dream.

He left the conference at lunchtime, hailed a cab like a real New Yorker, collected his bags at the hotel, and soon was on his way back to JFK. He now thought of himself as a seasoned traveler, confidently using the self-service check-in kiosks and taking off his shoes and belt to be X-rayed, while he stood with his arms above his head in the body scanner. After only half an hour of standing in various lines, he found himself in the departure area, faced with an array of shops and with time to kill. Everything was on sale and duty-free, and the temptation was too great. He had to buy gifts for the family.

For the girls, it was easy. He bought them each an "I Love New York" T-shirt with a picture of the Statue of Liberty on the front. For his mother, he bought a silk scarf with rainbow colors. It wasn't really a souvenir from America since it was made in China, but he thought she'd love it anyway. It was a present for Joy that posed a real problem.

First, he thought perfume would be good, but he wasn't sure what she liked. Then he passed a jewelry store and spotted a pair of twisted gold earrings marked 50 percent off. These he knew she would adore. Even with the discount, they were expensive for a Botswana detective. The shop assistant noticed his hesitation and said, "Shall I gift wrap them for you, sir? No extra charge." Kubu grimaced and nodded.

THE FLIGHT HOME was much better than the journey out. Not only was the jet stream helping, but the flight to Johannesburg was nonstop, so it seemed much shorter. Best of all, there was a vacant seat next to Kubu, so he could spread out, lean his pillow against the window shade, and doze from time to time.

Nevertheless, by the time he arrived in Johannesburg, he was pretty shattered. Once more, he had to negotiate customs, immigration, and security, but all continued smoothly, and, for once, Air Botswana was on time. I'll be home for dinner, he thought. Or is it lunch?

In any case, it was only a few more tiring hours before he carefully negotiated the steps down to the runway in Gaborone and was hit by a blast of dry hot air. He smiled. Fifteen minutes later, he had a child in each arm and a wife and mother whose smiles looked as though he'd just returned from months in the wilderness.

"Daddy, Daddy, we missed you," Tumi yelled. "Did you take pictures? Did you bring us presents?" Joy started to scold her but then just laughed. In the meanwhile, Amantle was looking hard at Kubu's face. "David, I can see your face is chapped from the cold. I told you that you needed a proper hat, but you didn't listen!"

"I'm fine, Mother, and anyway I bought a hat," Kubu said. To cheer her up, he added, "But it was very cold. Much colder than any of you can imagine." He gave a theatrical shiver, much to the delight of the girls.

Once they got to the car, there was a huge welcome from Ilia to finesse, but eventually they were all settled with Joy driving, Kubu in front holding the fox terrier, and Amantle in the back with the girls talking nonstop.

And half an hour after that, he was home.

CHAPTER 45

As Mabaku drove to the Department of Mines, he planned the coming meeting. He was a straight shooter. He liked to say what he meant and mean what he said, and he disliked lying under any circumstances. He didn't do it and wasn't going to start now. In any case that might be ruled entrapment. What he intended to do was to be selective with the truth, and he had no great problem with that.

A twinge of doubt remained. Zanele had told him that there was a very high probability that the voices were the same, and then she gave him a lecture on key frequencies and confidence intervals and continuity measures. The bottom line was that she thought Newsom's recording was genuine and that the participants were Mopati and Shonhu. That was good enough for him, but if Kubu was right about Newsom being CIA, then it was just possible they were falling for a scam. Another reason to be careful in the interview.

As soon as Mabaku arrived at the office of the director of mines, he was shown in. Mopati greeted him and ushered him to his meeting table. He reminded Mabaku that they'd met before at a government function and offered coffee.

Was there an undercurrent of nervousness below the friendliness? Mabaku wondered. He thought there was, but maybe he just saw it because he expected it.

Until the coffee was served, they compared their plans for the *kgotla* at Shoshong on Sunday. Then Mabaku got down to business.

"Director, I know you must be very busy, so thank you for seeing me at such short notice. The reason I asked to see you urgently is to brief you on certain important matters that we've discovered since the Shoshong riot. The minister and even the president may need to know, so we felt you must be completely in the picture. Before I do that, however, I'd like to get a little more background from you. Some points are confusing us, and I'd like to be sure we understand the situation properly." Mabaku paused until Mopati nodded his agreement.

"I understand there are at least two applicants for a mining lease over the contentious area in Shoshong. Is that right?"

Mopati hesitated. "That's correct. This is confidential, of course, but I have no problem sharing it with you. Both the Konshua Mine and an American company have applied for the lease. They have both been involved in prospecting the area. Konshua is proposing a large expansion of their existing operation; a US junior, UNE—Uranium and Nickel Exploration—wants to start a new open pit in an overlapping area. We need to choose which one to award the license to."

"But all this depends on the people of Shoshong?"

Mopati nodded. "Both developments will dispossess a significant number of people. Whoever wins the lease must come to a settlement with them."

"Konshua tried and apparently—at this point—failed. What about the American company?"

"It's a bit technical, Director Mabaku. Konshua's view was that if they could get approval from the people and if they had a strong economic case for Botswana in terms of jobs and revenue, they would have a big advantage. They were probably right. But as it turned out . . ." He shrugged. "They made what I felt was a generous offer. I was most surprised by what the chief decided. It was a big mistake, I think."

"It certainly was for him," Mabaku commented dryly. "And the US company?"

"They're applying for the lease subject to *subsequent* approval from the community. And they have the US embassy backing them with offers of all sorts of support. The US is lagging China in investment here, and they're obviously keen to catch up."

"And how will you decide between the two applications?"

Mopati frowned. "There are many issues, and the minister has the final say, of course. I don't believe it will be helpful to go into the details of the process now."

I'll bet you don't, Mabaku thought. "The minister will presumably follow your recommendation?"

Mopati nodded. "Probably. That's why I have this job."

Yes, thought Mabaku. A very senior and quite well paid position. But it's not enough for you, is it? "Let me explain my interest, Director," he said. "There are several issues that have arisen during our investigations. In the first place, it's possible that Konshua was doing more than making promises. Julius Koma—the chief's son— was clearly compromised. He negotiated with the mine management behind his father's back and used every opportunity to push the mine's case. He even advised people to show displeasure if the chief ruled against them—mainly unemployed young men. As a member of the chief's council that wasn't ethical."

"True, but unless the mine was paying him off, it wouldn't have been inappropriate on their part."

"There's more. Two of the men arrested for committing murder during the riot claim they were paid to cause serious trouble if the chief rejected the mine's offer. That included bringing knob-kieries with them and jumping onto the stage to threaten the chief and elders. Also, they handed out sticks and alcohol to friends at the *kgotla*, friends who supported Konshua."

"That's much more serious. Do you have proof that the mine was behind this? It would be very foolish of them. Isn't it possible that these men are making this up as a mitigating circumstance for their crimes? There was nothing in the papers about people jump-ing on the stage and inciting the crowd."

"They claim that the crowd surged forward without them hav-ing to do anything. And, no, we don't have proof at this stage. Nor have we been able to identify the man who paid them as yet."

"Maybe this Julius Koma was behind that too. It sounds as though he's playing a dirty game."

"It's possible, but either way you should be aware that there was inappropriate pressure being applied in Shoshong. That was at least partly responsible for what happened at the *kgotla*."

Mopati nodded. "I appreciate that," he said. "I understand that the press is calling for an inquiry into the police reaction, suggest-ing that it too was partly responsible for the disaster."

"That's possible," Mabaku said shortly, and changed the subject. "Now there's another matter, equally serious, we believe. Do you know a man named Peter Newsom? An American?"

"Of course. He's the front man here for UNE. He's been coor-dinating their efforts to secure the license."

Mabaku paused, carefully picking his words. "What I tell you now has to be in strict confidence because the matter is still under investigation. But I have to tell you that in looking into Good-man Kunene's death, we've discovered that he was working for Newsom."

Mopati looked shocked. "Working for Newsom? What do you mean? He was my assistant director!"

"I mean that Newsom was paying him—at least for information, but perhaps more. It's possible he was also trying to sabotage Konshua's application. We really don't know the extent of the corruption involved at this point."

Mopati shook his head. "I'm really shocked. Goodman was a trusted colleague, a friend . . . I can't believe it."

"Did Kunene ever try to influence you about the decision? In a way that went beyond what you would expect from his role in your department?"

Mopati hesitated. "I have to say that he did favor the US bid whenever the issue came up."

Mabaku nodded. This was exactly what he expected to hear, whether or not it was true.

"Is what you say definite? Do you have proof?" Mopati asked.

"I'm afraid so. The investigation is still going on, but we have bank records, and Newsom has pretty well admitted it."

"Will you charge him?"

"He's in the US. We think he has some security service role there. Perhaps the CIA, but that's just a guess."

"That's amazing! You realize this will pretty well exclude the UNE application? But we will need firm proof."

"We can't supply that at the moment, but we expect the minister will want to delay the lease decision. The president will say something along those lines when he speaks at the *kgotla* next Sunday. Of course, he won't say why. The deaths will be reason enough to delay."

"Very wise," Mopati said, nodding. He picked up his empty coffee cup and examined it. "Does this affect the issue of Goodman's death at all?"

He's not much of an actor, Mabaku thought. "Based on the circumstances of his death, the most probable cause is suicide."

"Perhaps the guilt of the betrayal . . ." Mopati put down his cup with a small clink.

He's learned a lot this afternoon, Mabaku thought. I wonder if

I can also learn something. "One thing really puzzles me, Director. Perhaps it isn't relevant, but I'm curious. With uranium in the doldrums, what's so attractive about this prospect? What's attractive enough to involve the US embassy and to persuade Konshua to make generous offers to the locals? What is so appealing about the area to be worth bribing government officials and paying off agitators? I don't get it."

Mopati leaned forward, suddenly alert. "It's all economics and politics, Director Mabaku. A bit out of your area of expertise, I would guess. A lot of people think that with global warming, nuclear power will be the only way to go in the end. That fossil fuel plants will only make things worse. Obviously, these companies subscribe to that point of view." He checked his watch. "It is getting late. I'm extremely grateful to you for filling me in on all these developments. Is there anything else?"

Mabaku got to his feet, accepting the brush-off. So Kubu is right, he thought. There's more going on here than the extension of an old uranium deposit. And Mopati knows all about it. Now we'll see if he takes the bait.

Mabaku shook Mopati's hand, wishing that he didn't have to, and took his leave.

MABAKU DIDN'T HAVE long to wait. By the time he was back at the CID, Edison was waiting at his office, bursting with excitement. "He must've phoned Shonhu pretty well as soon as you left. They think it was from his car because the signal was a moving location. The number he phoned wasn't the one Shonhu usually uses, though. Obviously, he has a special phone for private conversations with Mopati. That's smart. But Mopati isn't that smart. He called from his own cell phone."

"Do you have the recording?"

"Yes, I'll go and fetch the recorder and get it set up."

The phone rang and Mabaku grabbed it. "Yes?"

"It's Kubu, Director. I've just got home."

"Ah, Kubu. Did you come back with an American accent?"

Kubu laughed. "Hardly, Director. I was only there three days. But my body doesn't know where it is."

"Well, the news is that I met with Mopati, and right after I left his office, he made a call to Shonhu. Edison's going to play it for me now."

"Excellent. Director, I just wanted to say it's good to be back."

"It's good to have you back."

There was a knock, and Edison bustled in carrying the recorder.

"Kubu, I'll speak to you in the morning. There's a meeting here at ten. Have a good night."

Edison apologized for the interruption, but Mabaku waved that away. "Let's listen."

For the next seven minutes, they listened to Mopati speak to Shonhu. They listened as Mopati explained that the police seemed to have accepted Kunene's death as suicide; they listened as he gloated about Newsom being caught out and the result being that the UNE application would be rejected; they listened as Mopati told Shonhu that he expected an even bigger return on his investment after this; and they listened as Mopati warned Shonhu that the police had their eye on Julius, and it would be best to keep him out of the picture. Finally, there was a click as he disconnected and the recording ended.

Mabaku allowed himself a smile. "We've got him!" he said.

PART 7

CHAPTER 46

As Kubu made his way to the meeting room, everyone he met stopped him and wanted to hear about his trip. It's as if I've been away for weeks on vacation, he thought. But as much as he'd resented being thrown out of Shoshong, he had to admit that the trip had been quite an experience. And, of course, he'd tracked down Newsom, although he suspected it was rather the other way around.

Mabaku came in not looking happy. Kubu's heart sank. Something's gone wrong, he thought.

The director took the seat at the head of the table and folded his arms. "I'm going to fill you in on what's happened over the last few days. But I want it absolutely clear that everything I tell you is in strict confidence. Is that understood?" He glared around the table until everyone had offered a nod. Then he laid out the whole story of Kubu's meeting with Newsom, the verification of the voices on Newsom's recording, the possibility of a much more valuable ore body than the Department of Mines had been led to believe, and, finally, the Mopati sting. "All Kubu's idea," he concluded generously, "and we pulled it off!"

There was a buzz around the table and broad smiles. Mabaku held up his hand. "But . . ." Everyone quieted down. "But I've been talking to the prosecutor and the commissioner this morning. It's not enough. It won't convict Mopati, because all this evidence is tainted by Newsom's illegal recording. It's likely we won't be allowed to use our own recording in evidence either because the authority to tap the phones was based on illegally obtained information. Anyway, Shonhu was careful about what he said. When Mopati told him that we thought Kunene's death was suicide, he said: 'That is good.' That's hardly an admission that he had anything to do with the murder."

Mabaku slapped his hand on the table in frustration. "These bastards aren't going to get away with what they've done. No way Mopati quietly resigns, or this Shonhu character gets deported. They're criminals—possibly killers—and they're going to pay for it."

There was silence for a moment before Mabaku continued, "We'll go after Mopati. Damn it, he must've left a paper trail. We can follow that. For a start we know about the payoffs. We should be able to trace them."

"Is it possible Mopati actually helped Shonhu with the murder?" Samantha asked. "They both had a motive, and it would've taken two people to set up the fake suicide."

Kubu shook his head. "It's possible but unlikely. People like Mopati don't get their hands dirty if they can help it. He'll have a watertight alibi, I'm sure." He took a sip of water and thought for a moment. "We mustn't see the Kunene case in isolation," he continued. "Somehow I'm sure they're all connected: the attack on Newsom, the shooting of Chief Koma, even the murder of my father. I'm not saying the mine was responsible for all of it, but I believe the mine's at the center of all of it."

Samantha joined in. "If our riot suspects were paid to cause trouble at the *kgotla*—that could be the link. I've got a webcam videoing people coming and going at the mine's admin building. Julius Koma went in and out twice over the last couple of days."

"I wonder what he was up to there," Mabaku said. "I don't trust him."

"I made blowups of pictures of all Batswana who visited the building and showed them to the suspects to see if they could pick out who paid them. It seemed like a good idea, but they haven't identified anyone yet. But we're sticking with it."

"I see a few scenarios," Mabaku said. "Now that we know the sort of things the mine is up to, I think it's likely that they arranged for the men to stir up trouble and for the chief to be shot. In that case, forget about finding the gun or the guy walking into the admin building and making an appointment to see Shonhu. But there's also a chance that Julius was behind it. Then the question is where did he get the gun? We should follow up on people who we know or suspect might be selling illegal weapons."

Kubu thought it was a long shot, but he didn't object. He didn't have a better idea. He took a deep breath and changed the subject cautiously. "I said my father's murder was also wrapped up in this somehow. I'm just guessing, but I do have a theory." He glanced at the director to see how this was being received. "My uncle told me that he thought my father had inherited something to do with land. When Julius came to see him, he told him about it. Suppose it was some sort of right over the area the mine wants or even an ancient mining lease? If so, my father would have been able to block the expansion if he'd wanted to. These people didn't know my father and wanted to make sure he didn't cause any problems. So they tried to get the document, if there was one. When they didn't succeed, they killed him." He paused. "Some of his papers, including his will, are missing. My mother and I believe they were stolen during the break-in after his murder."

"Have you done anything about this?" There was a growl in Mabaku's voice.

Kubu shook his head. "No. It's only an idea. I've been thinking it through since I learned about the rare-earth possibility. Suddenly, all the stakes are much higher."

Mabaku mulled it over. "I think it's a very long shot, but we'll look into it. It's not the way mineral titles work here, certainly not anymore. But if such a document existed, then there must be a record of it somewhere."

"I can check," said Edison. He liked ferreting out information.

Mabaku looked around, but no one else had anything to contribute. "I have a hunch Kubu is right about the mine being at the center of all these issues. But I've no idea what the connection is." He shrugged. "Okay, let's get to work."

HOWEVER, THE DAYS passed, and no breakthrough occurred. There was a feeling that the case was slipping away from them. At any time, Shonhu might vanish back to China, and the common link with Newsom and Mopati would be gone. Eventually, Kubu couldn't take it anymore. He went to see the director.

"Director," Kubu said as he sat down, "what has Edison come up with? He was going to follow up on all sorts of things. Has he done that?"

Mabaku nodded. "He did, but there's nothing there," he growled. "The Nigerian bank was a dead end. We need to put a request to the Nigerian police through Interpol. That will take forever. We don't have that much time. He checked the bars along Kunene's route. Nothing. And the big disappointment is the phone tap. Nothing more of any use. Just Mopati informing the Chinese that the decision about the new mining concession has been delayed a couple of weeks. The Chinaman didn't make a single call since the one last Friday."

They sat in silence for a few moments. Then Kubu asked, "What about my father's case. Is anyone doing anything about it?"

Mabaku took a deep breath. "Kubu, at the moment we have

nothing new to go on. I know you think all the cases are connected, but we've no idea how."

"Edison was going to look for land records. Did he do that? I could—"

"You'll do nothing! Edison has spoken to officials in the Department of Lands and talked to several elders in the area by phone. Nobody knows anything about a document your father may have had. In fact, only one of the elders had even heard of a Bengu family from Tobela. I never believed that idea would go anywhere." He shook his head.

Kubu was silent again. He still felt he should be more involved. Edison worked hard, but he might miss things—especially about his father. "Damn it, Jacob. We can't let them get away with this!"

"And what do you suggest we do, Kubu? Tell me where I'm going wrong." The sarcasm wasn't wasted on Kubu. He sighed.

"I'm sorry, Director. I know everyone's doing their best. But we need something soon, or everything we've done will be wasted."

Mabaku nodded. They needed a break. But how were they going to get one?

MABAKU CALLED A meeting for Friday afternoon. He wanted a report back from everyone and hoped a little pressure might get things moving.

"Well?" he growled. "Has anybody got anything more?"

Nobody answered.

"Edison. The phone tap?" Edison shook his head.

Mabaku turned to Samantha. "Any progress on who paid the men to incite violence? Or who may have sold the handgun?"

"There's quite a long list of people who we suspect of being able to supply firearms of different sorts. I've spoken to over half of them, threatening them with all sorts of bad things. They all deny it, and the bad news is that I believe them. To be certain, I've shown the two men who say they were paid to cause trouble photographs of everyone I've spoken to. But they haven't recognized anyone. I'll keep on it, but I'm not really optimistic we'll find the man."

Mabaku turned to Zanele. "If we start from the assumption that Shonhu was the murderer of Kunene, what can we get from the forensic evidence?"

"We got a partial fingerprint from the hose that was put in the exhaust pipe. If that matched Shonhu's prints, we'd have strong evidence."

"I presume we tried the database?" Mabaku asked.

Zanele nodded. "Nothing. But you often don't get matches to a partial anyway."

Kubu looked thoughtful. "We know he'll be at the *kgotla* next Sunday, Director. Can't we make an excuse to give him something to look at or something? Maybe a vendor asks him to hold a curio or something?"

Zanele looked glum. "It won't work with a partial," she said. We really need a decent set of prints for comparison."

Mabaku frowned. "What about the bullet that killed the chief?"

"It's badly fragmented and distorted from hitting the spine. We won't be able to match it to the gun." She shrugged.

"Zanele, didn't you find a hair in the car?" Samantha asked.

"Yes, I did. It could've been from someone from the East. Possibly a Chinaman."

"How can we get one of Shonhu's hairs?" Edison asked.

There was a silence in the room.

"If we had a search warrant for his house, we'd find one easily enough," Kubu said. "But I don't think we'd get one just yet."

Mabaku shook his head. "Definitely not."

He looked around the table, but no one had anything more to contribute. "Well, there's not much more we can do at the moment," he said. "We'll just have to be patient. That's what this business is— paying attention to detail and patience. If we're lucky something will break."

"Director, are you sure we can't go after the Chinese with what we have now?" Samantha asked.

"I'm sure, and the prosecutor is sure. All we'd do is alert them, and we'd not be able to stop them heading back to China. Then we'd have nothing. No, we must be patient, as hard as that is."

"And so, if nothing breaks, they walk away?" Samantha's voice was husky with anger. "That's not right!"

"Right or not," Mabaku responded, "that's the way it is. It's not easy to swallow seeing people you know are guilty getting away with what they've done. Unfortunately, it happens all the time. But what's worse is when they get off because the police have screwed up. So we just have to keep plugging away and hope we find something or someone that helps us."

He looked around the table. "Kubu and I are going to Shoshong on Sunday for the president's visit. We know that the mine officials will be there, and I'm told the Chinese ambassador will be too. That's how important this is. Normally, he wouldn't go to a thing like this, but obviously he has pressure from above in China. If you find anything new before I leave, absolutely anything, phone me on my cell phone. I'd love an excuse to talk to them."

He stood up. "Kubu, I'll pick you up at your house at one on Sunday. There's no way I'm driving that far in your Land Rover."

"Yes, Director," Kubu said. "I'll be ready."

As Kubu and Samantha walked back to their offices, Kubu remarked that Samantha must look forward to having a weekend off at last.

"I am," she replied. "I'm way behind on my volunteering at the women's shelter. They need all the help they can get."

Kubu looked at her. "You really believe that women are treated badly in Botswana, don't you?"

She stopped. "Don't you?" she snapped, and walked off.

Kubu stared after her. What an unusual woman, he thought.

CHAPTER 47

Kubu was delighted that Mabaku wanted to drive. The trip to Sho-shong was long and boring, and Kubu was beginning to lose count of the number of times he'd done it recently. Better still, Mabaku drove a relatively new Toyota Camry with air-conditioning—something that Kubu's Land Rover didn't have. Kubu wasn't sure why the commissioner wanted Mabaku there when the president addressed the *kgotla*, and he didn't know why Mabaku had insisted on Kubu joining him. Perhaps it was no reason other than for company on the five-hour round-trip.

For the first half hour or so, the two detectives talked about the various unsolved cases they had before them, but they made no progress in figuring out how they could move the cases forward other than methodically following up every potential lead. They were already doing that. Then they lapsed into the relaxed silence of two people who knew each other well.

At last Kubu said, "I wonder if the president is worried about another riot today if he doesn't give the mine the go-ahead."

"I don't think so," Mabaku replied as he slowed down for cows that had wandered onto the road. "I'm sure he's confident that he can calm things down. Anyway, the army will be out in force, I'm sure, and no alcohol or weapons of any sort will be allowed. If anyone so much as thinks about disrupting proceedings, they'll be hauled off."

A MILE BEFORE they reached Shoshong, they were stopped by a military roadblock. After examining their credentials, the sergeant told them where to park, just a few blocks from where the president was going to speak, which was not at the *kgotla* itself, because it had too many bad memories, but on the primary school's soccer field.

"Everyone who's not from here must sit in a reserved area to the right of the stage," the sergeant said. "It'll be cordoned off, and my men will be there to make sure nothing happens to you."

Even though it was still an hour before the president was scheduled to speak, the roads were packed with people. To Kubu's eye, the atmosphere was subdued—few were talking, and there was a noticeable lack of laughing and singing that typically accompanied groups of Batswana going to a meeting.

"At least no one is carrying a knobkierie," Mabaku said. "The army must be doing its job."

"I hope nobody has a gun in his pocket," Kubu muttered.

AFTER THEY PARKED, Mabaku and Kubu were escorted to the visitor enclosure, which had space for about forty people and was roped off from the rest of the seats. A rioting mob wouldn't even notice the ropes, Kubu thought, but the presence of at least a platoon of armed soldiers gave him confidence. Mabaku led the way to the back row. "We can keep an eye on things better from here," he said.

Kubu recognized some of the other people nearby, mainly

journalists, and Mabaku pointed out representatives from several foreign embassies, South Africa, the UK, Australia, and the United States among them. Countries with mining interests, Kubu thought. There were also a few people from a variety of human rights NGOs. The Chinese ambassador was also there with an older and a younger companion. The older, Kubu assumed to be the mine manager, Hong, and the younger to be their man of interest, Shonhu.

Kubu gazed at him. He was stocky, looked to be in good shape, and was constantly scanning the crowd. Suddenly, he turned around, and their eyes locked. Then Shonhu turned and whispered something in Hong's ear. Hong turned, looked at Kubu, and turned away. There was another whispered discussion.

Julius must have told them about me, Kubu thought. Probably nothing true. But they're soon going to find out what sort of person I really am.

A few minutes later, the director of mines arrived. As he walked to his seat, he acknowledged the three Chinese. Then he noticed Mabaku and Kubu and nodded a greeting. Little does he know what is ahead for him, Kubu thought. He's probably feeling pretty good right now.

AT QUARTER PAST four, the presidential helicopter flew overhead and landed in a field at the edge of the village, sending a cloud of red sand billowing into the air.

When the president arrived at the meeting a few minutes later, Kubu was surprised to see who climbed the steps to the platform. He could understand a couple of elders being there, including Nwako, the fortunate elder who had missed the ill-fated *kgotla*. He'd also expected the commissioner. But he did not expect Julius. But there he was, looking appropriately somber, as he followed the president up the stairs.

Kubu was even more surprised when Julius stood in front of the microphone and told the gathering that he was acting chief and there on behalf of the people. He introduced the president and welcomed him to the *kgotla*. At least he showed good taste and didn't make a speech, Kubu thought.

For the next fifteen minutes, the president extolled the virtues of the *kgotla* system, saying that it had stood the test of time and served Botswana well. Then he admonished the people of Shoshong for reacting to the old chief's decision in the way they had.

"It is not the way we do things in Botswana," the president said. "Even if you disagree, there are established ways of handling that."

This didn't go down well with the younger crowd, and Kubu heard a number of very disgruntled comments.

"At the same time," the president continued, "I fully understand that you want to work, and there is little or no work for you here. Expanding the mine would have provided several hundred jobs, which is what Shoshong needs. I can't guarantee how many jobs there will be in the future, but I will tell you that whatever company gets the mining lease, it will provide a lot of jobs. I will direct the minister of Minerals, Energy, and Water Resources to make that a prerequisite for getting any lease."

For the first time since he stood up, there was an approving murmur from the crowd. Kubu glanced at Mopati, who sat with a big grin on his face.

"In addition, because it is necessary to delay the decision on granting the lease for a couple of weeks, I have instructed that the road between Mahalapye and Shoshong be upgraded immediately. The Department of Roads will start work sometime this week and will need at least fifty strong men to help." There was another murmur of approval.

"I know it is not enough, but it is a good start." He looked at the crowd. "And finally, I have instructed the Department of Tourism to make Shoshong a priority cultural tourist destination—after all, it is one of the most prominent towns in our country's history. This will entail training several of you to be tour guides, as well as hiring some of you to upgrade the cemetery and other historical places." He paused. "Please be patient as we implement these initiatives. We will do whatever is possible to get you work. Finally, I want to extend my deepest sympathies to all who lost loved ones in the troubles. And that includes the police who died in the line of duty. Thank you."

This time the crowd applauded warmly. The president had the reputation for keeping his word, so there was optimism that jobs would start becoming available quite soon.

Julius jumped up and thanked the president. "Thank you, Mr. President. Thank you. We need the jobs badly." He turned to the crowd. "The president has kindly agreed to take your questions. If you have one, please come to the microphone next to the stage, say your name, and ask your question."

He looked around expectantly.

For a few moments, nobody moved. Then a young man in a dirty T-shirt came forward.

"*Kgosi*," he said. "My name is Dume. I thank you for coming to Shoshong to help us. I listened carefully to you this afternoon and how you thought the *kgotla* was a good system. The problems we had last time were because the chief didn't understand what was happening. He was living in the past. So my question is this: because things change so quickly these days, wouldn't it be better to run the *kgotla* in a democratic way? The chief and elders would still provide their wisdom, but decisions would be made by democratic vote. Thank you."

Mabaku leaned over to Kubu and whispered, "I bet he wasn't prepared for that question! I wonder what he'll say."

The president took his time moving to the microphone. "Rra Dume, thank you for your question. It shows me that the community here is thinking about how we, as a country, best govern ourselves."

"He's stalling!" Kubu said.

"For the first time since I have been president, I am beginning to hear people say that we should think about the system we have now, which is different from most democratic countries. They want the same as America or Germany or the United Kingdom. They want to get rid of a system that made Botswana strong."

He picked up a glass of water and took a deep drink.

"As you know, we have two systems working at the same time—the national legal system, based on English law, and the traditional system such as we have here today. If we were to be totally based on the English system, all crimes would be tried in court, often nowhere near where the people live. The court wouldn't know them, their families, or their histories. The traditional system attempts to operate as a family, where everyone knows everyone else. It is not perfect, but it generally works well."

Dume put up his hand. The president nodded to him to take the microphone again.

"But, *Kgosi*, it is not a good family when the father ignores what all the children want. That only makes the children want to leave or disobey the father."

"It is a good point, Rra Dume. Thank you. I will have my staff see how strong the support is for a change. Any other questions?"

A middle-aged woman moved forward. "*Dumela, Kgosi.* Thank you for letting me speak. I am Alice Moyo. My son was killed at the riot last week. Not by the crowd but by the police. What is the country coming to when the police shoot their own people, people they know and are neighbors with? And what is going to happen to the police who shot at the crowd?"

Kubu looked around and saw that the crowd was unsettled by the question. Probably bringing back bad memories, Kubu thought.

"Mma Moyo. You have my condolences. I am sorry that your son had to die, particularly shot by a policeman. That must be terrible for you and your family." He pointed to the commissioner sitting behind him. "I have instructed the commissioner of police to open a public inquiry into the police behavior on that day. Based on the findings, we will take steps to prevent it happening again."

And so the questions went on, about ten in all, but none very aggressive.

The offer of immediate jobs has helped keep the meeting on an even keel, Kubu thought. The president has handled the situation well.

Finally, Julius took the microphone again and thanked the president for his wisdom and for taking the time to come to a small village. Again there was applause—quite warm, Kubu thought.

With a wave to the crowd, the president left the stage and, with the commissioner, headed back to his helicopter.

Kubu and Mabaku watched the crowd disperse. "They look happier than before the meeting," Kubu commented. Then he nudged Mabaku and nodded toward the exit of the visitor area. Shonhu had held back when the ambassador and Hong had left and was listening to an animated Mopati, who was whispering into Shonhu's ear.

"I wish I knew what that's about," Mabaku said.

"Something about money, I would bet," Kubu answered. "Lots of money. It makes me so angry that we can't do something about it."

Mabaku stood up. "Patience, Kubu. Something will turn up. Let's go. We've another long drive ahead."

CHAPTER 48

The Chinese ambassador, Hong, and Shonhu walked back to the visitor parking lot. When they reached it, the ambassador told Shonhu to go on ahead. He wanted to speak to Hong alone and would drop him off at the Chinese compound a little later. Shonhu was unhappy about leaving his charge but could do little about it. He couldn't disobey the ambassador.

As he walked to Hong's car, he talked himself into a bad mood. Why had he been excluded from the conversation? Didn't the ambassador know that it was he who was really in charge at the mine? Didn't the ambassador know that Hong was a dolt? What, in fact, did the ambassador know about anything? He'd just started considering whether he should send a report back to Beijing about the situation when his cell phone beeped. He looked at the text.

Want you back visit me tiger

Shonhu stared at the phone. Maybe that's what I need, he thought. Get rid of my bad mood.

After a few moments, he replied, *15 minutes.*

Too bad she's not like Li back in Shanghai. She can take it.

As he drove to her house, Shonhu thought about Jasmine. She'd approached him shortly after he arrived and offered her exclusive services. He refused, scared of AIDS. But she persisted, offered to take an AIDS test, and promised she would sleep with no one else. Eventually, he relented, missing what Li had provided for several years, and decided he'd have to use a condom. Jasmine was quite different from Li. She was tall, big-breasted—enormous compared to Li—and uninhibited. Li was short, compliant, and resilient.

When he'd tried to persuade Jasmine that he wanted to fuck her for free before making a commitment, she laughed. "Three months in advance," she said. "You will be pleased."

And he had been. She was very good in bed, quickly learning what made him happy. And she always seemed happy too. Happy to see him. Happy to do what he wanted.

Except for one thing.

She wouldn't let him tie her to the bed.

Last time, he was so angry when she refused, he'd taught her a lesson.

"Get out!" she'd screamed. "Get out!" She threw some money at him and swore that she'd never see him again.

He was surprised she'd contacted him again. Surprised but pleased. She must be missing me, he thought. Or the money.

He smiled and climbed into the manager's car.

WHEN SHE OPENED the door, she was wearing a simple cotton dress in a colorful African pattern. He caught his breath, as he always did. The dress revealed nothing, but only hinted at what lay below.

She smiled. "Ni hao, China boy. I have tea ready."

He grabbed her and pulled close. "No tea today," he grunted. "Need you now."

He pushed her into the small bedroom. "Today I tie you up."

He crushed his mouth against hers to stop any objection. She tried to struggle free, but he was far too strong. They fell onto the bed, and he straddled her, putting one hand over her mouth and holding one of her arms with the other. The other arm, he pinned under his knee.

"No make noise," he hissed. "Else I hurt you."

She struggled, trying to buck him off. He slapped her across the face. "Quiet!"

She managed to free the arm that he'd trapped under his knee. She tried hitting him, but he just laughed. He hit her across the face again, this time much harder.

She grabbed at the hand over her mouth and managed to get hold of a finger. She pushed it back, forcing the hand away from her mouth. She screamed. He punched her in the face. "I kill you."

She screamed again.

He grabbed her throat and squeezed.

Suddenly, there was a banging at the front door. "Is everything okay?" a male voice called. "Police. Open the door."

He let go of Jasmine and ran to the back door. He opened it and peered out. Nobody there. He went out and looked around the corner of the house. Still no one. He heard voices inside and ran to the car, hoping there was only one policeman.

He jumped into the car and raced away.

Fucking police, he thought. Didn't they know she was just a whore?

CHAPTER 49

I seem to spend all my time in this meeting room, Kubu thought. All we hear is that there's no progress on anything. We'd be better off shaking the bushes to see what slithers out.

He looked around at the group—all good at what they do, all working hard, but seemingly unable to break the cases. He wondered whether they would ever solve any of them—none looked promising at the moment—and the least promising was the murder of his father.

"Where's Detective Khama?" Director Mabaku asked as he walked into the room. "She's always on time. Has anyone heard from her?"

There was silence from around the table.

"She'd better have a good excuse." He sat down and spent a few minutes giving an account of the president's visit to Shoshong. "I think he calmed things down, but unless the jobs appear very quickly, the situation could turn ugly again."

"What about the Chinese?" Edison asked. "Were they there?"

Mabaku nodded. "Including the ambassador. And Shonhu was as thick as thieves with the director of mines as they left. Probably talking about how much money they were going to make now that the American company was out of the running."

"When will the decision be made?" Zanele asked.

"I'm not sure," Mabaku replied. "Probably next week sometime. And given our current lack of progress, they'll probably be uncontested and get permission to expand."

"Can't you go and talk to the Minister of—" Before Zanele could finish her sentence, the door to the meeting room opened, and Samantha walked in with a tall woman who looked very uncomfortable at being there. There was a gasp from Zanele, who was the first to react to the woman's swollen and bruised face.

"I'm sorry I'm late, Director," Samantha said, "but I was helping my friend here. This is Bongi Modongo—she goes by the name Jasmine." She introduced all of the detectives at the table and indicated to Jasmine that she should sit. "Please sit down," she said quietly, and sat down beside her.

"What is she doing here, Detective Khama?" Mabaku was obviously not impressed.

"I've been so frustrated about our lack of progress," Samantha replied, "that I wanted somehow to help things along. The only thing I could think of was the hair Zanele had found in Kunene's car. But we had nothing to match it with. So I decided to see if I could get a hair from Shonhu's head."

She rummaged in her purse and pulled out a plastic bag. "I did it!" she said, pulling a plastic bag from her purse and holding it up. "I got a hair from Shonhu. Two in fact."

"And how did you do that?" Mabaku asked acidly. "And who is this woman?"

"Director, you may not know that I volunteer every weekend at a women's shelter. Most of the women who come in have been assaulted, either by their husbands or boyfriends. But many of the women who come in are prostitutes. The men who pay them think that assault is included in the price."

She paused.

"Of course, the police do nothing about most of these cases. Probably because the police also beat up on their women." She looked around at the men. "Or they think it is a traditional Botswana value," she added sarcastically, "and not worth pursuing."

She put her hand on Jasmine's arm.

"So I called the Mahalapye shelter on Saturday and asked if any of the prostitutes who had come to them for help had ever mentioned having Chinese clients. They told me that Jasmine had come in a few times, badly bruised, complaining about her Chinese lover."

She took a sip of water.

"I called her, and she told me that the Chinaman was, in fact, Shonhu. I explained our situation and asked her to invite him back to try and get some of his hairs. When I promised that the police would take her seriously and that we'd prosecute the man, she agreed.

"One of the Shoshong constables and I waited in the neighbor's house in case there was trouble. When she screamed, the constable rushed over, but it was too late. Jasmine had been punched in the face and kicked, and Shonhu had fled through the back door."

She turned to Mabaku. "I can't tell you how sorry I am that she got hurt. That was never meant to happen. Her injuries are all my fault. We need to make it right for her."

She lifted the plastic bag. "So it was actually Jasmine who got the hairs, not me."

"He could have killed her," Ian said. "Has she seen a doctor?"

Samantha nodded. "I took her to the hospital in Mahalapye. She has a slight scratch on her cornea and those bruises."

Kubu looked at Mabaku, who was clearly furious. Will Samantha still have a job here tomorrow? Kubu wondered.

Mabaku stood up. "The meeting's over," he said. "Zanele, get the hairs from Detective Khama, and see what you can find. Get back to me as soon as possible." He turned to Samantha. "Take this woman to Princess Marina for another check; then come and see me as soon as you get back."

When Mabaku, Samantha, and Jasmine had left, the room buzzed. The general reaction was that Samantha had done a very stupid thing but could possibly have broken the case open.

Kubu stood up. "Don't get too excited," he said. "Hair matches are often not conclusive, so I'm not sure we'll be able to use them anyway."

He walked toward the door, then turned to the group.

"However, as Samantha says, just because Jasmine is a prostitute, that gives no one an excuse for violence. So we can go after Shonhu on an assault charge! Then we can get his fingerprints and search his home. And only then, we may have him."

With that, he turned and walked out.

MABAKU GLARED ACROSS his desk at Samantha. "So what did the doctor say, Detective Khama?"

"She confirmed what the doctor in Mahalapye said. A slight scratch on the cornea of Jasmine's left eye and facial bruising."

"So, what the hell did you think you were doing? This man Shonhu could be a murderer. You could've got that woman killed."

"We weren't getting anywhere, Director," Samantha replied. "You said yourself that they'd get away with it unless something turned up. I made it turn up. Jasmine knew exactly what she was getting into and was prepared to take a chance to get Shonhu charged. So I thought—"

"But you didn't think this *thought* of yours was worth discussing with anyone?"

"When I had the idea, it was already Saturday," Samantha replied.

Mabaku whipped out his phone and held it in front of her face.

"This, Detective Khama, is called a cell phone. I have it with me at all times. I often wish I didn't, but it's part of my job." His voice rose. "In case you hadn't noticed, my job is to direct the CID. That means *I* make the decisions about operations. We don't all just do what we think is a good idea at the time. We work as a team."

Samantha leaned forward and asked, "And if I *had* asked you, Director? Would you have allowed me to do it?"

"No! Absolutely not. This man is probably a trained killer. Putting a civilian woman at risk? She was lucky to get away so lightly. And what if she had been killed? We'd have been taken to the cleaners by the law and by the press. And you'd probably be off the force."

Mabaku battled to get himself under control. "What you did was incredibly stupid. CID work isn't about daredevil antics and flashes of brilliance. It's about working as a team, planning, attention to detail, one step at a time. And you're part of that team."

"But we weren't getting anywhere! We had the tapes, but Shonhu wasn't giving himself away. He's too clever for that. We had to have some physical evidence. And I was the only one who could do that."

Mabaku shook his head. "You're not hearing me, Samantha. Here at the CID, we do things . . . BY . . . THE . . . BOOK." He thumped the table in time with the last three words. "I'm going to let this go because I think you could become a decent detective. But never again. The next time you get a great idea . . ." He held up his cell phone again. "And if you don't, you'll be directing traffic in Ghanzi."

Samantha swallowed an angry retort; she still felt she deserved credit for what could be their first real breakthrough on the case. She started to say so but was interrupted by Mabaku's desk phone ringing. He grabbed it, listened for a moment, and said, "Send her in."

Zanele came in, smiling. "It's a match, Director. I think those hairs are from the same person. I've sent Samantha's samples and

the hair found in the car to Johannesburg, where they have a specialist on this sort of thing, but I'm convinced. I checked all the key
features under a comparison microscope, and they all matched."

Mabaku nodded. "Can we do a DNA match as well?"

Zanele shook her head. "The hair found in Kunene's car didn't
have follicle cells attached."

Mabaku shrugged and turned back to Samantha. "Kubu suggested we use your fiasco to our advantage. Go and lay a charge
against Shonhu for assaulting Jasmine. We'll pull him in on that
count. Then we can take his prints and get as many hairs as we
want. And we'll see if the commissioner can swing us a search warrant for Shonhu's home and office in case he's left something there."

He pulled a folder toward him—a sure signal that the meeting
was at an end.

"And if the fingerprints match," he said as the two women
reached the door, "it won't be long before we'll have Shonhu singing like a bird about his boss, Hong, *and* about the director of the
Department of Mines."

CHAPTER 50

The next morning Mabaku drove to Shoshong once again, this time with Kubu and an interpreter. Kubu knew that Shonhu could handle English, but other senior mine management probably could not, so they'd borrowed Liz Linchwe for the day from Foreign Affairs. She sat quietly in the back, not attempting to join in the discussion between the detectives.

"We should've alerted the border posts," Mabaku said.

"Shonhu's not going anywhere, Director," Kubu replied. "He doesn't know we're onto him yet. Others in the mine management might take off once we arrest him, but there's not much we can do about that—we've got nothing on them—and Shonhu may have been acting on his own, in any case."

"I don't believe that for a minute," Mabaku replied. "Hong is the head man there. He must know what's going on. But I'll settle for Shonhu first, as long as I get Mopati and Hong later. At this point, we say nothing to Hong about anything other than the assault."

That made sense, and Kubu nodded. They passed Tobela, and

he felt a pang. Nothing had been found suggesting that his father had any involvement here. Was he wrong? Was his father's murder just a random act of violence, never to be resolved?

At the turnoff to Konshua mine, a police van with three uniformed constables from Shoshong joined them. Kubu wasn't sure what to expect at the mine, and he wasn't going to take any chances. Also, he wanted the road blocked. No one was leaving the mine without Mabaku's permission.

They drove in a convoy up to the security gate, where a surprised Chinese guard stopped them.

"I am with the Botswana police," Mabaku told him in English, offering identification. "I am here to speak with the manager, Mr. Hong, and some of his staff."

The man said something in Chinese, so Liz rolled down the back window and explained what they needed. There were a few exchanges between them before he returned his attention to Mabaku.

"You wait, please," he said. Returning to his post, he grabbed a phone and had an agitated conversation. Eventually, he hung up and let them through, pointing toward the administration block.

The constables remained at the gate, and the others headed for reception. Hong met them there and carefully checked their identification himself. "Director Mabaku, why this?" He struggled for a few seconds to find the right words, until Liz said something to him in Chinese. He turned to her with relief, and Liz translated for Mabaku. "Mr. Hong asks what this is all about? He is very busy this morning and would have preferred that you phoned for an appointment."

"We want to speak to Mr. Shonhu," Mabaku said.

Hong frowned and responded in Chinese. Liz said, "Mr. Hong asks why you want to see Mr. Shonhu. He says that if it's a matter concerning the mine, he can answer all your questions."

"It is not about the mine. It's a matter involving Mr. Shonhu personally," Kubu interjected.

Hong looked from one to the other. "I call him to my office," he said slowly in English.

"Just take us to him," Mabaku instructed.

Hong hesitated, then nodded and signaled for them to follow. When they reached the office, Shonhu looked up from his laptop with surprise, and there was a quick exchange between him and Hong before Shonhu turned to the detectives. "We go to meeting room," he said. "Then you explain what you want."

You're the one who'll be doing the explaining, Kubu thought, as they all moved to a bigger office.

"We want to speak to Mr. Shonhu alone," said Mabaku, dismissing Hong. The mine manager protested but left when Mabaku insisted.

"Now, what do you want?" Shonhu looked from Kubu to Mabaku and back.

Mabaku let Kubu take the lead. "Mr. Shonhu, would you tell us what you were doing on Sunday afternoon?"

"I was at *kgotla* with Mr. Hong. You saw me there."

"And after that?"

"After that, I came back here."

"Did you meet a woman after the *kgotla*?"

Shonhu shrugged. "Perhaps I saw a woman. What is this about?"

"You met a woman for sex. Is that right?"

Shonhu frowned. "She is my girlfriend."

Kubu consulted his notebook. "She's not your girlfriend. She claims that you pay her to be your woman. But she won't let you tie her to the bed. When she refused again yesterday, you assaulted her, punched her in the face, and kicked her."

"No! Never hit her."

"Let me ask again. Did you hit her when she refused to let you tie her up?"

"No. Never hit anyone."

Kubu took a sheet of paper from a folder. "This is a copy of the doctor's report. She confirms damage to the left eye and bruises on the face. So the woman is not making the story up. She *was* viciously attacked. Also, she gave a very accurate description of you in the complaint. Are you sure you don't want to reconsider your story? It will be best if you admit you did it." He shrugged. "Perhaps something can be worked out."

But Shonhu didn't take the bait. He shook his head firmly. "This is all bullshit! She fell over a table. You waste time on this woman's lies? You have nothing important to do? I'm busy!" He stood up as if to leave.

"Sit down, Mr. Shonhu," Mabaku said. "We're not finished."

For a moment, Shonhu looked as though he would ignore Mabaku, but then he sank back into his seat. "What else?" he demanded.

"Where do you live?"

"At the Chinese village down the road. All the Chinese people live there."

"Take us to your house," Mabaku told him. "We need to search there."

Shonhu jumped up again. "Search my rooms? What for? This is bullshit!"

"Nevertheless, we want to take a look."

"No! It's private. You don't go there."

Mabaku dug in his jacket pocket and passed the search warrant to Shonhu, who glanced at it, then threw it on the floor.

"You don't understand," he said angrily. "This is *Chinese* mine. China is big." He demonstrated with wide-open arms. "Botswana is small." He used thumb and forefinger to show how small. Then he squeezed them together as though crushing an insect. "Don't fuck with me!"

Mabaku jumped to his feet. "Mr. Shonhu, I'm arresting you for the assault of a Motswana woman. We don't allow assault in little Botswana, whatever you do in big China!"

Shonhu ignored him and moved toward the door. Kubu also jumped up, moving surprisingly quickly for his bulk.

"Get out my way, fat man!"

But Kubu stood firm. He was holding his service pistol and was ready to use it. *I'm no match for him in a fight*, he thought. *If he rushes me, I'll have to shoot.*

He felt his heart pounding, but the gun was steady in his hands.

When he saw the gun, Shonhu froze. A moment later, Mabaku had a handcuff on his left wrist and dragged the arm behind his back. The snap of the second cuff closing on his right wrist signaled the end of it. Kubu lowered the gun and let out the breath he hadn't realized he'd been holding.

Mabaku turned to Liz, who had pressed herself against the far wall. This wasn't the usual fare at Foreign Affairs. "Go and call the constables," he said to her. "They can take him to a nice, small Botswana jail."

She nodded and slipped out of the room.

Mabaku focused on Shonhu again. "Now, Mr. Shonhu, you are under arrest for the assault of Bongi Modongo. You don't have to say anything, but anything you do say will be noted and can be used in evidence at your trial."

Shonhu just glared at him.

ONCE THE CONSTABLES had dragged the still protesting Shonhu out of the building, Mabaku asked the shocked receptionist to call Hong. He appeared a few moments later, looking flustered and upset. "Where Shonhu?" he began. "What—"

"Let's go to your office," Mabaku interrupted.

Once there, the director explained that Shonhu was being held for the assault of a woman after the *kgotla*. It was slow going since everything had to go through Liz, but during the conversation,

Hong's loud interjections and head shakings slowly gave way to puzzlement. At last Liz said, "Mr. Hong says that he is very surprised and shocked and doubts that Mr. Shonhu would behave in this way. Nevertheless, he understands the position."

Mabaku nodded. He asked a variety of questions about where Hong was after the *kgotla* and what he'd seen. It turned out that Hong had been talking to the ambassador in private about the mine expansion, and Shonhu had been left on his own to drive the car back.

There was a pause, and then Mabaku said, "Tell Mr. Hong that we're concerned that Mr. Shonhu has behaved badly before with women. Also, ask him if he knows where Mr. Shonhu was on the night of February sixth."

Liz did as he asked, and they could see that Hong was disturbed by this new line of questioning. "Thursday three weeks ago," Mabaku prompted.

Hong sat very still, his hands folded in his lap. At last he shook his head and replied.

"Mr. Hong says that he and Shonhu always play mah-jongg together on Thursday nights," Liz translated. "They haven't missed a game for a long time. So Shonhu was here on the evening of the sixth."

So Mabaku was right, Kubu thought. They *are* in it together. Hong has given Shonhu an alibi, and, no doubt, Shonhu will return the favor for Hong.

Mabaku nodded. "Thank you, Mr. Hong. That is very helpful." He stood up. "We will need to take Mr. Shonhu's computer with us, and we want to search his house." Liz translated, and Hong burst into a stream of Chinese with more head shaking. Mabaku didn't wait for the translation but took out the search warrant and passed it to Liz. "Read it to him in Chinese. Tell him that men who beat up women often leave a trail of pornography sites on the Internet. That is why we want the computer."

Liz did as he requested, and Hong was speechless by the end of it. At last he nodded and led the way back to Shonhu's office. Kubu picked up the laptop and asked Hong how to find Shonhu's house. Hong muttered directions to Liz and offered to send someone with them, but Kubu brushed that aside. "We'll find it," he said. He didn't want Hong's people watching over his shoulder.

As they headed back to the car, Liz whispered to Kubu, "I'm very impressed that the police are going to so much trouble to catch a man because he beat a woman, even if she was a prostitute. I'm glad to be helping you with this."

Kubu just smiled. He suspected that Samantha would have a few things to say about this comment if she were present.

MABAKU COMMANDEERED ONE of the constables and followed Liz's directions to the Chinese compound, not far from the mine. Again they were stopped by a guard at the entrance.

"He says no one can come into the compound here unless they are with one of the residents," Liz told them.

"Tell him to open the gate at once!" Mabaku said angrily. "Who do these people think they are?"

"I told him," Liz replied. "But he says he doesn't care. He says we must go back to mine reception."

"Tell him to open the gate or he'll be arrested!"

The man listened to Liz but then shook his head firmly and started walking away.

"You open it," Mabaku instructed the constable.

The man clambered out and started pushing the gate, but there was a shout, and he turned around to find the guard holding a gun on him. Mabaku was too flabbergasted to react, but Kubu grabbed his service pistol and aimed it at the guard.

"Tell him to drop the gun," he said to Liz. She shouted something in Chinese, and the man looked around. When he saw Kubu's gun, he hesitated. Liz shouted again, and he lowered the pistol.

"Tell him to drop it," Kubu said. A third shout, and the man did as he was told. The constable ran over to him and handcuffed him, none too gently, and scooped up the gun.

"Tell him he's under arrest," Mabaku said. Liz did so, and the man just nodded as they led him to the car and cuffed him. He sat there with his shoulders slumped.

In fact, he turned out to be useful. He knew where Shonhu lived and walked them there from the gate. And he had a master key to let them in. After that they sent him back to the car with the constable, while Kubu, Mabaku, and Liz entered the small prefabricated building.

The house comprised a small lounge with two easy chairs and a table, a bedroom with a single bed and built-in cupboard, a bathroom with a shower and toilet, and a small kitchenette. Probably very luxurious by Chinese standards, Kubu thought as both detectives pulled on latex gloves.

Mabaku made his way to the bathroom. He recognized toothpaste, shampoo, and a packet of condoms, but the small medicine cabinet contained a variety of other items all labeled in Chinese characters. Since he had no idea what might be of interest, he decided to collect everything, packing it all into evidence bags.

Kubu started in the lounge area. He lifted the chair cushions and felt around the edges of the furniture. There was nothing there.

On the table was a cardboard box with the remains of a Chinese meal. Perhaps he doesn't enjoy his own cooking, Kubu thought. There was also a framed picture of a proud young man in military uniform between an older man and woman. Young Shonhu with his parents, Kubu surmised.

There was nothing of interest in the kitchen area either, so he moved to the bedroom and opened the cupboard. The right half was shelves, neatly packed with clothes. He sorted carefully through them but found nothing there either.

The left side was hanging space, containing several jackets and pairs of slacks. Below them was a selection of shoes on a shelf. There was also a pair of boots. Kubu picked them up and turned them over. They were made in China. He took a deep breath. Could these be the boots Zanele was looking for? The boots his father's murderer had been wearing? He put them carefully into a large evidence bag.

He noticed that the shoe shelf was above the floor of the room by about six inches, but the shelves on the right side reached down almost to the floor. That's odd, he thought.

Kubu asked Mabaku to join him. "Why do you think the shoes aren't at floor level?" he asked.

"Maybe something to do with the plumbing? The bathroom's behind that wall."

Kubu took a look in the bathroom. "No, the pipes are on the outside wall," he told Mabaku. He returned to the cupboard and took out the shoes and boots one by one. Then he examined the bottom of the cupboard carefully. It felt a bit loose, but then so did one of the doors and some of the shelves. Poor workmanship had gone into the building of the compound. Kubu pulled the clothes out of the bottom shelf and put them on the bed. Then he examined the screws holding the shoe shelf in place. One was loose to the touch, and the other had a fresh scratch. Mabaku, spotting what Kubu was up to, dug in his jacket and came up with a Leatherman. He passed it to Kubu, who battled to find the screwdriver on it. At last it clicked out. Do-it-yourself was hardly Kubu's thing, but he had no trouble removing the screws, and the shelf lifted out at once.

"Look at this, Director," he said. Mabaku came over and examined the exposed space. It contained several small boxes, a packet of latex gloves, and some clothing, including a ski mask. Kubu picked up the top box—surprisingly heavy—and opened it. It contained a pistol of a make he didn't recognize and several boxes of 9 mm ammunition. Mabaku opened another box and found that it contained a variety of knives. He closed the box with a snap. "I want Zanele and her people to go through everything here. We'll leave the constable here to prevent anyone entering the room. You can sit in the back to keep an eye on the guard until we get him to the Shoshong police station." Kubu nodded as he packed the contents of the compartment into evidence bags and stowed them in a duffel bag.

"A good morning's work, Kubu. We can add possession of a firearm to the charges against Shonhu." Mabaku smiled. "Our Mr. Shonhu is in very, very deep trouble," he added with relish.

CHAPTER 51

On Tuesday afternoon, after Jasmine had formally identified him, Shonhu was driven to Gaborone in the back of a police van. He cursed and struggled as he was taken into the Gaborone police station, resulting in a few bruises from the unsympathetic constables. There, he was charged with the assault. He was fingerprinted, and more hair samples were taken. After that he was left to fume in a cell—a small one—while Forensics worked through all the potential new evidence. Several promising liquids found in his house were sent for analysis. His clothes and shoes were checked for bloodstains, the boxes hidden in the cupboard were examined for fingerprints, and the knives were checked for both. The handgun was of Chinese manufacture, and they fired multiple rounds through it to see if there was a match with any of the bullets recovered from a variety of crimes.

Despite his impatience, Mabaku left Shonhu to stew on Wednesday. The director wanted to gather as much forensic evidence as possible before they confronted him with it. Mabaku hoped that, faced with what they'd found, he'd break down and confess. Then Hong and Mopati would go down too.

By Thursday morning, they thought they had enough. Mabaku and Kubu agreed to meet at nine, plan the interview, and then grill Shonhu. Both felt confident about the outcome. But as they were walking to the interview room, Miriam ran up behind them, calling to the director.

Mabaku stopped. This wasn't at all the way Miriam normally operated. She was organized and efficient, and she knew they had a crucial interview ahead.

"I'm sorry, Director," she told him. "I just had a call from the commissioner. He's been summoned to the president's office, and he wants you there."

"When is this? What's it about?"

"In half an hour, Director. He didn't say what it's about. Just to make sure you were there."

Mabaku swore. He'd been looking forward to seeing Shonhu squirm, but he had no option. "Kubu, I don't want to delay things anymore. Next thing, Shonhu will get out on bail. Grab Edison and take him with you. Best if there are two people, but you handle the interrogation. Shonhu's hired a lawyer now. A good one."

WHEN KUBU ARRIVED at the interview room, he was not pleased to see the lawyer. He'd had dealings before with Jeffrey Davidson, widely regarded as Botswana's best criminal defense attorney. Kubu had seen more than one guilty man walk free after Davidson's intervention. But Zanele's people had been working flat out for the last day and a half. Shonhu and Davidson had some unpleasant surprises ahead.

Kubu gave Davidson a terse greeting and introduced Edison. Then the two detectives seated themselves opposite Shonhu, who was sitting handcuffed and not looking happy. Kubu was pleased about that.

"Mr. Shonhu, this interview is being recorded," he began. "You've already been cautioned, and you have your lawyer present. You've been charged with assault, but we want to interview you about another matter—the murder of Goodman Kunene."

Before he could continue, Davidson held up his hand. "Assistant Superintendent, my client is already charged with a serious crime. I think we need to discuss that before we start on something new."

"There's nothing to talk about. The director gave you a file specifying the details of the crime. You can read the victim's statement. And you can see the pictures of the woman's injuries."

"I've seen the pictures and read the statement from this Jasmine woman. Certainly her face shows signs of bruising. The issue is whether they were caused by my client."

"She identified him, and the police saw his car outside her house!"

"Yes. So she did, but, of course, Mr. Shonhu claims she fell over a coffee table and hit her head. We also want to know why there was a policeman waiting next door. It seems that my client was set up by the police and this woman so that you could get him into custody to grill him about this other matter."

Kubu battled to keep his temper. "Mr. Davidson, if you want to challenge the evidence and make speeches, save it for the trial. We want to interview Mr. Shonhu about the death of Goodman Kunene."

"I certainly will raise it in court. I've asked for an urgent bail hearing, and we'll see what the judge thinks of these goings-on. Mr. Shonhu is a senior executive at the Konshua Mine—hardly a flight risk. In addition, my client claims he was manhandled by the police."

Kubu suppressed his irritation and concentrated on Shonhu. "Do you know Mr. Goodman Kunene?" he asked.

Shonhu glanced at the lawyer, who nodded.

"Yes. He worked in the Department of Mines for the head, Mr. Mopati. But he's dead."

"Did you ever meet him?"

"One time. I went with Mr. Hong to see him about the mine expansion."

"When was that?"

"End of January. I can't remember date."

That was a couple of weeks before Kunene was killed, Kubu thought. "What car did he drive?" he asked.

"Car? I know nothing about his car."

"A sample of your hair was found in his car after Kunene was killed."

"Impossible!" He hesitated, then added, "Maybe from documents I gave him?"

"And your fingerprints were found on the hose used to gas him!"

Davidson held up his hand again. "Do you have a question for my client or are you just listing alleged forensic facts that he's unable to challenge here? If the latter, I will advise him not to answer any further questions."

"All right, I have a question for him," Kubu said. "Where were you on the night of February sixth? The night Mr. Kunene was murdered."

"I play mah-jongg with Mr. Hong. We play every week on Thursday. Sixth of February is Thursday."

"Who won?" Edison asked.

Shonhu paused and looked at him. "I don't remember. It was weeks ago. We play for fun. Not to win." He shrugged.

"So my client has a solid alibi," Davidson commented. "He was in Shoshong. Kunene died here in Gaborone. This is just a fishing trip, gentlemen. Is there anything else?"

"Oh, yes, there's a lot more," said Kubu. "Mr. Shonhu, I'd like you to tell me about the various items we found under the false bottom of your cupboard."

"What items? I know nothing about this."

"Don't waste our time, Shonhu. Among other things, we found knives and a firearm. Do you have a permit for that, Mr. Shonhu?"

Shonhu shrugged. "You make up another story like the assault? I have no gun."

Kubu took out his notebook. "It's a Chinese-manufactured QSZ-92 pistol, common in the Chinese military. Director Mabaku, our interpreter, and myself were all present at the time it was found."

Shonhu shrugged again. "If this true, maybe man who lived there before left it. He is in China now. Perhaps you can ask police in Shanghai to find him."

Kubu glanced at Davidson, who obviously wasn't pleased by this new revelation about the hidden weapons.

"One of the knives we found in the cupboard in your room has traces of blood on it. Whose blood is that, Mr. Shonhu?"

Davidson jumped in. "How would my client know that? He's already said he knows nothing about what you claim you found in his rooms."

Kubu fixed his attention on Shonhu. "So you say that you know nothing about the hidden compartment? That you didn't know it existed?"

"Yes. That's what I said."

"Then how come we found your fingerprints on an item inside that compartment? Did they get there by some form of Chinese magic, perhaps?"

Kubu was delighted to see the smug look drop from Shonhu's face. Yes, you made a mistake, didn't you? he thought. And if you made one mistake, you made others.

"Impossible!"

"The box of latex gloves, Mr. Shonhu. You handled the box to get the gloves out. You shouldn't have put it in the compartment."

Shonhu turned to Davidson. "He's making it up. This isn't true! Why would I have gloves, guns, knives? I'm engineer, not a criminal."

Davidson now looked really sour, and Kubu pressed his advantage.

"Why did you have Rohypnol in your bathroom, Mr. Shonhu? What was that for?"

"What is Rohypnol?" He seemed genuinely puzzled.

"Rohypnol is a drug. Sometimes, it's called a date-rape drug because men who can't get a girl to agree to sex use it to knock them out. But you can use it to knock a man out too. Like Mr. Kunene. Is that what you used it for?"

"Oh," Shonhu said to the lawyer. "He means . . ." and he used a Chinese word. "It's to make me sleep. I don't sleep well."

Kubu shook his head. "Let's go back to the knife. The knife with blood on it that we found in the compartment. Was that the knife you used to attack Mr. Peter Newsom? We're tracing Mr. Newsom and will soon have a sample of his DNA to confirm that. Then we will charge you with that attack also. I'm not surprised you don't sleep well with all the vicious crimes you commit!"

"I don't know this man, Newsom."

"Mr. Shonhu, I think you know that Mr. Newsom represents the American company that is in competition with your mine for the land in Shoshong. He was an obstacle to your plans, wasn't he?"

Shonhu didn't respond.

Kubu leaned forward and raised a finger. "One. We've already charged you for the assault on Mma Jasmine Modongo."

He raised a second finger. "Two. We're also going to charge you with the murder of Goodman Kunene."

He raised a third finger. "And, three, when we have a DNA match from the blood on the knife we found in your room, we'll charge you with the attempted murder of Mr. Peter Newsom."

He leaned back and glared at Shonhu. "Your lawyer will confirm that murder is a capital offense in this country, Mr. Shonhu. That means we execute people in this country for murder. Isn't that so, Mr. Davidson?"

Shonhu looked at his lawyer, who barely nodded.

"I strongly advise you to tell us what happened, Mr. Shonhu," Kubu continued. "Admit what you've done. It will be best for you."

"I want to talk to my client alone," Davidson interjected.

Shonhu ignored him and stared at Kubu, expressionless. "You think you scare me, fat man? I not scared. Nothing you say is true. I admit nothing."

Kubu felt a wave of anger. Shonhu was the murderer! The hair and fingerprint placed him at the scene of Kunene's death, and Rohypnol was found in Kunene's body. And surely the blood on the knife belonged to Newsom. Zanele had confirmed it as human blood. Who else? Unless . . . unless it was his father's blood! Suddenly, he recalled the boots. *Those* Shonhu couldn't deny.

"We found a pair of boots in your cupboard. Chinese make," he said in a voice suddenly hoarse. "Are those yours?"

Shonhu looked surprised. "Yes, the boots are mine. Not allowed to have boots in Botswana?"

"What size are they?"

"Seven."

That was the size Zanele had estimated from the boot prints near where his father had died! Now Kubu was absolutely certain that he was sitting opposite his father's murderer. His anger turned to uncontrollable fury.

"You killed my father!" he yelled at Shonhu. "You killed Wilmon Bengu with that knife, didn't you? Wearing those boots? Admit it! Admit it, damn you!" He leaned across the table to grab Shonhu by the shirt.

"Who is Wilmon Bengu?" Shonhu asked, pulling back, and then everyone was talking at once. The lawyer was objecting; Kubu was shouting about his father; Edison was shouting at Kubu. Then Edison grabbed Kubu by the arm and dragged him from the room, still yelling accusations.

CHAPTER 52

When Mabaku was shown into the office of the president of Botswana, he knew immediately why he was there.

"Director Mabaku," the president said, "may I introduce you to Ambassador Jiu from China. You know the commissioner of police, of course. Please sit down." Mabaku shook hands with the other two men and settled himself in the only remaining chair.

"Ambassador Jiu has come to see me because he says that the police arrested a Chinese national on Tuesday on a trumped-up charge of assault," the president continued.

Mabaku remained impassive and said nothing.

"He also says the police dragged this man from his office in Shoshong. Then they threw him in prison here in Gaborone and treated him badly."

"Does this Chinese national have a name, Mr. President?" Mabaku asked.

"His name is Shonhu Wei Long," the ambassador said. "He is a senior official at the Konshua Mine."

"How does your country treat men who beat up women, Mr. Ambassador?" Mabaku asked angrily.

"In my country, entrapment is not allowed, Director."

"What does that mean?" spluttered the commissioner.

"Apparently, one of your detectives lured Mr. Shonhu into having sex with a prostitute so they could arrest him."

The commissioner turned to Mabaku. "Is that true?"

Mabaku shook his head. "Absolutely not, Commissioner. No policeman or policewoman spoke to or contacted Mr. Shonhu about having sex with any prostitute. Mr. Shonhu has had a longtime association with a prostitute and has assaulted her on several occasions. He visited her on Sunday and assaulted her again. She has a damaged eye and bruises on her face. We arrested him for that."

"But the police were waiting there."

"It is the job of our police to protect all our citizens—and visitors—irrespective of their profession."

"Mr. Ambassador, we will obviously get to the bottom of this. It seems most irregular," the commissioner said. "But let me ask you a question. How was Mr. Shonhu mistreated?"

"Mr. Shonhu says he was beaten."

"Have you seen Mr. Shonhu, Mr. Ambassador?" Mabaku asked.

"Not in person. His lawyer gave me a note he had written."

"Let me tell you, Mr. Ambassador, the Botswana police do *not* mistreat prisoners." Mabaku's anger showed. "If you provide proof that someone mistreated him, we will make sure that person is disciplined appropriately. Do you have such proof?"

The ambassador shook his head.

"How well do you know Mr. Shonhu, Mr. Ambassador?" Mabaku demanded. "Do you normally spend time with men who commit murder? With men who try to kill their competitors? Who incite locals to violence?"

"Director Mabaku," the commissioner intervened, "calm down. Your accusations are very serious. Can you back them up?"

For the next few minutes, Mabaku laid out the evidence that Shonhu murdered Goodman Kunene.

"We've determined that the assistant director of mines, Goodman Kunene, did not commit suicide as reported in the media. He was murdered. He was sedated with a drug called Rohypnol. Then he was left in his own car with the exhaust fumes being fed inside through a hose attached to the muffler. When we searched Shonhu's home, we found Rohypnol." He looked at the ambassador. "What would a mining executive do with something that is regarded as a date-rape drug, Mr. Ambassador? Also, a partial fingerprint on the hose matches Mr. Shonhu's right thumb and a hair found in Mr. Kunene's car matches samples taken from Mr. Shonhu's head."

Mabaku stared at the ambassador. "Would you like me to go on, Mr. Ambassador?"

The ambassador didn't reply.

"And what's more," Mabaku continued, "we may have a second assault charge filed against Shonhu—a knife attack on an American citizen who was representing a mining company in competition with the Konshua Mine. We found a knife at Mr. Shonhu's home with traces of human blood on it. The blood type matches that of the victim, and we're going to do a DNA analysis to confirm it."

The ambassador shook his head.

"I'm not finished, Mr. Ambassador. I want you to know everything about this man who is accusing us of mistreating him. When we searched Mr. Shonhu's rooms, we also found a firearm. Does he have a permit for it, Mr. Ambassador? You can guess the answer. He does not. Why would a mining executive want a firearm in Botswana, where it's illegal to have a handgun?" Mabaku paused, then continued, "I don't think Mr. Shonhu is a mining executive, Mr. Ambassador. I think he's a thug, who's here in Botswana to intimidate people to do what's in the best interests of China."

"If what you say is true, Director Mabaku," the ambassador said quietly, "then Mr. Shonhu must be punished. We will deal with it immediately. He will go before a tribunal in Beijing, and I'm sure if they find he has dishonored his country, then the punishment will be severe."

"Mr. President," the commissioner said, "that is not how we see justice done in Botswana. Mr. Shonhu will have a *fair* trial. If he's found guilty, he'll be punished accordingly. If he is found innocent, he'll go free. But it is important that the trial is held where the alleged crimes took place."

"Director Mabaku," the president said, "you also mentioned earlier that Mr. Shonhu may have incited men to violence. Is that in connection with the riot at the *kgotla* at Shoshong?"

"Mr. President, we've arrested two men on charges of murdering people during the riot. They've told us they were paid to cause trouble. At this time, we've no proof that the mine was involved, but the biggest beneficiary of getting rid of the old chief *is* the mine. It would not surprise me if Mr. Shonhu was involved in that too."

"The mine would never do such a thing," the ambassador said.

"I didn't say the mine, Mr. Ambassador," Mabaku retorted. "I said it wouldn't surprise me if *Mr. Shonhu* was involved."

"The mine manager, Hong Zhi Peng, would have told me about this," the ambassador said. "I spoke to him just this last Sunday."

"Ah, you mention Mr. Hong!" Mabaku interjected. "It would be a surprise if he did not know what Mr. Shonhu was up to, don't you think, Mr. Ambassador?"

He turned to the president. "Mr. President, I would like your permission to take Mr. Hong's passport. He'll be an important witness at Mr. Shonhu's trial, and I regard him as a flight risk. I would also ask you to get the ambassador's word that Mr. Hong will remain in Botswana until we say he can leave."

"Mr. Ambassador?" the president asked.

The ambassador took a moment, then nodded.

"In which case, I think everything is settled," the president said. "Thank you all for coming to this meeting."

Mabaku and the commissioner left together, not saying anything until they had left the building.

"The ambassador is as guilty as the rest of them," Mabaku said. "He didn't even ask why Shonhu would be doing such things. He knows there are rare earths in Shoshong. He knows how important they are for China. That's why he wanted to get Shonhu out of the country. I want Hong's passport for the same reason."

"Wise move," the commissioner responded. "And you're probably right about the ambassador, Jacob. It seems the Chinese want to take over the world."

"And they don't care who they hurt on the way."

WHEN MABAKU RETURNED from the president's office, Edison immediately apprised him of what had happened. Mabaku went straight to Kubu's office and flung open the door. Kubu was sitting at his desk with his head in his hands. He looked up at Mabaku, who was so angry he couldn't speak.

"I don't know what came over me," Kubu said. "One moment everything was going okay, the next I knew with absolute certainty that Shonhu killed my father. He stalked him with one of those knives and stabbed him to death. I just don't know why. Why did he do it? Why?"

Mabaku collapsed into a seat and took a deep breath. "You've damaged our case, Kubu. Shonhu may get away because of what you did. Davidson will have a field day." He sighed. "What made you think Shonhu killed your father?"

"It's obvious," Kubu said slowly. "The tread of his boots matches the pictures of the boot prints Zanele and Samantha found near my father's body. Remember the man seen running from the scene wearing a hood? And the knife had human blood on it. My father's blood . . ."

"Kubu, he had a strong motive to attack Newsom. What possible motive could he have to attack your father?"

"I don't know. I don't know why he did it."

Mabaku sighed again. "Kubu, go home and stay there."

"Am I suspended?"

"Yes! And if I see you anywhere near here until I tell you otherwise, you'll be more than suspended. You'll be fired!"

Kubu just nodded, heaved himself out of the chair, and started collecting his things.

"I'm sorry, Jacob. I'm sorry I let you down. I really am."

Mabaku said nothing more but walked with Kubu to the parking lot and watched as he drove off in his Land Rover. He shook his head. Then he went back into the CID and arranged to resume the aborted interrogation of Shonhu.

THEY RECONVENED AFTER lunch, Mabaku with Edison, and Shonhu with Davidson, who had recovered his earlier confidence.

"Director Mabaku, it seems the whole CID has some personal grudge against my client. Detective Bengu's involvement in the search and arrest on Tuesday voids any evidence you found, in my opinion. If I were you, I would keep only disinterested detectives on the case. If you have any."

"Don't tell me how to run my department, Davidson," Mabaku said through clenched teeth. "And I won't tell you how to run your law practice." He turned to Shonhu. "For the record, I want your answers to the following questions. Were you involved in the murder of Wilmon Bengu?"

Shonhu shook his head.

"Say it!"

"No!"

"Where were you on the first of February?"

"I was at the mine, like always."

"Did you see anyone that night?"

Shonhu took a few moments to reply. "Was Saturday. I don't think so, but it was weeks ago!"

"Did you attack Peter Newsom with a knife?"

"No."

"Where were you on the night of the twelfth of February?"

"At the mine compound. Alone, I think."

"Your fingerprints are on the hose that was used to get the gas into Kunene's car. How do you explain that?"

"I don't believe it."

"Our forensic experts have confirmed it!"

Shonhu shrugged and said nothing.

And so it went for over an hour. Mabaku whipped between cases, throwing evidence at Shonhu, asking the same questions different ways, looking for a slip as the trap of tiredness closed. But he got nothing.

Eventually, Davidson intervened. "You're asking my client the same things, Director Mabaku, and he's answered all of them. Do you have any witnesses to any of these alleged crimes?" He paused, and when Mabaku said nothing, he continued, "No, I didn't think so. I think this is enough for today, don't you?"

Mabaku gave a curt nod and yelled for the guard to take Shonhu back to his cell. He left the interview room angry and frustrated. He'd hoped that Shonhu would break down, and then they'd have enough to go after Mopati, but Shonhu had persisted in denying everything. Not only that, Davidson might well be right: Kubu might indeed have compromised the case. How could a day that had started out so promising end in such a mess?

Mabaku strode back to his office, slamming doors on the way. Nailing Shonhu was something, but he really wanted to get Mopati.

Anyone in government who was corrupt deserved to be put behind bars for a very long time.

He went to the window and gazed out, not even seeing the baboons playing on the cars below. After a few minutes, he realized he had only one chance left. Shonhu's boss, Hong, had lied when giving Shonhu an alibi. They should bring him in and charge him as well. Maybe something would break.

CHAPTER 53

"Commissioner, I have to alert you to the fact that I have just ordered that the manager of the Konshua Mine in Shoshong—a
Mr. Hong—be driven to Gaborone to answer questions about the
murder of Goodman Kunene, the assistant director of mines."
There was distinct satisfaction in Mabaku's voice. "He's lied about
where he was and what he was doing on the night Kunene was murdered. We believe that he accompanied Shonhu to Gaborone and
helped him in asphyxiating Kunene in his car. He's on his way to
Gaborone, as we speak, and I'll interview him this afternoon.
Perhaps you should let the president's office and Ambassador Jiu
know."

"Goddammit, Jacob. Are you trying to cause an international
incident?"

"No, Commissioner. I think he's involved, so I need to talk to
him on the record."

Mabaku listened to a prolonged silence. "You really think he's
involved? This isn't another one of Kubu's infamous fishing trips."

"I'm sure he's involved, Commissioner. And Kubu is no longer on the case. In fact, I have suspended him." Mabaku went on to explain what happened during the Shonhu interview. "As much as he brings to our investigations, in this case he's a liability. He thinks everyone and everything is related to the murder of his father. I can't have him screwing things up. I just hope he hasn't already done that."

"All right. Go ahead, but let me know what's happened before you go home this evening."

MABAKU OPENED THE door to the interrogation room and was met with a barrage of Chinese.

"Mr. Hong, please sit down," Mabaku said. "This is Detective Banda, and you've met our interpreter, Liz Linchwe. You can voice any objections in a minute." He turned to Liz. "Please tell him that this is a formal interview; it will be recorded, and anything he says can be used in a court. Also tell him he can have an attorney present, if he wants one."

Liz and Hong went back and forth for several minutes. Then Liz turned to Mabaku. "Mr. Hong says he has done nothing wrong, so he does not need an attorney."

Mabaku nodded and indicated that everyone should sit down. "Please tell Mr. Hong that I'm turning on the recorder."

Liz did that, and Hong just nodded.

"Mr. Hong, as you know we arrested Mr. Shonhu on Tuesday on a charge of assault."

Hong nodded, after Liz translated.

"He says it is a terrible thing," Liz said after Hong's response.

"Not as terrible as the next charge we've laid against him."

Hong frowned after the translation.

"He is now also charged with the murder of Goodman Kunene . . ."

Hong jumped to his feet. "Not true! Shonhu with me when Kunene died."

"Sit down!" Mabaku snapped. "So you understand English! That's what you told us on Tuesday, but it was a lie."

Hong opened his mouth to object, but Mabaku told him to shut up and listen.

"We found a hair in Kunene's car that came from a Chinese head," Mabaku continued, stretching the truth a little. "After we arrested Mr. Shonhu, we were able to compare one of his hairs with the one we found. They matched. We also found a partial fingerprint—actually a thumbprint—on the hose going into Kunene's car. Yesterday our forensic experts confirmed that it matched Mr. Shonhu's right thumb. We also found the same drug in Mr. Shonhu's home that was used to knock Kunene out. So we have proof that he murdered Kunene. We also have a motive. It turns out that Kunene was being paid for information by a Mr. Newsom, whom I'm sure you know. He represents the other company interested in getting a mining lease. Getting rid of Kunene would greatly help your chances of winning. And we have the word of the director of mines, Mr. Mopati, that Kunene was opposed to you getting the new lease."

He took a drink of water while Liz translated.

"So, you're here, Mr. Hong, because I'm going to arrest *you* too—as an accessory to murder."

"I don't understand," Hong said.

Mobaku turned to the interpreter. "Explain it to him."

There was a prolonged exchange between the two, with Hong's voice getting louder and louder.

Eventually, Hong turned back to Mabaku. "Not true."

"He says he had nothing to do with Kunene's murder," Liz said.

"But you lied about playing mah-jongg with Mr. Shonhu on the night Kunene was murdered. So all we can do is assume that you helped him. The two of you drove to Gaborone. You followed Kunene and Mr. Shonhu down near the yacht club. You helped Mr. Shonhu set up the car to look like suicide. Then the two of you drove back to Shoshong. And it was you who lied to the police."

He stood up. "Mr. Hong, I'm arresting you as an accessory in the murder of Mr. Goodman Kunene." He pulled out a pair of handcuffs.

Hong shot to his feet as Liz translated. "Not true. Not true." He turned to Liz and spoke.

"He says he didn't know Mr. Shonhu killed Kunene. That he had nothing to do with it."

"Tell him I'm going to repeat the question I asked on Tuesday. Where were you on the night Mr. Kunene died?"

Liz translated and Hong replied.

"He says he was in Shoshong."

"Playing mah-jongg with yourself?" Edison interjected.

Hong spoke to Liz. "He says he was by himself. He didn't know where Mr. Shonhu was. He says Mr. Shonhu asked him to say he was in Shoshong."

Mabaku stared at him. "I don't believe you."

"He says he was reading a book."

Mabaku sat down and waved at Hong to do the same.

"Mr. Hong, let me tell you your options. If you tell me the truth about what happened on the night Kunene died, we will reconsider charging you as an accessory to murder. If you continue to lie, we will charge you, and we will win, and you will spend many years in a Botswana jail." He flipped through the pages of his notebook. "But I should also tell you that I had a meeting with Ambassador Jiu yesterday. He wants to send you back to China right away. I assume you will have to answer to somebody there about how you have failed."

Liz translated, and Hong jumped up again. In an agitated voice, he spoke to Liz.

"He says you must not send him back. He's afraid for his life if you do."

"Then tell us what really happened."

Hong sat down, shoulders slumped, and admitted that Shonhu

had asked him to drive him to Gaborone on the night Kunene died.

"What was Mr. Shonhu doing in Gaborone?" Mabaku asked.

When Liz translated, Hong shook his head. "He doesn't know," Liz said. "Shonhu told him that it was important business."

"Why did you have to go with him?" Mabaku waited for the translation.

"Mr. Hong says Shonhu said he needed Mr. Hong's help. That he must come."

"Exactly where did you go?"

Hong shook his head when Liz translated, and then he spoke for some time.

"He says he doesn't know. Shonhu directed him, and they went into a residential area. Then Shonhu told him to stop, and he got out carrying a bag. Mr. Hong doesn't know what was in it. Then Shonhu told him how to get back to the main road and told him to drive to Game City shopping mall and wait there until he called."

"What happened after that?"

Again there was an exchange in Chinese. At last Liz said, "He had a long wait. More than an hour. Then Shonhu phoned and told him to drive south on the main road and meet him at the turnoff to the yacht club. Mr. Hong picked him up there, and they drove back to Shoshong. It was very late when they got back."

Mabaku thought about it. It added up, but surely Hong knew what was going on?

"When you heard that Kunene had died that night, didn't you think there could be a connection? Didn't you ask? After all, you're his boss."

Liz translated, and Hong shook his head. After a few moments, he spoke, glancing around fearfully.

"He says he is head of the mine, but Shonhu is the boss. He is with Chinese intelligence. He says when they discovered rare earths, suddenly everything changed. He wasn't talking to Shanghai anymore; he was getting orders from Beijing. And they sent Shonhu to make sure that they got control of the new prospect—whatever that took. He knew Shonhu may have been involved in Kunene's death but couldn't ask."

"Rare earths?" Mabaku asked. "Nobody has said anything about rare earths. Your application was to mine uranium, not rare earths."

Liz translated, and Hong looked as though he was going to collapse.

"He says they couldn't say anything about rare earths. The Chinese government didn't want anybody to know. Particularly the Americans. Rare earths are very important for Chinese security."

"And how were you going to get them out of the country?" Edison asked.

"He says Mr. Shonhu has a friend in the Department of Mines. He would certify that what was leaving the country was uranium. Nothing would be said about rare earths. They would just be shipped to China with the uranium. Then they would be sold as Chinese."

"Another fucking corrupt official! We'll get him too!" Edison could see that Mabaku was furious. "Mr. Hong, I don't believe a word you are saying. You're the manager of the mine. Mr. Shonhu would do nothing without you telling him." He turned to Edison. "Detective Banda, please go and phone the Chinese ambassador and tell him to come and take this bag of shit away. He must be out of the country by tomorrow night."

When Liz translated, Hong jumped up. "No, no. Please. I die if I go back."

"I couldn't care if they stick a pole through you and roast you over a fire. You lied to me, and now you are going to pay." Mabaku stood up, while Liz translated.

Hong fell to the floor. "Please. Please. Please. I tell truth."

"It's too late!" With that, Mabaku turned and left, followed by Edison and Liz.

When they were outside, Liz said, "Director Mabaku, sir. You won't really let the ambassador send him back to China, will you? They'll kill him."

"Ms. Linchwe," Mabaku replied with a grin, "of course, I'm not going to send him back. I just want him to think I will. We'll let him stew for a few hours. Then we'll talk to him again. I think we'll get what we need."

IT WAS FIVE hours later by the time Mabaku, Edison, and Liz returned to the room in which Hong had been confined.

"I'm sorry to keep you waiting, Mr. Hong. I had to make special arrangements with Immigration to let you out of the country."

"No! No! I tell everything."

After another twenty minutes of cross-examination, Mabaku was convinced that Hong did not, in fact, know that Shonhu had gone to Gaborone to kill Kunene. Hong had driven the car when Shonhu was spiking Kunene's drinks, but he wasn't involved in the killing.

"So, why did Mr. Shonhu want to kill Mr. Kunene anyway?" Mabaku asked.

"Mr. Hong says that Kunene was corrupt," Liz translated. "He was taking money from the Americans, and he was spying on the director of mines, Mr. Mopati. He was making it difficult for the Chinese to win the new mine."

"I don't understand," Mabaku said. "Are you saying that Kunene was paying Mopati to fix the bidding in favor of the Americans?"

Hong shook his head and spoke rapidly to Liz.

"He says if you promise that the ambassador does not send him back to China, he will tell you the truth."

"Tell him I know what happened, but I want to hear it from him."

Hong clutched his head, then spoke rapidly. Liz translated.

"He says that Kunene had found out that the mine was paying

Mopati to fix the bidding. They didn't think anyone would find out because they were very careful . . ."

"Tell him we know Mopati was paid from Shanghai into a bank account in Nigeria. This is not difficult to find out."

When Liz translated, Hong's face was pure astonishment. "You know this? You find out?"

Mabaku nodded. "The Botswana police are very good."

Hong just shook his head.

"Here's what I have to offer, Mr. Hong," Mabaku said. "You will testify that the Konshua Mine bribed the director of mines, Mr. Mopati, to fix the bidding process so that the Konshua Mine would be able to expand. You will provide any evidence that you can to support that. In return, we will drop the charge of accessory to murder and charge you instead with corruption and obstructing justice. You will probably only spend four or five years in a Botswana jail, if convicted. After that, I will ask Immigration to allow you to stay in Botswana."

When Liz finished translating, Hong blabbered, "Yes, I do. Thank you. Thank you."

Mabaku nodded at Edison. "Take care of the details. I don't want him out on bail."

WHEN HE RETURNED to his office, Mabaku looked out the window at Kgale Hill. *Things have turned out better than I imagined they would*, he thought. *And best of all, I now can go after the director of mines. Little does he know what's ahead of him.*

He picked up his phone and dialed a familiar number. "Kubu," he said, "I have some good news for you."

PART 8

CHAPTER 54

"I'm looking for Lamado Emefiele," Samantha said as the door to the small house opened.

A shirtless man, wearing shorts and sandals, looked her up and down. "Well now. And who are you?"

"Detective Khama, Botswana Police." She held out her ID. "Do you know where he is?"

He broke into a smile. "Come in. Would you like a cup of tea— or a beer?"

"No, thank you," she snapped. "Do you know where I can find Lamado Emefiele?"

"And what do you want with him—if you find him?"

Samantha glared at him. "Tell him I may be able to work out a deal for him." She pulled out a card and gave it to him. "Ask him to call me, if he's interested." She turned to leave.

"Wait a moment."

She stopped and turned.

"What sort of deal?"

"We know that he's been importing goods from Nigeria without a permit and then selling them without being registered for tax. The Revenue Service is looking into prosecuting him on various related charges."

"So what's the deal? I will give him your message."

"I can only negotiate with Rra Emefiele in person."

The man looked around anxiously.

"I am Emefiele! What do you want?"

"Rra Emefiele, you're in a lot of trouble. I may be able to help you."

"How?"

Samantha quickly explained that she was looking for the man who had paid the two men to disrupt the *kgotla*. "They tell us that the man was foreign. You're Nigerian, right?"

He nodded. "But what does that prove?" he asked.

"I'm not here to prove that you did it," she said. "I'm here to find out who *paid* you to do it. If you can tell me that, we'll ask the revenue service to give you a warning rather than prosecute you."

"How do I know that you're not bullshitting me?"

"You're probably not used to trusting people, but you're going to have to trust me. If I walk away from here with nothing, I can't help you. You probably saw that one of your compatriots was recently sent to jail for six years for tax evasion."

The man stared at her for what seemed like minutes.

"I think you *are* bullshitting me. I don't know what you're talking about. Good-bye."

He shut the door in Samantha's face.

"DID YOU GET a good shot?" Samantha asked Edison when she returned to her car.

Edison nodded. "Good enough for anyone to recognize, anyway," he said as he took the long lens off the camera body. "That's the third today. Let's drop them off and pick up the prints after lunch."

After a leisurely meal of a hamburger and fries, they returned to their offices at Millennium Park and picked up an envelope at Reception. The prints inside were very sharp—three of Emefiele, and two each of the other two men they'd visited, both from South Africa.

"Okay," Samantha said. "Let's see if our men recognize any of these."

They showed the first suspect the photos, and he immediately pointed to Emefiele. "He's the guy that paid us," he said. "Where's he from?"

"Nigeria," Samantha answered as she walked out of the cell.

A few minutes later, the second suspect corroborated what the first had said.

"I don't believe it," Samantha said. "All that work, and we've finally got something. I think it's time to visit Rra Emefiele again."

"HELLO, RRA EMEFIELE."

"I told you I wasn't interested!"

"Well, now you have no choice! I'm arresting you on charges of incitement to violence and of disturbing the peace. Edison, please handcuff him."

"What do you mean? I've done nothing. I want to talk to my lawyer."

"Save your breath," Edison said. "Two men independently identified you as paying them to cause problems at a *kgotla* in Shoshong. You can call your lawyer after we've booked you."

"And then we'll let the revenue service know that we have you," Samantha interjected. "They're going to be pleased."

"I've done nothing, and you know it. I'll be back here by evening."

"Dream on," Samantha said. "You're going down for a long time now." She turned and walked away, leaving Edison to drag Emefiele to the car.

"KUBU? THIS IS Director Mabaku."

"Yes, sir. What can I do for you?"

"I'm lifting your suspension for the rest of today only. I want you to come in and interrogate a Nigerian Samantha located. He apparently was the man who paid our suspects to cause troubles at the *kgotla*. They've identified him from photos. I want you to have them identify him in a lineup. If they both ID him, interview him and find out who paid him, when, how much, and so on. This could strengthen our case against Shonhu, because I'm sure he was behind it."

"Yes, Director. I'll come in right away."

"Two things, Kubu. First, remember this has *nothing* to do with your father's murder. This is about the murders at the *kgotla*. Second, Samantha has some dirt on the man that you may be able to use to persuade him to tell us what happened."

"Yes, Director," Kubu said. "I promise I'll behave."

"MR. EMEFIELE. MY COLLEAGUE, Detective Khama, has already told you how much trouble you're in. Unfortunately, she's an inexperienced detective and missed the most important charge."

Emefiele frowned.

"If you don't tell me who paid you to get those two men to stir things up at the *kgotla*," Kubu continued, "I have to assume that *you* wanted to cause the trouble in Shoshong. If that's the case, I have to charge you as an accessory to the murder of two policemen, of the chief, and two elders. That can carry a very long sentence, Mr. Emefiele. Much longer than you intended to stay in Botswana, I'm sure."

"I don't know anything about Shoshong," Emefiele said. "I don't know what you're talking about."

"Mr. Emefiele. Where were you on the afternoon of Saturday, February fifteenth?"

Emefiele smiled. "I was in Johannesburg. You can check my passport. I couldn't have been at Shoshong as well."

Kubu nodded. "What do you say to the fact that two of our suspects identified you as being the man who paid them to cause trouble?"

"They're lying!"

"I don't think so. They're willing to testify that it was you."

"You've made some sort of deal with them to set me up."

"No, Mr. Emefiele. They are being charged with murder no matter what they say about you." Kubu stood up and turned to Samantha. "Go and charge him as an accessory to the murder of those who died at the *kgotla*."

"Yes, sir!" Samantha jumped up eagerly.

"Wait!"

Kubu and Samantha both turned back.

"A man gave me money to get the men to cause trouble."

"His name?" Kubu asked.

"I never asked for it. He came to my place, just like you did." He pointed at Samantha. "Told me what he wanted and left."

"How much did he give you?" Samantha asked.

Emefiele hesitated. "Five thousand pula," he said.

"Nice profit, seeing as you only gave the men a thousand each," Samantha said.

"What did he look like?" Kubu asked.

Emefiele shrugged his shoulders. "Black man. A Motswana, I think. Maybe thirty years old. I don't know."

"You're sure he didn't give a name?" Kubu demanded.

"I'm sure."

"What sort of car did he drive?" Samantha asked.

Emefiele was silent for a few moments. "A silver car. A Toyota, I think."

"Julius!" The name popped out of their mouths at the same time.

"Samantha, go and get Julius's photo," Kubu said eagerly. "And the photos of another four or five men about the same age. Let's see if he can pick him out."

"WE'VE GOT HIM!" Kubu could barely contain his excitement as Emefiele pointed to the photo of the late chief's son. "Julius. I never trusted him."

He turned to Emefiele. "Thank you. We'll speak to the revenue service and ask them to drop their charges." He walked to the door. "Constable," he said to the man standing quietly in the corner. "Constable, take this man to the cells and book him as an accessory to murder."

Emefiele jumped up. "You promised—"

"I promised to speak to the revenue service about your tax problems. That's all," Samantha chimed in. "You helped get several people killed. That's what we're charging you for."

"But I didn't hurt anyone." Emefiele had started to whine. "This Julius must have killed the men. I sold him a gun too!"

There was silence in the room.

"Say that again," Kubu said quietly.

"I said that the man who paid me also bought a gun. A .22 handgun."

"Oh my God!" Samantha said. "Julius murdered his own father!"

CHAPTER 55

When the police came for him on Friday afternoon, Julius was meeting with two of his friends at his house. They were finalizing their strategy for the election—now only a week away—that would make Julius chief. The elders were scared; they knew there would be more trouble if Julius wasn't elected and that the trouble would be directed at them. So Julius had the numbers he needed, and if it was more because of fear than respect, he had no problem with that.

But Julius was worried. The papers were full of the story of Shonhu's arrest, and Hong hadn't returned his calls. When he'd phoned that morning, he'd been put through to someone he didn't know, who said that Mr. Hong would be away for some time. What if Hong started talking about their cozy deal?

He tried to relax and concentrate on the discussion. After all, why would Hong bring that issue up? It looked like he had much bigger problems.

"*Kgosi*," one of the friends called out. "There're some people driving in here." Julius went to the window to take a look.

Two vehicles had pulled into the driveway: a police van and an unmarked car. Julius felt a flush of panic, but it was too late to run; he'd have to wait and see what it was about.

He opened the front door and waited for the policemen. Three uniformed constables climbed out of the van, and the man getting out of the car was the police station commander. He'd always been a supporter of the old chief and never shown Julius the respect that he felt was his due. At least the fat man from Gaborone isn't with them, Julius thought. Who would've thought that the senile old fool in Mochudi would have a sharp detective for a son?

The station commander offered no greeting. "Julius Koma, I have here a warrant for your arrest for the murder of Rra Rankoromane Koma." He paused and then added caustically, "Your *father*." Julius was too shocked to respond. He saw the disgust in the man's face and the scorn in his eyes.

"You don't have to say anything, but anything you say will be noted and may be used at your trial. Do you have anything to say?"

Julius shook his head, still speechless.

"No, I didn't think you would. You must come with us. You'll be taken to Gaborone. You better get what you'll need."

The station commander followed him into the house with one of the constables. The others remained outside.

"You must go," he said to the two men gawking at their leader. "At once. I have a search warrant for the house, and I'm to secure it until the forensics people arrive." They gathered up their belongings and headed for the door.

"Wait!" Julius called after them. "I need a good lawyer. They're trying to frame me! It's all a lie. Do you understand? Please!" Neither looked back. A few minutes later when Julius was brought out in handcuffs and roughly shoved into the back of the waiting police van, there was no sign of either of them.

• • •

AN HOUR LATER, Zanele arrived with the forensics team. She knew the responsibility was on her to get the evidence required to convict Julius. So far he had motive and opportunity, but they needed a clear connection to the murder. She intended to find it.

Her team put on their overalls, gloves, and booties, and spread out, doing their work efficiently. She headed straight for the main bedroom, carrying a close-up that Mabaku had given her of Julius at the *kgotla*. He was wearing a gray sports coat and charcoal pants. It only took her a few minutes to find the jacket, and she carefully took it off its coat hanger. She felt through the pockets—they were empty—but the lining on the right-hand one felt different, coarser. She paused, then turned it inside out and checked the stitching. It was obvious that the pocket had been replaced. The color had been well matched, but the material was of a different quality. She smiled. "You thought that was good enough, Julius," she said aloud. "Just replace the pocket. Too stingy to throw away a nice jacket." She knew that jacket would take Julius a step nearer to the gallows. She folded it neatly and zipped it into an evidence bag.

There were several pairs of jeans and a variety of belts. One of the brown belts had a darker rust stain on the rough inside of the leather. She collected it, but at first, thought nothing of it. She knew Julius's clothes would have bloodstains. He'd lifted his dead or dying father. But then she rechecked the picture. It was hard to be sure, but it appeared that Julius was wearing a black belt with his gray pants at the *kgotla*. Maybe the stain wasn't blood? But then she came across a black zip-up rain jacket with a hood. She bagged that also. Maybe that stain was blood after all. Just not Chief Koma's blood.

She stood back from the cupboard and thought it through. Maybe Julius was careless about his clothes or maybe he was just careless, period. Careless and stingy. And in that case, there might be more to find. She felt a touch of excitement as she returned to her careful search, and she was rewarded by the discovery of a small safe fixed to the back wall. She looked at it for a few seconds, wondering where she might find the key. They could get a locksmith, but somehow she didn't think Julius would have hidden the key well. And she didn't think he'd carry it with him.

It was Meshak, one of her men, who found it in a desk drawer under some papers.

"A burglar would never look in the desk drawer," she said sarcastically. "I don't know why he bothered with a safe at all." She shook her head. "Bring the camera and video me opening it, Meshak."

The first thing she saw when she opened the safe was the revolver. She reached in carefully and used one finger to lift it out by the trigger guard. She took a closer look. "The serial number's been filed off, but that's not going to make any difference. Can you believe he was stupid enough to keep it?" Meshak shook his head, but in his experience most criminals were stupid, and the smarter they thought they were, the stupider they turned out to be. "He'll probably have his prints on it too," Zanele continued. Before she passed the gun to Meshak, she checked the cylinder. "Be careful. It's loaded." Meshak took it gingerly.

"Don't forget the ammunition," Zanele added. She lifted a box of .22 ammunition out of the safe by its corners and passed it to Meshak for fingerprinting.

Neither of them had any doubt that they'd found the gun that had been used to kill Chief Koma at the *kgotla*.

CHAPTER 56

When Kubu left home on Monday morning, he was feeling cheerful. He'd enjoyed a good breakfast of eggs, toast, and coffee and had pleased Joy with his relatively enthusiastic eating. And he was looking forward to the interview with Julius. Mabaku had been delighted with the evidence from the Nigerian and immediately ordered the arrest of Julius, whom they left in a cell until Monday morning while Zanele saw what she could do to link him to the revolver. Mabaku's enthusiasm had even run to lifting Kubu's suspension, and the two of them had agreed to meet at eight a.m. to plan the interrogation; Mabaku would lead, and Kubu would back him up.

Also, at last Kubu felt he was coming to terms with his father's murder. He remained convinced that it was Shonhu who had plunged a knife into his father's chest. However, Shonhu refused to say anything about the murders, so they might never know the true reason why. Whether his silence was due to loyalty to his masters in Beijing or fear of them, they didn't know. When told of Hong's betrayal, Shonhu had sneered, "He's scared to go home.

He'll say anything." No doubt Davidson would try to exploit that at the trial, but it wouldn't wash. There was no doubt that Shonhu would be convicted of the Kunene murder. And if they never proved the Wilmon case, well, a man can only be executed once.

However, when Kubu reached Mabaku's office, he knew at once that something was wrong. Mabaku returned his greeting and invited him to take a seat, then sat for a few moments saying nothing. When he did speak, the tone was somber.

"Kubu, something came up over the weekend. Zanele worked like a dog as usual, and she played a hunch that turned out to be right."

This sounded like good news, so Kubu nodded and waited for the director to continue.

"She has Julius's prints on the gun and ammunition, and the jacket he saved from the *kgotla* is positive for powder residue. He shot his father with that gun in the jacket pocket. No doubt." He paused. "But she found something else. There was blood on one of his belts. She got the South Africans to do a rush job over the weekend. It was your father's blood." Mabaku paused again and waited for that to sink in. "She also found a hooded rain jacket. And Chinese boots, size seven."

Suddenly, it all seemed so obvious to Kubu. He should've known that Julius had murdered his father. Julius had admitted to visiting Wilmon, and they'd quarreled over some sort of land issue, and Julius was, after all, the only connection to the mine.

Kubu took a deep breath. There was still one huge question.

"Why?"

Mabaku shook his head. "I don't know, and we may never know unless Julius tells us. We can't make a case on the bloodstain alone."

Kubu started to protest, but Mabaku held up his hand. "We've got him for his father's murder. He may well come clean. I'll interview him with Samantha; she can link in the Nigerian."

Kubu swallowed a wave of resentment. Samantha replacing him! But Mabaku was right. He'd been right from the beginning, and the proof was in the outburst of last Thursday. In his father's case, he couldn't rise above his emotional involvement. "Yes, Director, I understand."

Mabaku nodded. "Good. I know how hard this is for you, Kubu, and I can't promise success, but I can promise we'll try our very best." Uncharacteristically, he rose and stuck out his hand. Kubu shook it and said, "Thank you, Jacob. You'll let me know as soon as you have something?"

"I can do better than that. We'll use the new interview room with the one-way glass. I want you to watch. You may be able to pick up something we miss."

Kubu thought that unlikely; that wasn't the reason Mabaku was doing this. "Thank you, Jacob," he said again. Mabaku nodded.

After Kubu had left, Mabaku asked Miriam to have Samantha come and see him so he could brief her. While he was waiting for her, he made a call to Ian MacGregor.

KUBU SAT IN the observation room facing the one-way glass panel looking into the interview room itself. It was like a vacant stage waiting for the play to begin and Kubu was the audience of one. But this play wouldn't have a happy ending. Maybe it wouldn't have an ending at all. The tension he thought he'd laid to rest had returned. He wanted to grab Julius and beat the truth out of him.

The door opened, and he looked around to see Ian MacGregor. The Scotsman smiled. "Fancy meeting you here, Kubu. How're you doing?"

"Ian! What brings you here?"

"You don't think I'm interested?"

"You have nothing to do today? No bodies?"

"They'll wait. They're not going anywhere." Ian paused. "The director thought you might appreciate someone to keep you company."

Kubu nodded. "Thanks, Ian. Bring any Scotch?"

Ian laughed. "For Julius's wake? Maybe a bit premature."

"Yes, maybe."

At that moment, the door of the interview room opened, and a handcuffed Julius was pushed in. There was another man with him whom Kubu didn't recognize, a lawyer presumably. Julius said something, but Kubu couldn't hear what. The room was sound-proof too. They'd have to wait until the recording started for the sound to be piped in.

Shortly afterward, Mabaku and Samantha came in, and the sound was switched on. Kubu and Ian concentrated on the pro-ceedings, staring through the one-way glass.

"Rra Koma," Mabaku began, "this interview is being recorded. You have been charged with the murder of Rra Rankoromane Koma, chief in Shoshong. You have been apprised of your rights. Do you have anything to say?"

"I certainly do! This is all a setup. You're trying to frame me for this so that the mine expansion is blocked. It's outrageous!"

Mabaku didn't react. "Let's go back a bit. Do you know a La-mado Emefiele?"

Julius shook his head, but Mabaku insisted on a formal answer. "No. I do not."

"He's a Nigerian. Maybe you didn't know his name. His address is . . ." Mabaku consulted his notes and read it out. Julius shook his head again.

"That's strange," Samantha put in. "He certainly recognized you. Picked you out from a selection of photographs with no trouble."

Julius shrugged.

"Do you own a gun?" Mabaku asked.

Julius hesitated and whispered to his lawyer. Kubu leaned for-ward, but of course that didn't help to hear. "Yes," he said at last.

"So," Mabaku commented. "I asked you that question once be-fore, and you lied to me."

"I don't have a permit for it. I wanted it in a hurry. There were threats made on my life, so I bought it illegally."

"You are admitting obtaining and keeping an illegal firearm?"

"Yes. I was scared. People had threatened to kill me!"

"And who were these people?"

"I'm sure it was the people opposed to the mine expansion. They knew I wanted what was best for Shoshong, but they had their own interests to serve."

"Did you report this to the police?"

"No. They wouldn't have done anything."

"So you took matters into your own hands. Did you ever fire this gun? At a shooting range, for example?"

"No."

"Did you carry it with you?"

"No."

"So you didn't feel that threatened."

"I thought they would come for me at home!"

"The mysterious 'they.' Where did you obtain this firearm?"

"I bought it from that man—Emfeely, whatever his name is."

"So you lied about that too."

"I didn't remember his name. I'm being honest with you here."

"Honest?" Mabaku said. "Hardly."

Kubu frowned with frustration. "He should be much more aggressive. He's letting him squirm out of it."

Ian shook his head. "Mabaku knows what he's doing, Kubu. Give him time. He's building a trap."

Yes, Kubu thought. He's already caught him in a lie. But I want it done. Over with. He just nodded in response to Ian's comment and shut up. He realized he'd missed Mabaku's next question.

"No!" Julius said. "I did not pay him to cause trouble at the *kgotla*. That's a lie! I paid him for the gun and nothing else."

"Don't you think it's odd that the two men Emefiele approached—and paid a thousand pula each—both identified him? Why would they lie about it?" Samantha chipped in.

"Maybe someone else paid him to do that. The mine people for example. You've arrested Hong and Shonhu for what they did to Kunene. Why not bribe someone to cause trouble also? Why don't you ask them?"

"He's clever," Kubu said. "He admits the things he knows they can prove and denies everything else." Ian nodded but didn't comment.

Mabaku changed tack. "How much did the mine people pay you for your *consulting*? For convincing your father?"

"They paid me for advice! I didn't bribe anyone. My father didn't listen to me anyway."

"Let's get back to the gun. Did you have it at the *kgotla*? In case you were attacked?"

"No."

"You're lying again. You used it to shoot and kill your father!"

"No! That's not true!"

"What about your jacket?"

"It got torn."

"How?"

"Maybe my father grabbed it when he fell. Or perhaps it was when the mob reached us. It all happened so quickly!"

"So what was torn?"

"The pocket was ripped off. I had to get it repaired."

"Oh, the pocket. That's what was torn off."

Julius was silent, perhaps realizing that he'd said too much.

"They've got him, Ian!" Kubu said. "He shot him through the jacket, then replaced the pocket. He's practically admitted it!"

"Has he, indeed?" asked Ian dryly.

The lawyer came to life. "Rra Mabaku, where is this going? My client has admitted to owning an illegal firearm. He was in fear of his life. Now you are making a fuss about a jacket pocket. Do you have a point?"

"Indeed I do, rra. You see your client fired his gun through that pocket. Our forensics people found gun residue on the inside of the pocket. So it's hardly surprising that he had to have it replaced afterward, is it?"

"That's not true!" Julius burst out.

"So how did the residue get onto the jacket?"

"Well, it must've been when my father was shot. Maybe the shooter was right behind me! I heard a bang, but I thought it was the police. Maybe he used a silencer."

"We shouldn't have given him the weekend to get his story straight," Kubu muttered.

Mabaku leaned back. "And crouched to get to just the right angle next to your pocket? Which was later conveniently ripped off? You seem to have an answer to everything, rra. What would your answer be if I told you that our pathologist found fibers from your jacket in the bullet wound?"

"Ian!" Kubu exclaimed. "Brilliant! How did you manage that? I wouldn't have thought it was possible."

"Probably isn't, Kubu. The bullet would burn a hole in the material, and, anyway, it would never carry fibers to the victim."

"But Mabaku said . . ." Then Kubu realized the director hadn't really said that, and Julius was floundering with the hypothetical question.

"Maybe the bullet went through my jacket," Julius said at last.

"And you didn't notice? Come on!"

Julius was silent, and Kubu was concerned that the lawyer would interrupt, but he didn't. Push your advantage, Jacob, Kubu silently encouraged.

"Look, Koma, we're wasting time. This is cut and dried. One, you obtained an illegal gun. Two, your father was shot with that caliber gun. Three, no one else had the opportunity. Forget about the mysterious assassin with the silenced gun. We have the photographs, remember? There wasn't anyone else close enough to fire a shot from that angle, let alone take out your pocket in the process. So we know you bought the gun from Emefiele. We know you fired the shot that killed your father through your pocket. Actually, two shots. You even left the spent cartridges in the revolver cylinder. We even know why you did it."

For a long moment Julius said nothing. At last he repeated, "Why I did it?"

"Your father was going to throw you off the council of elders, wasn't he? You knew he'd turn down the mine's offer. But that wasn't the real reason, was it? You were going to lose all that money from the mine. And even that wasn't the main reason."

"It wasn't?" Julius was transfixed now, as though watching a snake.

"No, the real reason was for the people of Shoshong. To preserve the town you loved and its young people. To make a future for them. That's why you did it."

Slowly Julius nodded. "Yes," he said as though recognizing a revelation. "That is why I did it."

The lawyer started to say something, but Julius brushed him aside. "There was no other way. I respected my father, but we had to move forward. There was no other way, was there?"

Kubu leaned forward, almost touching the glass. His mouth was slightly open.

Mabaku shook his head. "No other way. He wouldn't listen to you, would he? He wouldn't accept that Shoshong would die without the mine expansion. Perhaps I would've done the same in your place." Mabaku nodded slowly.

"He's overdoing it," Kubu muttered. "Julius is too smart. He'll wake up."

But he didn't. Over the next half hour, he told a rambling story. How his father had always despised him, always blocked his ideas, always lived in the past. How Julius had seen a way forward with the mine. It was a story he wanted to tell. His lawyer was flabbergasted and tried to shut him up, but Julius ignored him, and so the whole story came out.

"That was brilliant," Kubu said at the end, breathless. "How did the director know?"

Ian thought for a moment. "Julius needed a justification for his hatred of his father, Kubu. Mabaku gave it to him, and he couldn't resist it."

CHAPTER 57

Mabaku allowed them all a half-hour break and suggested to the lawyer that he advise his client to get everything off his chest. The lawyer nodded nervously, wondering what further revelations lay ahead. Julius was turning out to be a nightmare client.

Samantha came into the viewing room with a big smile and accepted Kubu and Ian's congratulations, telling them that Mabaku had gone to phone the commissioner. Julius's confession would finally put the *kgotla* riot case to rest, but the tension around the mine expansion and the issue of the new chief would remain, of course.

The break was soon over, Samantha rejoined Mabaku, and Kubu realized that the main act was about to begin. He felt a little light-headed as he anticipated knowing at last what was behind his father's brutal murder. However, things started slowly.

"My client has nothing more to say," the lawyer announced. "He's told you the circumstances behind his father's death. That's it."

Mabaku ignored the lawyer and focused on Julius.

"Tell us about Wilmon Bengu," he said.

"I've told you everything before," Julius said, and went on to summarize the story of their meeting.

"What about the second meeting?"

"I didn't see him again."

"We found Rra Bengu's blood on a belt you were wearing. How do you explain that?"

Julius seemed thrown by the question. Kubu leaned forward so far that he almost touched the glass.

"All right, there was a second meeting. But I didn't kill him! I found him lying on the ground. I thought he'd collapsed, so I tried to help him up, and my hand came up covered in blood. That must've been how I got it on my clothes."

"He's lying!" Kubu said. "Why can't he just tell me what happened? I have to know!" Ian put his hand on Kubu's shoulder. Julius glanced up at the mirror, as if he'd heard something. Then he returned his attention to Mabaku.

The director stared at him for so long that eventually Julius dropped his eyes and looked away.

"Start from the beginning. How did you arrange this second meeting? I thought Rra Bengu wasn't too keen on your visits."

"The same way as before. But I told him the chief himself wanted to meet him. That if he proved what he said, the chief would use it to block the mine's expansion. That's what they all wanted, these old men . . ."

"And did Chief Koma know about all this?"

"Of course not. I wanted to see it myself."

"What was it you wanted to see? What Rra Bengu claimed? And what was that?"

Julius put his head in his hands. They came away wet with sweat.

"The deed. The deed that he had rights to use much of the land where the mine was going to expand. My father had said he remembered such a usage grant, and Bengu confirmed it the first time I met him."

"Did you tell your father that?"

"That would've been crazy! He'd have used it as an excuse to block the mine! But Bengu was an old-timer. He had great respect for the chief, so he agreed to meet with him and discuss the situation. So I set up the meeting, and he promised to bring the document to show the chief."

"Go on."

"I've told you! When I found him, he was dead. Murdered."

"Why didn't you tell us this before?'

"You wouldn't have believed me."

"No," Kubu muttered. "You're damn right about that. And I don't believe you now, you bastard."

Mabaku took his time. "Did you tell anyone else about this land title?"

Julius hesitated. "I told Hong."

"Why did you do that?"

"They needed to know. It was important information for them."

Julius didn't sound convincing to Kubu, and clearly Mabaku felt the same way.

"No, it was important for *you*, Rra Koma. If you could get your hands on that document, the mine would have to negotiate with *you* to keep it secret."

Julius shrugged. "Shonhu must've got to him before I did. Killed him and took the document. Probably he destroyed it. There wasn't any other record of the land grant. I checked."

"Did you know his house was searched the next day? Was that also Shonhu?"

Julius waited for so long that Kubu thought he wasn't going to answer. When he did answer, he said it almost too softly for the mikes to pick up. "No, that was me."

"Why search his house if you believed Shonhu already had the document?"

"I thought maybe the old man had left it at the house by mistake. He was senile. It was possible; worth checking before his wife found it. And I knew the house would be empty after the murder."

"And did you find anything?"

"No. So Shonhu took the document. He probably destroyed it."

"Did you ask him?"

"No. I was scared of him. By then I'd learned that they'd stop at nothing to get what they wanted. That's the real reason I got the gun. I was scared of Shonhu!"

Kubu shook his head and said to Ian, "He's forgotten that having the gun for protection was part of the other set of lies. We're long past that."

"When did you tell Hong about the second meeting with Bengu?"

Julius shook his head. "I was going to look at the document and see what to do. Then I would have spoken to Hong. Maybe the whole thing existed in the old man's head. I didn't want to get them upset for nothing. I told you they're dangerous!"

"So how did they know where to find Rra Bengu? How did they know he'd have the document with him?" It was Samantha who delivered this question.

Julius looked at her as though noticing her for the first time. Then he looked back to Mabaku and spoke to him. "They must've tapped my phone."

Samantha spoke again. "No, Rra Koma. You never called Rra Bengu from your phone, or we'd have been onto you long ago."

Julius glanced at her and again addressed Mabaku. "I don't know how they found out! I don't know. Why don't you ask them?"

Mabaku folded his arms. "Oh, we'll do that, Rra Koma. But they won't know either, because that's not what happened at all. You set up the meeting, and you *did* meet Rra Bengu, and you *did* ask him for the document. But he didn't trust you, did he? He wanted to see the chief. He wouldn't show you the document. In fact, he hadn't brought it with him. You discovered that after you killed him. That was a mistake, wasn't it? Because after that you couldn't ask him where it was!"

"No, no! You're wrong. I didn't—"

"Come on, Julius, get it over with. You've already admitted killing your father. What does one more old stick-in-the-mud matter? Let's finish this now."

However, that seemed a step too far for Julius. He denied it and denied it. And he kept glancing at the mirror as though he knew Kubu was there, waiting to pounce when the words of admission finally came out of his mouth.

At last Mabaku called it a day. "Rra Koma, I'm charging you with the murder of Rra Wilmon Bengu, an old man who'd done you no harm, but who you thought stood in your way, so you killed him. Be glad his son isn't sitting here instead of me. He'd tear you apart. I'm tempted to do that myself."

He rose to his feet and signaled Samantha that they were leaving. "Take him back to his cell," he called to the guard as he slammed the door.

In the observation room, Kubu sat stunned. "He didn't admit it. He admitted killing his own father, but not my father. Why not?"

Ian shook his head. "Humans are strange, Kubu. Who knows what goes on in their heads? But it doesn't matter. Mabaku painted him into a corner. Julius set up the meeting, and his story about telling Hong makes no sense. So no one else knew about the meeting. He admitted being there with Wilmon's body. Obviously, he demanded the document and stabbed Wilmon when he refused to give it to him. He must've searched the body—that's how he got blood on his clothes—and the next day, he searched the house. Maybe he found the document and destroyed it, but I don't think so. He's a hoarder. He even kept the coat he used when he shot his father. He would've kept the document in the safe with the gun." He paused. "You never heard about this land grant? Maybe it didn't even exist."

Kubu shook his head. He had no idea how to answer.

Then Mabaku came in with Samantha, and Kubu realized that the last act of the performance was over.

CHAPTER 58

Kubu felt a pang of loss as he and Joy climbed the stairs to the veranda of his parents' home. It was the first time since Amantle had
moved back to Mochudi that his family had driven up for their
weekly Sunday visit. Normally his father would be sitting there,
quietly awaiting their arrival, but today his chair was empty.

Ilia, too, knew something was different. She yapped excitedly
as she bounded ahead of Kubu to where Wilmon usually sat, but
then stopped and looked around for the man who loved to rub her
ears. When she didn't see him, she sat down and whined.

"Hello, Mother. We're here," Kubu shouted as he was overtaken
by Tumi and Nono, who ran straight into the house.

A few moments later, Amantle appeared, each girl clinging to
a hand, pulling her outside.

"*Dumela*, Mother. How are you?" He wanted to hug her, to help
close the void he'd felt since his father's death. Instead he extended
his right hand, touching his right forearm with his left hand in the
traditional way.

"*Dumela*, my son," Amantle said, letting go of the girls and taking his hand. "You are welcome in our home, and . . ." She stopped abruptly, then continued, "You are welcome in *my* home, and . . ."

It was too much for her. She hung her head in confusion and burst into tears. Before Kubu could react, Joy took her in her arms.

"Don't worry, my mother," Joy said. "It doesn't matter. For us, it will always be your and Wilmon's home. He's here in spirit anyway." She patted Amantle on the back. "Come, let's go and prepare lunch. I've brought some cold meats and a potato salad."

Amantle nodded, unable to speak, and the two women went inside to prepare the food.

As usual, Kubu stayed outside, except, this time, his father wasn't there to talk to. Kubu stood at the railing, lost in memories of his father.

"Daddy, Daddy, can we go and play in the garden?"

Kubu didn't hear Tumi's request.

"Daddy, Daddy, can we go and play in the garden?" This time Tumi grabbed Kubu's arm and shook it.

"Yes, my darling, but don't pull any plants out," Kubu said, coming out of his reverie. "See how many names you can remember and teach them to Nono."

With squeals of delight, the two kids ran to the back of the house, where Wilmon had tended a herb and vegetable garden ever since Kubu could remember. It had been Wilmon's passion.

What's going to become of it now? Kubu wondered, realizing that his mother knew nothing of gardening. It would be a shame to see it overtaken by weeds. He shook his head. So much is going to change, he thought.

"DARLING, PLEASE GET the girls. Lunch is ready," Joy called from inside the house.

"Yes, dear. We'll be right there."

Kubu went down the stairs and walked around to the back of

the house. As he neared the little fenced garden, he was pleased to hear the girls giggling. It was a blessing that they got on so well.

"Come on, Tumi. Come on, Nono. Lunch is ready."

"Coming," the girls called in unison.

They came out of the garden and carefully closed the gate as Wilmon had shown them so many times. They ran over to Kubu with their hands behind their backs, laughing uncontrollably.

"What's going on?" Kubu asked, sensing trouble.

"Nothing," Tumi said.

"We have a present for you," said Nono with a huge smile. "A lunch present!"

Kubu frowned. What were they going to make him eat? he wondered.

"A present? I can't wait," he said. "Let's go."

The two girls ran ahead of him, careful to keep what was in their hands hidden.

When Kubu arrived at the table, everyone was already seated.

"David, please say a prayer."

"Yes, Mother. Hold hands, everyone."

When everyone was ready, Kubu spoke quietly. "Lord, we thank you for the food on this table and for the family we enjoy. We ask you to give us good health and to look kindly on the soul of Amantle's husband and my father—Wilmon Bengu. Amen."

Nobody said a word for a few moments as they reflected on changed times. Then Tumi couldn't restrain herself anymore.

"Daddy, Daddy, we've got a present for you."

She handed Kubu something wrapped in a piece of newspaper.

"I've got one too," Nono said, jumping up and handing Kubu her newspaper.

Kubu warily unwrapped one of the packets while the girls watched as they jumped up and down. In the center of the paper was what looked like a dry piece of wood.

"Eat it, eat it," Nono shouted.

"It's from Grandfather," Tumi yelled.

"What do you mean, it's from Grandfather?" Kubu asked.

"Grandfather told us that a friend of yours gave it to him to give to you."

Kubu had no idea what was going on. He looked at Joy and Amantle, but they just shook their heads.

"Did Grandfather tell you who gave it to him?"

Tumi shook her head. "I can't remember the name. It was difficult."

"He said he was a friend of yours when you were little," Nono interjected.

Kubu frowned. "Did Grandfather tell you what this is?" Kubu asked, pointing at the contents of the newspaper.

"He said it was called hoody," Nono said.

"Grandfather said it will make you small like your friend."

Joy burst out laughing. "It's *hoodia*, Kubu. That's what the Bushmen use to suppress their appetites when hunting. It must have been Khumanego who gave it to him."

Kubu didn't know whether to laugh or be angry. Neither his father nor Khumanego had ever mentioned being concerned about his size, but apparently they'd been plotting behind his back.

He picked up the crumpled newspaper and pressed it flat on the table. The date was May 1989.

"Father kept this for twenty-five years!" Kubu said. "I wonder if he was ever going to give it to me."

"He never said anything to me about it," Amantle said. "He was always one to keep a secret if he wanted to."

"I thought the two of you shared everything," Joy said. "You always seemed to know what the other was thinking."

Amantle shook her head. "I did not know everything. I did not know about this. I did not know about what he was doing when he was killed. Maybe there are other things too."

"Tumi, where did you find these presents?" Kubu asked.

"In the box in the shed."

"What box?"

"There's a box behind the shelves. Grandfather showed it to us and said we had to keep it a big secret."

"Will he be angry because we've told you?" Nono said, wide-eyed.

"I don't think so," Joy said.

"Is the box big?" Kubu asked.

"No, Daddy. I can lift it easily," Tumi replied.

"Well then, please go and bring it here."

The two girls ran off, skipping as they did.

BY THE TIME the girls returned, Joy had cleared part of the table and covered it with a more recent newspaper, in case the box was dirty. The girls put the box down. It was about the size of two shoe boxes and was made from corrugated cardboard. Wilmon had covered it with plastic, presumably to protect it from damp.

Kubu gingerly lifted the top. In the box were two more bundles of paper similar to those the girls had brought in. He took them from the box and placed them on the table. Then he took out a small book, also covered in plastic.

"It's a savings book from Barclay's Bank," Kubu said. "Mother, did you know if he had a savings account?"

She nodded. "We have had one for many years. I have the book in my bedroom cupboard. Do you want me to fetch it?"

Kubu shook his head, then opened the one in his hand. "This is a different account. There's over twenty-five thousand pula in it." He flipped through the pages. "He's been putting money into this account since you were married. Five pula a week for the first twenty years, and then ten."

Amantle burst out crying, and Joy put her arm around her.

"He was such a wonderful husband," Amantle sniffed, dabbing at her eyes. "He was always thinking of me."

Kubu placed the book on the newspaper next to the packages. Then he lifted out a stained envelope. "That's the last thing," he said.

He opened the envelope carefully and pulled out two sheets of paper.

"Aha!" he exclaimed. "Here's his will. He didn't keep it in the house with the other papers. For some reason he hid it in his shed."

He read the page quickly. "Mother, with one exception, he's left everything to you, as you would expect. You don't owe anything on the house. It's fully paid for." He paused. "He left me one thing. Let me read it: 'To my son, David Bengu, I leave the attached legacy. It must always remain in the family.'"

He unfolded what looked more like a parchment than a piece of modern paper and read it silently. When he reached the end, he laid it on the table and put his head in his hands.

"What is it, Kubu," Joy asked.

He didn't reply.

"What does it say?"

When he didn't reply, she stood up and put her arm around him. "Please tell us."

Kubu lifted his head and picked up the paper. Joy could see that it was handwritten in an elaborate cursive script. Kubu took a deep breath and started reading.

I, Khama the Third, in recognition for the healing he provided to my people during the Great Drought, do hereby grant to Rra Mephato Bengu, his family, and heirs, the right to graze his cattle on all the land west of the Bonwapitse River and east of Tobela village, and north of Tobela village to the hills, from this day for one hundred and twenty-five years.

Signed: Khama III

14 April 1887

"That's where the mine wants to expand," Kubu said quietly.

"But the rights expired two years ago," Joy said. "Why are they relevant now?"

"It was his Alzheimer's. He remembered he *had* the rights but couldn't remember they'd expired, which happened only a few years ago. That's why he insisted on giving it to Chief Koma. He thought the grant was still in place."

"You mean this deed was worthless? He could have given it to Julius and still be alive?"

Kubu nodded.

For a few moments there was silence around the table as the adults pondered the unfairness of life.

"Daddy, Daddy, eat the hoody! We want to see you small like Grandfather."

Kubu took the two girls in his arms. "Grandfather wasn't small, my darlings. He was a much bigger man than me."

AUTHOR'S NOTE

The idea for this story originated during a trip Stanley made through northern Namibia and Botswana.

In Namibia, even in the smallest towns, he noticed a proliferation of Chinese-owned shops. He also saw several instances of local Namibians joking with the Chinese, who appeared not to want to join in the fun.

When Stanley was driving between Katchikau and Goma Bridge in northwest Botswana—a road we've both driven several times before—he found the road now paved, with no economic reason justifying the upgrade. Then he saw a new, small village next to the road—a Chinese village—surrounded by a barbed-wire fence.

Subsequent research showed that many infrastructure projects were being done by Chinese companies that imported Chinese labor, ignoring the locals.

So there was the situation that locals were being sidelined by the Chinese, the Chinese were making no attempts at integrating with the locals and were isolating themselves, and the natural friendliness of the locals was being rebuffed by the Chinese.

What a good backdrop for a murder mystery!

Few people outside Botswana have heard of Shoshong, yet in its day it was a very important town in southern Africa—much more so than the current capital of Gaborone (which hardly existed at that time). Founded in the mid-nineteenth century, it was chosen for two critical reasons: it was protected on the north by a horseshoe of hills that are difficult to climb because of dolerite scree and it had comparatively plentiful water from the Bonwapitse River, which flowed into the town through a gorge in the hills. Sekgoma I chose it for his capital in 1849, and his son, Khama III, consolidated and built Shoshong into an important center of approximately thirty thousand people.

The town thrived because it was strategically placed on the main road between Zimbabwe and southern Botswana. It became an important trading center and was host to hunters, missionaries, and famous explorers—including David Livingstone. Some Europeans settled there, and traces of their tin-roofed rectangular houses and artifacts have been found in the area.

However, the river dried up, and a prolonged drought forced Khama to abandon the town in 1889. Little is left of old Shoshong—only the remains of a few stone walls and the graveyard. Even though the town was resettled and is quite a bustling little place these days, it never regained its importance.

There are significant mines in the area, but, of course, the Konshua Mine of our story and the friction with the local people are entirely fictitious.

ACKNOWLEDGMENTS

Many people in Botswana have generously given us their time to make this book as authentic as possible. In particular, Andy Taylor, headmaster of the wonderful Maru-a-Pula school in Gaborone, has been extraordinarily patient with all our questions and requests and invaluable for introducing us to people in the know. Alice Mogwe gave us insights about the Chinese presence in Botswana.

Eileen Pooe helped us with Setswana colloquialisms and found us the funeral song. Dr. Tom Combs helped us with medical issues. Finally, Patti Weber helped us a great deal to understand the role and methods of the CIA.

We were very fortunate to have a variety of readers of drafts of this book giving us input and suggestions and catching errors. Our sincere thanks to Jacques de Spoelberch, our agent, Steve Alessi, Linda Bowles, Pat Cretchley, Pat and Nelson Markley, Steve Robinson, and the Minneapolis writing group—Gary Bush, Sujata Massey, and Heidi Skarie. With all their comments, it is hard to believe that the book still has mistakes. But it probably does, and we take responsibility for any that remain.

We are grateful to our editor, Marcia Markland, for her confidence in Kubu, and also to Carol Rutan for the excellent copyediting of this version of the book.

GLOSSARY

bakkie	Slang for pickup truck.
Batswana	Plural adjective or noun: "The people of Botswana are known as Batswana." See Motswana.
biltong	Salted strips of meat, spiced with pepper and coriander seeds and dried in the sun.
borra	Setswana for gentlemen.
Debswana	Diamond mining joint venture between De Beers and the Botswana government.
dumela	Setswana for hello or good day.
hoodia	Cactuslike plant, eaten for energy and as a hunger suppressant (*Hoodia gordonii*).
ke a leboga	Thank you in Setswana.
Kgosi	Hereditary Batswana chief.
kgotla	(1) Assembly of tribal chief and elders; (2) the place of assembly.
knobkierie	A short club made from hardwood with a knob on one end, used as a weapon.

kubu	Setswana for hippopotamus.
Landie	Term of affection for a Land Rover.
lobola	Bride-price (originally in cattle) paid to the bride's parents in African tradition. Sometimes used to set up the newly married couple.
mah-jongg	Chinese game.
malva pudding	Sweet pudding of Cape Dutch origins made with apricot jam.
Mma	Respectful term in Setswana used when addressing a woman. For example, "Dumela, Mma Bengu" means "Hello, Mrs. Bengu."
Motswana	Singular noun or adjective. "That man from Botswana is a Motswana." See Batswana.
muti	Medicine from a traditional healer. Sometimes contains body parts.
pap	Smooth maize meal porridge, often eaten with the fingers and dipped into a meat or vegetable stew.
pula	Currency of Botswana. Pula means "rain" in Setswana. One pula equals one hundred thebes.
quelea	A small bird (*Quelea quelea*) that occurs in large flocks. They fly in tight formation, seeming to move as one.
rooibos	Literally, "red bush." A bush tea common in Southern Africa.
Rra	Respectful term in Setswana used when addressing a man. For example, "Dumela, Rra Bengu" means "Hello, Mr. Bengu."
samp	Dried corn kernels that have been stamped and chopped until broken, and the coatings removed. Usually served with beans.
seswaa	Fatty meat, usually beef, boiled until tender with salt, then shredded or pounded.

Setswana	Language of the Batswana peoples.
Shake Shake beer	Beer made from sorghum or corn. The name Shake Shake comes from the fact that solids separate when the beer carton is standing. The drinker needs to shake the beer before drinking.
shebeen	Originally a place serving illicit alcohol. Now, usually a licensed establishment.
skelm	A bad person.
steelworks	Drink made from kola tonic, lime juice, ginger beer, soda water, and bitters.
thebe	Smallest denomination of Botswana currency (see pula).
tsimaya sentle	Farewell in Setswana.
ubuntu	Humanness. The philosophy that we are all tied together and should support each other.

ABOUT THE AUTHOR

Michael Stanley is the writing team of South African natives Michael Sears and Stanley Trollip. Sears lives in Johannesburg and teaches part-time at the University of the Witwatersrand. Trollip was on the faculty at the universities of Illinois, Minnesota, and North Dakota, and at Capella University. A full-time writer, he divides his time between South Africa and Minneapolis, Minnesota.